Praise for Rebecca Kertz
and her novels

"*Jedidiah's Bride* reminds readers to count their
blessings despite life's hurdles."
—*RT Book Reviews*

"The caring nature of the Amish community...is well
demonstrated."
—*RT Book Reviews* on *Noah's Sweetheart*

"*A Wife for Jacob* is sweet and reminds readers that
love is a gift."
—*RT Book Reviews*

Praise for Alison Stone and her novels

"Unusual twists...[make] this a delightful read."
—*RT Book Reviews* on *Plain Threats*

"[A] well-researched tale with an engaging pace...
it contains sweet romance, palpable suspense."
—*RT Book Reviews* on *Plain Peril*

"Stone is off to a strong start... e Inspired
Suspense ...
Pursuit

Rebecca Kertz was first introduced to the Amish when her husband took a job with an Amish construction crew. She enjoyed watching the Amish foreman's children at play and swapping recipes with his wife. Rebecca resides in Delaware with her husband and dog. She has a strong faith in God and feels blessed to have family nearby. Besides writing, she enjoys reading, doing crafts and visiting Lancaster County.

Alison Stone lives with her husband of more than twenty years and their four children in Western New York. Besides writing, Alison keeps busy volunteering at her children's schools, driving her girls to dance and watching her boys race motocross. Alison loves to hear from her readers at Alison@AlisonStone.com. For more information please visit her website, alisonstone.com. She's also chatty on Twitter, @alison_stone. Find her on Facebook at Facebook.com/alisonstoneauthor.

REBECCA KERTZ

Jedidiah's Bride

&

ALISON STONE

Plain Threats

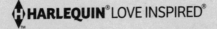

HARLEQUIN® LOVE INSPIRED®

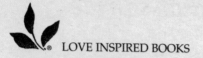 LOVE INSPIRED BOOKS

Recycling programs for this product may not exist in your area.

ISBN-13: 978-0-373-83817-2

Jedidiah's Bride and Plain Threats

Copyright © 2016 by Harlequin Books S.A.

The publisher acknowledges the copyright holder of the individual works as follows:

Jedidiah's Bride
Copyright © 2014 by Rebecca Kertz

Plain Threats
Copyright © 2015 by Alison Stone

www.Harlequin.com

Printed in U.S.A.

CONTENTS

JEDIDIAH'S BRIDE

Rebecca Kertz

For Evan…for believing.

Stop and consider the wondrous works of God.
—*Job* 37:14

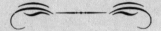

Chapter One

❧

Late May, Kent County, Delaware

"Sarah! Are all the baked goods in the buggy?"

"*Ja, Mam.* I put them carefully on the backseat." Sarah returned to the large white farmhouse where Ruth Mast stood inside the front screen door. "Everything is ready to go."

"*Gut,*" Ruth said. "Iva will keep me company today. Mary Alice will help you at the Sale."

Sarah nodded without argument although she knew that the day would be eventful with two wild boys to mind at the Sale. She worried about her mother, who had been feeling unwell for some time. Her *mam* hadn't been out of the house except for Sunday services for months. Aunt Iva had taken *Mam* to the doctor's last week, but *Mam*'s refusal to share the results of that visit frightened Sarah.

A black buggy drew up and parked in the barnyard, and Iva Troyer and her daughter Mary Alice stepped out of the vehicle.

Sarah waved a greeting to her aunt and cousin as she searched for signs of her brothers. "Timothy! Thomas! Time to go to Spence's!"

"Coming!" a young voice cried.

The boys came barreling around the house. Their straw hats flew off as they bolted toward the buggy, revealing twin mops of bright red hair. Her brothers looked disheveled as they halted before Sarah, out of breath.

"Boys! Your hats! Get them and quickly!" Sarah narrowed her gaze as her brothers obeyed and then approached. "You clean enough for town?" she asked, examining each with a critical eye.

"Ja," Timothy said as he jammed his hat back onto his head.

"Only our hands are a little dirty," Thomas added, "but they don't look it."

"Nay, they are clean," Timothy insisted. "We washed them in the pond."

"Let me see." The twins stuck out their palms for her inspection. "You've been playing with frogs again," she guessed, and saw Timothy nod. "Go wash your hands with soap." She kept her smile hidden as they scampered toward the house. "And comb your hair!"

The boys weren't gone for long. "Bye, *Mam!*" they cried in unison as they raced by their mother and out of the house.

"In the buggy, boys!" Sarah instructed. "And don't touch the baked goods." She turned to lock gazes with her mother. "I'll make them behave."

Her mother managed a slight smile as she opened the screen door and stepped outside. "I know you will, daughter," Ruth replied as she watched her youngest sons scurry into the buggy.

Sarah hesitated as she eyed her mother with concern. *Mam* wore a royal-blue dress. The dark color emphasized Ruth's sickly pallor. The white *kapp* on her head hid the gray in her dark hair.

"She'll be fine," Iva assured her. Iva Troyer, *Mam*'s sister, was a large, strong woman with a big, booming voice.

Sarah nodded. As she hugged her overly thin mother, she gave up a silent prayer. *Please, Lord, make* Mam *well again.* She caught her aunt's glance and relayed her silent gratitude. Iva gave her a slight smile as she steered her inside the house to rest.

"My *mam* will take *gut* care of *yours,*" Mary Alice said as she climbed into the Mast family buggy.

"I know she will." Sarah joined her cousin in the front seat. Mary Alice was tall but thinner than Iva. She wore a green dress without an apron, and a white *kapp* over her sandy-brown hair. "I appreciate your help today."

Mary Alice shrugged. "I like going to the Sale. I'm getting a barbecued-pork sandwich for lunch."

Sarah smiled, grabbed hold of the leathers and then steered the horse toward Dover. "Sounds *gut* to me."

Early morning at Spence's Bazaar was a beehive of activity as vendors and folks set up tables with their items for sale and prepared for the crowd that the warm spring day would bring.

Jedidiah Lapp arranged brightly painted birdhouses, stained and varnished shelves and other well-crafted wooden items on his uncle's rented table. He set some of the larger things, such as side tables, trash boxes and potato bins, on the ground where potential customers could readily see them. Finished, he turned to review his handiwork.

"Looks fine, Jed." Arlin Stoltzfus joined him after a visit to the Farmers' Market building across the lot. "Here." The older, bearded man smiled as he handed his nephew a cup of coffee, and Jed nodded his thanks. "You finish unloading the wagon?"

"Ja," Jedidiah said. "Almost everything you brought today is out and ready to be sold." He reached into a cardboard box beneath the table to pull out two cloth nail bags. *"Dat* gave us these to hold the money." He handed one to his uncle.

"Your *vadder* is a wise man," Arlin said as he stuffed dollar bills and coins into the bag's sewn compartments. "Where are all of your *mudder*'s plants? I don't see many."

Jedidiah shrugged before he adjusted his straw hat. "I put the rest under the table. I can put out more later after we sell these."

"Nay," Arlin said. "We'll put more out now." He shifted things about to make more room for his sister's plants. "Your *mam* will be hurt if we don't sell every-thing she gave us."

Jed smiled. "We'll sell them." He helped his uncle rearrange the plants before he reached beneath the table to withdraw more of his mother's plants. "The sage look healthy."

"Ja, and the vegetable plants are thriving." Arlin looked pleased by the new display.

"*Mam*'s kept busy in her greenhouse ever since *Dat* and Noah built it for her."

Arlin grinned. *"Ja."* He lifted a hand to rub his bearded chin. "She gave me ten tomato seedlings and four green-pepper plants," he admitted. "And she says she'll have more for our vegetable garden next week."

"You've got a fine selection of wooden items." Jed admired his uncle's wares.

"Enough, I think." The older man moved a trinket box to the front of the display.

Jed agreed. Arlin had crafted enough items to stock several shops back home in the Lancaster area, including Whittier's and Yoder's Stores. He'd spent weeks building birdhouses out of scrap lumber donated by the Fisher wood mill. Besides trinket boxes, he'd built hanging shelves that he'd carved and painted, vegetable bins, side tables and fancy jewelry boxes that would appeal to *Englischers*. Arlin had hospital bills to pay; his daughter Meg had suffered from some health issues. His Amish community in Ohio had held fund-raisers to help with Meg's medical expenses. Once Meg was well, Arlin moved his family to Happiness, where his sister lived. While he was grateful for his new community's help, Jed's uncle felt it was his responsibility to pay off the remainder of his debt. Someone had told him that he'd sell a lot of his handiwork at Spence's Bazaar Auction in Dover, Delaware.

Jed set down his coffee cup. "We're all glad you decided to move back to Happiness, Arlin." Their village of Happiness was in Lancaster County, Pennsylvania.

Arlin's stern face warmed with a smile. "I'm glad, too. Missy's *mudder* and *vadder* can't understand why their daughter converted to Old Order Amish. They are *gut* people, but they expected us to go against our beliefs and have electricity and a phone." He looked sad as he shook his head. "They wanted to buy us a car. I couldn't stay there any longer, and your aunt Missy understood. I prayed for the Lord's guidance and decided to come home. Missy and the girls love Happiness, and Meg is thriving."

"They are happy to live in a community who readily accepts them." Jed thought of his cousins and grinned.

Arlin frowned. "Still, I worry about my girls. Who is going to keep a watchful eye on them while we're away?"

"Your sister. You know *Mam* will be there to help Aunt Missy. She may not have teenage daughters, but she has enough experience with her sons to handle any boys who come looking to spend time with my cousins."

A middle-aged woman came to their table, her arms laden with her purchases, and bought several of *Mam*'s herb and vegetable plants. Jed offered to carry them to her car. "Thank you," she said with a smile. Jed followed her to her vehicle and set the bags carefully inside before closing the trunk.

A dog barked, followed by a horn blast. He heard someone scream with alarm and then the rumble of tires spinning against gravel. Jed turned in time to see two young boys bolt out into the parking lot after a dog, into the path of an oncoming car.

"Schtupp!" he cried as, reacting quickly, he snatched the two boys, one in each arm, out of harm's way. Heart thundering in his chest, Jed set them down. He studied them carefully, noting the startled look on identical twin

faces beneath their black-banded straw hats. "Are you all right?" he asked. They nodded, and Jed released a relieved breath. "Come with me."

"Are they hurt?" Arlin asked with concern as Jed steered the boys closer to their table.

"*Nay*. Where's your *mam*?" He searched the area for their mother. The youngsters appeared too frightened by their experience to answer. Suddenly, he saw her, rushing toward them.

The young mother had bright red-gold hair beneath her white prayer *kapp*. Her eyes were the vivid blue of a clear sky on a cloudless day. She wore a dress the same blue color as her eyes with a white cape and apron. Judging by her horrified expression, Jed realized that it was her scream that he'd heard.

Sarah gave each of the twins a fierce hug before she released them. "You know better than to run out into the parking lot!" she scolded. "You could have been killed!" She grabbed each boy by the hand. "You're to stay here next to me," she stated firmly. "*Don't move.* Do you understand?" They nodded silently and cast their eyes downward. Obviously, they were too upset by the near-accident to say a word. She then took several deep calming breaths before turning a grateful gaze toward the man who'd saved them. "*Danki,*" she said softly, studying the rescuer for the first time. "They escaped so fast, I didn't know where they'd gone."

"We just wanted to pet the puppy," Thomas explained and his brother nodded in agreement.

"Still, you know better than to run into the parking

lot," Sarah reminded them firmly. "And to leave without permission."

"They are young boys eager to explore," the man said quietly.

"Ja," she replied, "and they are a handful on their best behavior." She closed her eyes briefly and shuddered. "I don't know what would have happened if you hadn't been nearby."

"The Lord planned for me to help." His soft answer touched a chord in her. "The boys learned a lesson and won't run into the road or parking lot without looking again…or without permission again. Will you, boys?" They looked up at their rescuer and nodded their agreement with their eyes wide.

Sarah smiled. It must be true. The Lord watched over her brothers and sent this man to help the boys when they were in trouble. She studied the man closely. "You don't live here in Delaware." The Amish man's clean-shaven face told her he was still single. "Pennsylvania," she guessed. At his nod, she asked, "Lancaster County?"

"Ja," he said. He studied her, his look making her feel warm inside. "But you live not far from here."

She blinked. *"Ja,* 'tis true…but what gave it away?"

"Your prayer *kapp.*"

Sarah smiled. *"Ja,* ours are shaped differently than the women from your area." The back of their *kapps* was round, while the women in Lancaster wore *kapps* with a back that resembled a seamed heart.

She had relatives in Pennsylvania, although it had been many years since she'd visited them. Lancaster County was home to the largest Amish population in the country. Lancaster Amish returned each week to run the shops at Spence's Bazaar Auction and Flea Market in the Farmers' Market building.

"You have a table," Sarah said.

"*Ja.* I came with my uncle to sell plants and his woodcrafts."

"Do you know anyone who runs a Farmers' Market shop?" She pointed toward a building that housed several mini shops.

"I don't know." He shrugged. "I haven't been inside the building yet."

"You should take the time to go inside," Sarah urged. "They have the best food. My cousin and I like the pork sandwiches from the meat shop." Her heart skipped a beat as cinnamon-brown eyes met hers. "This is your first time here."

"*Ja.* That is my uncle and this is our table." He gestured behind him to where an older man stood helping an *Englischer* buy a jewelry box. "Arlin made all the wooden items. I brought plants from my mother's greenhouse." He introduced his uncle as Arlin Stoltzfus.

"You both should do well here," she said after she and Arlin had greeted each other. "*Englischers* love to buy plants for their flower and vegetable gardens at Spence's." She glanced toward the man's table and spied a potato bin among the items for sale. She turned back to smile at the man. "I'll have to come back later to shop."

The man studied her with an intentness that made her nape prickle. His dark hair under his straw hat was cut in the style of Amish men. His bright brown eyes, square, firm jaw and ready smile made her tingle and glance away briefly.

Her gaze settled on his shirt. She couldn't help noticing the way his maroon broadfall shirt fit under his dark suspenders and the long length of his tri-blend denim pants legs. She had to look up to meet his gaze. He stood at least eight inches above her five-foot-one height. His arms looked firm and muscled from hard work. Sarah felt her face warm and she quickly averted her gaze.

Thomas tugged on her arm. "Can we go back to our table now?"

"We promise to be *gut* and sit nicely in the chairs," Timothy added.

Sarah studied them a moment, until she realized that they were sincere. "Go ahead. Make sure you listen to Mary Alice…and sit and behave!"

With a whoop of joy, the boys scampered back to their table. Sarah watched with relief as they kept their word and sat in their chairs. Mary Alice was busy selling baked goods. There were several people waiting in line to make a purchase. "I should get back—my cousin needs help selling our cakes and pies." She also didn't trust her brothers to behave for much longer. "*Danki* for rescuing the boys—"

He smiled. "Jedidiah Lapp."

"And I am Sarah Mast." She returned his smile. The intensity of his regard made her face heat. "I hope you sell everything you brought today, Jedidiah Lapp."

"I hope all of your cakes and pies sell quickly," he replied.

She was conscious of the man's gaze on her as she hurried back to her table. A pie, she mused. She'd bring him a cherry pie in appreciation. Perhaps purchase some plants from him for their vegetable garden.

She chanced a quick look toward his table, watching as he helped a customer make a purchase. *Jedidiah Lapp,* she thought, intrigued. He remained in her thoughts as she worked with her cousin to sell the rest of her baked goods.

As the day went on, Sarah couldn't help the occasional glance toward his table to see how Jedidiah was doing. *Normal curiosity about the man who saved my bruders,* she told herself when she caught herself looking toward him often. *Or is it?*

Later that afternoon, when she'd sold all of her baked goods but one, Sarah picked up the cherry pie she'd saved for Jedidiah and headed toward his table.

"I see you sold most of your items," Sarah said with a smile as she approached.

With an answering grin, Jedidiah came out from behind the stand. "Most, but not all. What we don't sell today, we'll sell tomorrow," he said. "Will you return?"

"Nay," Sarah said, feeling suddenly disappointed. "We had a *gut* day, too. Sold everything we intended." She handed him the pie. "I saved this for you. I hope you like cherry."

Jedidiah looked startled. "It's my favorite. How did you know?"

"I didn't," Sarah said, pleased by his reaction. "I'm glad to hear it." The man's eyes suddenly focused on something behind her. She turned and saw her young brothers as they approached.

"They don't seem too upset by the experience," Jedidiah said as he met her gaze.

"Not a bit," she agreed with a half smile. "But I can't say the same for you or me."

"When are we going for ice cream?" Thomas asked.

Timothy jerked a nod. "*Ja,* when can we go?"

"Is that any way to greet Jedidiah?" Sarah scolded.

They looked at Jedidiah and grinned. "*Hallo,* Jedidiah. Have you seen the puppy?"

"Timothy!" Sarah exclaimed, embarrassed.

The man laughed. "I'm sure my brothers and I were just like them." He tugged on the brim of the boy's hat. "Afraid I haven't seen the puppy, but don't worry—I'm sure he's all right."

Both brothers looked relieved. "We don't have a dog," Thomas said. "We want one, but *Dat* said it wouldn't be *gut* for *Mam*."

Jedidiah studied her with a curious frown. Sarah looked away, unwilling to satisfy his curiosity. She wasn't going to tell him about her ill mother. She'd come not only to give him the pie but also to make a purchase. "I'd like four pepper and three tomato plants." She drew money from her apron pocket. "And that wooden bin."

He quickly placed the plants in a plastic bag. After the exchange of money, Jedidiah picked up the vegetable bin. "May I carry this to your buggy?"

Sarah nodded, pleased. "That would be helpful." She gestured to her brothers to follow and led Jedidiah to her family's buggy, where Mary Alice stood outside waiting.

"Jedidiah, this is my cousin Mary Alice Troyer. Mary

Alice, this is Jedidiah Lapp from Lancaster, Pennsylvania."

"Jed," Jedidiah invited, meeting Sarah's gaze with a warm smile before turning toward her cousin. "Jed is fine."

After her cousin and he greeted each other, Jedidiah leaned inside to place the bin toward the rear interior of the vehicle and straightened. "There you go."

Sarah nodded her thanks. "*Gut* sales tomorrow." She climbed into the buggy and took up the reins.

"Behave and keep out of trouble," Jedidiah said with a smile to the twins, who assured them they would try. "You should mind your *mam.*"

"We will!" the boys said simultaneously.

Sarah urged the horse on and with a wave she steered the buggy out of the Spence's lot, then left onto the paved road. She glanced back once to see Jedidiah—*Jed,* she thought—still standing in the same spot. She hesitated and then waved a second time. She saw Jed lift a hand again in a silent farewell before he returned to his stand.

As she steered the horse toward home, Sarah thought of Jedidiah and sighed with regret. *Too bad I'll never get to see him again.*

Chapter Two

Saturday, after a day spent at the Sale, Jed and Arlin returned to their cousin's house and pitched in to ready the Miller property for tomorrow's church services. The bench wagon had been pulled up to the barn. Services would be held in a large open area in the new building. Jed grabbed a bench, carried it inside and set it down. "This in the right place?" he asked their cousin and host, Pete Miller.

"*Ja,* that is *gut,*" Pete said. "We'll need all of the benches in the wagon and some of the chairs from inside the house. We have guests coming from another district. I hope we have enough room."

Jedidiah studied the huge barn that had been cleared for tomorrow's use and nodded. "Looks to me like you'll seat fifty to sixty easily. Will there be more than sixty coming?"

"*Nay.*" Pete took off his straw hat and wiped his brow with his shirtsleeve. "Maybe just under fifty."

"No need to worry, then," Arlin said. "You'll have plenty of room without the chairs."

Jedidiah, Arlin and Pete made several trips with benches. Pete's two eldest sons pitched in to help finish the job, as did two other churchmen who arrived a half hour after they had. It wasn't long before the room was set up with benches on three sides facing the area where the appointed preacher would stand and speak. The women would sit on one side, the men on the other. Women with their children would remain together, listening and singing the hymns sung every church Sunday. After services, the church community would gather outside to enjoy the midday meal. The women had prepared food prior to Sunday, and cold meat, salads, vegetables and desserts would be shared among the families. The men usually ate first, with the women and children taking their meal afterward, but tomorrow would be different. The church elders had decided that families would be allowed to eat together this church Sunday.

After they'd finished with the benches and brought in the *Ausbund* hymnals, the men lingered outside and enjoyed glasses of lemonade from the pitcher that Pete's daughter Lydia had brought them. As they quenched their thirst, they chatted about Sunday services, the weather and the crops they'd planted this year.

"Pete! Arlin! You bring Jed and the others in for supper!" Pete's wife, Mary, called out to them in the yard. She stood inside the screen door and redirected her attention to Ned Troyer as he climbed onto the bench wagon and took up the leathers. "Ned, come inside to eat." She stepped out into the yard and approached.

"I appreciate the offer, Mary," Ned said, "but Sally is waiting for me at home." He leaned over the side of the wagon and lowered his voice. "She's made some *gut* strawberry jam." He grinned. "I convinced her to make tarts for tomorrow."

Mary smiled. "Tell her we look forward to tasting her tarts. The berries are extra sweet this year. I haven't made jam yet—we've been too busy eating the fresh berries."

"Ja," Ned said. "Strawberry shortcake…fresh strawberries and cream. A *gut* year for Delaware strawberries!" He clicked his tongue and steered the horse toward the road. "See *ya* tomorrow."

"Ja," Pete said. He turned toward his cousins as Ned headed home. "Jed, there will be a singing here tomorrow night. I think you'll enjoy it."

Jed nodded. He enjoyed singings. Back home in Happiness, Pennsylvania, he'd been the one to lead the first hymn. He liked gathering with friends, spending time with the young people in his community and those nearby. He was now older than many who attended. His brother Noah married last year. He was twenty-two and should be wed himself by now, but he hadn't found the right woman. He'd thought for a time that she might be Annie Zook, but there seemed to be something missing between them. Annie would make a wonderful wife, but she wouldn't be his. When they discussed their relationship, he and Annie had reached the conclusion that they would be better friends than sweethearts. There were other girls who watched him as if interested, but Jed didn't have strong feelings for any of them. He wanted to find a love like his brother Noah had. He longed to find a woman who fully captured his heart and loved him completely in return.

Someone is out there waiting for me. He knew it. He

hoped he'd find her sooner than later. He wasn't getting any younger. He was the eldest son of Katie and Samuel Lapp, and he wondered if he'd ever find love… a love like Noah and Rachel's…a love like his *dat* and *mam*'s. He wasn't going to settle for anyone just to wed, even though he knew that many who married eventually came to love his or her spouse. It wouldn't be fair to marry any woman unless he truly loved her.

Sunday morning, Sarah sat in the back of the family buggy, a pie and a cake cradled on her lap. "You all right, *Mam?*" she asked as she leaned toward the front seat.

Her mother turned to smile at her. "*Ja,* I'm fine, Sarah. Stop your worrying."

Her *dat* glanced back briefly to meet Sarah's gaze before turning his attention toward the road. Sarah knew *Dat* was as concerned as she. It had been too long that her mother felt poorly. *Mam* was pale and constantly tired. She prayed that God would make her well soon.

"It's a lovely day for church services," Sarah said to fill the silence.

"*Ja,*" her mother agreed. "It's nice to get out and about. I look forward to visiting with our friends after church."

Sarah felt the same way. She was glad *Mam* was feeling well enough today to visit. She never missed a Sunday church service, but *Dat* usually took her home immediately afterward.

The only sound for a time was the clip-clop of their mare Jennie's hooves on the paved road as they headed toward the Millers' farm, the location for this Sunday's church services. Sarah's young twin brothers were surprisingly silent beside her. She glanced over and realized why. Just that quickly the boys had fallen asleep. Each child looked nice in his white shirt, black vest and black pants. They had managed to keep their clothes clean this morning and their usual wild mop of red hair beneath their black Sunday-best hat neatly combed. She smiled; they were miniature versions of their father. They were *gut* boys and they did listen and obey her, but still, she didn't always know what to expect from them.

There was a shift in the direction of the vehicle as Daniel Mast steered the horse onto the dirt lane that led to the Miller farm. Suddenly, *Mam* turned toward Sarah. "I don't want you to fuss over me," she said, holding her daughter's glance before shifting to send the same message silently to her husband.

"You will tell us if you're tired?" her father asked softly.

"Ja," she said. "I will come to you or send someone to find you."

"Fair enough, then," Sarah's *dat* replied as he pulled the horse into the Millers' barnyard and parked the vehicle within the row of family buggies on the left side of the dirt drive.

Dressed in his black Sunday best, Jedidiah stood on the Millers' front porch and watched as buggies rolled down the dirt lane to the farmhouse and parked in the barnyard.

"Do you know anyone?" Jed asked his uncle, who stood beside him.

"A few," Arlin said. He ran a hand over his bearded

chin. "I recognize the Samuel Yoders. That's Samuel getting out of that buggy near the barn. He has five sons and a baby on the way. He lives on the neighboring farm."

"Is that his oldest son?" Jedidiah asked, studying a lad of about twelve years old.

Arlin rubbed his beard as he followed the direction of Jed's gaze. "*Ja,* that's young Abe."

Jedidiah instantly thought of his mother and wondered how she'd coped when he'd been that young age with four brothers not long behind him. It couldn't have been easy for Katie Lapp, but his *mam* had taken joy in raising her sons. It had never occurred to him how much work *Mam* had endured as a mother to five sons. And since then, she'd given birth to two more sons and a daughter.

Another vehicle pulled into the yard. Jedidiah watched casually as the driver stopped the buggy and climbed down from the carriage. The bearded older man went around to the other side to help someone out of the vehicle, while a young woman climbed from the backseat on the driver's side, a dish in each hand.

He felt his heart give a lurch, then pound rapidly as he noted the shock of red-gold hair peeking out from beneath her black bonnet. *Sarah Mast,* he thought. The young mother stood with her hands full near the buggy while her sons Thomas and Timothy scurried out after her. He saw her bend to speak briefly with the twins, watched as the boys nodded before racing toward a group of youngsters who stood waiting outside the barn for church services. He saw the driver—Sarah's husband? *Nay,* her *dat,* he suspected—had helped someone out of the carriage. *Sarah's mother?*

Jed frowned. *Where is Sarah's husband?*

He watched Sarah pause to wait for the other woman to catch up before they headed toward the Miller farmhouse together. The older woman carried a basket. Jedidiah didn't know what possessed him to move in her direction, but within seconds, he was reaching out to relieve the frail older woman of her burden. "Let me," he said with a smile. The basket wasn't heavy.

Sarah's mother looked up at him and responded in kind. "'Tis nice of you," the woman gasped, out of breath.

Jed turned toward her daughter. "Sarah," he greeted. "I didn't expect to see you here."

"Jedidiah." Sarah looked surprised to see him. Her voice was soft and slightly breathless. "I thought you would have gone home by now."

"*Nay.* We leave tomorrow." He could sense Sarah's *mam*'s curiosity. He nodded at the woman respectfully.

Sarah made introductions. "*Mam,* this is Jedidiah—" She paused a second. "Jed—"

"Lapp," he supplied, amused.

"*Ja.*" Sarah nodded and Jed saw her blush as she looked away. "We met at the Sale. He's from Lancaster. Jed was the man I told you about—the one who grabbed the twins before they got hit by a car." She turned to Jed. "Jed, this is Ruth Mast, my *mam.*"

Jed took off his hat. "Nice to meet you."

Her mother stopped to study him more closely, making Jed slightly uncomfortable under the intensity of her regard. And then the woman smiled, and Jed relaxed.

"Thank the Lord that you were there to save my sons," she said. Unlike Sarah's red-gold hair, Ruth's hair was dark brown with streaks of soft gray. Sarah had inherited her mother's features—nose, chin, smile, but not her hair or eye color. Ruth's eyes were green, while Sarah's gaze was a vivid shade of bright blue.

Jed glanced over to check on Ruth's progress. Satisfied that she was managing, he held out a hand for Sarah's cake plate. With Ruth's basket in one arm and Sarah's cake plate in the other, he escorted the two women to the Miller house. Mary Miller came to the door as they climbed the porch steps.

"Ruth! Sarah!" Mary greeted as she came forward to accept the family's food offerings.

"Ruth's," Jed explained as he handed his cousin the basket and gave Edna Byler, a neighbor who'd followed closely behind Mary, Sarah's cake. "I will talk with you later," he told the two women.

"Will you sit at our table for the midday meal?" Ruth asked.

Jed smiled. "I would like that."

"We will see you then," Sarah's mother said as she carefully climbed the porch steps.

Sarah nodded as Jed met her gaze before she followed her mother into the house. Jed looked back to see her standing at the screen door. She quickly moved inside and disappeared from sight.

Sons? He suddenly realized what Ruth had said.

Thank the Lord that you were there to save my sons. The twins weren't Ruth's grandsons, nor were they Sarah's sons, Jed realized. They were Ruth's sons...and Sarah's brothers!

And now he understood why there was no husband in sight for Sarah. She wasn't married and didn't have children! Jed suddenly felt elated.

I'll be eating at Sarah's table. Jed was pleased at Ruth's invitation. He was leaving tomorrow, but until then, he could enjoy the day, learning more about Sarah Mast. He grinned happily, buoyed by the prospect.

Soon, the community and their guests gathered for church inside the Millers' new barn. The service began with a hymn from the *Ausbund.* Jed realized that his community back in Happiness, Pennsylvania, sang the same hymn during services, but the melody was different. Still, Jed was able to catch on quickly, and he sang the hymn with confidence with the rest of the congregation.

Jed saw Sarah, who was seated beside her mother and twin brothers, listen intently as Preacher Byler addressed the church members. He couldn't help look her way from time to time until he saw her glance in his direction and then back over her shoulder as if she could tell someone was watching her.

He focused his full attention on the preacher and didn't gaze in Sarah's direction again...although he was conscious of her for the rest of the service.

Sarah tried not to look in Jedidiah's direction, but a prickling along the back of her neck made her wonder if he'd been watching her. Several times she glanced his way only to see that he paid strict attention to Sunday services. Sarah realized that she must have imagined his stare. But then the feeling of being watched came back so strongly that she took a quick look behind her. If Jed wasn't studying her, then who was?

Jed stood outside the barn door as Sarah left with her twin brothers. "May I help carry out the food?" he asked.

Sarah shook her head. "We can manage. You'd best join the men. There's my *dat*. You can sit at that table. The rest of us will join you shortly." She watched as her two older brothers sat down near her father. "There is Toby and Ervin. They are older than me."

Jed studied the two young men who sat across from their father. "How many siblings do you have?"

"Besides the twins and the two eldest?" she asked. He nodded. "I have an older sister. Emma married and moved to Ohio with her husband, James."

"I see." Jed seemed thoughtful as he looked away briefly. "Then you are the only daughter at home." He focused his eyes on her.

"Ja," Sarah admitted. Jed's intense regard made her quickly look away.

"Your *mam*...she is unwell?"

Taken off guard, Sarah flashed him a look. "She says she is fine."

"But you don't believe it." His voice was soft.

Sarah sighed as she felt the warmth of his concern. *"Nay.* She has been tired and sick for weeks now."

His expression filled with sympathy. "Is there anything I can do?"

His response surprised her. "I appreciate your kindness. *Ja,* there is something you can do...pray for her."

"I shall keep her in my prayers," Jed said quietly.

Sarah blinked back tears. *"Danki."* She took a deep

breath and pulled herself together. "I must go inside. Please…feel free to sit at our family table. I can introduce you first if you'd like."

Jed suddenly grinned, and Sarah felt her face warm. "Go help inside. I can introduce myself." He turned and headed toward the table.

Sarah stood a moment as she saw Jed speak with her father and brothers, watched as her father gestured for Jed to sit across from him. Her brothers shifted on the bench to make room for Jed, who then sat next to her eldest brother, Ervin. Relieved at how well her family appeared to receive him, Sarah headed toward the Miller farmhouse.

Sarah felt a lurch in her chest as she entered the house with thoughts of Jedidiah. Women filled Mary's kitchen, working to unwrap food that had been prepared previously. She attempted to force Jed from her mind. "What can I do to help?" she asked as Mary set a casserole dish on the counter.

"You can start with those," her mother said, gesturing toward platters of meat and bowls of salads. She uncovered a bowl of potato salad and moved to place it next to the casserole dish.

Mary gestured for her mother to sit. "Ruth Mast, don't you overdo!" She smiled at Sarah's mother. "We like having you here."

Sarah was happy to see her mother take a seat. "I'll be careful," *Mam* said.

Pleased that her mother was able to join the day's meal, Sarah made numerous trips outside as she carried platters of cold meat, bowls of homemade potato salad and coleslaw, and dried corn casserole to the food tables. She was glad that Mary refused to let her mother carry anything, happier yet to note that Ruth Mast didn't object but remained seated in the kitchen until all of the food had been uncovered or unearthed from the gas refrigerator and brought outside. After the meal, they would take the leftovers inside and return to put out the desserts.

Men, women and children mingled, enjoying the food. Sarah set down the last dish on the food table. Where was Jed? She didn't immediately see him at her family table. She searched the grounds until she found him standing by a tree not far from the table as if he was waiting for her. His eyes brightened as Jed watched her approach. He nodded as she drew closer.

"Hungry?" he asked.

Sarah inclined her head. "You?" His answer was a slow smile that did odd things to her insides.

The food was set up as a buffet for folks to fill their plates. *Should I ask him what he wants to eat?* she wondered. She needed to fix a plate for *Mam*. Then her thoughts centered on the brush of his hand on her arm, the touch of his arm against hers, as they walked side by side toward the buffet tables. Sarah felt her heart pumping hard and she had trouble concentrating as she followed behind Jed and they each filled plates. She was puzzled at first when she saw Jed fix a second plate, asking her opinion as he chose food. It was then that she realized that he was filling a plate for her mother. Touched by his thoughtfulness, she blinked back tears.

They went back to the table to find two seats vacant across from each other. When Jed set the plate before *Mam,* then took his seat, Sarah's mother seemed as moved by Jed's kindness as Sarah had been.

Sarah enjoyed the cold roast beef, dried-corn casserole and potato salad, while Jed, she noted, had chosen a slice of ham, sweetened green beans and a huge helping of macaroni salad. They looked at each other's plates, saw the differences and chuckled.

"I like it all," Jed said.

Sarah nodded, but she realized that he had chosen carefully for her mother. "I love those beans, but I get them whenever I want, since I made them using *Mam*'s recipe."

Jed's eyes flickered. "You bake *and* cook."

Sarah nodded. "*Ja,* of course." She didn't want to tell him that she'd been doing all of the cooking these past few months, that *Mam* was too tired and feeling poorly to do much more than peel potatoes or snap the ends off store-bought fresh green beans. She saw that he'd guessed the truth by the way he studied her.

Everyone enjoyed the meal. Sarah was pleased to see how at ease Jed seemed in the company of her family, and she smiled and laughed as her father told stories of her twin brothers' antics on their farm. For Sarah, the meal passed too quickly.

Chapter Three

"I'll be going home tomorrow," Jedidiah said to her family as they lingered over the remainder of their meal. "Arlin and I came to Spence's Bazaar—the Sale, you call it?" Sarah nodded. "We had many things to sell—and we sold everything we had. My uncle is eager to head back to his family. He has five daughters, and he worries about them."

Sarah silently wished he could stay longer.

"I understand that Arlin made Ruth's new vegetable bin," Daniel Mast said.

Jed paused in the act of eating potato salad. "*Ja.* Arlin works well with wood. Just like my *vadder* and my brother Noah."

"How many brothers and sisters do you have?" her mother inquired.

"Six brothers and a little sister. My *mam* keeps busy but she enjoys all of us. *Mam* grew the vegetable plants Sarah purchased in her greenhouse."

Sarah checked her mother's reaction. She smiled as

if she enjoyed hearing about Jed's life in Pennsylvania. Sarah didn't like the thought of him leaving.

"There is Arlin by the barn talking with Ned Troyer." Jed flashed her a grin, and Sarah blushed.

"I'd better help bring out the desserts." She stood and resisted the urge to straighten her bonnet.

"I'm eager for a slice of your pie, Sarah," her *dat* said.

"Me, too." Jed's soft voice vibrated down her spine.

Sarah hesitated when Arlin stopped by to chat. Jed introduced Arlin to her family. "*Mam* likes the vegetable bin I bought for her," she told Jed's uncle with a smile. "Hers needed replacing, and yours is well made."

Arlin looked pleased. "I hope it gives you many year's of *gut* use."

"I'm sure it will," *Mam* said.

Soon, Arlin left to rejoin his cousin Pete at another table, and Sarah grabbed leftovers from the food table to carry inside. After the desserts were put out, she returned to her family…and Jed.

"Dessert!" Timothy exclaimed, climbing over the bench and running toward the food. Thomas jumped up and raced after him, eager to get there first.

Ervin stood and straddled the bench, watching his young brothers choose sweets from the dessert table. "*Mam, Dat,* want anything in particular?"

"I'd like to try one of Sally Troyer's strawberry tarts," her *mam* said.

Sarah started to rise. "I'll get it."

She shook her head. "Sit. Your brother will get it for me." She flashed Ervin a smile.

Ervin rose and Toby followed. "I'm thinking of chocolate cake," Toby said, and his older brother grinned.

Feeling Jed's gaze, Sarah shifted uncomfortably on the bench. "*Mam,* can I get you some lemonade?" She wasn't used to sitting. It made her feel guilty when she knew how much her *mam* needed her.

Timothy and Thomas returned to the table, each carrying plates that threatened to tip and spill. "Jedidiah!" they cried in unison, "we got cake!"

"Looks good!" Teasingly, Jed reached out as if to grab Thomas's plate. "What is that? Carrot cake?" he asked.

Thomas nodded and cradled his plate protectively. "It tastes good. Want me to get you some?"

"It looks delicious, but I'll go over and get some myself—when your sister Sarah is ready for dessert."

The boys turned to Sarah. "There are lots of cakes and pies, Sissy," Timothy said.

Hearing her name on Jed's lips infused her with pleasure. "I'm thinking about chocolate-cream pie," she said. She could feel Jed's regard, and although feeling a bit shaky, she managed to smile at him. "I'm ready for dessert. Shall we go?" She stood and smoothed out her apron.

Jed grinned and rose. "Chocolate-cream pie?" he asked as they headed toward the dessert table.

"Maybe," Sarah said with amusement, "or maybe not. I won't know what I want until I see it."

He chuckled. "I'm thinking I'll have more than one thing."

"I may, too," she replied with a sudden feeling of gladness. The day was bright and sunny, and life was good.

The lingering memory of Jed's answering laughter did strange things to her insides as Sarah selected a slice of chocolate-cream pie and a piece of peanut-butter fudge.

Jed, she saw, chose peach cobbler and a piece of her cherry pie. *His favorite kind of pie,* she remembered, pleased.

Sarah enjoyed spending the day in Jed's company. She liked seeing him with her family. She knew her parents well enough to know when they liked someone, and they liked Jedidiah. It was too bad that he lived in Pennsylvania. She reminded herself that this was simply a day to remember. Tomorrow Jed would leave and Sarah would never see him again. It was just as well, since she needed to be near for *Mam.*

Soon it was afternoon and the women had begun to clean the tables and collect the leftovers. Sarah rose. "Time to help Mary in the kitchen." And it was time to check on her mother, who had gone inside moments earlier.

"I enjoyed spending time with your family," Jed said, his brown eyes glowing.

Sarah averted her glance from the warmth in his gaze. "It was a nice day."

"Sarah!" *Mam* stood at the screen door. "Would you please bring in the rest of the desserts?"

She smiled in her mother's direction. *"Ja, Mam."*

"Please see me before you leave," Jed said. "There is something I'd like to talk with you about."

Warmth curled in her belly as she nodded. "Is everything all right?"

"Ja, of course. I want to talk with you about the singing here this evening."

A singing, she thought. It had been a long time since she'd attended a singing. But thoughts of her mother's health tamped down her joy. How could she leave *Mam?* She heard Jed talking with her older brothers as she headed toward the house. Wouldn't it be nice to spend a few more hours with him before he left for home?

Later, after the women had cleaned up after the meal and put away the food, Sarah came out of the Miller house and spied Jed seated in a chair on the front porch.

He stood when he saw her. "I spoke with your brothers. They are attending the singing tonight. Will you come?"

"I don't know if I can.... *Mam*..."

Jed nodded as if he understood.

"I'd like to come," she was quick to add. "I'll be sorry to see the day end." Then she glanced away as she wondered how he might have interpreted her words.

"The day is not over," he said softly. "Your mother seems well today."

"*Ja,* 'tis true." Sarah wanted nothing more than to stay. "I'll check with *Mam* to see if she needs me."

"Your brothers will be there," he told her. His voice dropped. "I'd like to take you home afterward."

Sarah's heart started to race. Wouldn't it be exciting to go to the singing and be driven home by Jedidiah Lapp! "I'll check," she said and fled back into the house to ask her mother. Her heart beat wildly as she entered the kitchen and searched for *Mam*. It had been a long time since she'd gone to a singing. For months now, concern for her *mam* had kept her home.

But *Mam* had done surprisingly well this day. Was

it possible that her mother would be fine and that she could attend?

She caught sight of her mother seated in a chair in the Millers' great room. *"Mam."* She approached, almost afraid to ask; she didn't want to be disappointed. "There is a singing tonight—"

"Ja!" Mary Miller said. "It will be *gut* for you to go."

Sarah didn't want to miss it, but she wouldn't put her wishes above her mother's needs.

"Sarah," her *mam* said with a smile, "you should stay." She frowned as if it had just occurred to her how much her youngest daughter had missed during these past months. "It's been a long time for you."

"It's all right," Sarah assured her. "I'll come home with you and *Dat,* but if you are feeling well enough, I'd like to return. Ervin and Toby are going. I can ride back with them."

"Or you could stay and one of my sons can take you home," Mary Miller said. "I'm sure P.J. would be happy to see you home."

"I'd be happy to bring her home," Jed said as he stepped into the room.

Sarah felt his presence immediately. It vibrated in the room, making her fully aware of him. She watched her mother study the young man and nod. "As long as you get home safely," Ruth directed toward her daughter. "Where is your *dat?*" She stood, wobbling a little on unsteady legs before righting herself.

"Daniel is outside near the barn with Pete, Arlin and Ned Troyer," Jedidiah offered. Someone called him from outside. "Arlin," he explained with a smile before he left to return to the men who were gathered out in the yard. Sarah felt the loss of his presence.

"And what of the twins?" her mother asked. As if exhausted, she sat down again. "Have you seen them?"

"They are outside with my two youngest." Sally Troyer reached back to retie her apron strings. "They are getting along just fine. Perhaps your boys would like to spend the night with my Joseph and John."

Her heart gave a little lurch. Without the twins to wreak havoc on the house, Sarah could attend the singing, leaving her mother to rest quietly with her *dat* nearby.

"I think Timothy and Thomas would like that," *Mam* said. She focused her gaze on Sarah. "You'd like to go?"

Sarah nodded. "*Ja,* but I can stay home if you need me."

"*Nay,*" she said, "there is no reason for you to stay. I will be fine. Now, where did you say Daniel is?" Her eyes lit up as she spied her husband out the window. "Ah, there he is!"

"I'll tell him we are ready to go," Sarah said with quiet joy.

Mam frowned. "I thought you'd stay."

Sarah shook her head. "I will see you settled before I return with Ervin and Toby."

Her *mam*'s expression grew soft. "You are a *gut* daughter." She stood a bit wobbly but managed to right herself without help. "I will come with you to get your *vadder.*"

"I can bring back clean clothes for the twins," Sarah offered as she helped her mother across the room.

"No need," Sally assured her. "They will be fine."

She grinned, apparently pleased with the turn of events. "I'll tell them they'll be staying with us tonight."

Sarah could hear her young brothers' whoops of happiness as she and her mother joined her father outside. "Sounds like they are excited to be spending the night with the Troyers."

Daniel grinned. "It will be a nice quiet evening for us," he said.

Her mother's smile was weak but genuine. "I did well today," she declared. With help, she climbed into the buggy and sat down.

"Ja, Mam." Sarah set a blanket about her mother's legs. "Time to go home and rest."

Once *Mam* was situated comfortably, Sarah climbed into the back and then gazed out the window as *Dat* pulled the buggy away from the farmhouse down the dirt lane toward the main road. She thought she'd caught a glimpse of Jed watching them as they drove away.

This evening, she would be spending more time with Jedidiah Lapp. Heart thumping, she thought of the evening ahead with barely controlled excitement.

Jed stood on the Millers' front porch and watched as buggies and wagons arrived with young people who had come for the evening's singing. There was still no sign of either Sarah or her brothers. Would she come or did her mother need her?

Why should I care if she stays home? It wasn't as if he'd ever see her again. Still, the memory of her smiling face and blue eyes lingered in his thoughts. He had enjoyed his time with her family. The afternoon had passed quickly—too quickly.

He shouldn't think of Sarah. He was too old for her. What was she? Seventeen? Eighteen? He'd thought he'd found someone he might love in Annie Zook, but he'd been wrong. If he'd hurt her, Annie hadn't shown it. Sarah was vulnerable. She'd spent a long time caring for her mother. She hadn't been to a singing in months. He had no right to monopolize her time, but he couldn't help himself.

If she comes, then I'll enjoy the evening with her and then say goodbye. She would find someone else here in Delaware to love. She would want to stay near her family, and he needed to be home in Happiness.

It was growing late and still there was no sign of any of the Masts. Jed stepped down from the porch and crossed the yard, more than mildly disappointed.

Suddenly, a buggy came barreling down the dirt drive to pull up quickly behind the line of vehicles. Jed saw Ervin and Toby jump down from the vehicle, but no sign of Sarah. He waited for the brothers to join him before entering the barn.

Just as he had given up hope of seeing her again, Jed watched Sarah climb out carefully after her brothers, balancing a plate in one hand. Ervin helped his sister, grabbing the plate from her hand. The siblings turned and spied Jed standing in the yard. Ervin waved, and Toby followed his eldest brother, while Sarah came slowly behind.

Jed felt a sudden lightening of spirit. Sarah was here, and he would get to spend more time with her, if only for a few hours.

He grinned at Sarah's brothers, and then he waited with a soft smile as Sarah caught up to them. "Nice night for a singing," he said, noting her flushed cheeks and sparkling eyes.

"Ja," she said. "It's been a long time since I've had the joy." She gestured toward the plate Ervin held out to her. "I brought cookies—chocolate chip."

"This will be a *gut* night, Sarah," he whispered as the brothers went into the barn ahead of them.

She gave a barely perceptible nod as they followed. Then, there were greetings from the others who had come. Jed noticed that his cousin P.J. seemed particularly happy to see Sarah. P.J., Pete's eldest son, was closer in age to Sarah than he. He tried not to be upset by the fact that once he left, it could be P.J. who would eventually keep company with Sarah and perhaps win her heart.

Don't let it bother you tonight, he thought. They had this one night together, and he planned to enjoy every single moment of it.

Chapter Four

Sarah felt gladdened by the greetings of her friends and neighbors as she entered the barn and took a seat across from Jedidiah. She was conscious of Jed's presence as she smiled and returned Miriam Yost's wave. She hadn't seen Miriam in a long time. She liked the young woman. Sarah suddenly realized how much she'd missed socializing with her friends since her mother had become ill.

"Sarah," Pete and Mary Miller's oldest son, P.J., greeted her. "It is *gut* to have you with us again."

She smiled at him. "It is nice to be here." She sensed Jed watching her, and she flashed him a glance.

His eyes warmed as their gazes met. He smiled, and Sarah felt her breath catch. His attention was focused on her, and she felt the touch of his brown gaze as if he'd brushed her arm or captured her hand with his fingers.

But there was nothing untoward in his regard of her, she realized. The thoughts—the feelings—were all hers, and she pulled herself together, prepared to enjoy the events of the night's singing.

To her surprise, P.J., also known as Pete Jr., began the singing with his choice of hymn from the *Ausbund*. He sang the first verse before everyone joined in. As Jed joined in, Sarah heard his pleasant, vibrant tone. She was pleased when he began the second hymn, the *Loblied,* his voice rising in praise of the Lord. She could feel his conviction, his passion for God, and Sarah knew that her thoughts of him were accurate. He was a *gut* man with a kind heart and true love for the Lord. She sang out happily, her voice rising with the others as they finished the hymn they had all sung that morning during church services.

After a third hymn, Miriam Yost's brother Joseph suggested they stop for some refreshment.

"You are always wanting to eat," his sister teased.

Joseph shrugged. "We can sing another hymn, if you'd prefer."

"I could use one of Sarah's cookies," Jed said.

Sarah flushed as everyone turned to look at her. Jed's smile put her at ease, and she sent him a silent message of thanks.

As it was, the majority decided light refreshments were in order before they continued with hymns and games.

Lydia Miller, Mary and Pete's only daughter, had made lemonade and iced tea for all to enjoy. Sarah helped Lydia to distribute drinks, before she grabbed her plate of cookies and a platter of lemon bars that Miriam Yost had made for the occasion.

Jed, Sarah noticed, was quick to choose one of her cookies. He took a bite and flashed her an appreciative smile. Everyone had left their seat to mingle in the open area of the large barn.

Jed took another bite of the cookie. "You will let me take you home tonight, won't you?" he asked.

"My brothers are here—"

Jed gestured toward where Ervin was deep in conversation with Elizabeth Yoder. Not far from Ervin, Toby chatted with Elizabeth's older sister Alice. "I think Ervin and Toby have plans to take those two home. Wouldn't you rather ride with me?"

Sarah hesitated. She knew she'd rather have Jedidiah take her home, but she didn't know if she should go with him. Yet, how would she feel riding along with her brothers and the Yoder sisters?

"I will ride home with you," she said quietly so that no one but Jed would hear.

Jed grinned. "*Gut!* I will look forward to taking you," he said as the others began to head back to their seats.

Sarah was conscious that Jed allowed her to precede him, and as she sat down, she tried not to look at him, but she couldn't help herself.

She found him studying her with an intensity that made her feel odd inside. She couldn't say that she disliked the feeling. Being the focus of this kind man's attention was not unwelcome. *He leaves tomorrow,* she reminded herself. *I will never see him again.*

Will he write? she wondered. She wasn't going to ask him; it wouldn't be right unless he mentioned it first.

As her friend Miriam chose and began the next hymn, Sarah decided to forget tomorrow and simply enjoy the evening…and the ride home with Jedidiah

Lapp. Riding home with a young man from a singing was a rare treat, and she savored the thought of it.

The singing flew by quickly, filled with song and games, and delicious food.

Sarah went to search for her brothers afterward to tell them that Jed would be taking her home. There was an awkward moment when P.J. Miller offered to bring her home. Sarah had to tell him that she already had a ride.

"Jedidiah is taking me," she said. She felt badly when she saw the young man's face fall. "Maybe another time?"

His quick look of gladness made her slightly uncomfortable. She shouldn't have said anything, but she hadn't wanted him to feel bad.

"Jed will bring me home tonight," she told Ervin.

Ervin didn't seem surprised. "That's nice, Sissy. We will be home as soon as we can." He glanced over to where Toby and the two Yoder sisters stood. "We will be making a stop on the way."

Sarah nodded, then teased, "Do not take the long way to the Yoder farm, Ervin Mast."

Ervin looked stunned at first by her teasing, but then he grinned, obviously pleased. "We don't appreciate you enough...what you do for *Mam*."

"I am the daughter, and I love *Mam*. Emma isn't here, so it is up to me."

Ervin leaned closer to whisper in Sarah's ear, "You must take time to enjoy your life, Sarah. I know your hard work is not merely a duty to you, but an expression of love. I will try to help more."

Sarah's eyes filled with tears. "I don't know what to say."

Ervin grinned. "There is Jed. He's brought the wagon around, and he is waiting for you. Keep your words for your ride home."

As she headed toward the wagon by which Jedidiah stood patiently waiting for her with his hat in his hands, Sarah thought of her brother's words and wondered what he meant by taking the time to enjoy her life more. She prayed to the Lord and did what she could to live life the way He would want it. She couldn't take time away from *Mam,* not until it was certain that she was well again.

Jed studied her expression as Sarah approached. She seemed upset. Why? He had seen her talking with his cousin P.J. Would she rather he was taking her home? His concern vanished as Sarah offered him a genuine smile as she reached him. He lifted his black felt hat, then set it back onto his head.

"*Ja.* I let Ervin know that I would not be riding home with him."

"And did he mind?" he asked.

The corners of her blue eyes crinkled. "*Nay.* As you suspected, my brothers will not be going directly home. They have plans that include stopping by the Yoder farm."

"And so you are stuck with me."

"*Nay,* I am not stuck, Jedidiah Lapp."

Her answer delighted him, and he studied her fondly. *"Gut,"* he said as his spirits rose with the prospect of spending a little more time with her. He would like the memory of the evening to take home to Happiness with him. He would like to see her farm, to picture her out in the yard or in the farmhouse, going about her chores, caring for the twins and her family.

He held out his hand, and Sarah looked at it a moment before their fingers touched as she accepted his help onto the wagon seat.

The night was a typical late-spring evening. The temperature was cool, but not cold. There was a full moon, which lit up the dark sky and shed a beam of brightness onto the yard. Jed felt sorry to release her hand as he climbed up onto the wagon seat beside her.

"All set?" he asked, and she nodded. "Are you cold?" She shook her head. "Are you going to be silent during the entire ride?"

"Nay," she said with what sounded like horror.

He laughed. "I am teasing you, Sarah Mast." Then with a click of his tongue and a flick of the leathers, he steered the horse down the long dirt lane and then turned right onto the main road. He glanced at Sarah and saw her look back as if seeking her brothers. "They will linger awhile before they leave," he said.

She nodded. "I didn't know that both of them are sweet on the Yoder sisters."

Jed shrugged. "Why would any sister know? Unless she can read her brothers' thoughts."

"Praise the Lord that I can't," Sarah said with such feeling that Jed laughed out loud.

He saw her lips curve before her laughter joined his.

"Shall we take the long way home?" he asked, expecting her to decline.

To his surprise, she said, "You are the driver." She frowned. "Do you know where I live?"

"*Ja,* I asked directions and realized that Arlin and I drove by on our way back from the Sale."

She seemed content with his answer, and he drove at the slowest pace he could manage with the horse. He wouldn't take the long way home; it wouldn't be fair to her when he was leaving tomorrow. He would enjoy this time with her, even if in silence. Having her on the seat next to him was enough to keep him happy.

He didn't like the thought of leaving her, of never seeing her again, but what could he do? They both had responsibilities and family in two communities a long distance from each other. If only she lived in Lancaster, or his family resided here in Kent County, Delaware.

But the Lord had granted him the pleasure of knowing her if only for a brief time, and he would pray to the Lord to help him when he was home again…to get on with his life…and find a woman to love and become his bride.

All too soon for Sarah, Jed was steering the wagon onto the driveway that led to her family farmhouse.

They had chatted easily, sharing stories of their siblings. As time passed and the Mast farm drew nearer, silence had reigned between them. Sarah wanted to say something, admit how much she'd enjoyed his company, but she was reluctant to do so. He knew her situation. Perhaps he was just being kind.

She was conscious of the sound of the wagon wheels over dirt and gravel as Jed steered closer to her house.

Soon, too soon, Sarah thought, the wagon was in her yard, at her front door.

Jed jumped down and rounded the vehicle to help

her. He didn't extend his hand as he had before. He simply reached up and grabbed her waist. She blushed, feeling the heat in her neck and cheeks, the tingling of his hands on her waist, as he promptly released her and stepped back. The action took only seconds, but Sarah knew she'd remember the moment for a lifetime.

"Home," he announced. It was the first time Sarah thought that he looked uncomfortable.

"I appreciate the ride," she offered shyly. "I hope God grants you a safe journey home tomorrow."

He hesitated a few seconds. "I will remember this night, Sarah Mast."

"As will I," she admitted, her heart beating wildly.

Neither spoke as they looked out into the yard as if studying the way the moonlight played on the barn and property. Sarah chanced a look at Jed. His handsome features were clearly visible under the bright moon-beam. She saw that he looked troubled.

"Is anything wrong?" she asked, knowing that she shouldn't ask.

Jed turned, then smiled, and suddenly it was as if she had only imagined his sadness.

The sound of a buggy coming down the dirt lane toward the house heralded the arrival of her brothers. She didn't want her last moments with Jed to be witnessed by her older siblings.

"Jed…" she began.

"I will miss you, Sarah," he said.

She blinked back tears. "And I will miss you." She bit her lip. "I had fun today and this evening. I will thank the Lord for the moment when you stepped in to save my brothers."

His smile was warm. "Did you know I first thought you were their mother?"

She looked stunned. "You did?"

"*Ja.* And I was disappointed, for I knew you must be wed."

Her brothers' buggy pulled into the barnyard. He glanced their way and seemed to feel the same urgency that she did. "I am glad you weren't wed or I would not have had this time with you." He grew quiet and then said, "I regret that the Lapp family farm is not in Kent County, Delaware."

Ervin and Toby had climbed out of their wagon and approached them.

"Farewell, Sarah Mast," Jed said, sending her a look that she would never forget.

"Farewell and safe journey, Jedidiah Lapp. Give my regards to Arlin."

He nodded and then spoke briefly to her brothers before he climbed back onto the wagon and turned the horse for the Miller home.

Sarah stood, watching as the wagon headed down the lane, overwhelmed by a bittersweet mixture of sadness and pleasure.

Ervin came to stand next to her. "You like him."

"*Ja.*"

"He lives far from Delaware."

"I know," she whispered, then managed to grin at her brother. "I don't know about you, but I'm ready for bed."

Ervin studied her a moment and seemed satisfied by what he saw. "I could use something to eat."

Sarah laughed. "What?"

"Pie?"

"There may be a slice of apple or chocolate cream left."

Ervin grinned. "Singing makes me hungry," he said as they headed into the house.

Toby had already gone inside. Apparently, the singing had made him hungry as well, for he was already in the kitchen, delving into the extra cookies she'd made yesterday afternoon.

Later that night, as she lay in bed unable to sleep, Sarah thought of Jedidiah Lapp and the time she'd spent with him. As she chose to remember the warmth of his cinnamon-brown eyes and quick, ready smile instead of the fact that tomorrow he would be gone, Sarah finally fell asleep with a pleased smile on her face.

But when she woke the next morning, she thought of him leaving…then she tried not to think of him any more as she went about her daily chores and checked to see if her mother needed anything.

Still, she couldn't get him out of her mind.

Chapter Five

Jedidiah Lapp had left Kent County a month ago, yet Sarah couldn't stop thinking about him. She recalled the warmth in his brown gaze, the dark brown hair beneath his wide-brimmed banded hat, his grin. She knew she should forget him, but spending time with him had been a wonderful experience. She had enjoyed his company, his smile…the way he'd made her laugh… his pleasant voice lifted in song when they'd attended the singing that evening. She and Jed had talked during the buggy ride home. She had loved every second she'd spent with him.

It was late morning and Sarah was upstairs making the beds in the twins' room. The sun shone brightly through the window and streamed golden against the sheets as she tucked them beneath the mattress. She picked up Thomas's blue shirt and hung it on a wall hook near his bed. Spying a straw hat, she bent to retrieve it. As she set the hat on Timothy's bed, she thought of her parents. *Mam* and *Dat* were sleeping downstairs now. Her mother's strength was weakening, and Sarah knew she'd have to discuss her health with *Dat* soon.

"Sarah!" Her older brother Tobias stood at the bottom of the stairs as Sarah came out of the twins' bedroom to the top landing. Toby had been working on the farm. He'd pushed back his straw hat and there was a streak of dirt across his forehead and on his left cheek.

"*Ja,* Toby?" Sarah descended the stairs.

Toby tugged on his suspenders. "*Mam* needs you." He readjusted his hat, pulling the brim low.

Sarah hurried down the rest of the steps. "Is she all right?"

Her brother shrugged. "Seems to be. Except for being tired all the time."

Sarah sighed as she left him, shaking her head as she crossed the family gathering area toward the small room where her parents now slept. At times she didn't know what to make of her older brother. Didn't Tobias realize their mother was ill? Their eldest brother, Ervin, understood the situation better than she'd expected, certainly better than Tobias did. Lately, she'd caught Ervin watching their *mudder* with an intentness that was telling. Last evening, he had discussed his concerns with her, and she'd been surprised that Ervin was worried about her as much as he was for *Mam*.

"*Mam?*" Sarah entered the bedroom, saw Ruth seated in a chair by the window. "Are you all right?"

She turned toward her with barely a smile and gestured for Sarah to sit on the bed. "Come in, Sarah. I need to talk with you."

Sarah felt her insides lurch as she nodded and sat

on the patchwork quilt. "Is it about your recent doctor's visit?"

"Ja." Ruth turned to fully face her daughter and reached to clasp Sarah's hands. "There is something I need to tell you." The daylight emphasized the tired lines in *Mam's* face. She looked exhausted and much older than her forty-three years. "I need heart surgery. The doctor believes he can fix it, but it will take me a while to recover."

"Surgery?" Sarah breathed. She could feel the weakness in her mother's grip. She fought to stifle her fear, to keep her thoughts hidden. "That is something," she murmured, "and I'll be here to help."

"Nay," Ruth said. "We're sending you with the twins to our cousins William and Josie in Pennsylvania."

"But *Mam*—what if you need me?" Send her away? No, she didn't want to go. How could she leave *Mam?* "Can't I stay?"

"Nay. It's best if you take the boys. I love Timothy and Thomas dearly, but they are a handful. Josie has boys near the same age. Your brothers will enjoy staying with them. I need you to go to make sure they behave."

"What about Emma?" she asked. "Can't she take the boys?" Her older sister was married but had no children. If Emma took the twins, Sarah could stay behind to care for *Mam.*

Her mother rubbed the back of her neck as if it pained her. Catching Sarah's concerned look, she smiled weakly and dropped her hand. "Your sister hasn't been married a full year. I don't want her to worry about your brothers. Soon, she'll have a brood of her own.

And Ohio is too far. I want you and the boys nearby, in case…"

"*Nay, Mam!* The Lord will heal you. We just have to pray." Sarah felt a weight settle in her stomach at the thought that her mother might not fight to get better. "You'll have the surgery, and you *will* get well. I'll do as you say and take the twins to William and Josie's until you call for us to come home." She bit her lip. "But you must have faith."

Her mother reached out to touch Sarah's cheek. "You are a *gut* and kind daughter, Sarah."

Tears filled Sarah's eyes as she reached up to cover her mother's hand, pressing it lightly against her cheek. "I wish I could stay," she whispered.

"I know you do," *Mam* said. "But your *dat* and I have discussed this, and we believe this is for the best."

Dat felt the same way? Sarah sighed inwardly as she resigned herself to the trip. She was a dutiful daughter; she wouldn't argue with her parents. "When do we leave?"

"The day after tomorrow. We've hired Mr. Colter to drive you."

Mr. Colter was their neighbor and an *Englischer*.

"So soon?" Sarah's spirits plummeted when her mother nodded. "We'll be ready," she assured her. "I'd better see that the twins' clothes are laundered for the trip." Sarah had to swallow against a painful lump as she rose to her feet. She bent to hug her mother. "I love you, *Mam*."

She gave her a genuine smile. "I love you, Sarah."

Lancaster County, Pennsylvania

Jedidiah pulled the family buggy to the front of the farmhouse and waited for his family to exit the residence.

His mother came to the door holding his baby sister. Little Hannah wore a lavender dress and white prayer *kapp,* and she was barefoot. "Have you seen Joseph?" his mother called.

"Not since breakfast," Jed replied. He wondered if he should get out of the vehicle and help search. He had just made up his mind to go when his *dat* left the house, followed by his twin brothers, Jacob and Eli, and their younger brothers Isaac and Daniel.

"Did you find Joseph?" Jed asked as his father approached the buggy.

"*Ja,* but he's managed to get his pants dirty. Your *mam* is making him change his clothes."

Jed's brothers Jacob and Eli climbed into the buggy's backseat. Samuel Lapp hoisted young Daniel into the buggy, urged him to sit between Eli and Jacob, and then offered his hand to Isaac.

"I can manage, *Dat,*" Isaac said as his father helped him into the backseat.

"*Ja,* I suppose you can, Isaac," Samuel said kindly, "but we're late leaving, and I'm expecting you'll have to find a quick seat and make room for Joseph. Hannah can sit on *Mam*'s lap."

Katie Lapp locked the house and approached with Hannah in her arms and holding five-year-old Joseph's hand. Joseph didn't look happy, but he was neat, clean and dressed properly, and his *mudder* was content.

"How nice you look, Joseph," Samuel said with a wink at his wife.

He hefted Joseph to sit between Isaac and Eli. The boys moved to accommodate their youngest brother. Samuel then took Hannah from his wife until Katie was comfortable in the front seat, then he handed back their daughter.

Jedidiah shifted to make room for his *dat*. "Visiting Sunday," he said with a smile as he picked up the leathers and spurred the horse on.

"Wait!" Katie cried, startling all of them. "The food!"

Jed laughed. "Not to worry, *Mam*. I took the salad and cake over to the Kings early this morning. They're going to bring them for us. I figured it'd be easier, and Mae offered yesterday."

Katie released a sigh of relief. "Mae does have the room since Charlotte married and Nancy left to visit relatives in North Carolina."

Hannah squirmed on Katie's lap, and automatically Katie shifted her daughter toward the window opening so that the little girl could look out.

"What kind of cake did you make?" Daniel asked his mother.

Katie straightened her *kapp*. "Upside-down chocolate."

"That's Noah's favorite," Isaac complained.

"It's my favorite, too," his father said, glancing back to meet Isaac's gaze.

"And mine," Daniel added.

"And mine," Eli said and Jacob agreed that it was his favorite, too.

His mother turned to eye her thirteen-year-old son. "You don't like chocolate upside-down cake?"

Isaac looked sheepish. "*Ja,* I love it." His cheeks turned pink beneath his black hat, and he squirmed uncomfortably in his seat.

Jacob scowled and reached over Eli to jostle Isaac with his elbow. "Then why all the fuss?"

Isaac shrugged. "I was just saying that chocolate upside-down cake is Noah's favorite."

"And the favorite of most of us," Eli pointed out with a shake of his head and a small smile.

My favorite is cherry pie, Jed thought, and immediately an image of a young woman with red-gold hair and blue eyes came to mind. He frowned, forcing the memory away.

Conversation came to a standstill as Jedidiah drove toward the Mast farmstead. He enjoyed visiting Sundays. He wondered who'd be attending today. The number of families who came varied from Sunday to visiting Sunday. It was a perfect day for an outdoor meal. He'd tossed a ball into the rear of the buggy with the thought that there'd be someone willing to play catch on the lawn behind William and Josie's farmhouse.

The Masts' driveway loomed ahead and Jedidiah turned on the battery-operated turn signal before maneuvering the vehicle left onto the dirt path. Rosebushes lined the side of the driveway as they drew closer to the house. The scent of the pink rose-blossoms permeated the air.

Gravel mixed with dirt crunched beneath the buggy's wheels as they approached the house and pulled into the barnyard. The side lawn was filled with neighbors.

Tables had been set up and covered with white-paper table liners.

"Looks like this will be a fine gathering," Samuel said as Jed noted the line of buggies parked on the grass and the folks in the yard. There were eight buggies. Theirs made nine. Nine families with numerous children. Plenty to play catch with or toss yard darts or any other game someone wanted to play, Jed thought.

"Look, there's Mae!" Katie said. "Jacob, would you please help her with the food? Take the cake and salad from her. It looks like she has enough to carry inside."

The King buggy was parked two vehicles down the row from them. Mae and Amos had gotten out of the carriage, followed by their sons John and young Joshua, who spied the Lapps and waved at them with excitement. Mae waved and grinned at Katie. Mae was Katie's closest friend and lived on the other side of the road from the Lapp farm.

"I'll go, *Mam*," Eli offered. He got out of the buggy and headed toward Mae.

"Me, too," Jacob said as he followed closely on his brother's heels.

"Why don't you both go?" Jed suggested loudly with barely concealed amusement. There were no girls in the King family buggy. Why the hurry to help out?

Jed climbed down from the front seat and took Hannah from his mother. *Dat* got out after him and then assisted his wife.

"Jed-ah," Hannah said as she patted Jed's cheeks.

"*Ja*, Hannah banana?"

She laughed, a babylike chuckle that warmed his

insides and made him smile. "I'm not Hannah-nana. I'm Hannah Yapp."

Jed kissed her baby-smooth cheek. "That you are, little one. Let's go, shall we? And see if we can find one of your little friends for you to play with."

"Morning, Jed, Samuel," Amos King greeted, and Jed saw that Samuel had caught up with him.

"Perfect day for a picnic," Jed said, smiling at his father's closest friend.

"Mae brought her famous sweet-and-vinegar green beans."

The Lapp men grinned in appreciation. "Katie made chocolate upside-down cake and ambrosia salad with extra coconut and marshmallows," Samuel said.

All three exclaimed with delight and then laughed. "You'd think we didn't often get such *gut* food, but we do all the time," Amos said. "Mae and Katie are the best cooks."

"Josie is a great cook, too," Samuel said. "I wonder what she's made for us today." The three men chuckled and continued on.

"Timothy, Thomas, I want you to behave today, do you hear?" Sarah stood over her young brothers, examining them with a critical eye. "We've only arrived at cousins Josie and William's two days ago. Don't make them sorry that we've come."

"We won't, Sissy," Thomas promised, and Timothy nodded in solemn agreement.

"Where are Will and Elam?" she asked, referring to Josie's six-and seven-year-old sons.

"Upstairs," Josie said as she entered the neat-as-a-pin

kitchen. She grinned at the twins. "Go up and urge them to come down, please. They're taking entirely too long up there. I can only imagine what they're getting into."

Sarah liked Josie Mast from the first moment she'd met her. It had been a long time since her parents had taken the family for a visit. Sarah had been the youngest then at only four. William and Josie hadn't met and married yet. William couldn't have picked a better wife, Sarah thought.

"I appreciate you having us, Josie."

"'Tis my pleasure," Josie said, and Sarah could tell the woman was sincere.

Sarah looked about the kitchen, anticipating what needed to be done. There was nothing on the stove, as it should be, since it was Sunday. The white countertops were clear except for a stack of white napkins, plastic plates and utensils. The prepared food had been stored in the pantry and in the refrigerator. "What can I do to help?"

Josie adjusted her white apron before she opened the pantry door. "Besides the rooms you cleaned, the pies you baked and the salads you made yesterday?"

"That's not much work," Sarah said with a smile. "At home, my chores keep me forever busy. Here, I feel like I'm on vacation."

"Gut." Josie reached into the pantry and took out the two pies that Sarah had baked the previous day. "The salads are in the refrigerator." She leaned over to glance out the kitchen window. "It looks like everyone is almost here. Oh, the Lapps have arrived! There's Jedidiah carrying his sister, Hannah."

Sarah froze while retrieving the potato salad from

the second shelf of the refrigerator. Heart beating wildly, she carefully put the bowl on the counter and then slowly, casually joined her cousin at the kitchen window.

Jedidiah Lapp? Was he the man who'd saved the twins and captured her attention back home? Josie shoved aside the white window-curtains.

And then Sarah saw him. It was Jedidiah. Carrying his little sister in one arm, Jed waved to family and friends with the other. He looked the same, only better.

Would he recognize her? Would he greet her as if they'd met before? Or had he forgotten all about the girl who spent one Sunday afternoon and evening with him in Delaware?

"Here we go, banana," Jed teased as he set Hannah on a bench to play with her little friends. There was a pile of crayons on the table. One of the children had drawn a tree and a flower on the white table covering. "You'll watch out for her, Rosie?" he asked Mae and Amos's five-year-old granddaughter, Rose Ann.

Rosie turned large hazel eyes toward him. "*Ja,* we'll have fun together." The other children nodded. At the table with Rosie and Hannah were three-year-old Benjamin Stoltzfus and four-year-old Susie Jane Miller.

Satisfied that his sister would be content, at least for a little while, Jed headed toward the porch where William and the other men had taken up residence on white wicker rocking chairs.

"Food will be ready soon," Josie said as she came out of the house with plates, napkins and utensils. "Jed. Samuel. Amos. Glad you could make it."

"Wouldn't miss your fine cooking, Josie," Amos said.

"Can't say I did much cooking for this occasion. My cousin did it all. Sarah, come out and meet Samuel and Jed. Amos, I believe you met yesterday." Amos nodded.

Jed stood and turned as a young woman with red-gold hair and a familiar blue gaze exited the house, carrying a huge bowl of potato salad.

"This is Sarah Mast, our cousin from Delaware. Sarah, this is Samuel, and his son Jed."

Jed felt warmth curl in his belly. "Sarah," he said. "It's *gut* to see you again."

"Ja," she replied, her cheeks turning a bright shade of pink.

Josie looked stunned. "You've met?"

Sarah answered, "Jedidiah was the one who rescued Thomas and Timothy at Spence's."

Josie nodded as if she'd heard all about it. "The incident with the car."

"It's young Sarah with the twin boys!" Arlin Stoltzfus climbed the porch steps.

Sarah smiled. "It's nice to see you again, Arlin."

Jed, caught up in the wonderful sight of her, could only stare and listen. He'd thought of her often since he'd left Delaware for home. He'd never before enjoyed an afternoon as much as the one they'd spent together at the Millers' after-worship services.

Sarah Mast, Jed thought. She was a long way from home.

She met his gaze, and he smiled.

Chapter Six

"Sarah." Jedidiah studied her. "Is your family here?"

The look in his gaze thrilled her. Sarah liked the sound of her name on Jed's lips. She shook her head. "*Nay*—just the twins. *Mam, Dat* and my older brothers are at home." She looked away as she became overwhelmed by thoughts of her *mam*'s heart surgery. The procedure was scheduled for this coming week.

"Are you all right?" Jed asked.

She looked at him and smiled. "I'm fine."

He studied her a moment, clearly concerned. Suddenly, she felt him relax. "Come meet my family," he urged, as if eager to introduce them.

"I'd best check on my brothers first." She searched for the twins. "Have you seen them?" She heard shouts, giving away the boys' whereabouts.

"They're over there." Jed grinned as he pointed to where the twins played with their young cousins. "They're having a *gut* time with Will and Elam."

Sarah nodded. Will and Elam were Josie and William's two youngest. "Do you think they can stay out of trouble long enough for me to meet your family?" she said with a smile as she regarded the exuberant boys fondly.

"Ja," Jed said. "They will be fine. Young Joshua King has been keeping an eye on them." He turned to regard her with amusement. "They will not get into trouble unless Joshua decides to join them."

Sarah widened her eyes. "Should I be worried?"

Jed chuckled as they approached the tables—and one in particular. "Joshua is a *gut* boy. They will be fine."

Sarah felt the barest touch of his hand brush her back as Jed steered her toward his parents.

"Mam. Dat. This is Sarah Mast. I told you about her." He gestured her closer. "Sarah, this is my *vadder,* Samuel, and my *mudder,* Katie."

Sarah nodded respectfully. "'Tis nice to meet you, Samuel. Katie." Jed's features, she realized, were a stunning combination of his parents'.

"You're William's cousin from Delaware." Smiling, Katie shifted to make room on the bench for Sarah to sit next to her.

"Ja." Sarah couldn't help smiling back as she sat down. "We've come for an extended visit. Josie has been kind to me and my brothers." She caught sight of Timothy and Thomas running in their direction. "Here they come now."

Jed chuckled. "Timothy and Thomas are Sarah's young, *active* twin brothers."

"That is a nice way of describing them," Sarah said, but she watched with love in her heart as the twins approached.

"Jedidiah!" Timothy cried as they reached the table. "Do you want to play ball later?"

Jed nodded. "After we eat."

Thomas grinned. "Sissy, can we get our plates and eat with Will and Elam?"

"*Ja.* But mind your manners and eat your meat and vegetables before taking dessert."

"We will," Timothy said, and Thomas nodded vigorously in agreement. Timothy noticed some adults studying them. "*Hallo.* We are Sarah's brothers. I'm Timothy and this is Thomas."

Sarah caught Katie stifle a grin. "It's *gut* to meet you boys. I'm Katie, Jed's mother. Do you know that I have twin sons? Only, my boys aren't identical like you."

"You do?" Thomas asked.

"*Ja.* See those two down the table? The one with dark hair is Jacob. The fair-haired one is Elijah."

"Jacob. Eli!" Katie called. "Come meet these twin brothers."

Jacob and Eli rose from their seats and approached. Introductions were made, and it was clear that the older Lapp twin brothers had impressed the young Mast twin boys.

Seated with Jed's family, Sarah felt the warmth and love of the Lapps surround her. They made her feel welcome.

Katie Lapp looked much younger than Sarah's mother. With eight children of various ages, she had to be the same age or older than *Mam,* Sarah thought, but poor health had taken its toll on her *mudder,* making her look older than her early forties.

Jed's mother's sandy-brown hair peeked out from

beneath the front of her white prayer *kapp*. She wore a dress of lavender with her white cape tucked in a white apron. There were soft laugh lines near the corners of her warm brown eyes and outside her mouth, which looked as if it curved upward often.

A woman who enjoys her family and her life. Sarah felt wistful. If only *Mam* felt well again… *Mam* had been full of life and laughter until she'd begun to feel ill. The exhaustion that had taken hold of her had stolen her strength and the worry had taken her smile.

Sarah closed her eyes briefly. *Please, Lord, help the doctor mend Mam's heart.*

"There's Hannah," Jed said, interrupting her thoughts as he pointed toward where his little sister played at a table with other young children. "She is growing up quickly."

"Ja," Katie said quietly. She addressed Sarah. "Hannah is my baby." She smiled brightly, and it was as if the sunshine had burst forth from behind a cloud. "My youngest and the only girl."

Sarah couldn't help grinning back at her, her brief moment of wistfulness gone. With Katie nearby, it was hard to feel melancholy. Jed's *mudder* reminded her of *Mam* during the early days, before and right after the twins' birth. "Hannah has many brothers to keep a watch over her," Sarah said.

"'Tis true." Katie watched her little daughter at ease with other children. "I suspect that she will be well able to handle herself as she gets older without her brothers' help."

A young couple waved as they approached. "This is

my brother Noah and his wife, Rachel," Jed told her. "Newlyweds."

Noah and Rachel each carried two plates covered with plastic wrap. "Rachel's been baking again," Jed murmured, and Sarah looked at him for an explanation. "My brother loves dessert, and he has a special liking for chocolate. Rachel indulges him with brownies, cookies, cakes and chocolate-cream pies."

"It sounds like she loves him," Sarah said and then blushed at how her words could be taken. She stood. "I should get back to help Josie in the kitchen." She paused a moment to meet Jed's gaze. "We can talk later."

Jed's slow smile did odd things to her insides. "*Ja.* I want to know what you've been doing since I last saw you."

Sarah gave a silent nod. Then with a fluttering heart, she intercepted the young newlyweds and requested the dishes from Noah.

"I'm Sarah Mast from Delaware." Sarah introduced herself, and Noah relinquished the plates to her with a lazy grin. He was a good-looking man, with sandy-brown hair under his banded straw hat and in the short beard that edged his chin.

"It's nice to meet you, Sarah." Rachel, a lovely young woman with dark brown eyes, wore a blue dress under her black cape and apron. A white prayer *kapp* covered her dark brown hair.

"You've been visiting with my family," Noah said quizzically.

"*Ja,*" she replied. "Jedidiah and I met when he and Arlin came to the Sale at Spence's Bazaar back home in Delaware."

"Jed mentioned you," he said with an intent look that made Sarah silently wonder what Jed could have said to his brother.

"Go visit with your family," Rachel urged her husband as she cast Sarah an understanding glance. "Sarah and I will help Josie fetch the food."

His expression softened as Noah glanced at his wife. "Hurry back," he said in a soft, warm voice.

Rachel's dark eyes beamed with amusement. "Go sit with your *bruders* and behave."

Noah headed toward his family's table as Sarah and Rachel walked to the house. The day was warm and sunny. The sky was a glorious shade of blue without a single cloud in view. A light breeze made it a perfect day to enjoy a meal outside. Everyone was in good spirits, Sarah noticed as she and Rachel walked side by side across the yard and onto the front porch.

"You couldn't ask the Lord for a nicer day," Rachel said, as if reading Sarah's thoughts.

Sarah chuckled. "I was just thinking the same thing." She hesitated as she grabbed the screen door and opened it for Rachel to enter first.

"Congratulations," Sarah said, "on your marriage." And then she worried if she should have mentioned it, but she felt at ease in Rachel's company.

"I never expected to be this happy," Rachel replied with a gentle smile.

Sarah and Rachel exchanged grins. "Praise the Lord," Sarah said laughingly.

"Sarah!" Josie called. "Would you get the food from the refrigerator?"

"*Ja,* Josie," she called back.

"What can I do to help?" Rachel asked.

"Help Sarah" was Josie's answer.

Rachel followed Sarah to the gas refrigerator, and Sarah bent inside to retrieve platters of cold meat and bowls of various salads, vegetables and puddings.

They chatted and laughed as they worked to bring all the dishes into the kitchen, where they set them on the counter. Several Amish women crowded into the room unwrapping the food to prepare it for the table.

"I remember when I first came to Happiness," Rachel said as they returned to the refrigerator for the last of the food. "Noah followed me back to the refrigerator to *help,* he claimed, during a visiting Sunday that was held at his house." Rachel's expression warmed with the memory. "I was upset with him at the time. I was bending inside searching for the potato salad when I heard his voice right behind me. I was so startled I bumped my head as I stood to confront him. He made me uncomfortable, and I wanted to run from him."

Sarah listened with interest as they stopped in the other room. "But you didn't—"

"Nay." Rachel chuckled. "I demanded the bowl back but he refused. He followed me outside and put it on the table. I was embarrassed—yet pleased. I shouldn't have been, but I was. I waited until he'd set the food down and then I left to return to the house. He stayed outside, and I was relieved. I never imagined that one day we would be man and wife."

Sarah tilted her head as she eyed Rachel with curiosity. "Why not?"

"'Tis a long story," the other woman said as she bent inside the refrigerator for the last bowl. With bowl in hand, she straightened and smiled at Sarah. "Would you like to come to our house and have tea one day this week? We can talk and get to know each other better. How about on Tuesday?"

Sarah was delighted. "I'd like that."

"Gut," Rachel said, looking pleased.

They returned to the kitchen, and Sarah grabbed two bowls to take outside. Rachel followed with two baskets of rolls and bread.

"Sarah, it wasn't long ago that I came to Happiness from Ohio, as the new schoolteacher for the community."

Sarah paused and looked back.

Rachel held her gaze. "There is happiness to be found in Happiness, Pennsylvania. I sense sadness about you. I believe you will enjoy your visit here for however long you plan to stay."

Rachel and Sarah carried the last of the dishes from the house. Sarah stopped. Jed had risen from his chair and was speaking with two young women.

"The Zook sisters," Rachel said quietly from behind her. "Anna and Barbara. Annie is the taller one and the eldest."

Sarah continued slowly toward the food table, trying not to glance toward Jed and the two women. "Does Jed like one of them?" she asked Rachel, who set the dishes she carried next to Sarah's.

Rachel was quiet a moment. "Everyone thought for a time that Jed and Annie were sweet on each other," she finally said, her eyes focused on the young women, who remained deep in conversation with Jed.

Sarah glanced over, saw Jed's relaxed stance, then

she quickly looked away. "Are they still seeing each other?" She waited with bated breath for Rachel's reply and finally faced her to read the young woman's expression.

"*Nay,* they have not been seen together in months. This is the first time I've seen them talking for any length of time. And Annie wasn't alone then. Barbara was with her."

Sarah wanted to study the three, but refused to appear too curious. What if Jed and Annie still cared for each other and had simply suffered a misunderstanding? She thought of her time with Jed, the light in his eyes when he looked at her. She didn't think Jed was thinking about Annie when he'd spent the day with her back in Delaware. How Annie felt was a different thing entirely.

"Let's go. Noah sees us and he is waving us over," Rachel said.

"I don't know…. I should sit with Josie and William," she began.

Rachel smiled at her knowingly. "It is up to you. We'd like you to sit with us, but I don't want you to feel uncomfortable." She paused and then quietly added, "Look, the Zook sisters have left Jed's company."

Sarah saw with relief that Annie and Barbara had rejoined their family. "I'll take the meal with my cousins," she said, "and sit with you while we eat dessert."

"*Gut,*" Rachel replied with a grin.

Jed was relieved when Annie Zook and her sister finally walked away from him. He saw Sarah and Rachel cross the yard, and he felt his day brighten.

Seeing Annie had been awkward. It should have been easy, as they were friends, but the fact that they had once almost been something more made him wonder if Annie had felt the same as he did when they'd discussed their friendship—or if she'd only agreed because he'd been the one to bring it up.

Annie had been pleasant, and he had detected no dismay for her sister in Barbara. They had chatted casually, talking about their families, the weather and their farms.

"Do you still have your dog, Millie?" he'd asked her.

"*Ja,* she is a joy to have in the house." Annie confessed that she was grateful that her parents allowed her to keep the dog inside. Animals were usually kept in the barn.

While he had nodded and smiled during the conversation, Jed had found his mind wandering back to Sarah. He'd caught sight of her and Rachel as they'd made numerous trips from the house to the food table.

Sensing Annie's gaze, he'd quickly smiled in her direction, and he'd realized that he'd given the wrong impression when he heard Annie's breath catch as their gazes collided.

Jed frowned. *We are friends, Annie. Nothing more. We'd agreed, remember? There is another waiting for you...someone to love you as you should be loved.*

He didn't love Annie Zook, and he wouldn't settle for anything but love.

"You've been busy," he said as he walked up to meet them, and Sarah nodded. "Are you hungry?"

"*Ja.*" Sarah suddenly looked uncomfortable. "I should eat with my cousins, but I promised Rachel I'd eat dessert with your family."

"I'll see you later, then." He'd rather have her return to share the end of their meal than have no time to spend with her.

Jed rose and meandered over to the food with Noah and Rachel. He filled his plate with a mixture of delicious dishes before he returned to his family's table.

He heard Sarah's laughter as he ate. He flashed a glance toward the Mast family table, smiled when he saw her chuckling, probably over something that Timothy, Thomas and their cousins—Will and Elam—had said or done.

Sarah looked carefree and happy. The darkness that had once shone in her blue eyes had vanished. She didn't look his way, although he willed it. He would have to be satisfied that she'd come back to his table to eat dessert.

"I've enjoyed talking with you," Sarah said as she rose after they'd eaten dessert together. She'd chosen a piece of apple pie, while Jed had enjoyed a slice of cherry.

Jed stood. "Will you walk with us later?" he said, shooting Noah a glance.

"*Ja,*" Noah added. "'Tis a beautiful day. Please join us." He looked at his wife.

"*Ja,* please do." Rachel flashed her a sincere, welcoming smile, her dark eyes crinkling with amusement.

Sarah grinned back. "I may do that, after I check with Josie to make sure she doesn't need me."

She cleaned up the food and packaged leftovers with the other community women. When she was done, she headed outside to find Rachel, Noah…and Jed.

The sun was warm on Sarah's face as she and the

three Lapps walked across the lawn and into the farm fields. A robin flew from a branch onto the ground ahead of them, chirping to its mate still up in the tree.

Sarah watched with a smile as another bird sat on the ground close by, and the two robins rooted about in the dirt, before taking flight.

"Couldn't ask for a nicer day," Jed said.

"Ja," Sarah agreed. "'Tis a lovely day for a walk."

"We should have gone for a ride." Noah stopped a moment as if to enjoy the scenery. He raised his wide-brimmed straw hat before setting it onto his head again.

Sarah watched as Rachel stood nearby, smiling at her husband. While Rachel and Noah seemed aware only of each other, she felt someone's gaze and looked to see that Jed studied her with an odd look that made her wholly aware of him. "Anything wrong?" she asked, wondering if she had a speck on her nose or a crumb near the corner of her mouth.

He shook his head slowly, his gaze warming, his lips curving upward, as he continued to look at her. "I'm glad you decided to walk with us."

Sarah tried not to let his study unnerve her. "Seems too nice of a day to stay inside."

"Will you come for a ride with me one day?" he asked, his expression suddenly unreadable.

She didn't want him to realize how much she would enjoy such a ride. "If there is time—"

"There is always time, Sarah Mast. The Lord gives us all we need. We just have to use it wisely." He held on to her gaze.

And riding with you would be a wise thing to do? She thought briefly of Annie Zook.

"Thomas and Timothy—" she began.

Jed smiled. "They can come with us."

His offer to take the boys warmed her. "We'll see what our days bring."

"*Ja,* of course, Sarah," he said, his lips quirking with amusement. "Until then, I shall appreciate today and our time together."

Sarah didn't want to ponder the idea of a relationship with Jed Lapp too deeply. She would be leaving soon— what possible chance would the two of them have if Jed actually wanted a relationship?

"Sarah, look! It's a red fox and her cubs!" Rachel cried suddenly, outwardly drawing Sarah's attention, but she remained overly conscious of the tall, dark-haired man beside her.

"It's a large one," Sarah commented and flashed Jed a look to see that his amusement had deepened. *As if he suspects I like his company but am trying not to show it.*

The two couples paused to watch the fox with its cubs as the animals crept unaware of the humans. Suddenly, the mother spied their presence and scurried her young ones into the brush away from watchful eyes.

"Shall we continue?" Jed asked her several moments later, his deep voice close to Sarah's ear. "There is a stream up ahead. Maybe we'll find some wildflowers."

"*Ja,* let's keep going!" Rachel answered while Jed stood silent within inches of Sarah.

Sarah felt the light touch of Jed's fingers as he urged her in the right direction before he withdrew. Although he didn't touch her again, she could still feel the sensation of Jed's hand as she walked beside him with Noah and Rachel. During the rest of their walk, Jed kept his distance from her, which disappointed her. He seemed too polite as he walked a few feet from her side.

Had she misread his attention? Had Jed's thoughts turned to Annie Zook and their earlier conversation?

Sarah swallowed hard. She reminded herself that it would be best if she forgot Jedidiah Lapp and her growing feelings for him. Soon she'd be leaving Pennsylvania…and Jed would stay here in Happiness to marry and build a life with his new wife.

There was no hope for them.

Was there?

Chapter Seven

The day was sunny and warm, without a breeze to stir the leaves on the trees and the wet laundry that Sarah and Josie hung to dry on the clothesline.

"These wet garments will dry in no time," Josie said. She bent and pulled a shirt from the wicker basket. Shaking out the wet green fabric, she secured it to the line with wooden clothespins.

"'Tis not as breezy as yesterday," Sarah agreed, "but the temperature is much warmer." She withdrew a small pair of tri-blend denim pants and threw them over the line, pinning them in place before reaching into her basket for an identical pair. "It feels good to be outside."

"Ja." Josie smiled in her direction. "We've been lucky this spring. God has been *gut* to us all season."

Sarah nodded as she met her cousin's gaze. "We accomplished a lot this morning," she said, pleased.

"No more chores for you after this." Josie pinned a blue dress into place. "You are having tea with Rachel later today."

"It will be nice to see her again." Sarah experienced

warmth as she recalled how she and her new friend Rachel had become fast friends. "Is the *schuulhaus* far?"

"Nay," her cousin said. "It's to the right and down the road apiece. Take the buggy, though, since it will be afternoon when you get there. You may want to stay and chat until late."

"I'd rather walk." Sarah grabbed a small maroon shirt from her basket, shook out the wrinkles and then pinned it to the clothesline before doing the same with its twin. "'Tis such a nice day, and I can use the exercise."

"You can walk if you'd like," Josie said. "The sun stays out longer these evenings. You won't have to walk home in the dark if you're invited to supper."

"I'll be home in time to help you with supper."

"No need." Josie tucked a stray lock of hair beneath her *kapp*; the tiny strand had come loose during morning chores. "You've done more than enough since you've been here. Enjoy your time with Rachel."

"I don't feel right leaving you with the boys." Sarah frowned as she thought of her twin brothers. "What if they misbehave?"

Josie chuckled. "What're two more unruly children?" With the last garment secured on the line, she picked up her basket and regarded Sarah with an assessing look. "You need not worry, Sarah. If I can handle my youngest two, I can certainly manage the twins." She waited as Sarah retrieved her empty basket and moved closer to her before they headed back to the farmhouse. "They get along well, don't *ya* think? There has been little trouble with the four of them, which amazes me."

Sarah followed Josie up the porch steps, pausing on

the last stair to lean forward and wipe her forehead with the back of one arm. She straightened her prayer *kapp*. "I did notice that they've been behaving lately. Do you think it's because they get tired with all the activity?"

Josie opened the screen door, and Sarah grabbed hold of the edge, allowing her cousin to precede her into the house. "*Ja*. They certainly go to sleep easily enough," the older woman said. "Not a peep out of them once they're in bed." Her tone softened. "I think coming here has been *gut* for your *bruders*…" Her tone softened. "And you."

"*Ja*. I'm grateful we had this chance to visit," Sarah agreed. "I only wish that *Mam* wasn't having surgery."

"I'm sure you'll hear from your *dat* as soon as he has something to tell." Josie entered the kitchen and set the laundry basket on the table bench.

"Josie, I'm frightened for *Mam*. I pray to the Lord daily but I'm still scared." She set her basket next to Josie's. "Does that make me an awful person? I know we should trust solely in the Lord's love, but this is *Mam*, and I can't help but be concerned."

Josie gave Sarah a hug. "*Nay,* you're not awful, Sarah. God understands that we are human. As long as we continue to pray to Him, He will be there for us. In the end, all will be well."

When her cousin released her, Sarah had tears in her eyes. "I hope you are right."

"The Lord loves us. He gave us life. He is there whenever we need Him. Rest assured that we are all praying for your *mudder*." Josie studied her with understanding. "Before you leave, would you check on the boys for me? They are either upstairs or in the barn."

Sarah climbed the stairs to check their bedroom. The second floor was too quiet as she approached; the boys couldn't be up here. She heard laughter outside and peered out the open window. She watched as all four boys spilled out of the barn and gave chase to each other onto the lawn and then into the backyard. No matter how hard it had been to leave home, she realized, coming here had been the best thing for Timothy and Thomas.

And for her. If she hadn't come to Happiness, she never would have seen Jedidiah again.

It was one o'clock in the afternoon as Sarah headed down the dirt lane and onto the main paved road toward Rachel's cottage. Before she'd left, she'd washed and donned clean clothes. Her morning chores of scrubbing, dusting, washing and baking had left telltale dirt streaks on Sarah's face and arms and across her cape. As she turned right and then crossed the road to walk facing traffic, she softly sang a hymn from the *Ausbund*. Swinging her basket, she studied the surrounding countryside as she sang and walked toward the community *schuulhaus* and the teacher cottage currently occupied by Rachel and Noah.

It took Sarah a half hour of walking before she saw a glimpse of the *schuulhaus* ahead. She didn't mind the journey. It was too nice a day not to walk, and singing made the distance shorter. She smiled. She looked forward to seeing her new friend. She and Rachel had shared an instant liking for each other. Was it because Rachel, too, had come from a different state? The only difference was that Rachel had come to settle permanently in Happiness, while Sarah had come only for an extended visit.

Soon, she'd have to return home, Sarah reminded herself. Any day her family would be calling her and the twins back to Delaware. Everyone in Happiness had been so kind and caring that Sarah knew she'd have liked to stay the summer, if not for her worry for *Mam* and the knowledge that her *mudder* needed her.

Who was keeping house at home? Who was there to clean and cook and feed *Dat* and her older brothers? Who was caring for *Mam* and making sure she had everything she needed? Who was available to her all day and night?

"Aunt Iva?" Sarah murmured. "Mary Alice?" She frowned. She should be there for *Mam*—not her aunt or cousin.

She stopped, closed her eyes and prayed. "Help me, Lord, to be a *gut* and dutiful daughter, to understand why I am here in Happiness with the twins instead of home in Kent County with *Mam* and *Dat*."

Sarah opened her eyes and continued down the road, aware of the sights and sounds of the spring season. Lush green grass carpeted lawns and extended yards, while pink, yellow and red roses grew in abundance along an *Englischer*'s driveway, the blossoms' sweet scent drifting to her nose. A child played happily in her front yard with a big yellow dog, while the girl's mother and father sat in cloth chairs, watching with fond smiles as they sipped from cans of iced tea.

She caught a glimpse of the *schuulhaus* ahead. Farther up the lane next to the *schuul* was the teacher's cottage—her friends' home.

The twins were doing well. *Thriving,* she thought with a slight smile. She was a dutiful daughter here where her parents wanted her. For now, she had to take solace that whatever happened at home, she had done the right thing and obeyed her parents.

Rachel opened the door as Sarah approached. *"Willkomm!"* she exclaimed. She grinned as she gestured Sarah into the house. "I'm so glad you've come. You walked?" she said with a smile as she turned on the gas stove under the teapot.

"Ja, it seemed too nice of a day not to." Sarah studied her surroundings, immediately liking the kitchen's cozy warmth. "Am I too early?"

"Nay." Rachel grinned at her as she set down two teacups with matching saucers on the kitchen table. "I've been eager to see you again."

"Me, too." Sarah handed Rachel the basket of treats. "Lemon squares." She paused. "For you. Someone told me that you liked them."

"I do." Rachel beamed as she accepted the basket, peeked inside to see the confectioner's sugar-dusted yellow squares. "But I didn't know anyone knew."

"Josie noticed you seemed to enjoy them during one visiting Sunday," Sarah said, glad that her cousin was an observant person…except when it came to guessing Sarah's own thoughts.

"I wonder what else she noticed," Rachel murmured.

Sarah shrugged. "I wouldn't know. Unless it pertains to William and her children." *Or the twins or me,* she mused.

The teakettle began to whistle, and Rachel removed it from the stove while Sarah sat down at the table. As

Rachel made tea, Sarah unwrapped the lemon squares. Leaving the tea to steep, Rachel set out a sugar bowl, a jar of local honey and a small jug of milk. It was only after the tea was poured and flavored did Rachel pause to study Sarah. "How are you making out at the Masts'?"

"They've been wonderful to us," Sarah said. "I like Josie. She is *gut* for William and a fine *mudder* to her daughter and sons."

"*Ja,* I like her, too." Rachel took a sip of her tea and then cradled the warm cup with her hands.

Sarah reached over to select one of Rachel's chocolate-chip cookies. "Tell me about you and Noah. About how you met and later married."

Rachel smiled, but there was a brief glimpse of something painful in her dark chocolate-brown eyes. "When I first arrived in Happiness, I learned that everyone thought that Noah and my cousin Charlotte would wed one day. Noah rescued me from a runaway buggy my first day in Lancaster County. He was wonderful and brave. Charlotte was with him that day, and I thought they might be sweethearts. I tried not to like Noah, knowing that he belonged to her, but I couldn't help it. You've met Noah. He is just too likable."

Sarah chuckled. "It's obvious he loves you."

Rachel's features softened. "*Ja,* but I didn't know it then. I lived with Charlotte and her family when I first came here. Noah came to the farm often." She sipped from her teacup before she continued, "I thought he came to see Charlotte. Noah and my cousin have known each other since they were infants, and it was obvious that they liked one another. Yet, once I moved into the teacher's cottage, Noah started to stop by at the cottage or the *schuul* instead, to ask if anything needed fixing or if I wanted help."

"Charlotte and Noah weren't sweet on each other?" Sarah asked, eager to hear more.

Rachel took a bite of a lemon square and a look of delight entered her expression. "This is *gut!*" she exclaimed before she went on. "They liked each other well enough. In fact, at one time, they did think about marrying, but then they realized that they didn't love each other that way. They were like brother and sister rather than sweethearts. Charlotte fell in love with and married Abram Peachy. I don't think you have met Abram yet, as the Peachy family is currently away visiting Abram's relatives in Indiana."

Sarah nodded. "And Noah?"

Rachel blushed. "Noah loved me."

"So all ended happily ever after," Sarah said with a smile.

"Not exactly," Rachel admitted. "You see, about a year and a half ago, I was in a buggy accident back home in Millersburg, Ohio. I was with a local boy, and the buggy slipped off the icy roadway and into a ditch when a car sped around a corner. Abraham was unhurt, and so was my brother, who rode with us as chaperone. I was in the hospital for a while. Abraham never came to visit me—not once—and I was heartbroken." She paused and drew a sharp breath. "I was severely injured—a broken arm, a couple of cracked ribs and… I hurt my abdomen." She closed her eyes a moment as if in pain. "The doctor didn't know if I'd ever be able to give birth, and although I loved Noah, I couldn't allow myself to care for him too deeply. He's good with children, Sarah. He should have a child of his own."

Sarah had felt a tightening of sympathy in her chest as Rachel told her story. "But you must have worked it out between you, since the two of you married."

"Ja." Rachel's lips curved into a soft smile. "Noah wanted me more than a child. But—"

Sarah sipped from her teacup and waited.

"I think I may be pregnant," Rachel confessed. "You're the only one I've told. I don't know for sure. I want to make certain first. I don't want to disappoint Noah—or his family."

Tears stung Sarah's eyes. She understood. There were other physical reasons that a woman might think she was pregnant and not actually be with child. "What did the doctor say…after the accident?"

Rachel's grin was wry. "That's it possible, but not likely. If I do become pregnant, I'll be considered high-risk."

"Rachel, I'm sorry…." Sarah rose from her seat, skirted the table and hugged her friend. "You haven't seen the doctor yet," she guessed.

Rachel inclined her head. *"Nay.* Noah will want to go with me. I need to be sure before I tell him."

Sarah returned to her seat.

"I don't know why I find it so easy to talk with you," her new friend said.

"I feel the same way about you. I told you about *Mam*'s surgery the first day we met." She had told Rachel all about *Mam*'s illness while cleaning up after dessert that day.

"Have you heard anything from your family?" Rachel asked.

Sarah shook her head. "Not yet. It's too early. The surgery is tomorrow."

"I'll pray for her, Sarah," Rachel promised.

"And I'll be here if you need me for any reason…as long as I'm not called home."

The sound of a screen door as it was opened and shut was followed by Noah's deep voice raised in greeting. "Rachel!"

"In the *kiche!*" The light of love brightened Rachel's gaze as she stood and waited for her husband. As Noah greeted his wife, his brother entered.

Sarah felt Jed's presence keenly; he seemed to fill up the room. He looked wonderful in his work clothes. She tried not to notice how his suspenders fit over his green shirt or the strength inherent in his muscled arms bared beneath his short shirtsleeves. Her heart pounded hard as he smiled in her direction and they locked gazes.

"Sarah." He seemed to be genuinely happy to see her.

Her heart raced faster. "Jed," she greeted, wildly pleased to see him. Her nape tingled as he pulled out a chair beside hers and sat.

"Would you like some tea?" Rachel asked the two men.

Noah nodded. "*Ja*…and something to eat. Jed's helping me with a delivery, and since we had to drive past here…"

"I'm glad you did," his wife said happily. "Would you like a lemon square?" she asked Jed. "Sarah made them."

Jed's smile was slow and heart-stopping. "*Ja*, I'd like

to taste one if Sarah made them," he said, while Noah reached for a chocolate-chip cookie.

Rachel poured each man a cup of tea, and Sarah watched as Jed added sugar but no milk. Sarah's gaze noted Jed's big, strong hands handling the teacup with extreme gentleness as he raised it to his lips. He captured her gaze over the rim of the cup, and Sarah looked away, embarrassed at having been caught staring.

"Well?" Rachel asked when Jed tasted a bit of a lemon square.

Jed turned to focus his gaze on Sarah. "Delicious," he said, and Sarah blushed but was unable to look away.

"Sorry, Sarah," Noah apologized, "but I'm partial to chocolate."

Sarah grinned at Noah. "So I've heard…" She chuckled. "And from more than one person."

Noah returned her grin. "Rachel's eyes resemble dark chocolate, don't *ya* think?"

"Noah!" Rachel blushed as she rose to put on the teakettle again.

Suddenly, Sarah's day brightened. She and Rachel enjoyed the brothers' company for the next half hour, and then it was time for the men to return to work. "That was unexpected," Sarah said once Noah and Jed had left.

"Hmm," Rachel said as she thoughtfully stared at the door through which the two brothers had departed. "Wasn't it just?"

That night, while she lay in bed with Ellen asleep beside her, Sarah thought back on the day with a strange sense of exhilaration.

She'd had a fine working morning, a nice afternoon tea at Rachel's, and… Jed had stopped with Noah to join them. *He likes my lemon squares.* Sarah made a mental note to make more of them for Rachel…and for Jed.

Sarah knew she was foolish to feel this way about Jedidiah Lapp. She would be leaving soon and it was unlikely that she'd ever see him again. The thought made her stomach burn suddenly and her heart ache.

Why did they meet again if the Lord didn't have something in mind for them?

She closed her eyes and prayed silently, vehemently, for the Lord's guidance and help during the rest of her stay in Happiness. *Lord, help me to know what to do. If Your plan for me doesn't include Jedidiah Lapp, please keep me from losing my heart to him.*

Chapter Eight

"Sissy, can we visit the Kings with Elam and Will? Cousin William's going to take us." Timothy beamed up at her with blue eyes a shade lighter than hers.

Thomas stood beside his brother bobbing his head. "Please, Sissy."

Sarah stopped sweeping the front porch to lean on the corn broom's wooden handle. "Does Josie know?"

"Ja," Timothy said. "William's gonna help Amos at the farm, and he'll bring us home."

"Then you may go," she replied, holding back a smile, "but remember to mind your manners and behave."

"Ja, Sissy!" This time it was Thomas who spoke up. "Joshua has puppies in their barn."

Watching as the boys ran to meet their cousins, Sarah recalled the trouble once caused by the twins' fascination with dogs. She shuddered whenever she thought of the near-accident when they'd chased a puppy into the path of an oncoming car. *Thank Ye, Lord, for Jedidiah Lapp's quick response.* The boys could have been seriously injured or killed if Jed hadn't been there to snatch them out of harm's way.

Her thoughts turned to *Mam* as Sarah set the broom in motion again. It was Thursday, and *Mam* had had her surgery yesterday. *Is she all right? Have the doctors successfully repaired her heart? Why hasn't* Dat *called to let me know?* Surely he would have called if her mother had taken a turn for the worse.

When she finished sweeping the front porch, Sarah went into the house and confided her fears to Josie. "I'm worried about *Mam*. What if something terrible went wrong during her surgery?"

Josie looked up from the sink and the basin of sudsy water filled with the canning jars. "You must not fret, Sarah," she said. "Ruth's surgery might have been scheduled for late afternoon. If so, wouldn't Daniel want to check on her this morning before letting you know? He'll call soon."

"I hope you're right." Sarah leaned the broom in a kitchen corner. Earlier, she had swept the first-floor rooms. She would tackle the upstairs tomorrow.

"You'll see."

Her cousin's matter-of-fact tone made Sarah relax. She approached the sink where Josie worked. "Shall I change the bed linens?" she asked. "Or do you want help here?"

"Bed linens. If you could start with the boys' rooms, that would be *gut*." The older woman grinned. "They'll be leaving shortly, and it will be quiet here today."

The corners of Sarah's lips curved upward. "A nice peaceful break from the boys?"

"For a short time," Josie said as she washed a jar,

rinsed it in hot water and then set it on a clean dish-cloth spread out on the counter. "I will miss them soon afterward. I always do."

"I know what you mean." Sarah extracted clean pil-lowcases and sun-dried sheets from the linen chest. "They are so much a part of our lives."

With Josie's agreement ringing in her ears, she climbed the stairs and entered the bedroom shared by the four boys. The day was cooler than it had been, and the breeze blowing in through the open window past the plain white curtains was refreshing. Working quickly but efficiently, she stripped each bed. With skill born of experience, she remade the beds with clean sheets, deftly tucking the bottom corners in and fluffing the newly encased pillows before setting them in place. When she was done, she smoothed out the quilts that she'd replaced on both beds.

She gathered up the dirty sheets and started down the stairs. When she heard a deep voice near the front door, Sarah paused on the steps. She detected the words *Sarah* and *mudder* and *phone call*. Her throat constricting, she rushed with sheets over her arms toward the front door, where Jedidiah Lapp spoke with Josie in the hall.

"Mam?" she managed to whisper.

"Ja," Josie said. "Jed was at Whittier's Store when the call came. He's come to take you. Your *Dat*'s wait-ing for your call."

"I have the phone number where you can reach him," Jed said, his quiet tone full of concern.

She locked gazes with Jed. "Did he say anything?"

"Nay," Jed replied. " Bob Whittier said your *vadder* wanted only to speak with you."

Tears stung her eyes as Sarah nodded. "I should go." She looked about, feeling lost, wondering what to do with the sheets she had draped over her arms.

"I'll take those," Josie said softly before she disappeared with the sheets into another room.

"Danki," Sarah murmured. Her stomach burned and her heart raced rapidly with fear.

"Sarah," Jed urged gently, "we should go."

She shook herself as if she had been in a trance. *"Ja."* She'd been waiting to hear about her mother, and now she was afraid of what she'd learn. *Please, Lord, let* Mam *be well!*

A warm, masculine hand reached out for hers. "Are you ready?"

Jolted from her thoughts, Sarah gave Jed a little nod.

"Sarah, she will be fine," he said softly.

She took strength from his strong but gentle grip as she was led from the house and helped into the buggy before he released her hand. Soon, Jed was steering the horse and buggy down the lane and onto the paved road toward Whittier's Store.

They were quiet for a time and then Jed said, "Sarah—"

"She had surgery yesterday," Sarah told him. "Heart surgery." She looked at him with tears in her eyes. "I've been waiting to hear." She drew a sharp breath. "What if something bad happened during the operation?"

Jed reached over to briefly place his warm hand over hers, and the simple touch comforted her. "Sarah, let's see what he has to say. It may be Daniel wants to talk with you…to tell you himself that Ruth is fine and to ask about the twins."

Sarah gave him a weak smile. "I hope you're right." Despite her concern, she was conscious of Jed's warm, strong fingers against hers, and when he removed them, she felt the loss.

Jed studied Sarah with concern. The only sound for a time was the clip-clop of the mare's hooves on macadam and the occasional engine of a car as one passed from either direction.

"We're almost there," he said softly.

"Gut." She sighed wearily. "I shouldn't worry, but I can't help it." Her bright blue eyes glistened with tears as she met his gaze, and he wanted nothing more than to take her into his arms and comfort her. He was glad he'd been at Whittier's when the call came. Now he would be near if she needed him. *Please, Lord, let Sarah's fears be unfounded.*

Spying the store ahead, Jed turned on the signal and waited for a car to pass from behind before he steered the buggy into an empty spot near the hitching post in the paved parking lot.

He quickly jumped down, tethered the horse and hurried to Sarah's side with his hand extended to assist her from the vehicle. She accepted his help with a nod of thanks, and he walked with her into Whittier's Store, which was a combination general store, eatery and tack-supply shop.

Jed reached into his pocket for coins and pressed them into Sarah's trembling fingers. "There's the pay phone," he said.

"Danki," she whispered.

"Is this the young lady?" Bob Whittier asked, and

Jed nodded. "No need to use the pay phone. You can use this one here." He gestured toward the phone sitting on the cashier's counter. "Don't matter if it's long-distance or not."

Jed watched Sarah lift the receiver and dial the number he'd given her with a shaking hand. She looked anxious as she waited for someone to answer.

"Dat?" he heard her ask. *"Ja,* it is Sarah. How is *Mam?"* Jed stood by as she listened intently. *"Ja?* She will be all right?" She frowned and Jed moved closer as if he could infuse her with strength. "She will be in the hospital how long?" She met Jed's gaze as she nodded. "I see." She paused, listening. "We are fine. The twins enjoy spending time with Elam and Will. Josie has been *gut* to us." She paused to listen. *"Ja,* I will tell them." She closed her eyes briefly. "I love you, too, *Dat.* Please tell *Mam* I love her and I hope she feels better soon."

She raised a hand to tug on a *kapp* string as she clutched the telephone. *"Ja,* I will. Tell Ervin and Toby I miss them. *Ja.* I will. I will wait to hear from you, then. *Ja, Dat.* I will talk with you soon." She set the handset carefully back onto its cradle. She stood a quiet moment, lost in thought. She approached Bob Whittier. "I appreciate the use of your phone," she said.

"No problem," the old man said gruffly. "Feel free to use it whenever you need."

Jed studied Sarah and waited silently for her to talk with him as they headed outside together.

"Sarah—"

She turned to face him, and tears coursed down her face, wrenching at his heart and silently urging him to take her in his arms. He didn't. "What's wrong?"

She shook her head. "*Mam* came through the surgery. Her doctors think she will make a full recovery."

He stared into the depths of her glistening blue eyes and realized that what she felt was joy. Her tears were from happiness, not from concern, as he'd feared.

"That is wonderful, Sarah." He smiled and touched her arm before quickly withdrawing. "Come. I'll take you home. Josie will want to hear your news."

He helped her into the buggy, untied the horse and climbed onto the seat next to her. He flashed her a quick glance, but she was gazing out her side of the vehicle. With a flick of the leathers, he spurred the horse on, back toward the Mast farm.

"I appreciate the ride," Sarah said softly after a time, interrupting the quiet previously broken only by the sound of the horse's hooves on the road.

"I'm glad I could help." Jed enjoyed looking at her, but didn't look for long. He knew she'd be uncomfortable if she caught him staring. Turning his attention to the road, he still had a vivid mental image of her… the lovely color of her red-gold hair…the shining vivid blue of her eyes…the smoothness of her white skin… the pink of her perfectly formed, sweet lips.

"I'm happy that your *mudder* is doing well," he said.

"It was bad at first, *Dat* said, but she came through and the doctors are hopeful."

Bad? he wondered. How bad? He didn't ask. "She is awake and doing better?" He flashed her a look.

Her smile was genuine. "*Ja.* Much better."

Jed felt a relief so powerful that it was as if his own mother had been the one to undergo the surgery. What was it about Sarah Mast that made him feel this strong emotional connection to her?

He had no right to think of her as often as he had been, to consider a relationship with her. She'd be leaving soon, and he'd be staying in Happiness.

His thoughts turned solemnly to Annie Zook. He feared he'd hurt Annie when they'd ended their relationship and talked about staying friends. How could he trust his feelings for Sarah when he'd been wrong about him and Annie? If he hadn't seen how happy Noah was in his marriage to Rachel, he might have courted and wed Annie and been content.

But then he'd met Sarah in Delaware, and he'd begun to wonder, although he'd known it was foolish when they'd only just met. Seeing her in Happiness stirred mixed feelings inside of him. He felt happy when he was with her. When he was with her, the time flew and it was as if their moments together went by too quickly. He thought of what life could be if they were man and wife.

He silently scolded himself. He had to stop this. Sarah had a family in Delaware, a mother who needed her help.

Jed was conscious of her beside him as he steered the horse down the road toward the Mast farm. It was quiet inside the buggy, but it wasn't an uncomfortable silence. For him, there was joy in being in her company, in accompanying her wherever she wanted to go.

The Mast farmhouse appeared ahead on the right, and Jed steered the horse onto the dirt driveway. He pulled the vehicle close to the house, jumped down, skirted the buggy and held out his hand to Sarah. He felt a jolt of happiness when she placed her fingers within his grasp.

Sarah smiled as she climbed down, and Jed felt his heart rate kick into high gear as she regarded him with warmth.

"*Danki,* Jed," she said softly as he reluctantly released her hand.

"I'm here if you ever need a ride." He gazed at her intently to gauge her reaction.

Her smile reached her eyes. "I will remember that."

"Sarah!" Josie came out of the house and onto the front porch. "How's Ruth?"

"*Gut!*" she called back. Sarah headed toward the house. She hesitated in her stride as if she'd realized that he hadn't followed her. "Coming?" she asked softly. "I thought we could have a glass of lemonade together."

"That sounds wonderful," he answered as he trailed behind her into the house.

"*Mam* is fine," Sarah told Josie as she approached the porch, conscious of Jed's presence behind her. She was glad when he followed her. She didn't want him to leave yet. It had felt good to have him near when she'd called her father. His presence, his kind words, had given her strength when she most needed it.

"Lemonade?" she asked Josie.

"*Ja.*" Josie called into the house, "Ellen, bring the pitcher of lemonade that Sarah made this morning." She smiled at Sarah and added to her daughter, "And some cookies, too!"

"Coming, *Mam,*" Sarah heard the young girl reply.

Sarah turned to Jed. "Would you like to sit inside or out?"

"On the porch," he replied, gesturing to a row of white wooden rocking chairs with white wooden tables between them.

"I'll help Ellen," Sarah said.

"*Nay,* you sit with Jed," Josie urged. "I'll go in."

Sarah sat in a rocker and Jed took a seat in the nearest one. "It is a lovely day," she said, "made better by the *gut* news about *Mam* I received today."

"*Ja,*" Jed said quietly.

She flashed him a quick glance at his tone. He studied her with a look that stole her breath and made her stomach flip-flop.

This is Jed, she thought. *Why do I feel nervous around him? It's not as if I haven't spent any time with him.*

They caught and locked glances. Finally, Jed released her gaze. "Sunday service is at the Amos Kings," Jed murmured conversationally. "Charlotte and Nancy will be home by then."

"They are Amos and Mae's daughters, and Rachel's cousins."

Jed nodded. "Charlotte is married to Abram Peachy. He is a deacon. They and their five children have been visiting Abram's relatives in Indiana."

"Five children!" Sarah was surprised. When she'd met them, she hadn't thought Amos or Mae old enough to have a daughter with five children.

Jed's lips curved. "They were Abram's before they were Charlotte's." When Sarah frowned, Jed chuckled.

"Abram was a widower. Charlotte loves his children as her own, but she hasn't given birth yet."

Sarah's eyes sparkled. "I see."

"Nancy lives at home with Amos and Mae, but she, too, has been away." He reached up and adjusted his banded straw hat.

"Here we are," Josie announced, carrying four glasses and the pitcher of lemonade on a tray. Her ten-year-old daughter, Ellen, smiled as she brought out a plate of various cookies and set it on a table between Jed and Sarah.

"You baked these?" Jed asked the young girl.

Blushing, Ellen shook her head. "Sarah did. She helps *Mam* a lot."

"You help her, too," Sarah said gently, noting the girl's discomfort.

"Indeed she does," Josie said with a smile for her daughter. "Would you run inside and get some napkins?"

Ellen nodded and scurried away only to return seconds later with a stack of white napkins, which she handed to her mother.

They sat enjoying the lemonade, the cookies and the day.

Josie stood first. "I'd better check on the boys—"

Sarah rose. "I'll do it."

"Nay," her cousin said. "You stay and keep company with Jed." She flashed him a smile. "Give my best to your *mudder*."

Jed nodded. "I will."

Suddenly, Sarah found herself alone on the front porch with Jedidiah Lapp. As she looked out over the yard and barn, she was conscious of him studying her. She faced him to meet his gaze head-on. He smiled at her, and she felt her heart pound. "Is something wrong?" she asked.

Jed shook his head. "I was wondering if you'd be staying for the singing on Sunday."

She blinked. "I—I haven't thought about it."

"Think about it and come," he urged softly. "I'd like to take you home again."

She couldn't help it—the memory made her smile. She had enjoyed her ride with him after the singing that night in Delaware. She knew she'd enjoy riding with him again, but should she?

"We're friends, aren't we, Sarah?" he said, as if trying to convince her of the innocence of his request.

Friends? Sarah thought. Yes, they were friends, but there was more…something she didn't want to ponder on too deeply. *"Ja,"* she said, "we're friends." As he and Annie were friends? she wondered, not liking the thought.

"Then you shouldn't be concerned with riding home with me."

"I'm not—" she began and then stopped, sighed. "I will come to the singing and ride home with you—" she hesitated "—unless you change your mind and want to take someone else home instead."

"Not likely," he said softly as he stood. "I have to get home. *Dat*'s waiting for me—"

Sarah hadn't thought of Jed's plans for the day or how she might have ruined them. "I'm sorry—"

His chestnut eyes twinkled. "Don't be. I'm not." He reached out and tugged on her right *kapp* string. Then with both hands, he adjusted her *kapp,* after which he cradled her head for several long seconds before letting go. Sarah could still feel the warmth of his fingers on her skin beneath the fabric.

"I will see you soon, Sarah," he said. "I enjoyed the lemonade and cookies."

"I'm glad you were there with me when I made the phone call." She was sure that he had no idea how much his presence had helped her through the difficult time of not knowing the outcome of her mother's surgery while they were on the way to Whittier's Store.

"It was my pleasure to take you, Sarah Mast."

With those words ringing in her ears, she watched Jed descend the porch and hurry toward his buggy. He climbed aboard, picked up the leathers and then waved before he drove on.

She'd never felt this strange in anyone's presence. She liked him—how could she not? But there was something more lurking inside her: fear, happiness, resignation. She was afraid that she was falling hard for Jedidiah.

But she was even more afraid that nothing could ever come of her feelings for him. Soon her family would call her home, and she would again be the dutiful daughter available to help *Mam* with the kids, the house and the chores.

Chapter Nine

The storm began with a distant rumble of thunder and a flash of lightning through the window glass. As the thunder strengthened, Sarah glanced over at the young girl in the bed next to her and saw that Ellen slept on peacefully.

There was no sign of Timothy or Thomas; no doubt they were sleeping, as well.

Sarah lay in bed, watching the play of bright light as it flashed through the window and onto the ceiling. She didn't mind the storm; she enjoyed the sound of rain on the roof, the droplets that spattered against the house. What she didn't like was if the lightning got too close or the thunder too explosive. Lightning could cause fire, and fire could cause loss of life and property. This storm was soft and easy, and it was just how Sarah liked it.

As the rain began to patter against the farmhouse, Sarah found her thoughts shifting in different directions. She thought of home and her family, her mother in the hospital, her *dat,* her older brothers, her sister, Emma, and her husband, James, in Ohio.

Was *Mam* getting better? It had only been two days since she'd spoken with *Dat*. He would have called again if something terrible had happened. Wouldn't he?

Sarah closed her eyes and said a silent prayer that her mother would continue to improve until she was well again. Thoughts of *Mam* brought her around to her presence in Happiness. She had enjoyed her time here. She had taken on some of the chores for Josie, who was appreciative. When Sarah had offered to do more, Josie had declined, saying that Sarah did more than her share of work, that she should take time to have fun.

Take time to have fun? It had been a long time since Sarah had done anything but chores...except during that one evening back home at the Millers', when she'd attended a singing and Jed had taken her home afterward.

Sarah smiled into the darkness. It had been a wonderful night. She had enjoyed her time with Jed. She'd never felt so lighthearted, so alive, so happy, and it was Jedidiah Lapp who'd made her feel this way.

When he'd left for his home in Pennsylvania, Sarah had never expected to see him again. She'd known that he lived in Lancaster County, but the county was huge, home to the largest Amish population in the country. She'd realized that the odds of seeing him in Lancaster were slim.

Prior to her departure from Delaware, when her thoughts had been concerned with her *mudder,* had she really given Jed much thought? Perhaps as a passing musing, but nothing more. She hadn't wanted to hope...

But that first Sunday when she'd discovered that Jed lived in Happiness, that he was a member of the same church district as her cousins, she'd been at first stunned and then inordinately pleased. Her pleasure became tempered by the fact that someday soon she would go home to Delaware, while he would remain here in Happiness.

Back home, she had suffered some heartbreak after Jed had left, but with God's help she was able to find the strength and determination to return to her life, a life in which she did all the chores, working from morning until night when she'd drop into bed, exhausted. It was only after she'd awakened first thing the next morning, ready to start her day again, that her thoughts would return with a pang to Jed. Another prayer to the Lord, and she was able to continue with her day with the peace of knowing that Jed was out there somewhere, living his life, alive, healthy, happy.

Tomorrow was Sunday services, and the singing for young people was in the evening. Jed had asked her to go to the singing, then to ride home with him afterward. Sarah smiled with delight. The prospect of riding alone again with Jedidiah Lapp filled her with joy.

She shouldn't allow herself to feel this way, but she couldn't help it. *Please, Lord, help me to choose the right path.*

The rain fell in torrents, pounding the house, creating a ruckus, but Ellen slept on and Sarah smiled at the deep sleep of a child.

She heard a soft tap on the bedroom door. Or did she imagine it? The tapping came again, louder. *Timothy? Thomas?* Sarah rose to open it.

Josie stood at the door, a stack of towels in her arms on which lay a flashlight. "Sarah, I'm sorry to bother you, but we have a problem with leaking windows when it rains this hard. William is planning to replace those windows. We've been waiting for the new ones to come in." She handed Sarah the folded towels. "Would you place these around the windows and on the floor? Here's a flashlight."

Sarah nodded and accepted the stack and the flashlight, which was turned off.

Josie hesitated. "Did I wake you?"

"Nay," Sarah assured her. Josie looked like a young girl in her nightgown with her hair unbound and flowing well past her shoulders. Without thought, Sarah touched her long golden-red hair self-consciously.

Josie smiled at her and thanked her for taking care of the windows. "I'm glad I didn't wake you."

"The boys are still asleep?" Sarah asked, knowing that Josie would have checked on the boys before coming here.

A lightning flash lit up Josie's grin. "Sound asleep. They did their chores and played hard yesterday."

"Ja." Sarah grinned back at her cousin.

The women exchanged good-nights, and then Sarah turned on the flashlight and went to the first of two bedroom windows. The windows were indeed leaking. A small bead of water ran from over the windowsill, down the wall and onto the floor. Sarah leaned the base of the flashlight against the wall and placed the towel stack within easy reach. She dried up the wet areas before she packed towels into the crevice between the window and the sill. When she was done, she laid the remainder of the towels on the hardwood floor.

The storm was beginning to pass. Satisfied that she'd done all she could to stop the leak, Sarah went back to bed and her thoughts returned to Jedidiah Lapp and the happy knowledge that tomorrow she would see him again.

Sunday morning began as a clear day, which quickly turned cloudy and proceeded to a driving rain that threatened all plans for any outside activity. Taking the Mast open family wagon was out of the question. The Mast family, including Sarah and her two young brothers, climbed into the buggy. The vehicle with its three rows of seats had been custom-made for when William's parents—Sarah's grandparents—were alive.

William and Josie sat up front. The four boys sat in the second seat, while Sarah sat in the farthest buggy bench next to Ellen in the back. Enjoying the ride despite the rain, Sarah wondered how much the weather would affect the day's events. Would service and the meal be in Amos King's barn?

Sarah had her answer as William drove the buggy down the King driveway toward the house. She saw several people dash from their buggies through the rain into the house. The service was to be held in the King farmhouse.

Soon, Sarah and her family joined the others inside. Furniture had been cleared from the large living room. Benches stood in place, ready for the services to begin. Mae King handed towels to the newcomers so that they could dry off before taking their seats.

A group of three men stood to one side, deep in discussion. Were they church elders? She knew back home in Kent County there was often some discussion to decide who would handle the services on a particular Sunday.

"The one in the middle," a familiar male voice said in her ear, making her gasp, "that's Abram Peachy. And that—" a long, masculine arm reached past her shoulder to gesture toward a young blonde woman on the other side of the room "—is Charlotte, his wife."

The moment she'd realized who stood behind her, Sarah's heart had leaped for joy. "Rachel's cousin," she said breathlessly. "Who is that next to her? Nancy?"

She could sense Jed's grin before she turned to face him. As their gazes collided, he nodded. "*Gut* guess."

Sarah felt a tingling along her nape as she gazed up at the man before her. She could drown in the depths of his eyes. Stunned by her reaction to him, she quickly glanced back toward the women across the room. Forcing herself to concentrate on what she was seeing rather than the man next to her, she watched the interaction between the Peachys and Nancy King.

Mae King joined her two daughters with a smile on her face. Sarah realized that Charlotte and Nancy looked a lot like their mother. "Mae looks happy to see them," she murmured. She frowned as her thoughts turned toward her own recovering mother.

Jed was quiet a moment. "Your mother will be all right, Sarah," he said softly, as if reading her thoughts. "You've done a fine thing by listening to your elders, despite your feelings about leaving home."

"If something happens," she began, knowing that she couldn't have done anything but listen to her parents.

He shifted closer, until their shoulders almost touched. "Then it is God's will."

She looked at him. His expression was filled with understanding and something more. She quickly glanced away.

She saw church members take their seats. "Time for services," she murmured. She started to move and join the women.

"Sarah." Jed's voice was the barest threat of sound. "With this weather, some of the day's events might be changed."

She wondered if he referred to the singing.

He nodded as if reading her thoughts. Sarah tried not to feel disappointment. There was still the midday meal to share with friends and neighbors. Just knowing that Jedidiah was here brightened her day, made her thankful to the Lord. "I understand," she said.

As the service began with this day's officiate, Abram Peachy, the deacon, Sarah offered up praise and thanks to God. Her mother had survived the surgery, and for however long she had here in Happiness, the Lord had brought Jedidiah back into her life.

The service seemed to fly by, and then suddenly the men were shifting benches in the room and the women were in the kitchen unwrapping the food.

"Sarah," Rachel said. "These are my cousins, Charlotte and Nancy. Cousins—" she grinned "—this is Sarah Mast, William's cousin from Delaware."

"*Hallo,* Sarah," Charlotte greeted, her expression warm. "How do you like our village of Happiness?"

"I've enjoyed my time here."

Nancy beamed as she greeted her. "I'm glad to be home. I know our *grosselders* enjoyed the trip to North Carolina but there is no place like Happiness. They are over there." She pointed to an older Amish couple. "Harley and Emma King."

Just then, four young boys burst into the kitchen. "Elam! Will!" Josie scolded.

"Timothy and Thomas!" Sarah added. She pointed toward the other room, where tables had been set up with benches. "Go and sit now!"

Sarah gave the three women she was with an apologetic smile. "My brothers and cousins."

Charlotte grinned. "I can see the family resemblance in your brothers."

"Ah, my red hair!" Sarah chuckled.

"Sarah." A male voice spoke from behind her.

"Hallo, Jed," Charlotte and Nancy said in unison.

"Charlotte, Nancy." He nodded toward each one. "Rachel." He paused. "May I borrow Sarah?"

Sarah blushed while the cousins nodded and eyed her speculatively. Despite the strangeness of his approach, she couldn't help but feel a tiny bit pleased that Jed had sought her attention.

She followed him off to one side. "Is something wrong?" she asked him.

He hesitated. "I… Bob Whittier just dropped this by." He held out an envelope toward her.

"On a Sunday?" she whispered.

"Ja. He received the mail late yesterday. It was mixed up with his. He was afraid it was important."

Heart pounding within her chest but for another reason now, Sarah accepted the envelope, read the name and return address. "It's from Ervin."

Jed nodded. *"Ja."*

Suddenly nervous, Sarah tore open the envelope. She scanned the page, reading her brother's hand, and then smiled.

Jed watched as Sarah read the letter. "Is everything all right?"

Sarah met his gaze and grinned. "Everything is fine. *Mam* is doing well. She will be coming home next week."

Did he say anything about you going home? Jed wondered silently. He wasn't ready for her to leave. They had only just met up again. He didn't want to be nosy but he needed to know. "Did he mention anything else?"

"Only that they are managing well. Aunt Iva and my cousin Mary Alice have been helping out in the house." She glanced down at the letter and then returned her gaze to Jed. She grinned. "Remember the two girls my *bruders* took home? They've been stopping by with food. Often." She laughed outright, and the sound lifted his spirits. "Ervin doesn't seem pleased by the frequent visits."

Jed understood the feeling. If it wasn't the right woman, then it might be overwhelming if she kept coming around to "help" out. *Not that I wouldn't be anything but kind to her.*

"So your family is managing," he said. "They have the help they need and all the food they could want."

Sarah nodded as she continued to study the letter. "It seems so."

"*Gut!*" He was glad it wasn't bad news for her. "Sarah—"

She looked up from the letter to meet his gaze. The impact of vivid blue stole his breath. *"Ja?"*

"There may still be a singing this evening, but with the rain, we may have company when I take you home."

Was that a flicker of disappointment in her gaze? "It's fine, but I didn't realize that you lived so close, Jed. I can get a ride with the Zooks."

"I want to take you home, Sarah." He wanted to do more with her—take long walks, spend hours talking with her, sharing a meal, holding hands.

"That sounds *gut,*" she said softly. "As long as it's not an inconvenience."

"Being with you is never an inconvenience, Sarah Mast," he admitted quietly, and the truth struck him full force. He had come to care a great deal about her. He just didn't know what he was going to do about it.

The men sat and ate first. When they were done, the women and children enjoyed the meal. Today was more formal than last Sunday, when everyone shared tables outdoors.

Soon, church members cleaned up and began to leave. Most families were eager to get past the rain and into the warmth of their own homes.

"You will come to the singing if we have it?" Jed asked.

Sarah nodded. She studied his expression but noted nothing unusual on his features.

"I can speak with the Zooks to arrange a ride in for you," he said.

She shook her head. She decided that riding with Annie Zook wasn't a good idea. "I'll see if William can drop me off. If not, I'm sure Josie will arrange something."

Josie and William were ready to go. Sarah helped to round up the four boys and Ellen, and soon they were on their way home.

It wasn't until they were inside the farmhouse that Sarah spoke with her cousin.

"There is a singing tonight," she began.

"Ja," Josie said. "You will go. William will take you. I'm sure you can get a ride home."

Sarah nodded. "Someone already offered to take me home."

Josie opened her mouth as if to ask who, but then she abruptly closed it again as if she felt she shouldn't ask.

Sarah was relieved. Her feelings for Jed were too new. She realized what it meant to ride home with a young man. But she didn't want to discuss it yet.

As it happened, a fierce thunderstorm rolled in, canceling Sarah's plans.

"I'm afraid there won't be a singing tonight," Josie said as she glanced outside at the intermittent bolts of lightning.

Sarah hoped that Josie was right. She certainly didn't want to go out into the storm, but she didn't want to miss an occasion to spend time with Jedidiah.

A clap of thunder startled her. If it frightened her, what would it do to a horse on the road? As she backed away from the kitchen window, Sarah felt the envelope in her apron pocket—Ervin's letter.

It had been kind of Jedidiah to bring it to her. It was nice of Bob Whittier to see that it got delivered on a Sunday. The Happiness community had been wonderful. She was enjoying her time here, and so were her twin brothers. She'd never seen them so happy and active, and such sound sleepers once they were tucked up in bed at night.

The rain continued well into the night, the storm rolling out and then back in again. Sarah said a silent prayer that the wind, rain and especially the lightning did no damage.

She couldn't sleep, so she decided to use the time to write her family. She turned on a flashlight and wrote separate letters to *Mam, Dat* and Ervin. By the time she was done, it was late. The rumble of thunder grew distant, leaving only the gentle patter of rain on the roof above her, and Sarah grew sleepy. Thoughts of Jed entered her mind. When would she see him again?

Next Sunday, she thought, which was a visiting Sunday, if not before.

She recalled his deep, soft voice in her ear, the muscular arm that pointed over her shoulder, the light brush of his arm against hers as they shared a view.

She was in trouble. Jedidiah Lapp was taking up a lot of space in her mind these days, and she didn't think that was wise.

Sarah was carrying clothes downstairs to be laundered when William walked into the house, followed by Samuel, Noah…and Jedidiah Lapp.

'Josie!" William called. "We're putting in the new windows and doors today."

Josie came out from the back of the house. "*Gut.* Any more rainstorms like the last couple, and we'll be needing boats instead of towels."

As she descended the stairs to the last step, Sarah caught Jed's gaze. His lips tilted upward. His eyes gleamed. He looked handsome dressed in a maroon shirt and tri-blend denim overalls. His black-banded straw hat sat on his dark hair with the brim pushed back, and she felt the full impact of his unshadowed gaze. She could feel her face heat as she greeted the men, before she hurried down the hall toward the gas-powered washing machine.

She lifted the machine's lid, and as she was stuffing the wash into the basin, she was overly conscious that Jed was nearby. She heard the rumble of male voices outside the nearest window, saw Noah and Samuel carrying a new windowpane toward the area below the old one and set it down on the lawn.

Sarah watched Noah and Samuel Lapp walk past outside, perhaps to fetch another window.

Where was Jed? Working at the front of the house?

She poured liquid laundry detergent into the bottle cap and then spread it over the dirty clothes. She turned on the machine and felt satisfied when she saw and heard the spray of warm water.

A light tap on the window drew her gaze. Jed pressed his face against the glass, his mouth curved in a wide grin.

Sarah laughed. She couldn't help it. There was something so playful about him; he made her feel good to be the focus of his attention.

He stood back and waved for her to come out. Should she go? She shook her head. She had chores to do.

He remained determined as he continued to gesture her outside.

Finally, Sarah shrugged, set the laundry basket on the floor near the washer and then stepped out into the bright morning sun—and into the direct line of Jedidiah Lapp's vision.

Chapter Ten

"Hallo." Jed gave her a tender smile.

Her heart skipped a beat. *"Hallo."*

"I didn't get a chance to talk with you since we made plans for the singing. I'm sorry it was canceled."

Sarah nodded. Should she confess that she was sorry, too? "That was a little more rain than I would have been comfortable driving in."

"Ja." He reseated his straw hat onto his dark brown hair. There was a tiny bead of moisture on the side of his face, and Sarah watched as he reached up to wipe it away.

She hesitated, unsure what to say. "I have work to do."

"I do, too," he murmured.

She heard a shout from the other end of the house. "My brother," Jed said. "I should go see what I need to do." He started to turn.

"Jed?" Sarah waited for him to stop.

He spun back and met her gaze. "It was nice of you

to offer to take me home after Sunday singing, even if we never got to go."

His eyes brightened and his grin widened. "There will be other singings, Sarah." And he left to return to work with his father and brother.

"If I'm still here for another singing," she whispered, wondering when her family would call her back to Delaware.

Ervin had written that *Mam*'s recovery would take time and that it was a great thing that the twins weren't at home to disturb her.

I may be here for another singing after all, she thought with gladness as she reentered the house to check on the laundry.

Sarah heard the men working as they pulled out the old windows and replaced them with the new. When the front door was removed, the four young boys in residence thought the open space a play pathway for running in and out of the farmhouse.

"*Schtupp,* boys!" Sarah scolded as she came out of the laundry to spy what they were doing.

Noah peered through the open doorway and grinned. "I know a way to keep them busy."

Sarah raised her eyebrows. "How?"

"They can pick up the wood scraps and set them in piles away from the house."

She smiled. "And won't they be underfoot while you're creating the scraps of wood?"

"*Nay,* I'll suggest they help Ellen feed the animals first."

Sarah laughed. "This will be interesting," she said before she turned away.

* * *

Jed heard her laughter as he rounded the house. He loved the way it sounded—pleasant, girlish, full of happiness. He'd like to hear her laughing more. If it had been anyone other than his brother Noah who had made her laugh, he might have not been so pleased. *Nay,* that wasn't right. Jealousy was a sin and not permitted. Nor was envy.

He reached Noah just as Sarah left. "You said something to amuse her, I take it?" he said.

Noah's warm brown eyes twinkled. "I told her I had a plan to keep the young ones busy so that they wouldn't be in our way."

Jed's lips twitched. "And what was that?"

Noah told him, and Jed laughed outright. "This should be interesting." Jed regarded his brother with amusement.

Noah frowned. "That's what *she* said."

As it turned out, Noah's plan to have the boys pick up wood scraps didn't materialize until much later in the day. With some instruction, they did go to the barn to help Ellen feed the animals and milk the cows, and then it was time for lunch and the young ones gathered at the Mast kitchen table to eat. Sarah took sandwiches and desserts outside to the men, who sat on the front porch enjoying glasses of iced tea that Josie had brought out to them earlier.

She handed Noah his plate first. "Ham sandwich on homemade German rye bread with Swiss cheese. Just a hint of mustard." She gestured toward the dessert on one corner of the plate. "Chocolate cake," she said, recalling his love of chocolate, and Noah grinned.

Next, she handed Jed his sandwich plate but his dessert was cherry pie. He glanced down at the pie, then looked at her with a grin.

She nodded. She'd remembered that it was his favorite.

Josie had brought out lunch for William and Samuel. The men sat on the porch and enjoyed the meal. When they were done, they were back at work, determined to install all the windows and doors that were to be replaced that day.

As she moved about the house and yard doing chores, Sarah was overly conscious of the men's voices as they worked, of the sound of hammering as they secured each window after they'd set it into place.

Sarah hung laundry, dusted and swept the rooms downstairs, and when she was done, she headed upstairs to clean the boys' room. She entered the bedroom to find Samuel and Noah inside at the window opening. Startled by their presence, she froze and watched as Noah and his father tugged on a rope to hoist a window up into place.

Noah held on to the window frame as Samuel untied the rope and dropped it to the ground. Then the younger man helped to fit the window more firmly into the opening.

Sarah heard a noise against the side of the house.

"Careful, Jed. Make sure it's secure. We don't want *ya* falling, now."

"Ja, Dat," she heard Jed say.

"I'll hold it steady." William's voice reached up from ground level.

There was the clink of shoes against metal as someone—Jed, she thought—climbed the rungs of the ladder.

Suddenly, he was there, in the window opening, grinning. He didn't see her at first. The men exchanged instructions, and soon the window was secure, and Jed was ready to climb down. It was as he started down that he saw her.

He lifted a hand to wave. *"Nay!"* she cried. "Hold on!" She didn't realize that she'd spoken out loud until the two men in the room turned to stare at her.

"Sarah," Noah said, "we didn't realize you were behind us."

"I didn't want to disturb your work." Sarah was glad to note that Jed once again put his hands on the ladder as he continued the climb down.

Noah narrowed his eyes as he studied her. "He's fine," he said, his voice quiet. "This isn't his first time on a ladder. Jed knows what he is doing."

She bit the inside of her mouth. "Is that the last of the windows?" Seeing Jed on the ladder had made her nervous. She felt foolish for unintentionally revealing her thoughts.

"Ja. All done." Samuel checked the window and then turned, appearing pleased. "We did a *gut* day's work today."

"Ja," Noah agreed as he slipped his hammer into the metal ring on his nail bag.

"I had no idea you could do all that in one day," Sarah admitted. She set the laundry basket on a bed and began to extract the boys' clothes. She placed them in piles, each one belonging to a different boy.

"We had a *gut* crew of workers," Noah said with a smile.

She nodded. "How is Rachel?"

"Wondering when you'll come for another visit." His eyes twinkled teasingly. At that moment, she could see his resemblance to his older brother.

"Tell her I'll come this week. Is there a day that's better for her?"

"Nay." He glanced down to straighten his nail bag before looking up. "She'll be pleased to see you whenever you can come."

"Wednesday?" Sarah suggested, allowing Rachel two days' notice before she stopped by.

"Wednesday sounds *gut.*" Noah looked pleased. "I'll tell her."

When Sarah ventured downstairs a while later, the Lapp men were getting ready to depart. She stepped out onto the porch to discover William and Josie chatting with Samuel, Jed and Noah. She quickly hurried inside and filled a plastic bag for each Lapp man with cookies, zucchini bars and fudge. She raced back through the house and slowed her steps only as she neared the front door—newly installed by the four workers.

"Here's a snack for the way home," she said as she distributed the bags of treats. All of them looked pleased as they accepted her offering, especially Jed. His look of pleasure made her stomach flutter.

After parting words, the Lapps moved toward their wagon.

"Jed." Josie called him back. "Would you wait a moment until I get something for Katie?"

"Ja." Jed approached until he reached Sarah's side,

where he waited while Josie hurried back to the house. Sarah felt his presence keenly, the height and strength of him, his muscled arms developed no doubt by hard manual farm or construction labor.

"'Twas *gut* to see you again, Sarah," Jed said softly.

Sarah flashed a glance at Noah and Samuel, who were looking over some papers with William. "You worked hard today," she said.

He shrugged. "One day of work is like another." He hesitated a moment. "Sarah—" he began earnestly.

"Here it is, Jed!" Josie returned, interrupting, making Sarah wonder what he was about to say. Josie carried a clear bag of what appeared to be pieces of evenly cut fabric. "Quilt squares," she explained. "I've put them in a plastic bag for you."

"They're beautiful," Sarah said. "I haven't seen these before."

"We hope to hold our quilting bee next week. Katie is keeping all of the squares for us. We'll meet at her house—yours," she said to Jed with a smile, "next."

At Sarah's insistence, she allowed her to take a closer peek.

Sarah saw that the fabric squares had been sewn in the Amish star pattern. "May I help?" she asked. It had been a long time since she'd had the pleasure of attending a quilting bee.

"We'd love the help." Josie turned to Jed. "Are you free tomorrow?"

"What do you need?" he asked.

"I need a few things from town. Would you mind taking Sarah to pick them up for me?"

Jed's eyes lit up with delight. "I'd be happy to."

"I'll get my list," Josie said before she again disappeared inside.

"We can make a day of it," Jed told Sarah while they waited for Josie's return.

"I don't know if I can," Sarah replied, although the idea tempted her. Josie had never mentioned needing any supplies.

"We can take the twins with us."

"That would be *gut*," she replied. "I worry that they'll misbehave if I'm not around to scold them."

"Who?" Josie said as she rejoined them.

"The twins. We thought we might take them with us." Sarah was startled when her cousin disagreed.

"I have plans for the boys tomorrow," Josie replied.

Plans? Sarah thought. What plans did Josie have that would involve four active young boys—the twins and Josie's two sons?

"You can take Ellen if you'd like," Josie suggested. "She would enjoy the outing."

"*Gut!* We'll do that," Jed said. He turned toward Sarah. "What time can you be ready?"

"Whenever you'd like to leave—"

"Nine o'clock?"

Sarah nodded. "Then I can help with the morning chores."

"Sarah," Josie said, "no chores for you tomorrow. You'll be doing the shopping—that is work enough." She addressed Jed: "Eight o'clock?"

"I'll be here." A small smile played about Jed's lips. "Sarah, I'll see you tomorrow, then." With their plans for the outing made, Jed joined Noah and Samuel in the wagon and moments later the men left, leaving William to return to the house.

Sarah watched as Jedidiah drove off, her heart beating with excitement about tomorrow's outing.

"Here." Josie held out the list toward her. "Jed will take you wherever you need to go."

"I didn't know you needed supplies." Sarah studied the list, noting the baking and cooking ingredients. There were also a few other household items that Josie apparently needed.

"I meant to tell you earlier. William is busy or I'd ask him to take you."

"I have money. I'll take care of this for you."

"*Nay,* Sarah. You'll keep your money and take ours to buy the supplies."

Sarah sighed, knowing that it was useless to argue with Josie, who looked ready to do battle. "Are you sure you don't mind having the twins? They can be a handful."

"They behave well with my two," Josie assured her. "I have a few chores for them, which I'm sure they'll enjoy. Don't worry about them." She paused a moment. "Ellen will be excited to go. You don't mind having her?"

"Of course not!" she exclaimed as she and Josie headed into the house. "I enjoy Ellen's company. She is not wild like my dear twin *bruders.*"

"It will be *gut* for her to have a day out, as well." Concern entered Josie's expression. "She is quiet at times. I worry about her."

"She is fine, Josie. I've seen her with the boys. She isn't quiet when she's with them. I've watched her on

Visiting Sundays. The *kinner* like her." Ellen played well with the other children. Sarah wanted her cousin to know that her fears were unfounded.

Josie beamed. "I'm glad."

"If I'm to be out and about tomorrow, I'd best get back to my chores."

"You've done plenty today already," her cousin insisted.

Sarah shook her head. "*Nay.* I need to finish up in the house and then I'd like to work in the vegetable garden. It's a beautiful day, and it will be nice to work outdoors."

The next morning, when she heard the sound of horse hooves and metal wheels turning on dirt, Sarah went to the window and saw Jed pull up his family's market wagon near the front door of the farmhouse.

He looked up as if he knew she was at the window and waved. She lifted a hand in response before she turned toward the young girl seated on the bed behind her.

"Ellen, are you ready to go?" she asked with a smile. She had rolled and pinned up the young girl's hair only moments before.

Ellen nodded as she reached back to tie her black apron strings. Sarah saw her struggle for a few seconds before she offered to help. Ellen turned and Sarah made quick work of it, and then stood back to eye the girl appraisingly.

"We'll have a *gut* time today." Sarah checked her cape and her own apron ties, glad to find everything in place.

"*Ja. Mam* says we'll be going to lunch."

Sarah inclined her head. "Maybe we'll have a snack, too."

Ellen grinned. "Ice cream or kettle corn?"

"I like both," Sarah said with a smile.

"Me, too." Ellen preceded Sarah out of the room and down the stairs.

Jed was waiting for them on the porch when Sarah stepped out of the house first.

"*Gut* morning," he greeted.

"It is, isn't it?" Sarah couldn't keep the wide smile from her face. She'd looked forward to the day since she'd first learned of the outing yesterday.

"Is Ellen coming?" Jed ran his gaze over the length of her.

"*Ja,*" Sarah said, noting his look, which thrilled her. She then moved to allow the young girl to step forward from behind her.

"*Hallo,* Ellen," Jed said softly. "Are you ready to have a wonderful day?"

Ellen nodded vigorously. She wore a green dress with a black full-length apron, unlike Sarah, who wore a black cape and half apron tied at the waist over a royal-blue dress.

"We'll have a meal and a snack later," Jed said, causing Ellen to grin and glance toward Sarah, who returned the smile.

Josie stepped outside as Jed helped Ellen onto the wagon before he held out his hand to assist Sarah. "Have *ya* got the list?" she asked.

"*Ja,*" Sarah said. "Can you think of anything else you want to add?"

"*Nay,* I think that's everything." Josie shaded her eyes from the sun with her right hand. "Mind Sarah while you're out," she told her daughter.

"*Ja, Mam.*" Ellen turned to Jed. "May I sit in the back?" she asked.

"I don't see why not." After shoving a toolbox out of the way, Jed helped Ellen to sit in one corner of the wagon with her back against the rear of the front seat. A blanket cushioned the wood behind her. Then he climbed up onto the seat beside Sarah.

Sarah noted the power in Jed's arms as he flicked the leathers to spur the horse on.

"Are you ready?" he asked casually. "Is that your list?"

She nodded. "*Ja.* Josie needs baking supplies, some herb plants for her vegetable garden, and she wants some fabric for the quilt." Sarah glanced over in time to see Jed nod.

"I know where to go." He turned from the road to gaze at her from beneath his wide-brimmed banded straw hat. "Where would you like to eat?"

"You know the area better than me. Why don't you choose?" Josie had given her money for the supplies and for lunch for all three of them.

They drove in silence for a time. Sarah was conscious of Jed beside her and Ellen behind her.

"Look!" Ellen exclaimed. "That horse!"

Sarah frowned as she realized what Ellen had seen. "Jed—"

"I see it," Jed said as he pulled the buggy off the road and onto the driveway that led to a farmhouse. "It belongs to David Troyer, one of our church members."

He stopped the buggy and got out. There was a horse caught in fence wire.

"Wait in the buggy," Jed said. "We don't know how he is going to react when I try to free him."

Jed approached the animal carefully. He didn't want to frighten it. He wanted the horse to stay calm while he reached over and freed its leg.

He hunkered down to study the situation. As he moved closer to untangle the mare's leg, the animal whinnied and moved anxiously. Jed stepped back.

"I don't want to frighten her," he said as he continued to study the situation.

"Jed," Sarah called out softly, "may I help? I can calm the horse while you work to get her free."

"How do you know it's a mare?" he teased. He looked at her and grinned before his expression became serious as he examined the animal. "I'd appreciate the help. Do you think you can stroke and soothe the horse while I try to free her?"

"Ja," she said. She addressed Ellen: "Stay in the buggy." Jed saw Ellen incline her head.

"Gut girl," he heard Sarah say.

She climbed down from the buggy and hesitated before she approached. "Do *ya* have anything to cut the wire if necessary?"

Jed frowned as he thought for a moment. "There may be something in the toolbox in the back of the wagon."

"I can look in the toolbox," Ellen offered softly.

"What do you need?" Sarah asked.

"Wire cutters or a razor knife." He waited with an eye on the horse for Sarah to reach him.

"Will these work?" Ellen held up a pair of tin snips.

Jed nodded. "Sarah, do you think you can get to the other side of the fence?"

There was a pause, and he looked over to see Sarah gauging the fence as if to decide the best place to enter the farmer's pasture.

"There," he suggested. "There's a gate there. You'll be able to get in as long as it's not locked."

Sarah hurried toward the gate. "It's latched but not locked. I can get in." She proceeded to slip inside the fence, shutting the gate behind her, before she carefully approached the horse.

"Can you get next to her?" Jed asked. He watched Sarah with concern. If anything happened to Sarah…

"Ja." She moved closer and the horse stirred restlessly. Sarah soothed her with soft words and gentle strokes along the animal's neck. With Sarah's help, the mare calmed and then stood docilely while Jed cut away just enough wire with the tin snips to free the horse's leg.

"Come on, girl," Sarah said, urging the mare away from the fence once she was free.

"Her leg is scratched but I don't think it's serious," Jed said. "Still, her wound needs to be tended. We'll ride up to the house and tell David. Sarah?"

"I'm coming," she assured him. He heaved a silent sigh of relief once she returned through the gate and joined him outside of the fence.

Chapter Eleven

Sarah was impressed with how quickly and efficiently Jed had freed the animal. The animal had been in pain, but she was obviously a good workhorse.

"I'll go up to the house," Jed said after driving the wagon up into the barnyard. He climbed down from the vehicle. "I'll be right back."

And then he disappeared from Sarah's view as he went to speak with the horse's owner, David Troyer.

He was back within minutes with a young man Sarah recognized immediately. She had seen him at Sunday church services. He had a wife and three children, although he couldn't be more than twenty-one years old.

"*Hallo,* David," she greeted.

"Sarah," he said with a nod. "You helped my horse. *Danki.*"

Her eyes met Jed's briefly. "I'm glad I could help."

"Ellen," David said, acknowledging the young girl.

Sarah smiled as Ellen said *hallo,* then the two men moved aside to talk quietly.

Soon, Jed climbed into the wagon next to Sarah. "He is going to see to his mare. I think she'll be fine."

"Ja," Sarah agreed.

"Now, Ellen, Sarah, are we ready to begin our day?"

"Ja!" Ellen exclaimed, and Sarah and Jed grinned at each other.

"Let's go, then!"

They went to the fabric store first, where Sarah bought Josie's quilting fabric. Sarah purchased three yards of three different colors—blue, burgundy and green—as well as three yards of unbleached muslin. While she was there, she purchased material for a new cape, apron and prayer *kapp* for herself and her mother.

Thoughts of her mother gave her pause. How was *Mam* faring? Should she ask Jed to take her to Whittier's Store so she could call home? Their neighbors, the Johnsons, would get a message to *Dat*…

"Sarah." Jed's voice interrupted her thoughts. "Are you ready for a snack?"

"A snack?" she echoed.

"Ja." His eyes lit up boyishly, and Sarah couldn't help but smile.

"Before lunch?" There was something so appealing about Jed as he stood there with Ellen by his side. He had a hand on the young girl's shoulder. She glanced toward Ellen to see that her eyes were lit up, as well.

"What are *ya* thinking?"

"Ice cream," they chimed in together.

"Ice cream." She saw their faces, and suddenly the thought of ice cream before their midday meal sounded like a wonderful idea. Sarah laughed. "Ice cream sounds *gut.*"

Jed grinned. Ellen exclaimed with joy, and then Jed took Sarah's fabric purchases from her and set them in the wagon before the three of them climbed in.

Jed drove them to a small ice-cream shop that had more flavors in one place than she'd ever seen. Back home in Kent County, Delaware, Sarah's favorite place for ice cream was Byler's General Store. Most of the time, her family kept ice cream in their gas freezer, but there was something special about going out for it. Today, she realized, that something special was Jedidiah Lapp driving her around town.

As she and Ellen sat across from Jed, Sarah enjoyed her treat and thought how fun it was to be eating it before the midday meal. They chatted conversationally while they ate, and then when they were done, Jed took them to a grocery store next, where Sarah bought all the baking and cooking supplies that Josie had requested. She spied fresh cherries in the produce aisle and decided to buy some to make a couple of chocolate-chip cherry pies, one for the family and one for Jed in appreciation for taking her into town.

Sarah paid for her purchases while Jed was wandering the store, gathering supplies for his mother. The cherries were bagged before Jed rejoined her, and she was glad because she wanted it to be a surprise.

"Did you get everything you needed?" Jed asked as he and Ellen approached.

"Ja," she said. She hesitated. "Do *ya* think we can stop by Whittier's Store?"

Jed smiled. *"Ja.* Would you like to make a phone call?"

Sarah nodded.

"We'll stop for lunch and to buy some kettle corn," he said with a smile at Ellen as he spoke. "Then we'll stop by Whittier's on the way back."

Seated across from Sarah as they enjoyed a midday meal, Jed found that he liked looking at her. She looked lovely in her royal-blue dress with black cape and apron. The small glimpse of hair pulled back from her forehead before it was hidden beneath her *kapp* was like spun gold that glistened with red warmth in the sunshine. He liked her company. If he wasn't careful, he'd find himself falling in love with her, but she would be leaving, and it would be wrong to start a relationship when they each had their lives in different Amish communities.

That doesn't mean I can't enjoy being with her now, he thought.

"I've had a *gut* time," Ellen said after she'd chewed and swallowed a bite of pizza.

"I have, too," Sarah said, and Jed felt enormously pleased that she had enjoyed the day as much as he had.

Soon, Jed was steering the horse into Whittier's parking lot. He climbed out and then held out his hand to Sarah. His heart skipped a beat as Sarah accepted his help and he felt the warmth of her fingers.

She stood waiting while Jed reached up and lifted Ellen down. Then the three of them went inside the store.

"Sarah." Bob Whittier greeted her. "Come to make a phone call?"

"May I?"

The man nodded. "Of course."

As Sarah went to the phone, Jed and Bob Whittier

chatted about the weather and the comings and goings of the Happiness community.

Ellen wandered about the store, looking at all the items that lined the shelves.

Sarah dialed the phone number where she could leave a message for her father and waited for someone to pick up. She kept an eye on Ellen as the phone rang on the other end of the line. She was about to hang up after several rings, when someone answered her call.

She recognized the voice as that of John Jacobs, the owner of the convenience store closest to Sarah's home. "*Hallo,* John? This is Sarah… Sarah Mast. I'd like to leave a message for my family."

"Sarah!" John exclaimed. "You called at the right time! Your brother Ervin is here in the store now."

She heard John call Ervin's name and then there was a rustling noise on the phone as John handed the handset to her brother. And then Sarah heard the wonderful sound of Ervin's voice.

"Sarah!" he exclaimed. "What a surprise! Is everything all right?"

"*Ja,* everything is fine," she assured him. "I'm calling about *Mam.*"

"Sarah," Ervin said, because he knew his sister well, "try not to worry. *Mam* is doing well. Resting as the doctor ordered. Iva spent the night the day *Mam* came home from the hospital, and since then, she and Mary Alice have been by daily to help out. Mary Miller and some of our other neighbors have been bringing food by for us. Lots and lots of food," he added, sounding amused.

"That's *gut,*" Sarah said, glad that everyone at home

was being taken care of. "Will you tell *Mam* that I love and miss her?"

"Of course, Sarah," he said softly, "but she knows." Ervin was silent a moment, as if he understood how hard it was for her to be away from home. "Are the twins behaving?"

"*Ja,* they are enjoying their time here."

"I'm glad," her brother said. "They will remember their adventures there."

"Ja," she agreed. *Just as I will,* she thought, thinking of her cousins' kindness, the warmth of the Happiness community—and her time with Jedidiah Lapp. Sarah stared at a bulletin board in the store as she and Ervin chatted for a minute more to catch up. "I'd better go, Ervin," she said as her gaze caught sight of the clock on the wall above the bulletin board. "Bob Whittier has been kind enough to let me use his telephone. It's not a pay phone." She paused. "I liked receiving your letter. I'll write to you and *Mam.* I think she might like that."

"She will," Ervin assured her.

After ending their conversation, Sarah hung up the receiver. "Thank you for the use of your phone, Bob," she said as Bob came to the counter to wait on a customer. "I hope I haven't stayed on too long. I can pay you for the phone calls."

"No, Sarah. It's fine," the storeowner assured her. He lowered his voice. "I have unlimited phone service, but don't tell anyone." The last was said with a twinkle in his dark gaze.

She grinned. "I won't tell." After Bob assured her that she could come back to use the phone anytime she needed it, Sarah turned to search for Jed and Ellen. She caught sight of Jed first. He was outside the store, talking with Annie Zook.

Jed's former sweetheart. She felt a burning in her stomach. He and Annie were smiling as they chatted. She heard Jed laugh out loud and saw Annie grin. Sarah suffered a little pang in the region of her heart as she turned to look for Ellen. She didn't have far to look. Ellen stood eyeing a display of candy and other treats. Pushing thoughts of Jed and Annie from her mind, Sarah smiled as she went to see whether or not Ellen would like any candy.

"Do you think the boys would like some?" she asked as she reached the young girl's side.

Ellen met her gaze as she inclined her head. "*Ja*. Can we buy some flavored sticks and some licorice?"

"Pick out whatever you think the family will like, and we'll purchase some treats for them." Sarah still had some spending money of her own. There had been little need to spend it since she'd arrived in Happiness.

Sarah paid for the treats and then glanced over at Jed to see if he was ready to go. Although he was talking with Annie, Jed sought her out with his gaze. Her heart gave a little jump.

Encouraged, Sarah urged Ellen to follow as she approached Jed and Annie with a smile. "*Hallo,* Annie," she greeted.

Annie nodded. "It's *gut* to see you again, Sarah."

"Annie and I were just talking about visiting this Sunday," Jed said. "The social will be held at our farm this weekend."

Sarah smiled. "Is there anything I can do to help?"

The community women often came by to help the hosting family get ready for the onslaught of guests.

"Would you make some of your delicious pies?" Jed asked.

Annie's expression gave no indication of her thoughts. "I've heard about your pies, Sarah," she said politely after a lengthy pause.

"I bake much like everyone else," Sarah said, uncomfortable with Jed's praise.

After another awkward silence, Annie said directly to Jed, "I'll stop by to see if your mother needs my help."

Feeling out of place, Sarah decided to wait by the wagon for Jed to finish his discussion with Annie Zook. She bid Annie farewell and returned to the vehicle with Ellen, giving Jed a few moments alone with his friend.

Jed joined them not long afterward. He grinned as he climbed onto the seat next to Sarah. "Are you ready to head back?" he asked.

"Nay!" Ellen exclaimed, and Jed laughed. The young girl leaned over the bench seat from the back of the wagon. "I had fun today."

"I did, too," Sarah said softly.

"Me, too," Jed said, his expression warm. Apparently unaware of her dismay, he picked up the reins and flicked the leathers. Under Jed's guidance, the wagon moved across the parking lot until it reached the main road. Jed looked both ways for any oncoming traffic. He waited as a car raced closer. "Would you like to do this again another day?"

"Ja!" Ellen answered, but Sarah remained silent. She didn't know how much longer she'd be in Happiness.

And the mental image of Jed talking and laughing with Annie Zook still upset her.

"Sarah?" Jed asked with concern. Although the car had passed, he didn't spur the horse onto the roadway.

Her eyes met his. "I don't know how much longer I'll be here," she finally explained.

Jed frowned. "Did you learn something distressing from back home during your phone call?"

She shook her head. "*Nay. Mam* is doing well. I was able to speak with Ervin. I suspect that it won't be long before I get a phone call asking me to come home."

"I hope not too soon," he admitted as he studied her intently.

She blushed and looked away. "I have enjoyed my time here in Happiness." *And spending time with you.*

Jed checked the road again before driving the wagon forward. He drove on in silence for a time before an animal crossed their path and he had to pull up on the reins to slow down the horse. "We may have to arrange another outing sooner rather than later," he said.

Sarah bit down on her lip, then released it. "It's nice of you to say so."

"It's not nice of me at all," he admitted. "'Tis how I feel." And with that remark, he turned his attention toward steering the horse down the road toward cousin William's farm.

When her day with Jed came to an end, Sarah felt disappointed. Jed was quiet as he drove the vehicle down the lane into the barnyard near the farmhouse. He stopped the wagon, jumped down and then extended a hand toward her.

Sarah silently accepted his help, nodding at him in

thanks before he turned to assist Ellen. He helped to carry in Sarah's purchases. Ellen tagged along behind them, bringing in the treats she had picked out for the boys and her family.

"How was your day?" Josie asked as Sarah entered the house.

"We had a nice time," Sarah said.

"A nice enough time to go again?" Jed queried with a hopeful smile.

Remembering him with Annie, Sarah was saved from replying at all when the twins and their cousins burst into the kitchen from outside.

"Jedidiah!" Timothy exclaimed. "I didn't know you were here. How come we didn't get to go into town?"

"Timothy!" Sarah scolded with a stern eye. Timothy wasn't fazed by his sister's tone.

"I had jobs for you to do," Josie said. "I needed you here."

"Ja!" Timothy said with bright eyes that lit up as if he'd suddenly remembered how he'd spent his day.

Thomas spoke up next. "We got to feed and brush the horses." He looked as if he'd enjoyed the chore.

"Ja! I like brushing the horses, but I needed help reaching the top of them, so William got me a stool to stand on."

Sarah smiled to see her young brothers' excitement. "I think you boys had a *gut* day right here."

They nodded vigorously. "We did," Thomas said.

Sarah smiled as she reached out, straightened Thomas's hat.

"Sarah." William came from outside behind them. "A letter came for you in the mail."

"A letter?" She had just spoken with her brother. He hadn't mentioned another letter. She accepted the envelope from William and stared at the return address with surprise. "It's from P.J. Miller," she said as William walked past and into the other room.

"P.J. Miller, my cousin?" Jed asked with a frown, and Sarah nodded.

She carefully undid the envelope flap and slipped out the letter. She unfolded the sheet of paper and began to read.

"Is everything all right?" Jed said with an odd tone in his voice.

"*Ja.* He is just writing to let me know how everyone is doing. He asked how I was and…" Her voice dropped off. She was surprised to hear from him.

"What else did he say?" Jed asked.

"He said that he—and everyone—misses me." P.J. was a friend and a nice man, but why should he miss her?

Jed listened to Sarah explain what was in the letter, and as she talked about P.J., he felt a burning in his stomach. He remembered his cousin's obvious interest in Sarah. P.J. was a good young man, and he knew that his cousin would treat Sarah right, but although he knew he shouldn't be upset, Jed found that his feelings for Sarah had grown the past few weeks.

"Are you going to write him back?" he asked her.

"I suppose I should. He took the time to write. I owe Ervin and *Mam* letters, as well."

"He likes you," Jed said, his mind still on his younger cousin.

"Who?" she asked distractedly.

"P.J." He studied her closely. There was nothing in her expression that gave away her thoughts or her feelings for P.J.

"I like him, too," she finally said. She watched as he set the packages he carried on the kitchen table. "He is a *gut* friend. Would you like a snack?" she asked.

He couldn't help but chuckle. "How could I possibly be hungry?" He regarded her with amusement.

Her eyes widened a second and then she laughed. "You're right. Ice cream, kettle corn and lunch." A beautiful smile played about her lips. "Would you like a drink, then? Lemonade? Iced tea?"

"Iced tea." He wanted to spend a few extra moments with her, and he didn't want to think about why.

Josie entered the kitchen. "Iced tea? Is there enough left for two more glasses?"

Sarah, who had retrieved the tea from the refrigerator, nodded. "There's plenty. I made more than one pitcher early this morning."

Jed watched as Sarah poured glasses of iced tea for Ellen, Josie, William and him, before pouring one last one for herself. He studied her hands, the careful way she took on the task. *She has nice hands,* he thought, *and a pretty smile.* She handed out the glasses and then suggested they sit on the porch to drink their tea.

He felt as if he could do this every day and evening as long as she was on the same porch with him, enjoying a bite to eat, a drink or simply some conversation.

He had a sudden mental image of Sarah sitting beside him on the front porch of a farmhouse, her face aged but still lovely as they watched a group of red-haired children playing out in the yard.

Jed mentally scolded himself, *What are* ya *doing?* Dreaming about something that will never happen.

Or would it?

After they finished their tea, Jed rose. "Time for home," he said.

"It was a wonderful day," Sarah murmured.

He grinned. *"Ja."* He stepped down from the porch and then turned to regard her with a feeling of inner warmth. "I will see *ya* on Sunday." She nodded. "Take care, Sarah."

"You, too," she said.

As he drove home, he took the memory of her sweet smile to last him until Sunday.

Chapter Twelve

During the days that followed the outing into town, Sarah found her thoughts returning again and again to Jed. What was it about him that had her envisioning her every moment with him? Yes, he was good-looking, but it was more than that. He had a kind heart. He had saved the twins, and he had taken the time to listen to her and be there for her whenever she needed someone.

Sarah frowned as she went about her chores on Wednesday morning. As she set the stainless-steel bucket under the cow's teats, she thought of her life back in Delaware, her family, who needed her, especially *Mam.* Soon she would leave. Soon she would get a phone call or letter that told her that it was time to go home. She wanted to see *Mam,* to see for herself that *Mam* was well. She wanted to see *Dat* and Ervin and Tobias.

As she milked the cow, she was barely aware of the sound of milk squirting into the metal bucket. She was torn. She wanted to see *Mam,* but she wanted to stay. She missed her family, but she knew that as soon as she left Happiness, she'd leave a large part of herself behind. Her heart.

The existence of Annie Zook in Jed's life made it hard, but Sarah kept recalling how his gaze had sought her out while he was talking with Annie. Was that an accident? Or something more?

By Thursday morning, Sarah was no closer to feeling any better about the situation. The twins were happy and healthy. Josie seemed to enjoy having them around. William was kind, a good husband to Josie, and Ellen, Will and Elam were well-behaved children who were loved by their parents.

"What's wrong?" Josie asked as she and Sarah pulled weeds from the vegetable garden.

"Why should something be wrong?" Sarah replied as she tugged on a clump of grass that had sprouted between green-bean plants.

"You've been quiet."

Sarah stood and wiped her moist forehead with her arm. "I'm listening to the silence," she said. "Hear the bees? And I can smell the honeysuckle. It's a nice day and I'm simply enjoying it."

Josie rose to her full height and captured Sarah's gaze. "I know it's more. You may be enjoying the day, Sarah, but I also know that you've been quiet ever since you came back from town with Jedidiah Lapp. Did something happen?"

"Nay." Sarah shook her head. "We had a nice time."

"But—" Josie invited.

Sarah sighed. "How well do you know the Zooks?"

"They are church members and friends. Why do you ask?" Josie brushed her hands down her apron before she reached up to tuck in a strand of hair that had escaped from the rolled hair under her *kapp.*

Sarah didn't say anything at first. She didn't want Josie to suspect how she felt about Jedidiah Lapp.

"I just wondered. We saw Annie Zook at Whittier's."

"Ah…" Josie flashed her a knowing smile. "You heard that Jed and Annie were once thought to be sweethearts."

Sarah bent down to hide her red face and check all the plants for anything that was ready to be picked.

"What?" Sarah said without looking up. "Were they sweethearts?" she asked casually, as if she wasn't eager to hear something that would prove the thought wrong.

"He took her home from a singing a time or two." Josie hunkered down to get back to work, and Sarah felt relieved. "I think he liked Annie at first, but once Noah married, Jed seemed to change."

"How?" Sarah kept her eyes focused on the task at hand, tugging gently on a stubborn weed near a bellpepper plant.

"I don't know. I can't describe it." Josie started to pick green beans. "*Restless* might be a *gut* word for it."

Restless? Sarah thought. "How so?"

Josie shrugged. "It was as if he wanted more from life."

Sarah remained thoughtful as Josie began to talk of other things. She perked up when she heard Josie mention Rachel.

"I know Rachel has been wanting you to visit again," she said. "Why don't you go today after the midday meal?"

"But we have pies to bake for Sunday's visit," Sarah began, although she wanted to visit Rachel.

"We have the cakes you baked in the freezer that we can take. Besides, we have all of tomorrow to make pies if we want."

Sarah smiled. It was hard for her to forget about work and leave. She knew it was because she'd spent so many months handling everything for *Mam*.

"I'd like to visit her," she admitted. Josie looked up from weeding around a zucchini plant and grinned. *"Gut."* She went back to inspecting the small green squash that would soon be ready to pick. "This will be a *gut* year for zucchini."

Sarah nodded. "I imagine the garden back home is thriving. Who will pick and can the vegetables there?"

"Sarah," Josie said softly but firmly, "didn't you say that your family was being well cared for?"

Sarah met her cousin's gaze and nodded. "I did."

"Then the work will get done whether you are there or not. Isn't it better to enjoy what time you have here than to worry about the work at home?"

Sarah knew Josie was right, but old habits died hard. "I will try."

Her cousin's lips twitched with amusement. "That's all I shall ask of you."

After sharing a midday meal of egg-salad sandwiches complemented by sweet pickles and sweet-and-sour chowchow, Sarah wrapped up some lemon bars and chocolate brownies to take to the Noah Lapp cottage near the schoolhouse a mile down the road from the Mast farm.

"It's a lovely day for a walk," Sarah said before leaving.

"Why not take the buggy to the *schuulhaus?*" Josie suggested.

"I need it," William said as he entered the room. "I'm heading over to help Amos King fix a section of his barn roof."

"Don't you be falling off that roof, William Mast," Josie scolded lovingly. "What of the young Lapp boys? Can't they fix it?"

"They're all busy today, and Amos says the barn has been leaking with every rainstorm. He's eager to get the work done."

Josie sighed. "Please be careful." She turned to Sarah. "You can take the courting buggy."

Sarah opened her mouth to refuse, but before she could utter a sound, William said, "I'll drop her by the cottage. I'll be going that way. It's just across the road from the Amos King farm."

Sarah smiled as she untied her apron strings. "I was going to say that it's a nice day for walking, but I'll take the ride and walk back."

"Gut." William nodded and Josie looked pleased. "I'll be leaving in five minutes. Can you be ready?"

"Ja. I'll just run upstairs and be right down." It would be better to take the ride to the cottage with the baked goods than to walk the distance.

As promised, Sarah ran upstairs to remove her cape and apron. She'd wear only her spring-green dress and white prayer *kapp.* On her feet she wore sneakers without stockings or socks.

She was outside next to the buggy when William

joined her. He raised his eyebrows when he saw her seated in the buggy with the baked goods on her lap.

"I've never known a woman to be ready so quickly," he said with a smile.

Sarah simply smiled in return.

William was quiet as he steered the horse and buggy down the road toward the Lapp cottage. It was a pleasant silence between them. Sarah enjoyed the warmth of the summer day as well as the scenery that never failed to make her smile.

How did *Englischers* live in their fast-paced world? Did they ever stop to notice the wildflowers along the road, the tiny sprouts in the tilled fields that hinted at a good year's crops? Did they ever pause to smell the honeysuckle or take long walks just to breathe in the fresh air? Did they take notice of every little bit of life that the Lord generously gave them? God's wonders, she thought.

Sarah felt wonderful this day, as she did most days since coming to Happiness. She couldn't think of a better name for this village.

"William," she said, finally breaking the silence as they neared the Samuel Lapp farm and soon the Noah Lapp cottage. "I appreciate you having us—the twins and me. I know the boys can be a handful, and I don't doubt that it's harder to have all of us underfoot."

William drew up the leathers as they neared the dirt lane next to the schoolyard. He steered the horse onto the lane and then stopped to give her an incredulous look. "Sarah," he said, his tone gentle, "you are family. It has been *gut* having you here. You are welcome for as long as you like." He grinned. "You make the best cakes and pies, but don't tell Josie. And the twins—they have been *gut* for Will and Elam. I've never seen them so happy." He clicked his tongue and spurred the horse on. "Josie loves having you, as well."

Sarah felt the sting of emotional tears. *"Danki,"* she said, murmuring the word they rarely spoke except on special occasions. They often showed with actions rather than with words their appreciation of someone's kindness.

William pulled up the horse near Rachel's cottage, and Sarah climbed out. "I will stop by when I leave to see if you want a ride home," he said.

Sarah smiled as she adjusted her *kapp.* "It is a nice day for a walk, but that will be fine."

As her cousin steered the buggy down the lane and then toward the Lapp farm, Sarah approached the cottage's front door and knocked. It was a few moments before Rachel opened the door. Her eyes looked red, as if she'd been crying.

"Sarah!" she exclaimed, happy to see her.

"Are *ya* all right?" Sarah asked as she stepped inside after Rachel opened the door wider for her to enter.

"I am fine," Rachel assured her. "I'm disappointed, but well."

"You're not going to have a baby," Sarah guessed. She set the plate she carried on top of a linen cabinet.

Rachel nodded. "I know I shouldn't feel this way, but…" She drew a sharp breath. "I was so hopeful. I so want to have Noah's baby. He will make a *gut* father, and I feel like I've failed him."

Sarah placed her arm around the young woman's shoulders and led her to a kitchen chair. "It will be fine,

Rachel. I feel it. The good Lord will provide." She sat down in another chair and leaned toward Rachel. "I will pray, Rachel. I feel He will give you the child you desire. You and Noah."

Rachel blinked back tears, sniffed and then smiled. "There is something about you, Sarah. You make me believe that God wants this for us."

Sarah nodded. "I believe it." She stood and looked toward the stove. "Can I make you a cup of tea?"

"I can do it." Rachel started to rise, but Sarah waved her to stay seated.

"*Ja,* but I'd like to make it."

"Then you may, certainly." Rachel wiped her eyes and then watched as Sarah made the tea, glancing toward her friend often as she worked.

"I brought lemon squares and chocolate brownies." Sarah went back to the linen chest and retrieved the dish she'd brought with her. She unwrapped the treats and set them on the kitchen table.

"You know us so well," Rachel said with a smile.

"I know you like lemon and Noah likes chocolate."

"I feel as if I've known you longer than just a few weeks."

Sarah understood. "I feel the same."

"I went to the doctor," Rachel admitted after they'd discussed simple things like the gardens, the weather and when school would begin again. "I drove myself."

"What did he say?" Sarah took a bite of a lemon square as she waited for Rachel to continue.

"That it is possible that I can conceive, but that it may be difficult."

"Then you will be carefully watched by a doctor when you do get pregnant."

"Ja." Rachel stood and took her cup to the sink. "I think Noah was disappointed."

Sarah shook her head. "Noah loves you. He would rather have you happy and healthy than have a baby." She smiled. "I've seen the way he looks at you."

"The same way that Jedidiah looks at you?"

Sarah felt a jolt. "He doesn't look at me that way."

An amused smile played about Rachel's lips. "If you say so." As if realizing that Sarah might feel uncomfortable discussing Jed, Rachel asked Sarah if she'd like to see the schoolhouse.

Sarah agreed. After they finished their tea, they walked over to the schoolhouse together.

Rachel pulled out a key and unlocked the door. "It seems so quiet with the children gone."

"But they will be back before you know it." Sarah enjoyed seeing all the wooden desks in rows that ran a few feet's distance from the teacher's station down the length of the room. She saw the alphabet and arithmetic charts on the wall. On each side of the door were two wooden cases with glass doors and books lining every shelf. Storybooks, Sarah suspected, as they didn't look like textbooks. When she relayed her thoughts to Rachel, she learned she was correct.

"The textbooks are in the bottom cabinet," Rachel said. "Those books are for the students to borrow and enjoy at home."

Sarah noted that the teacher's desk was particularly well made. When she commented on it, Rachel admitted that Noah had made it for her.

"He is a talented craftsman," Sarah said.

"The Lord gave him a wonderful gift," Rachel agreed.

They wandered about the classroom for a time, looking at some of the papers the students had written, the letters the younger ones had penned.

Rachel locked up the school when they were done, and they entered the yard to take a look at the swing sets. "The children enjoy them at recess," she said. She was quiet as she and Sarah walked back to the cottage. She paused near the cottage door. "Sarah, will you be staying the summer?"

"I don't know," Sarah admitted with a little pang. She was bothered by the fact that she'd be leaving soon. As much as she wanted to see her family, she wanted to stay here in Happiness.

"Will you write to me after you've gone home?" Rachel asked as she opened the door and they returned inside.

Sarah was touched. "I will be happy to." She bit her lip and then admitted, "I'll miss you and everyone in Happiness. This has become like home to me during the short time I've been here."

"Maybe one day you can come back for a visit," Rachel said.

"I'd like to." It all depended on *Mam*'s health and how much her family needed her.

How does *Jed look at me?* Sarah questioned later as she walked down the road, after a delightful afternoon spent with Rachel.

She liked Jed. The idea that he might like her as well thrilled her.

She'd never cared for a man like she cared for Jed, and she'd never had a man return her feelings.

Did she love Jed? *Ja, I love him,* she realized with a suddenly rapidly beating heart.

She thought of stopping at the Amos King farm to tell William that she was leaving, but she didn't want to bother him. *And what if Jed happens to be there?* Was she ready to see him so soon after coming to realize her love for him?

Sarah paused on the side of the street and closed her eyes. A car horn tooted, startling her, and she gasped. The weather remained lovely, and she looked around her. This was why she'd wanted to walk, wasn't it? To enjoy the wonders of God's work along the way?

Birds sang in the treetops. The scent of rose blossoms filled the air as she passed by a hearty bush. Children played on an *Englischer*'s lawn, laughing and running, and yelling, "You're it!" as they engaged in a game of "tag." A soft breeze blew across her skin, making her smile.

Life was beautiful. God had given them all wondrous things. God had given her Jed when she'd needed him most. She shouldn't worry about the future. She should trust in the Lord's love.

And she should protect her heart and keep her love for Jedidiah Lapp to herself.

Chapter Thirteen

L̲ate Sunday morning, Sarah, the twins and the William Masts climbed into the family buggy and then headed toward the Samuel Lapp farm for a day of visiting. The day started out unusually warm. Sarah wore her lavender short-sleeved dress with white cape and apron. On her feet, she wore white sneakers. She'd washed her hair when she'd first risen at dawn, and after it had dried sufficiently, Sarah had rolled and pinned up the red-gold strands in the traditional Amish way. Then she'd covered her hair with the new white prayer *kapp* she'd made earlier in the week.

"Will," Timothy said from where he sat in the seat directly in front of hers, "do you think Jacob and Eli will play ball with us today?"

"If we ask them." Young Will, William's oldest son, grinned beneath his black-banded straw hat. "Someone will play with us."

"Maybe Jedidiah," Thomas said.

Sarah's heart skipped a beat at the mention of the one man she longed to see.

"He might," Elam said. "He's played with us before. Joshua King will play. So will David Schrock and Nate Peachy."

As the discussion continued around her, Sarah couldn't stop thinking about Jed. She'd always been comfortable with him. Should she allow the information Rachel had revealed change that? She knew she'd be watching him closely to see if she could see what Rachel had glimpsed—that Jed had feelings for her.

"Will there be a large group here today?" she asked conversationally, hoping to get her mind on other things.

Josie smiled as she glanced back to where Sarah sat in the farthest backseat. "Large enough. The Lapps have plenty of room."

"The Amos Kings, the Abram Peachys, the Eli Shrocks and the Joseph Zooks will be there," William said. "It will be a nice day for all."

"Ja," Sarah said, thinking of Jed and his promise to give her a tour of the farm.

Rachel and Noah had just arrived when William pulled their buggy into the yard near the farmhouse. Tables had already been set up outside. Children ran about the lawn, playing. A young girl with a rope about her waist pretended to be a horse while a boy held the two ends of the "reins" as they both ran among the others, who laughed and played and had fun.

Sarah was glad to see Rachel as she stepped from the buggy. She felt a feeling of warmth when she realized that her new friend was waiting for her.

"You look well today," Sarah said.

"I feel better than I did," Rachel admitted. "I appreciate your encouragement the other day."

"I didn't do anything." Sarah fell into step with Rachel, her arms cradling a basket of fresh-baked muffins and rolls. Josie and Ellen went ahead with the two pies and a chocolate cake that Sarah had made yesterday.

"*Ya* did a lot." Rachel placed a hand on Sarah's arm, halting their progress. "You reminded me how much Noah loves me and all the things I should be grateful for."

"What things?" Sarah said with a frown, then she laughed.

"I talked with him about it." Rachel paused. "You are right. He loves me. He said so from the first. He told me we could adopt if we couldn't…" Her voice trailed off as if it was too painful to actually say the words.

Sarah glanced back toward the buggies. "Here comes Noah now," she whispered.

Noah had stopped to talk briefly with William, probably to ask him how the windows and doors were holding up, Sarah suspected.

Now he reached the two women and placed a hand gently on his wife's shoulder. "I enjoyed the brownies the other day, Sarah," he said with the boyish grin that she'd come to associate with him.

Sarah smiled. "I'm glad you liked them."

With his hand still touching Rachel, Noah leaned forward to take a sniff. "What's in the basket?"

"Not much," Sarah said. "Just some muffins, biscuits and rolls."

Noah grinned. "I like muffins, biscuits and rolls." He tried to take a peek. "Are any of them chocolate?"

Rachel chuckled. "Would you refuse a corn or blueberry muffin if it's all she brought?"

"*Nay.* I love them, too," he said.

Sarah exchanged grins with Rachel. "I just happen to have a dozen chocolate-chip muffins in here." She held up the basket.

Noah closed his eyes in gleeful anticipation. "May I have one now?"

"Noah!" Rachel scolded lovingly.

Sarah lifted the tea towel she'd placed over the basket of baked goods and allowed Noah to select a chocolate muffin.

His obvious delight was his thanks. "You are a *gut* friend to us, Sarah."

Katie Lapp came out of the farmhouse and headed in their direction.

"Hallo!" She smiled at her son and offered the same generous warmth to Rachel and Sarah.

Josie had disappeared inside to put the cake and pies out of the sun until they were ready to enjoy them later that afternoon.

Josie exited the house in time to see one of her sons running with a big stick in his hand. "Elam! Drop that stick. You'll fall on it and poke yourself."

Sarah heard a *"Ja, Mam"* in a subdued voice before the boy obeyed his mother, dropped the stick and rejoined the other boys.

"Boys," Sarah said with a smile.

"Ja," Katie agreed. "I've seen enough accidents to make you shudder. But now they know better. Even Joseph, my youngest, understands the danger of running with a stick. He's had his share of tumbles and accidents." Relieving Rachel from the burden of her casserole dish, Jed's mother gestured toward the house.

"Come inside. Mae, Charlotte and Nancy are in the kitchen."

Rachel looked pleased. "Come, Sarah. I've introduced you to my aunt and cousins, haven't I?"

"*Ja.* I had the pleasure of meeting them at Sunday church services."

"I haven't seen them since," Rachel said. "I'm eager to talk with Charlotte."

As she followed Rachel and Katie inside the house, Sarah recalled that Rachel had believed that Charlotte and Noah were sweet on each other at one time.

Her thoughts turned to Jed, and she turned to quickly search the yard for him. But he was nowhere to be found. She frowned. Where was he?

Jed heard the names Josie and William through the open window and he went to peer outside from his second-story room to look for Sarah. He knew she would be with them...unless she had gone home. *Nay,* she would have come to say goodbye, wouldn't she? They were friends, but in his mind, she meant more to him.

He found her standing with his sister-in-law Rachel and *Mam,* as if she enjoyed the women's company.

Should he head down now? She'd been on his mind a lot lately. He wanted her to keep company with him. He had promised to take her on a tour of the property—a good excuse to spend time alone with her, coupled with a genuine wish to show her their land.

He had enjoyed their day in town together. He'd loved watching her face light up as she'd eaten her ice cream, and had found it endearing the way she ate her lunch and later her bag of kettle corn.

The only awkward moment had been when they'd stopped at Whittier's Store for Sarah to call home. He hadn't expected to see Annie there. They had chatted a bit—it was the polite thing to do—but his thoughts had been with Sarah and her phone call.

He had laughed at something Annie had said, but he couldn't remember what she'd said or why he had laughed. He'd wanted to wander the store with Sarah and Ellen. He'd wanted to stay near in case Sarah received bad news about her mother.

Eager to see her, Jed hurried down the stairs and headed toward the kitchen. He recognized her voice before he entered the room. He stood a moment, enjoying the soft, feminine lilt of her words as she talked with the community women, as they took care of the food. Eager to see her, Jed moved forward and made his presence known.

"It smells *gut* in here," he said as he joined the women.

"Jed!" Josie smiled as she gestured toward the desserts. "We have a lot to enjoy today."

"As we do every Sunday," he replied with a grin.

The other women greeted him, and then Jed made his way toward Sarah, who stood at the other end of the counter, placing rolls, biscuits and muffins from a basket onto a platter.

"*Hallo,* Sarah," he said softly, studying her fine hands as she worked, her profile, her beautiful red-gold hair pulled back and mostly hidden beneath her prayer *kapp*. He could see the delicate skin at her nape.

"Jed." She flashed him a quick smile before she continued the job at hand.

"May I show you around the farm later?" he asked, waiting eagerly for her answer.

"I'd like that," she said without looking up as she uncovered a bowl of potato salad and set a spoon into the potatoes.

Rachel approached. "What shall I carry?"

"The muffins and rolls?" Sarah suggested as she picked up the container of chocolate pudding. She glanced at Jed and held up the bowl. "The refrigerator?"

"In the back room." He smiled. "Follow me."

Sarah's gaze met Rachel's as the two women passed each other. Sarah saw amusement in her friend's expression, and she raised her eyebrows.

The refrigerator was in a back room next to a chest freezer. Jed opened the door, shifted a few things around and then held out a hand for the pudding bowl.

Sarah nodded her thanks, handed him the bowl and turned to leave.

"Sarah—"

The sound of his soft voice made her tingle. *"Ja?"* She didn't turn.

"Can *ya* eat dinner with me today?"

Sarah turned to him. "Josie…"

"I understand," he said softly, but there was a hint of something in his eyes. Disappointment? Longing?

She jerked with surprise. *Affection?* Could this be the look that Rachel had seen?

"But you can still show me around the farm," she murmured, suppressing the urge to touch her *kapp* to make sure her hair was neatly tucked inside.

She saw him study her, felt his interest in her as

keenly as if he'd told her he liked her outright. She was suddenly conscious of her own feelings for him.

Nay, she thought. *I shouldn't do this. I'll be going home soon.*

Enjoy your time with him, her heart said. Tomorrow she might get that phone call or letter, making today their last day together.

"I'll see you later," she said quickly and then turned to hurry back into the kitchen—and the safety of the women's company.

Jed didn't follow her into the room. But when she went outside carrying items for the food table, she saw him seated at a table with his aunt and uncle and their five daughters. Jed spoke in earnest with his uncle, and Arlin seemed intent on whatever Jed was saying.

What were they discussing? Sarah wondered, and then she scolded herself for being so vain to think the topic of discussion was her. Vanity was a sin, and she knew the two men had more important things to discuss between them. *Lord, help me to know what is right. Help me to be strong, whatever happens.*

Jed sipped from a cup of coffee as he reached for a muffin on the food table. He chose a cinnamon-crunch muffin, and as he took a bite, he thought of Sarah making it, with flour on her apron and a bit of baking powder in her hair.

He would love to watch her bake. She was good at it, and somehow he felt she'd look content as she measured out the ingredients, stirred them in.

But it wasn't Sarah's baking skills that drew him to her. It was her inherent sweetness. She'd sacrificed much to take care of her mother, and did so with love. Her concern for her family's welfare and the welfare of others was a glimpse into what made up Sarah.

He looked for her and saw her seated at a table with her cousins. She was leaning close to Ellen to listen carefully to what the young girl was saying. Sarah smiled and nodded as she straightened in her seat.

Jed felt a tight feeling in his throat as he studied her. He couldn't help himself; something drew him to her. He didn't know if he'd be welcomed or not, but he continued on.

His mother approached the other side of the table from the opposite direction. Jed paused, wondering if he should go on, but he kept going.

"Jed!" Katie Lapp said. "Would you mind helping your *dat* set up the badminton set?"

Jed saw the way Sarah went still as his mother mentioned his name. "*Ja, Mam.* Where is he?"

"On the back lawn."

He nodded. Before he left, he said, "Sarah, will *ya* be ready soon for that tour?"

She turned slowly, awarding him a glimpse of those bright blue eyes and sweet pink lips. But before Sarah could answer, Katie said, "We'll be sharing midday meal soon, Jed. Why not wait until after we eat, when you can take your time showing her the farm and property?"

Sarah's blue eyes met his as he nodded. He saw an answer in her expression, and he saw agreement in her features…and a smile meant only for him. He felt his heart slam in his chest as he turned to leave. While he assisted his father, he thought of Sarah, the heady knowledge that he would be spending time with her soon. It seemed like ages ago when they'd gone into town, although it had only been a few days.

"Where did you get this?" he asked his father as they stretched out a net with a pole on each end.

"Rick Martin," Samuel said. "He dropped it by this morning. I would have put it away so that we could set it up for next Sunday, but Isaac and Daniel saw it and pleaded with me."

Jed grinned. "And so you had to put it up today."

"I think the Lord will forgive me this one little chore, don't *ya* think?" Samuel waved Isaac over and instructed him to hold one pole while Jed held the other. Next, he placed thin ropes about the top of each pole and grabbed the first of four stakes that would keep the poles standing up and balanced. Samuel extended his hand toward the ground for his hammer.

"*Dat,* let me," Jed said, grabbing the hammer. Samuel nodded and took Jed's position at one end of the net. Jed bent and quickly hammered two stakes at one end before securing the other two at Isaac's end.

"Can we play now?" Isaac asked when they were done.

"You can play now, but *Mam* may have other ideas. It's about time for dinner. You may play afterward," Samuel said.

Isaac looked disappointed for only a second. "I am hungry," he confessed.

"Didn't you have a biscuit or muffin?" Jed asked, lifting the boy's hat playfully before setting it back onto his head.

"That was two hours ago!" his brother said.

"Oh," Jed said with great understanding. "Then you definitely should get something to eat first."

Samuel and Jed exchanged amused looks as they walked back to the community area. Jed went into the barn and put away his *dat*'s hammer before returning in time to share in the meal that the Lord had blessed them with.

The deacon prayed over the food, and then the midday meal was shared in companionable enjoyment for all. Sarah, seated at the table with Josie, William and the children, rose to get her food. Josie and Ellen followed closely behind her.

As she picked up a plate and started down the food line, Sarah was startled when Josie said, "Sarah, you don't have to sit with us all the time."

Sarah looked at her. "Whom else would I sit with?"

"Rachel. Noah. *Jed,*" her cousin suggested.

"Josie—"

"Jed will be taking you on a tour of the property, *ja?*" Josie speared a piece of cold fried chicken with a fork and placed it on her plate.

Sarah spooned a helping of potato salad. "*Ja,* Jed has offered to show me around." Why was her cousin bringing up Jed?

"Then why not sit with your friends? It's not every Sunday you can do so."

On church-service Sundays, the men ate together first, and when they were done the women and children sat down to eat their meal.

Visiting Sundays, at least, here in Happiness, Sarah noted, were more relaxed in their eating arrangements, as it was in her particular church community back home in Kent County, Delaware. Every church had its own set of rules. Their beliefs and teachings were the same, but as far as the way they dressed or the things they were allowed to do, the community's church elders decided those things.

"I told Jed that I'd be eating with you," Sarah admitted. She added some sweet-and-sour chowchow to her plate.

Josie was silent for a moment. "I see."

Sarah flashed her a glance. "What do you see?"

Josie smiled. "You are worried about the twins again."

Sarah remained quiet. It was the first time that she hadn't thought of the twins, and she felt guilty for forgetting them in light of her feelings for Jed.

"They are fine with us." Josie chose a piece of frosted raisin bread.

"I know they are." Sarah chose a couple more food items, including a scoop of the green-bean salad and some dried-corn casserole. "I'm surprised at how well your two and the twins get along and behave together."

Josie laughed as she assisted her daughter Ellen with a helping of pasta salad that was just out of the young girl's reach. "I may have put the fear of God into them the first day they were here."

Sarah raised her eyebrows as she faced her. "How?"

"I told them that the Lord was everywhere, His gaze especially on young, active boys who get into trouble. I said the Lord gives special blessings to those who are *gut,* do their chores well and play nicely with each other."

"And that worked?" Sarah was flabbergasted that so simple a warning had done so well.

"Well…" Josie grabbed a napkin and eating utensils before turning to head back to the table.

Sarah fell into step with her. Ellen had gone ahead.

"I hear a note of *but* in your tone," Sarah said before she sampled a sweet-and-sour cauliflower that was part of the chowchow mix.

"Actually, I told them that if they didn't behave, I'd send them over to help Jake Stoltzfus slog out his hog houses."

Sarah laughed. "The stench alone would be punishment enough for naughty boys. Would you have really sent them?"

"I am a woman of my word, Sarah. What do you think?"

Sarah was still chuckling as she sat down at the table while Josie and Ellen joined them. William flashed them a funny look, and Sarah could only grin at him. "Your wife makes me laugh" was all she told him.

William glanced at his wife, saw the amusement shimmering in her hazel eyes and said, "I don't want to know, do I?"

Josie smiled sweetly at him. *"Nay."*

Sarah became more acquainted with everyone who visited with the Samuel Lapps this day. The Eli Shrocks were Charlotte and Nancy's oldest sister, Sarah; her husband, Eli; and their children, David, John and Rose Ann.

Sarah had enjoyed a piece of coffee cake that Sarah King Shrock had made for dessert.

The Abram Peachy family consisted of the church

deacon, Abram Peachy; his wife, Charlotte King Peachy; and the five Peachy children—Jonas, Nathaniel, Jacob, Mary Elizabeth and young Ruthie.

She saw the Joseph Zooks. She'd already met Annie and her sister Barbara. Horseshoe Joe and his wife, Miriam, had two sons as well—Josiah, who was older than Barbara but younger than Annie, and young Peter. She learned that the eldest Zook daughter had married and moved out of state.

She'd met Jed's uncle, Arlin Stoltzfus, in Delaware and since coming to Happiness, she'd became acquainted with his wife, Missy, and each of their five daughters.

"Sarah." Jed's deep voice coming from behind her startled her at first as it shivered along her spine. "Are you ready for the tour?"

Sarah rose from the table. *"Ja."* She picked up her paper plate and plastic utensils and put them in the garbage bag set outside for the day's event.

There was little to bring inside. Sarah looked at the dessert table and wondered if she should carry something.

"I'll clean up," Josie said as she carried her own plate to dump into the trash bag next to Sarah.

"Are you sure?" As much as she wanted to go, Sarah was reluctant to run off without helping.

"Ja." Josie waved for her to leave. "There is little enough." She turned to smile at her daughter, who had come up behind them carrying not only her own plate but also several others from the table. "Ellen will help me with the desserts." The girl nodded.

Jed waited patiently, leaning against the massive

trunk of a tree, not far from the Mast table. He pushed off at Sarah's approach. "I'll show you the house first, and then we can see the rest of the property from inside our buggy."

Chapter Fourteen

Jed gave Sarah a narrated tour of the farmhouse first. He took her through the first floor and gave his version of how the family utilized the space. Afterward, he led her up onto the second story, scooping up Hannah, who'd been napping in the first room and was now awake.

Sarah listened to Jed explain who slept where, while he carried Hannah comfortably in his arms. The way the little girl rested her head against Jed's shoulder as he walked told Sarah that Hannah had been picked up and held by Jed many times. It gave Sarah a warm feeling to see Jed holding his little sister so tenderly.

"This is where the twins and I sleep," Jed said, stopping before a door to a bedroom with four beds and a dresser. "Noah used to sleep here, too, before he got married."

Sarah looked quickly and then turned away, eager to move on. Jed must have sensed her mood because he continued on.

"This room is where the youngest sleep—Daniel,

Isaac and Joseph. That's *Mam* and *Dat*'s room across the hall. Hannah is the only one with her own room, and you saw how tiny it is. It's just big enough for her crib and when she is old enough, a twin bed." Jed stopped and smiled down at her, making Sarah's heart race and her stomach flip-flop.

"I like your home," she said, meaning it. The house looked well lived-in and loved. She could tell the Samuel Lapps were a loving family who cared about each other and their home.

Jed showed her Katie's sewing area—a small room off his parents' bedroom—and the upstairs bathroom before they headed down the stairs.

Sarah thought of her parents in their makeshift downstairs bedroom, and thoughts of her *mam* reached in and squeezed her heart. *She will get well,* Sarah had to remind herself.

"Shall we go outside?" Jed said. She looked up and saw him eyeing her with a concerned frown.

She smiled. *"Ja."*

"Are you interested in the barn?" he asked as he shifted Hannah to his other arm.

"Of course. An important part of any farm is its barn."

"And *Mam* has a greenhouse."

Sarah was eager to see it. "I remember. Does she have anything growing in it?"

"I'll show you after we tour the barn."

After setting Hannah down on his mother's lap, Jed took Sarah through the barn and saw how impressed she was with the building's cleanliness and the condition of the animals. Next he brought her to Katie's greenhouse. Inside were different plants in various stages of growth.

"I can understand why your *mudder* enjoys working in here." Sarah bent to examine an unfamiliar plant more closely. The label called it *Aloysia citrodora*.

"Lemon verbena," Jed explained. "It smells like lemons."

She leaned close to catch the scent. "You can make syrup out of it, can't you?"

"So I'm told. It's good over ice cream and probably other things, as well."

"And tea." Sarah took another whiff and then smiled. "I'm sure I've had tea made with lemon verbena." She looked about the greenhouse. "Katie has a large selection here, but I don't see any parsley or sage."

"Sold or given away," Jed explained. "Many of our church members come in the spring to purchase her herbs and seedlings, but *Mam* also gives a lot away— especially to family."

Sarah faced him with a smile playing about her lips. "I like your *mudder*. She is a kind and caring woman."

Jed grinned. "I like her, too."

Sarah chuckled. "I should hope so."

At Jed's invitation, Sarah preceded him out of Katie's greenhouse.

"I'll bring the buggy around. I think you'll enjoy a ride through our property."

Sarah nodded. She waved to Rachel and Noah, who approached. "Jed is going to take me for a ride through the property," she told them as they drew near.

"We'll go with you," Rachel said.

Noah gave her a wry smile. "*Mam*'s suggestion."

Jed brought the buggy around, and Rachel and Noah climbed into the backseat, while Jed helped Sarah into the front before joining her. If he felt bothered by his brother and sister-in-law's presence, Jed didn't show it.

The day was warm but not overly so as Jed steered the horse and buggy down the dirt driveway from the farmhouse to the main road ahead. He turned left onto the paved road and drove a distance before turning onto the road that ran past the school and cottage and continued down a length of Lapp property.

He stopped the buggy, climbed out and secured the horse to a small nearby tree. Noah got out the same side as Jed and helped Rachel out from the back. Jed skirted the buggy to assist Sarah.

"There is a stream just past that windbreak," Jed said, gesturing toward the line of trees to the right.

Noah and Rachel headed toward the trees, and as Sarah was about to follow them, Jed grabbed her hand and gently tugged her in another direction before releasing it. "I want to show you something."

His smile did odd things to her heart. The warmth of his fingers about her hand remained long after he'd released it. Sarah wished that he hadn't let go.

In silence, Jed led her farther down the dirt road. Sarah studied her surroundings as she followed his lead. To the left, corn grew in acres of farmland. To the right, the windbreak of trees had thinned. Sarah could see through the trees to farmland beyond. She wasn't sure, but it looked as if the field was filled with lush tall grass.

Jed stopped. With a light touch of her shoulder, he gestured toward the break in the trees. He started through the opening first, stopping as he reached the stream. Here the water width was so narrow they could easily jump across.

"Come," he said. He jumped over the water and then held out his hand to her.

Sarah looked at the stream and then his hand, and accepted his help. She felt the exact moment when his hand surrounded hers. This time he didn't let go. He laced his fingers with hers as they walked into the field, then paused. She studied the scenery before her and smiled. "It's beautiful here."

She glanced over in time to catch Jed's soft expression. "I bought this land from William and Josie. It once belonged to Josie's brother. He purchased it with the hope that he would build on it one day and bring a wife and family to live here."

He turned to eye the farmland, his brown eyes intent. "When he passed, Josie and her father came out from Indiana to see the land and decide what to do with it. It was during her time here that William and Josie met and fell in love."

"I didn't realize that Josie had lost her brother," she murmured, unable to break away from Jed's gaze.

"*Ja.* And she was heartbroken. She loved her brother, and it upset her that he never got to realize his dream."

"He never brought his wife?" Sarah finally looked away, her gaze returning to the land.

"He never married. He died in a farm accident in Indiana."

Sarah inhaled sharply. "How?"

"The horse attached to his plow spooked. He wasn't plowing the fields at the time. James's hands got caught in the reins. It happened so quickly that he couldn't get free."

Sarah closed her eyes, imagining the rest. James, she realized, had been dragged by his horse and caught under the plow. "I'm sorry." It had nothing to do with Jed, but she felt Josie and her family's pain.

"When Josie married William," Jed continued, "her family entrusted the land to the two of them. Later, when they decided to sell—especially since it was some distance from William's property—I asked if I could buy it from them. I had money saved from some construction work I did. I used it as a deposit and I continue to make payments. The land will be paid off next month."

Jed watched the play of emotion cross Sarah's face as he told her about the land and how he came to buy it. Did she have any idea what he was thinking?

He wanted a family and a home—with her. He knew her life was complicated and that he couldn't ask her to stay here and leave her family. But he had to let her know how he felt....

"Someday, I'm going to build a farmhouse on this land. I'll bring my wife here and together we'll raise our children."

Jed watched her closely as he spoke. He couldn't read her expression, and it bothered him. He had never told anyone about this land, certainly not Annie Zook. The only ones who knew were Josie and William, his parents and, more recently, his brother Noah, who was allowed to tell Rachel but no one else.

"The woman you marry will be happy here," she finally said. She released his hand to walk farther down the length of the field. "How far does it go?"

Disappointed in her reaction, he followed her. "It runs that way," he said, gesturing away from the main road by which they'd come, "to another road on the other side. The land starts here and goes there."

Sarah nodded politely. "So it starts here and heads away from the *schuulhaus*."

"*Ja*."

She paused and turned to him with a smile that didn't quite reach her eyes. "I hope you and your wife will be happy here."

"Sarah—"

"We should go," she said, turning to head back the way they had come. "Rachel and Noah will be wondering where we've gone."

Jed felt a burning in his stomach as he nodded. "I wanted you to see this."

"It is beautiful. You will have a *gut* farm."

But not with you, Jed thought.

Surely she knew how he felt about her, but apparently her desire to go home was uppermost in her mind.

"Sarah—"

"Please, Jed. Don't!" she cried and hurried on, sprinting over the stream, through the trees and back onto the dirt road where the buggy lay ahead.

Jed followed slowly until he saw Noah and Rachel appear through the windbreak. He didn't want them to know what had happened. He needed to talk with Sarah, to make his love for her known, to see if there was a way for them to be together.

* * *

"It's wonderful here, isn't it?" Rachel gushed with a warm look at her husband. "The water is cool, but refreshing."

Sarah looked down and saw that her friend and Noah were carrying their shoes. "You went wading in the stream!" she exclaimed.

"A favorite pastime of ours," Noah said with an affectionate smile for his wife.

Sarah tried to chuckle, but her thoughts were in a whirl after learning of Jed's land and his future plans. Why was he telling her all this? Was he trying to let her know that after she went home, he and Annie were to be married?

She recalled the way their hands had entwined, how comfortable it felt to have him close, the warmth of his body radiating as he stood next to her.

Why did he bring her here? Because of Annie? She recalled Josie's claim that Jed had realized that Annie wasn't the one he wanted to marry.

Yet she recalled Jed deep in conversation with Annie…the laughter the two of them had shared while she'd looked on from a short distance away.

Soon she and the others got back into the wagon. She sneaked a quick peek at Jed, but she couldn't read his expression. She felt tension emanating from him, and she felt no comfort, no warmth that she'd felt before in his company.

She stared straight ahead as Jed continued to steer the buggy down the dirt road, which circled behind his father's farmland until they reached another dirt lane, which brought them onto the other paved road that Jed had mentioned. But instead of turning right to show her the land from the other side, he steered the horse left until he reached the lane that would take them back onto the farm and toward the farmhouse.

As Jed steered the buggy back into the barnyard, Sarah felt disappointed that the outing had come to an end. Something with Jed had changed during the ride.

He got out of the vehicle and then went around to her side. Extending a hand to her, he helped Sarah climb down. Silently, he started to turn.

She felt her stomach burn at the distance between them. "Jed—" she began.

He stopped and faced her, his expression unreadable.

"I enjoyed the day." She bit her lip, and it seemed as if he watched her closely. Noah and Rachel had left the vehicle and waited not far, but out of earshot. "If I said something wrong," Sarah said, unable to control the tears that stung her eyes, "I'm sorry."

His expression softened. "You said nothing wrong, Sarah." He sighed. "The fault was mine."

Sarah frowned. "I don't understand."

"I thought you might like the land that I purchased—"

"I do!"

"And the fact that I plan to bring my future family there."

"It's a *gut* plan," Sarah said softly, trying hard to smile, but not succeeding.

"I thought so…"

Sarah hated this tension between them. "Jed, I'll be going home soon, and I don't want things to be bad between us." If he was with Annie, she couldn't ask him to write. The thought saddened her.

"That will never happen," he assured her, and she heard his sincerity. He studied her a moment. "I need to go see to Janey, our mare."

Sarah nodded. "The dessert has been brought out."

Jed glanced toward the tables set up in the yard. "I see that."

"Sarah," Rachel called to her, "are you coming?"

"Ja!" Sarah looked back toward Jed, but he was already moving away to park the buggy and take care of the horse.

She approached Rachel. Noah had gone ahead. "Where is Noah?"

"Abram Peachy asked to have a word with him."

Sarah followed the direction of Rachel's gaze as her friend glanced toward her husband. Noah was deep in conversation with the deacon and his wife, Charlotte, who was Rachel's cousin. Charlotte left moments later to join her mother at the food table.

"I have a feeling they have work for him," Rachel said with a smile. "While we wait for the men to join us, shall we head to the dessert table?"

"Ja." With a heavy heart, Sarah followed Rachel toward the food. While Rachel selected a couple of delicious-looking items for her and Noah, Sarah chose a piece of carrot cake for herself, and just in case Jed did return, she sliced him a good-size piece of the cherry pie.

Noah approached Rachel and Sarah a few minutes later. "You are the best wife," he told Rachel when he saw the desserts she had chosen for him. "I'm glad I married you."

"It's not hard to know what to get for you," Rachel replied. "As long as it's chocolate."

Sarah grinned as the two sparred teasingly before Noah actually sat and began eating the rich chocolate cake on the same plate as the chosen chocolate brownies and fudge.

Jed returned to find them as she continued to laugh at Noah, who heartily dived into the chocolate goodies. Sarah didn't have to look at Jed to feel his presence. She met his unreadable gaze before looking down to see the plate of cookies he'd brought.

He set the cookies down in the center of the table between them. "I brought these to share," he said directly to her.

Sarah felt a warmth spread through her belly as she slid the cherry pie across the table to him. "I thought you'd enjoy this."

His sudden grin warmed her heart and made her feel giddy inside. "Your cherry pie," he said before he dug into the flaky crust with a fork and brought a mouthful of the dessert to his lips.

"Your favorite," she murmured as she watched him enjoy his first bite.

"You are a keeper, Sarah."

His comment startled her.

"Perhaps you should marry her," Noah joked.

Jed's face suddenly became expressionless, and Sarah's spirits plummeted.

Rachel, immediately sizing up the situation, spoke

up. "You say that to everyone," she told her husband teasingly.

"Can I help it if I want everyone to enjoy married life as I do?" Noah bit into a piece of fudge made warm and gooey from the day's heat.

"That's sweet of you, but you're embarrassing Sarah." Rachel smiled at her friend.

Sarah offered a half-hearted smile in return. Sensing Jed's gaze on her, she flashed him a glance and saw a glimpse of something she couldn't identify, since it came and went so quickly. *Longing? Pain? Disappointment?* She couldn't tell.

The discussion turned to a different topic as Noah talked about the work Abram wanted done.

"While Charlotte was nearby, he asked for a new front door. After she left, he told me what he really wants—to surprise Charlotte with a rocking chair," he said.

"She'll love that," Rachel commented. "She appreciates quality furniture, and you always put a lot of time and care into everything you make."

Sarah took a sip from her glass of iced tea before setting it down. "I saw the desk you made for Rachel. It's lovely."

Noah frowned a moment before his brow cleared. "Ah, the teacher's desk," he said with a twinkle in his warm brown eyes.

"Well, she's the teacher, isn't she?" Jed said after happily swallowing a mouthful of cherry pie.

Noah bestowed a loving look on his wife. "That she is," he murmured, "and a *gut* one." He clearly enjoyed it when Rachel blushed.

The rest of the afternoon went by too quickly and soon Josie called out to Sarah, "We'll be leaving in a half hour."

"I'll be right there." Sarah stood. She should help to finish up in the kitchen. She mentioned it aloud.

"Nay," Rachel said. "We did what we could, and Katie and the others expect no more."

Sarah frowned. "But—"

"Sarah," Jed said softly, "you've done so much for so many months. Listen to Rachel. I'm sure Josie wants you to relax. In fact, I *know* she does."

Sarah felt warmed by Jed's tone and the way he looked at her.

"Jedidiah!" Timothy called as he ran toward them with Thomas fast on his heels. "Will you play ball with me?" The boy's gaze settled on Noah. "How about you, Noah? Will you play, too?"

Agreeing to play, the two Lapp brothers stood and followed the young Mast twins to the lawn, where Sarah saw other children waited to play, including the Peachy boys, David Shrock, Joshua and John King, and the younger Lapp brothers—Isaac, Daniel and Joseph.

Sarah watched them for a while, a smile on her face. She was pleased to see how good Jed was with the children. After a turn, she smiled at Rachel. "I should get up to help—"

"Nay. Jed is right, Sarah," Rachel said. "You've been working hard to help Josie. She told me so herself." She stood and picked up the empty plates. "You know that when you go home again, you'll be busy." She dropped them in a nearby trash can before returning to the table.

"It's hard to sit and not work—"

Rachel shrugged. "Enjoy it. It's Sunday and not a time for work. There is little to do. Let the others handle it."

They were silent as they watched the ball game in progress. Someone had brought out mitts and a bat. The game became a true baseball game with Jed pitching first and Noah in line to bat. Jed threw a pitch that had Noah swinging and grabbing only a little of the ball, which went careening off to the side.

"Foul ball!" Isaac Lapp shouted. He stood behind "home plate" as acting umpire.

Noah got ready for the next pitch. "Give it your best shot, *bruder*," he taunted Jed.

Jed merely grinned and then pitched the ball. Noah swung, hit the ball hard, and sent it flying over the heads of John King and Timothy in the outfield.

Sarah laughed when she saw Jed shrug briefly as he looked her way.

"You like him," Rachel said, drawing her attention away from Jed.

"Who?" she asked but she knew what her friend was saying. She had realized only recently that her feelings for Jed had strengthened well beyond friendship.

Rachel's expression was knowing but warm. "Jedidiah."

Sarah frowned. "Rachel, please don't tell anyone."

"It's not my secret to tell," Rachel said with a seriousness that reminded Sarah when Rachel had revealed a secret from her own past to her.

Sarah reached out to touch Rachel's hand briefly. *"Danki."*

I'm going to miss you when you leave." Rachel studied her with an intensity that spoke volumes.

"I'll miss you." Sarah swallowed against a suddenly tight throat. "I've been here longer than expected, but not long enough."

Rachel smiled as she reached for her iced tea. "The weeks have gone by too quickly." Her gaze went back to the boys playing baseball. "It's been *gut* for your *bruders* to be here." Jed shouted out encouragingly as a ball went sliding on the ground toward second base. "And you've been *gut* for Jed."

"I don't know about that," Sarah said, her eyes intent on the man she loved. "He's been nice to me because he knows I'll be leaving soon. I think he still cares for Annie Zook."

Rachel watched Jed closely before turning back to Sarah. "*Nay.* I know for a fact that he watches you when you're not looking."

Her friend had hinted at this before, but it was the first time Rachel seemed sure of the way Jed studied her.

Sarah glanced his way, but Jed was focused on the game. She turned back to Rachel. "He does?"

"*Ja.* All the time."

Sarah was surprised. She had caught him looking at her in the past, but things had changed between them this week, ever since he'd taken her to Whittier's Store and encountered Annie Zook.

"Annie Zook didn't stay long today," Sarah said.

"*Nay,* her *grossmudder* is feeling poorly. She went home to stay with her." Rachel hesitated before continuing, "Her *grosselders* have had their share of trials this past year. Margaret Hershberger has been in and out of the hospital, and her husband has had a difficult time with his wife ill."

"Hershberger?"

Rachel's lips twitched. "You've met Alta Hershberger? She is Joe's sister-in-law. Joe and Miriam brought Miriam's parents to live in the *grosselders'* house when they moved to Happiness. They originally lived just north of Lancaster City. Joe's parents passed early on, so the house was ready and perfect for them."

"Barbara, Josiah and Peter are still here," Sarah noted. The three were Annie's siblings.

"Annie, Barbara and Miriam take turns caring for Miriam's *mudder*. It's a *gut* arrangement and seems to work out well."

Except Annie had to leave while Jedidiah remained behind.

"Does Jedidiah truly watch me when I'm not looking?" Sarah asked, loving the thought.

Rachel nodded. "*Ja,* he does."

Sarah recalled the way Jed had held her hand long after he'd helped her cross the stream. She felt confused. Jed was a sincere, kind person; he wouldn't have held her hand if he didn't like her.

But liking isn't the same as loving.

Chapter Fifteen

Sarah moved about the worktable, cleaning up after a morning of baking. The scent of homemade bread and chocolate-chip cookie bars filled the kitchen, tempting one to take a sample.

Josie wiped the table while Sarah washed bowls, utensils and pans. "I can't wait to try the cookie bars."

"I'm wanting a taste of bread with a pat of butter." Sarah rinsed off a soapy bowl and placed it in the dish drainer. She washed out a bread pan next. Three loaves sat on cooling racks on the counter. She dipped the pan into the sudsy water and used a pad to scrub off the residue left by the baked bread.

When she was done cleaning their workspace, Josie grabbed a towel and began to dry the dishes Sarah had washed. "The boys loved those cherries you brought back from town last week."

Sarah shot her a wry look. "I had planned to make a couple of chocolate cherry pies with them—one or two for the family and one for Jed. I wanted to show my appreciation for taking me into town."

Josie grabbed the newly rinsed bread pan. "You bought the cherries with your money," she scolded.

"*Ja,* of course. This was to be my gift to you and William…and Jed."

"I'll give you the money to buy more—" Josie began.

"*Nay.*" Sarah washed the last of the dishes and emptied the plastic sink basin. "You all enjoyed the cherries, didn't *ya?*" Josie agreed that they had. "Then the cherries were as *gut* as the pie."

"Except that Jed didn't get any."

Sarah shrugged. "I've given him a pie before. I'll think of something else to make him."

A car horn beeped outside. Sarah and Josie looked out the window just as a black SUV pulled into the yard and came to a stop not far from the farmhouse.

"Who is that?" Sarah asked.

Josie hurried to the door with dish towel in hand. "Let's go find out."

Sarah followed behind Josie as she stepped out onto the front covered porch and waited for the occupants of the vehicle to alight. A young Amish man stepped out first and then reached in to help a woman out.

"Oh, my!" Sarah gasped. "It's Emma!" The woman was her older sister, Emma, the man Emma's husband, James. It had been over a year since she'd seen the Yoders. She ran to her sister and grabbed her hands. "'Tis wonderful to see you!" Emma pulled her into a quick hug. "What are you doing here?" Sarah frowned. "Is it *Mam?* She's taken a turn for the worse! You've come to take us home!" Her stomach clenched with terror.

"*Nay,* Sissy, *nay,*" Emma said, grabbing her by the shoulders and giving them a squeeze. She gave Sarah a warm smile. "*Mam* is fine. She is mending nicely. She has weeks of recuperation yet, but the doctor expects her to make a full recovery."

Sarah closed her eyes and prayed. "Thanks be to God." She opened her eyes to see James taking a suitcase out of the hired car. "You're staying?"

"*Ja.* Josie was nice enough to invite us." Emma turned to grin at her husband as he carried their suitcase toward them.

"How did you know where we were? Why have you come? How do you know that *Mam* is well? How long will you stay?"

"I knew you were here because *Dat* told me. I know that *Mam* is well because I asked *Dat.*" Emma smiled at Josie, who didn't look surprised to see her, Sarah noted. "And I'm here to see you and the twins."

As if mentioning them called them by name, the twins, followed by Josie's two young sons, burst out of the house and headed toward the barn. Timothy grabbed Elam's hat and started to run; the others gave chase.

"Boys!" Sarah cried.

Thomas stopped without turning. "*Ja*, Sissy?"

"Come say *hallo* to your sister."

"Emma?" Thomas saw his eldest sister and let out a whoop. "Timothy! Emma is here." He saw her husband beside her. "And James!"

Timothy, who'd been laughing and holding Elam's hat out of reach, paused and without thinking lowered his arm.

Elam quickly grabbed his hat and placed it back on his head. He scowled at Timothy. "Who is Emma?" he said, as if he'd just noticed Timothy's expression.

"My sister," the twin whispered. "Emma?" he said more loudly. He approached and saw that the dark-auburn-haired woman was indeed his eldest sister.

Emma gave him a scolding look. "What were you doing with that hat?"

Timothy dropped his eyes as he came closer. "We were just playing."

Elam and Will followed behind Timothy, curious to see what was going on.

"Ja," Elam said, as if he realized that his cousin Timothy might be in trouble. "We were just playing."

Emma eyed the boys sternly for a minute before she grinned and extended her arms. "Well? Aren't *ya* going to give your big sister a hug?"

Timothy nodded happily and then ran into Emma's arms. Emma looked at Thomas over Timothy's head. "What about you? Too big for a hug?" Holding Timothy with one arm, she extended the other to his brother. Thomas shook his head, grinned and ran in for a hug. "You're getting so big! What happened to my baby brothers? You're growing up too fast!"

"Ja," Thomas said proudly as his eldest sister released them. *"Dat* measured us last month. We growed an inch!"

Emma studied him seriously. "I can see that. It looks like you grew a foot since I last saw you." She addressed Josie: "We appreciate the invitation."

"My pleasure." Josie waved the boys to go back to their play. "I thought your sister might enjoy the visit."

Sarah flashed Josie a wide-eyed glance. "You knew she was coming?"

"Ja. I wrote and invited her." Josie wiped her hands

on the kitchen towel. "I'm happy that you came," she said to Emma and James.

"And the timing was *gut*," James said as he set down the suitcase and straightened.

"We are pleased that we could both come," Emma said with a loving look at James.

"I'm stunned," Sarah admitted. Now that she knew *Mam* was fine, she was excited to be able to spend time with her sister. She had missed Emma since her sister had married and moved to Ohio. "How long will be you be staying?"

"A few days," James said. "I can't stay away from the farm much longer."

"Come inside," Josie invited.

Sarah followed her family into the house. Her thoughts went to Jed, as they often did during the day and every day since she'd first seen him. She wondered if she'd get to see him again soon and what her sister would think of the kind, young man to whom she had lost her heart.

"Sarah's sister has come to visit." Rachel moved about the cottage's kitchen, making lunch for Noah and Jed, who was helping his brother at the shop this day.

"Sarah has a sister?" Noah asked. "I thought she only had brothers."

"*Ja,* she has one older sister," Jed said, revealing the fact that he knew a great deal about the red-haired girl. "Emma. She lives in Ohio with her husband—James, I think his name is."

Rachel looked at him knowingly. "It is James."

"Is she glad to see her?" Jed raised a glass of iced tea to his lips.

"*Ja,* it's been over a year since she's seen Emma." Rachel set a sandwich plate before each man. "I'm sure she's missed her."

"I can only imagine what Sarah must have thought when Emma arrived. With her mother recovering from surgery, she must have thought her *mam* had taken a turn for the worse."

Rachel nodded. "I stopped by yesterday and that's exactly what Sarah told me."

Jed felt a tingling warmth as Rachel spoke of Sarah. Poor Sarah! How worried she must have been!

It had been three days and forty-five minutes since he'd last seen her. He missed her like a flower missed the sunshine. He had kept his distance intentionally. Did she miss him? When he'd showed her his property and told her of his plans, she'd seemed a bit cool, unaffected, and he'd been hurt. These past days he'd thought that by staying away he'd get over her, but he was proved wrong.

Sarah Mast was constantly in his mind from the time he woke up in the morning until bedtime, and during the night he often dreamed of her: her lovely face smiling as she stood next to him by the stream that bordered his new property, on the front porch of a new farmhouse cradling an infant—their infant—in her arms.

"Do the sisters look alike?" Noah asked after chewing and swallowing a bite of roast-beef sandwich on homemade German rye bread.

"There is some resemblance. Emma's eyes are green. Emma's hair is a dark red, while Sarah's—"

"Is red kissed golden by the sun," Jed finished. He averted his gaze from Noah's knowing glance.

"So when are you going to meet her sister?" Noah asked.

Jed hesitated for only a second. "After we're done at the shop." His brother was a skilled cabinetmaker who created furniture to order. Noah had needed a little help to get caught up on a few orders. They'd accomplished a lot that morning, but there was more work to be done.

"You've worked enough today." Noah took a sip of lemonade. "In case you'd like to visit after lunch."

"I can work a little longer." Jed grabbed a cookie and took a bite.

"*Nay,* brother," Noah said. "You'd better get over to the Masts' this afternoon. It's the best thing to do, for all of us."

"Why?" Jed bit into a cookie.

"Because we're tired of seeing your unhappy face, that's why," Noah said. "And the Lord wants you to visit her."

Jed frowned. "How do you know?"

"Because I've seen how you are with her. Any woman who makes you happy whenever you're with her is a gift from God. We should always accept what the Lord wants for us."

"Is that how you felt about Rachel?" he asked, turning to study his sister-in-law, who came out of a back room.

"*Ja,* it's exactly how I felt."

Jed pushed back his chair and stood. He grabbed his straw hat from a wall hook and set it on his head.

"Lunch was *gut*," he told Rachel with a smile. Then he turned to his brother. "And so was the advice."

Jed hurried home to clean up before heading out to the William Mast farm to visit Sarah.

Seated at the kitchen table with Emma and Josie, Sarah heard the clip-clop of horse hooves on dirt and the sound of turning buggy wheels in the yard.

"William must be back from Abram's." Josie set a cup of tea before Sarah's sister.

"That was fast." Sarah gratefully accepted a cup for herself. "I thought he had a full day's work there."

Josie shrugged. "They must have finished sooner than they thought."

Emma bit into a cinnamon-streusel muffin. "These are delicious, Josie."

"Sarah made them." Josie pulled the platter of muffins closer and selected one to put on her own plate.

"Sarah did?" Emma studied her sister.

"*Ja.* She's been doing all the baking since she's come."

"You're a *gut* baker, Sarah." Emma took another bite.

"She's a *gut* cook, too," Josie said. "She's been a blessing to us all. It's been wonderful having her here."

Footsteps resounded on the front porch. "Jedidiah!" Sarah heard Timothy exclaim. Josie's boys and Thomas echoed Timothy's greeting. "You want to play ball?"

She heard the rumble of Jed's familiar deep voice in answer. "Not today, but we can play another day." She heard the agreement among the children and then the sound of a knock on the door.

Her heart started to pound. Jed was here? It had been

days since she'd seen him, since the awkwardness had happened between them after he'd taken her on the tour of his family's farm and told her about his plans with Annie as he'd shown her his property.

Had he expected her to be happy about his relationship with Annie? When she loved him herself? *But he doesn't know I love him.*

Sarah rose and went onto the porch. "*Hallo,* Jed." He looked wonderful, she thought with a pang of longing.

"Sarah! How are you? I've come to visit you." He smiled and stepped up onto the porch to stand next to her. "I've missed you," he said softly.

She stared at him, startled by his admission. "I've missed you, too."

His grin did odd things to her. "Do you have time for a walk? If you're not too busy…"

Sarah wanted nothing more than to walk with him. "My—"

"*Hallo.*" Emma had stepped outside and was eyeing Jed curiously. "You must be Jedidiah Lapp. I've heard a lot about you."

"From who?" Sarah frowned. She hadn't told her sister about Jed.

"*Mam* and *Dat.* Who else?" Emma smiled at the man Sarah loved. "You rescued my brothers."

"'Twas nothing—"

"It was definitely something," Sarah insisted. She was surprised to see him blush. "Jed, in case you haven't figured it out—this is my sister, Emma."

Emma came closer and smiled. "Nice to meet *ya,* Jed."

"*Gut* to meet you, too." He studied her sister. "You look a lot like your *mudder*," he said.

"So I've been told." Emma glanced back as Josie exited the house.

Looking distracted at first, Josie smiled and the frown on her brow cleared. "Oh, *hallo,* Jed. How's your *mudder?*"

"She's well. She wanted me to remind you about the quilting bee tomorrow. She's sorry she had to cancel it for today, but Joseph has a doctor's appointment she'd nearly forgotten."

"Tomorrow is better for me anyway."

"Sarah and I are going for a walk. Would you care to join us?"

Sarah sent her sister a look. "*Nay,* but it was nice of you to ask," Emma said. "I've got laundry to do, and I promised to help Josie with her mending."

Sarah was relieved. It wasn't that she didn't want to spend time with her sister, but she didn't know how much longer she would be in Happiness, and she wanted to spend as much time as she could with Jed—alone.

Josie looked off in the distance toward the pasture. "If you're heading toward the back fields, would you tell William and James that we're holding their lunch for them?"

"*Ja,* of course," Sarah said. She looked to Jed.

Jed agreed, "We'll find them."

Emma and Josie returned inside, and after a quick greeting, the boys had returned to the barn where they'd been grooming the horses.

"Are you ready to go?" Jed asked softly.

Sarah nodded and fell into step beside him as they walked past the barn and into a farm field.

Chapter Sixteen

They walked in silence for a time. The day was hot, but not uncomfortable. Birds chirped in the nearby trees. A bee buzzed in a honeysuckle bush. A soft breeze tousled the bushes and leaves and even the grass that carpeted the surrounding area of the house and barn.

Sarah could feel Jed's presence keenly. The warmth of his nearness, his clean masculine scent, made her overly aware of his movements beside her.

"I should have been by sooner." Jed stopped and faced her. "I was upset the other day—"

"Jed." She put her hand on his arm, feeling the muscle, and then quickly released it. "I'm not certain what happened, but something changed between us during our tour of the property."

Jed inclined his head. His expression was somber. Sarah loved everything about him: his dark hair beneath his straw hat, the way his cinnamon-brown eyes studied her. He wore a royal-blue shirt and dark blue tri-blend denim pants with black shoes. She couldn't help noticing the way his shirt fit him under his black suspenders.

"I'm sorry about that day, Sarah. I wasn't in the best mood, and I don't want anything to ruin our friendship."

"I don't want anything to ruin it, either," Sarah breathed.

Jed grinned. *"Gut."* He gestured ahead. "Let's tell William that Josie is waiting for him at the house, and then we'll go back and head in the opposite direction."

Sarah enjoyed her walk with Jed. They chatted about many things, including the sale at Spence's Bazaar in Dover, Delaware, and the Plain and Fancy restaurant in Bird-in-Hand that offered delicious family-style food to the locals and tourists.

"'Tis *gut* to spend time with you," he said as they changed direction toward the north pasture, where William and James examined one of William's cows.

"I've enjoyed it, too." She hesitated. "I wasn't sure I'd see you before I left."

"You're going home?" He studied her with a frown.

"I don't know. Emma said that *Mam* is doing well and everyone at home is well taken care of."

She was pleased when she sensed him relax. *"Gut.* Then maybe you'll get to stay longer."

"Maybe." She gave him a slight smile. She quickly changed the subject, because the thought of leaving upset her. "So now you have met my sister."

"Ja. You have the look of sisters between you." Jed waved at William, who had caught sight of them. He then turned to grin at her. "You may have a family resemblance, but I find I favor golden-red hair and blue eyes."

Sarah's cheeks bloomed bright red. Her cousin and

brother-in-law were just up ahead. "William! James!" she called as they approached the two men.

"Hallo!" William rose from his hunkered-down position near the animal. "Jed, what brings you out this day?"

"'It's been a while since I visited." Jed flashed Sarah a glance, and her face grew warm again.

"Josie's been keeping lunch for you and James," Sarah told William, enjoying the knowledge that Jed had come to the farm to see her. She was so caught up in Jed's presence that she nearly forgot to introduce him to James.

"James, this is Jedidiah Lapp. Jed, this is my *bruder*-in-law, James Yoder."

The two men greeted each other. Each appeared to size up the other and apparently liked what each saw.

"So, you're the one I've been hearing so much about." James took off his hat to wipe the perspiration from his forehead. A short sandy-brown beard edged his jaw, a testament to his newlywed status. "From Emma's parents. We visited there before we came here."

Sarah was stunned. "Emma didn't tell me you went to see *Mam*."

"Ja, well, we were only there two days—just until we could see for ourselves how she and the family are managing."

"And?" Sarah narrowed her gaze as she studied her brother-in-law.

"They are doing well. We haven't seen *Mam* for over a year—since the time we last saw you." James set his hat back on his head and readjusted it. "Emma was eager to see her."

Sarah frowned. "But she's well?"

"*Ja.* According to Iva, Ruth has her color back. She's moving slowly, as she should, but she has more energy and she smiles often. She's able to breathe more easily."

Sarah relaxed. She needed to have a discussion with her older sister. She and Jed exchanged glances. "Shall we tell Josie that you're on your way?"

"*Nay.* We'll head back now." William turned to James and gestured toward his animal. "So what do you think?"

"She looks fine to me," James said. "Whatever bothered her previously seems to have resolved itself."

James, Sarah knew, had a herd of dairy cows. He was knowledgeable regarding the animals, and William must have sought James's opinion on this one.

William ran his hand along the cow's back. "Let's go," he said to James. "Have you eaten?" he asked Jed and Sarah. Both nodded.

William and James accompanied Sarah and Jed back to the farmhouse.

As they neared the barn, they heard a loud cry. "Help!"

Jed looked and saw one of the twins hanging from the barn-loft window, barely able to hold on. "Dear Lord, please help him," he heard Sarah gasp.

Seeing the danger, he reacted immediately. "Stay below in case he falls," he called out to James and William, who looked for something to catch him in the event the boy fell. He ran into the barn. Spying the ladder, he hurried up the rungs and urged Timothy away from the loft window and his twin brother, who was barely able to hang on.

"Help!" Thomas cried but only weakly. "I'm...losing...my...grip!"

Jed approached carefully, quickly sizing up the situation from above. "Thomas, you trust me, don't you?" He saw it in the boy's eyes as he met Jed's gaze. "I'm going to grab hold of your hands and pull you up. Don't panic, all right?"

"Ja." It was barely a whisper.

Praying silently, Jed reached down to grab hold of the boy's wrists, which wasn't easy, since Thomas dangled by his fingers. *Please, Lord, help me to save Thomas!* He made a grab for the boy's wrists and tugged hard, wincing when he heard the scrape of body against wood as he pulled Thomas up and into the loft. With his heart beating wildly, Jed hugged the trembling boy hard before he picked him up and brought him to the top of the ladder.

At the bottom, Sarah looked frightened. "Thanks be to God!" she cried as she examined her brother, who stood within Jed's arms, before she met the gaze of the man she loved.

"Sarah, can you climb up and help Thomas down from below?" Jed said. "I'll be above ready to catch him if he starts to fall."

She nodded. "Thomas, listen to whatever Jed says."

"Ja, Sissy," her brother said weakly.

Jed turned to Timothy behind him. "Can you climb down by yourself?"

Timothy gave a nod. "I can do it."

"Gut boy!" Jed applauded him. He released Thomas

and helped the still-shaking boy onto the ladder rungs. "I'll be right above you. I won't let you fall."

With Jed's watchful encouragement from above and Sarah's position below as the boy climbed down, Thomas was soon on the ground, where he began to cry. Sarah reached out to hold him, her face crumbling at her brother's obvious fear and remorse. He could tell that any urge to scold him had promptly died as Thomas cried.

William had run inside the house for a blanket, and soon Josie, Ellen and Emma were outside watching Jed's rescue of Thomas from below. They each had hold of a blanket edge, ready to catch the boy should he fall.

With her arm about Thomas, Sarah watched as Timothy climbed easily down the ladder. When both boys were safe, she released her traumatized brother, who ran to his older sister, Emma.

Sarah approached Jed, who studied the Mast family as they rejoiced over the little boy's safety. "Jed?" she said softly as she drew near. "It seems like you are always there to rescue my *bruders*." She met his gaze, her blue eyes bright with tears. Jed caught his breath at what he saw in the depths of her glistening blue orbs. She touched his arm. *"Danki."*

He swallowed hard. "I'm glad I was here to help."

"I don't know what I will do without you when we go home."

Jed glanced down at her hand. Her touch felt warm and wonderful on his biceps. *I don't know what I will do without you, either,* he wanted to say, but he kept silent instead. This wasn't the time or place to be having a discussion of his feelings for her.

The others entered the farmhouse, including the twins and Will and Elam, who had been upstairs in their bedroom. They'd hadn't known about Thomas's near-accident until they'd heard the commotion outside the same time as their mother had.

Jed stayed outside with Sarah. He had suggested a walk in the other direction earlier, but now it was too late and he had to return home to help his father. "Sarah, I have to go. May I visit another day?"

Sarah inclined her head. "*Ja*. I'd like that. It was *gut* of you to come—"

"I wanted to," he replied, and he saw her expression soften. "I wish I could stay longer."

He felt warm inside. He loved her smile, the way her vivid blue gaze regarded him with understanding and gratitude. There was something about her that made him want to stay and just stare at her all day long.

"I need to talk with Emma." Her smile turned wry. "She never told me that she visited *Mam*—"

"Hmm." Jed was thoughtful. "I wouldn't be upset with her. She may have decided you'd worry more if she told you of her fears. I can understand that she had to see for herself how your mother was recovering."

"But she could have told me she'd gone—"

Jed placed a hand on her shoulder. The warmth of her reached up to tug at his heart. If he wasn't careful, he might say something he wasn't quite ready to say and she wasn't ready to hear. He quickly released her.

"Sarah," he began softly, "you've been there for your *mudder* since she became ill. Emma was miles away with her new husband. You told me yourself that Ruth didn't want Emma to worry about the twins, since she was newly married. I'm sure she didn't tell her how ill she was, either, until she had the surgery and then someone was forced to tell her."

Silent, Sarah stared off into the yard. "I would be upset if *Mam* had kept her illness from me." She met his gaze, her expression serene. "I didn't think of this."

"Talk with Emma."

She nodded. "I will."

"*Gut.* I will see you tomorrow at the house." He wanted to capture her hand, give it a squeeze, but he wouldn't. The last time he'd held hands with her he'd told her about his dreams to marry and build a home. When she looked at him in question, he said, "The quilting bee *Mam* is hosting?"

"*Ja, ja,* of course."

"I will see you soon, Sarah." He gave in to the urge to briefly touch her cheek.

"*Gut* day to you, Jedidiah," she murmured.

Jed climbed into his buggy, took up the reins and urged the horse to move. He glanced back over his shoulder several times and was happy to note that she continued to watch him as he drove the buggy down the lane toward the main road.

Chapter Seventeen

The next day, Sarah and Emma, along with Josie and the four young boys, who tagged along with them, went to the quilting bee at Katie Lapp's. As soon as they arrived at the Samuel Lapp farmhouse, the children ran to find Jed's youngest brothers—Daniel, Isaac and Joseph—while the women went inside.

"Hallo," Katie greeted them with a warm smile. "I see you brought a cake."

"Sarah made it," Josie said, holding up the plate.

Sarah, who was looking about for a glimpse of Jed, heard her name and smiled at her hostess. "I enjoy baking," she said.

"You'll make some lucky man a *gut* wife someday." Katie accepted the cake from Josie and gestured for the women to enter the great room.

"I'm afraid I wasn't able to bring down the quilting frame. My sons were busy this morning, but some have returned. I'll see that they set it up for us."

"Can I help?" Sarah asked.

"Nay, but I appreciate the offer. It's a bit cumber-

some. Jacob and Eli will take care of it for us. They've done it before."

Where is Jed? Sarah wondered. He'd told her he'd see her here today.

Jacob and Eli entered the great room and greeted the women. "You must be Sarah's sister," Jacob said.

Emma nodded. "It's nice to meet you."

"Jed said that he met you." Jacob studied Emma and then compared her to her sister. "*Hallo,* Sarah."

Sarah smiled. "Jacob," she greeted. "Eli."

Katie came out of the kitchen with a pitcher of iced tea. "Jacob, Eli, would you set up the quilting frame for us?"

"*Ja, Mam,*" Eli said and Jacob agreed. They apparently knew where to find it, as they immediately left the room and Sarah could hear their footsteps as they climbed the stairs to the second floor.

Emma watched as the young men left. "How many sons do you have?"

"Seven. Seven sons and one daughter."

"*Seven sons?*"

Sarah saw Katie smile at her sister's startled look.

"*Ja.* Jacob and Eli are third-born." Katie grinned. "Actually, third-and fourth-born but on the same day."

"They're twins, Emma," Sarah said with a chuckle. "Fraternal twins." Jacob's hair was dark brown; he looked a lot like his older brother Jedidiah. Eli was fair-haired, and he had his mother's eyes and her warm smile.

Rachel entered the room and greeted everyone. "Where is Jed?" she asked Katie conversationally after a quick knowing look at Sarah.

"He had to work today. A local company called him for a new construction job. It was unexpected. Samuel didn't need him on the farm today, so Jed went."

Sarah's excited anticipation of seeing Jed again dissipated. "Does he like the work?" Emma asked.

Curious herself, Sarah waited for Katie's reply. "*Ja,* he doesn't mind it. Jed is a hard worker. Like his *vadder* and *grossdaddi,* he is *gut* with his hands. Samuel's *dat* was a cabinetmaker, although his age has slowed him down."

"Noah learned woodworking from his *grossdaddi,*" Rachel said.

"*Ja,* Noah's furniture shop is doing well." Katie set the pitcher of tea on a table near clean glasses and a plate of baked goods. "Samuel's *vadder* helps out Noah if he is feeling well enough. And Jed works at the shop from time to time, whenever Noah needs an extra hand."

Jacob and Eli returned, carrying lengths of one-by-three boards, which they promptly laid out on the floor to form a square. Katie exited the room for a moment and returned with a neat stack of the quilt squares hand-sewn by the community women. "I stitched them together with my sewing machine. Rachel, would you get the rest of the quilting material from my sewing room?"

Rachel agreed, and Sarah asked, "Can I help?" Her friend nodded. Sarah followed Rachel upstairs to Katie's sewing room, where they found a large piece of fabric to be used for the quilt backing, created by sewing together three lengths of the same material. Several bags of batting lay on a table next to Katie's treadle sewing machine.

Rachel picked up the fabric. "Can you manage the batting?"

"*Ja,* I've got it." Sarah balanced all the bags in her arms and followed Rachel down the steps.

The two women returned to the great room to find that many other community women had arrived and were discussing their families, the day and the quilt they would be stitching.

Jacob and Eli helped Rachel and Sarah set up the backing, batting and top layer of quilt squares stitched together by Katie. They stretched the quilt-to-be over the rack and pinned each layer into place on each length of the four boards secured together with C-clamps. Soon the women were seated around the quilting rack, talking and laughing and telling tales.

Later, on the way home, Emma expressed her enjoyment of the day. "The Lapps are a wonderful family."

"*Ja,*" Josie said, "and they are *gut* neighbors and friends."

"Their little Hannah is a darling," Emma commented softly as she gazed out the buggy window opening.

Sarah smiled, recalling how Jed's little sister, Hannah, had walked up to Rachel and held out her arms to be picked up. Rachel had immediately obliged by lifting the child onto her lap and cuddling her.

"I don't know when I last went to a quilting bee," Emma admitted softly. "Back home, in Delaware, it was. I wonder if any of the women near Millersburg would be interested in working together on a quilt."

"I'm sure they will. Some of the women may get together already to quilt once a week or month."

"*Ja,*" Emma said. "I supposed that's true." She was

quiet for a time until they arrived home and entered the house. "Sarah, we'll be leaving tomorrow. Would you help the boys pack their things?"

Sarah felt a clenching in her stomach. *"Ja."* She headed upstairs with an overwhelming feeling of sadness. The time had finally come to head home. Should she look for Jed and tell him she'd be leaving? Then she recalled what Katie had said about Jed working the new construction job. He'd be on-site long hours for the next few days. How could she say goodbye without disturbing his sleep? Should she leave him a note?

She couldn't see herself leaving a quickly penned note for him. She could write him a long letter once she got home, telling him how much she'd enjoyed her time with him, wishing him all the best with Annie as his bride.

Sarah moved about the boys' room, finding their garments, glad that she'd washed their clothes the day before so that most—if not all—were clean. She packed the twins' shared suitcase, leaving out only their nightshirts. If they didn't get too dirty this afternoon, they could wear the same shirt and pants that they had on today. When she was done, she went downstairs to help prepare supper.

The family soon joined them for the evening meal. The twins and Josie's two sons were excitedly relaying the events of their day. "…And we got to play on the swings at the *schuulhaus,*" Timothy said. Jacob had taken the four boys with his three youngest brothers to the schoolyard at the edge of the property to play on the swing sets.

When the boys were done with their tale, Emma informed them that tomorrow morning they'd be leaving Happiness.

The twins were upset. "We'll never see Elam and Will again!" Timothy cried.

"*Ja, ya* will," Emma assured them. "They are your cousins. They'll come visit you, and one day you can come back for a visit."

Josie smiled at each twin. "This isn't *gut*-bye for always."

Sarah's young brothers looked sad until William distracted them with ice cream.

The next morning, Sarah was packing the last of her belongings when Ellen came into the room and sat on the bed. "Breakfast is ready," she said.

Sarah shut her valise and offered a small smile. "Did you help your *Mam* this morning?" she asked.

Ellen nodded. She was quiet a moment. "Sarah, I'm sorry to see you leave. I liked sharing my room with you."

"And I liked staying here with you." Sarah thought back on the time she'd spent fixing Ellen's hair, tying her apron strings, sharing stories of Delaware and teaching the young girl how to bake Sarah's favorite recipes.

"Sarah! Ellen! Breakfast!" Josie called up from downstairs.

"Coming!" Sarah gave Ellen a hug. "I'd like you to come for a visit. I think you'll enjoy meeting my *mam* and *dat,* and my brothers Ervin and Toby."

"I'd like that." Ellen pushed off the bed and headed toward the door. "I wish you didn't have to leave."

Sarah picked up her valise and followed close behind. "I do, too."

"Will you come back for a visit?" the young girl asked.

"If I can." As she descended the stairs, Sarah thought of her mother and her duties at home. She had been away a long time. She wondered if her family could ever manage without her. She set her valise next to her brothers' suitcase near the door.

Moments later, when she entered the kitchen, everyone was seated at the dining table. Plates of muffins and rolls with platters of eggs and ham and bacon covered the surface. There was a gallon of orange juice and a pot of tea. Josie had also made fresh coffee, and the rich aroma competed with the delicious scent of bacon and freshly baked goods.

Sarah enjoyed her last meal with her cousins. She was sad to go and especially saddened by the knowledge that she'd never again see Jedidiah Lapp.

"I put my valise beside the door near the boys' suitcase," Sarah said after the boys had left for one last romp outside with their cousins.

Emma frowned. "Why did you do that?"

"Where else would you have me put it?"

Josie poured Sarah another cup of tea. "How about upstairs, where it—and you—belong?"

"I don't understand." Sarah enjoyed the warmth of her teacup as she cradled it with her hands.

"Sarah, you're not coming with us," her sister said. "I thought you understood that I'm taking the twins to Ohio for a couple of weeks."

"Ohio?" Sarah echoed, wondering if she was hearing correctly.

"Josie thought—and I agree—that you should stay

here. In Happiness." Emma spread butter over a piece of toast. "Sarah, I had no idea how hard you had to work while *Mam* was ill. I think you should remain and enjoy yourself. Josie loves having you, and I think that maybe you're not unwilling to stay."

"I love it here," she confessed. "I do miss *Mam* and *Dat* and Ervin and Toby, but Happiness also seems like home to me."

"Then stay. *Dat* will send for you when he wants you to come home," Emma said. "Until then, you can help Josie here and take every moment you can just being a young woman without the extra burden of too much responsibility."

"I love *Mam* and *Dat*. I'd do anything for them," Sarah said.

"*Ja,* I know. And they appreciate all you've done. Without the boys to disturb her rest, *Mam* will be fine without you. You'll have enough to do once you are home again."

Sarah blinked back tears. "Are you sure it's all right?"

"I wouldn't have it any other way," Josie told her with a smile.

"Emma?" Sarah watched her sister closely.

"Stay. Enjoy your life, Sissy. Make a memory of every moment to last you a lifetime."

"I'll unpack," she said after she helped clear the table and wash the breakfast dishes. Her heart felt light. She would see Jed again. "When I come down, I'll do the laundry."

When Sarah returned, however, Emma, James and the twins were outside waiting to say goodbye. A car was parked near the front door. The travelers' suitcases were already in the trunk.

"Give me a hug, you rascals," Sarah told her brothers. The boys obliged by running into her arms and hugging her tightly.

"We'll miss you, Sissy," Timothy said, his light blue eyes overly bright.

"Lots and lots," Thomas added.

"I'll see you again soon." Sarah released them and ruffled their hair. "Where are your hats?"

"I've got them." Emma approached with a small black-banded straw hat in each hand. She set one on each little red-haired boy's head. "Give your cousins a hug," she instructed.

As the boys obeyed, Emma approached Sarah. "I love you, Sissy."

Sarah sniffed. "I love you." She hesitated. "Are you sure you want to take them?"

Emma smiled. "Do you mean because trouble follows them everywhere and Jed won't be around to rescue them?"

"They can be a handful," Sarah warned. She watched as the boys ran about the yard, giving chase after Elam and Will.

"I'll manage." Emma paused and looked regretful as she studied her sister. "Sarah, I'm sorry I wasn't there to help with *Mam*."

Sarah waved away Emma's concerns. "It's fine, Emma. Don't you worry. *Mam* didn't want you to know."

"I realize that, but it wasn't fair to you."

"You were newly married. *Mam* wanted you to have a chance at happiness."

"What about your happiness?"

"Mam needed my help," Sarah said simply. "I'm happy."

Emma shook her head. "*Nay,* but you'll be happy one day." She grabbed Sarah in for a hug. Rounding up the boys, she and James saw the children seated in the backseat of the car between them.

"Bye, Sissy!" the boys cried out the open window.

"Be *gut* for Emma!" Sarah called back. She lifted her hand to wave. "Love you!"

She watched as the driver of the hired car drove down the lane and off the property before she went inside to help Josie with the morning chores.

Jed rapped on the door to the teacher's cottage until Rachel opened it. "Jed!" she greeted with a smile. "What a nice surprise!" She suddenly frowned as she saw his troubled expression. "What's wrong?"

"They left, Rachel!" Jed exclaimed. "Sarah and the twins! Gone with their sister, Emma. I didn't even have a chance to say goodbye! I needed to talk to Sarah. There is so much I wanted to say, but it's too late because she's gone!"

"Jed—"

"Is Noah here? I have to ask him if he saw them. I don't know how long ago they left. Jacob thought he saw the twins in a car early this morning—" He felt ill. He couldn't believe he wouldn't see Sarah again.

"Jed." Rachel's voice was calm, her smile serene, as she stepped aside, allowing Jed a glimpse of the kitchen.

Jed felt a jolt. Seated at the table sat Sarah, who met his startled gaze with a surprised look of her own.

"Sarah." He rushed past Rachel and into the room. "Why are you here? I thought you had left. Are the twins here? What about Emma and James—did they leave or stay?" Eager to learn more, Jed fired one question after another until Rachel began to laugh at him.

"Sit down, Jed," she urged, "and give Sarah a chance to answer."

Sarah, who had stood when Jed entered, sat down again. "Emma took the twins to Ohio. I'm staying with Josie and William for a while."

Jed sat close to her. "Praise be to God!" he whispered, his heart filled with gladness. He was pleased to see Sarah's blue gaze brighten.

"Why not have a seat and a cup of coffee?" Noah suggested with wry humor.

Jed glanced at him and grinned. "*Ja,* I'd like some coffee." He sat down next to Sarah.

A cup was set before him. A plate was pushed in his direction but he was too busy gazing at Sarah to pay any attention to anything else. Noah cleared his throat, finally drawing Jed's attention.

Jed looked at his brother, who stood, his expression unreadable, with his arm about his wife. He stared at them a moment. "What's going on?"

"Do you want to tell him or should I?" Noah asked.

Rachel leaned into her husband. "You tell him."

Jed narrowed his gaze. "What is it? Is something wrong?"

"*Nay,* Jedidiah," Noah said, his warm brown eyes

sparkling, his lips curving upward. "Rachel and I are going to have a baby."

Jed blinked. "A baby?" He jumped up from his seat, grinning from ear to ear. "Congratulations!" He hugged Rachel and then slapped Noah on the back before he gave in and hugged him, too. "When is the happy event?"

"April," Rachel said. "Or March—we're not exactly sure yet."

Chuckling as he studied the parents-to-be, Jed resumed his seat next to Sarah. "I'm happy for you." He studied Rachel carefully. He wondered how Rachel's accident would affect her pregnancy. "You will take care of yourself?"

Rachel inclined her head, her expression turning serious. "I'll be watched closely."

Sarah was silent as she watched him digest the news of his upcoming niece or nephew's birth. "Will you continue to teach school?" she asked her friend quietly.

"For a time, unless the doctor says differently. Eventually, we'll have to find someone to take my place." Rachel cradled her abdomen, as if her touch could somehow protect her child and ensure a safe birth.

"Who?" Jed asked.

Rachel smiled when Noah's hand covered hers on top of her belly. "I haven't given it much thought, but my cousin Nancy would be a *gut* teacher, if she wants the position."

"That's an excellent idea." Jed studied his surroundings—the warm, cozy kitchen with its whitewashed walls and cabinets. He thought of the rest of the house—the bedroom, bathroom, living room and pantry that he'd helped to build. He thought of his own house, the one he wanted to build for Sarah. "You'll need a house. We'll have to find you property."

Noah looked startled. "*Ja,* I suppose we will."

"Nancy lives nearby." Rachel stood to heat water on the stove. "She won't need the cottage right away. She may want it eventually, but we'll be able to stay after the baby is born." She reached into a cabinet for the box of tea bags.

Jed became caught up in the excitement of Rachel and Noah's news as the morning lengthened. Sarah's presence was the highlight of his day, and his sister-in-law's pregnancy had increased his joy.

"I should get back," Sarah declared after a time. "I promised Josie I'd do laundry." She rose from her chair. "I didn't expect to be gone this long."

Jed stood. "I'll take you home." To his delight, she accepted his invitation. "The wagon is outside."

Rachel and Noah followed them out of the cottage. Sarah hugged Rachel and Noah and waited while Jed congratulated each one again.

"Sarah, I'm glad you're staying," Rachel said. "Jed, it was *gut* of you to stop by." Her dark eyes twinkled as she flashed a look from Jed to Sarah.

"You don't know how glad I am to see you," he told Sarah as he helped her into the wagon. He climbed in the other side and faced her; he was in no hurry to go.

Sarah looked at him, her blue eyes glistening. "Early this morning, I thought I was leaving and that I'd never see you again, but then the Lord had other plans for me."

"Thanks be to God," he said softly. He captured

her hand and laced his fingers through hers. Her touch warmed him and he felt an overwhelming tenderness for her.

God had chosen her for him; he was sure of it.

Chapter Eighteen

Jed didn't say a word as he steered the horse past his parents' driveway and down the road toward the William Mast farm.

Sarah wondered what he was thinking. He'd been upset when he thought she'd left for Delaware without telling him. Her world brightened. *He cares about me.*

Suddenly, he flashed her a glance and looked away again. "Sarah, could you be happy in Happiness?" He kept his gaze on the road as he waited for her reply.

Sarah saw the tension in his face and the hands holding the leathers. *"Ja,"* she confessed. "I could be happy here. Your village, your community, is aptly named. Everyone is caring and concerned for one another. Happiness has been like a second home."

"Sarah," he interrupted, "about the other day…when I took you to see my land"

She frowned. *"Ja?"*

"I didn't tell you everything about my plans."

Sarah braced herself. *"Ja,* I know," she said softly. "You plan to live there with Annie."

He pulled up on the leathers to stop the vehicle on the side of the road. "What did you say?" He studied her carefully, as if he were memorizing her features, imprinting each one lovingly into his mind.

She swallowed hard. "I know you plan to build a house and live on your land with Annie Zook," she said.

Jed shifted in his seat to face her fully. He placed his warm, firm hands gently on her shoulders. "I have no intention of living on that land with Annie. I have no intention—nor have I ever had any intention—of asking Annie Zook to marry me." He leaned in close so that his nose touched hers. She could feel his breath against her chin, her neck, and she felt a shiver of delight.

"I don't understand."

"It's simple, Sarah. How can I ask Annie to marry me when there is someone else in my life, in my heart, who I love more than anyone?"

Sarah placed a hand over her rapidly beating heart. "Who?"

"You," he whispered. "I love you, Sarah. I wanted you to see my land because it's *you* I want to spend the rest of my life with, *you* I want to build a house for and have children with, and love forever and ever."

Overwhelmed with emotion, Sarah felt her eyes fill with tears. "Oh, Jed, you know I'll have to go home eventually."

"We have today and tomorrow and each day after that, until that happens." He narrowed his gaze as if trying to read her thoughts. She must have worn her heart on her sleeve, because he shot her a smile so full of happiness and love that Sarah caught her breath.

"I love you, Jedidiah."

"I was hoping you'd admit it," he teased.

Sarah chuckled until the look in his eyes made her stop and stare. "I want all the things that you do," she said gently, "but I can't stay and neglect my family." She was torn between her desire to stay and her need to be there for her *mam* and family.

"I'm not asking you to."

"What are we going to do?"

"We'll enjoy every moment we can together." He paused and frowned. "I have this job to do. I can't avoid it. When it's done, I'll have enough money to make that last land payment."

"*Ja,* you must finish the work," Sarah said. Knowing that Jed loved her the way she loved him would make those moments apart from him bearable.

He took her hand and cradled it between his palms. "Will you allow me to court you?"

Her throat felt tight. "I may only be here a short time."

"How long?" Jed furrowed his brow.

"Two weeks? A month?"

His expression brightened. "Long enough for me to court you," he declared.

"But when it's time to leave—"

He shook his head as if denying the moment when she would have to return to Delaware. "Then I will go with you."

Stunned by his declaration, Sarah could only stare at him.

He looked alarmed by her silence. "Sarah—"

She cried out and leaned in to hug him hard before

pulling back quickly. "I will be happy to be courted by you."

He was grinning from ear to ear as she sat back in her seat. "*Gut!* You've made me a happy man."

"Jed, we should keep our courting secret," she suggested, "at least, for now. Until we know what will happen...when I'll have to go."

Jed didn't look too happy about it, but he agreed. "I will spend as much time as I can with you. Will you allow that?"

Sarah grinned and wrinkled her nose at him. "Just let anyone try to keep us apart," she said, which seemed to please him immensely.

Sarah was feeling happy and excited as Jed pulled the buggy onto the road again. He had to return to the farm; she had to get back to help Josie.

He pulled into the William Mast barnyard and then turned to study her. "I'll see you again soon," he promised.

Emboldened by the knowledge of his love, Sarah dared to reach out and run her fingers along his jaw. She saw his eyes gleam a moment before she smiled and withdrew her touch. "I'll look forward to it."

He came around to the other side of the buggy and helped her to alight. "Think of me," he whispered.

"As if I can do anything else," she whispered, and then she waved as he got into the buggy and steered the horse back the way they'd come.

Sarah was feeling giddy as she entered the house and then the kitchen.

"Sarah?" Josie called as she came down the stairs from the second story. "Is that you?"

"*Ja,* Josie! Are *ya* ready for me to do the wash?"

Josie came around the corner from the steps toward the back of the house, where Sarah stood near the linen chest. "Did you have a nice visit with Rachel?"

Sarah went to grab Josie's armload of sheets. "*Ja.* Noah was there, and Jed stopped by for a visit." She hoped there was nothing in her expression or tone to give away what had transpired between them.

"Jedidiah Lapp just happened to stop by, eh," Josie said, watching her closely.

Sarah blushed and looked away.

"He's sweet on you, and you on him. He told you how he feels, didn't he?"

Sarah flashed her a startled glance. "I—"

"I knew it! I've known all along how the two of you felt about each other. I told Emma so, and she agreed. She saw it, too."

Horrified by how transparent she must be, she could only gape at her cousin. "Oh, dear. Does everyone know?"

Josie gestured Sarah toward the kitchen. "*Nay.* Emma saw only because I told her. I saw it because I've come to know you well. Jedidiah is a fine man, Sarah. I am happy that the two of you care for each other."

"I care for him a great deal."

Josie's lips twitched. "You love him."

Sarah released a sharp breath. "*Ja.*"

She set the sheets on the table a moment and turned to plead with Josie. "Please don't say a word to anyone. I have to go home soon, and I don't know what is going to happen."

"You're meant to be together," Josie insisted. She

grabbed the laundry from the table and carried it to the washing machine. "Emma and I felt you should stay here in Happiness to decide what you want for your life. If it's Jed Lapp, then all the better."

Sarah followed Josie to the gas-powered washer, measured out the laundry detergent and dumped the soap into the basin as the machine filled with water.

"I know that I love him, and he says he loves me, but we want to keep our relationship a secret for a while." Sarah touched Josie's arm. "Can you do that for me? Keep this secret?"

Josie chuckled. "I've kept it thus far, haven't I? And I knew it before you did."

Sarah felt herself relax. *"Danki,"* she whispered.

"No need. This is the way of the good Lord. Thank Him. I believe He has *gut* things ahead for you."

Sarah enjoyed every moment in Jed's company. He worked during the day, but come early evening, he managed to get away to meet her at the edge of the Mast farm. Once there, they would walk together, talking about their hopes and dreams, pausing from time to time to gaze into each other's eyes and smile.

The first week went by quickly. Sarah was happy to see the start of another week with no letter or telephone message from Delaware calling her home.

On Saturday, Jed took her again to see his property. This time Sarah was able to envision a house. Her home with Jed.

She began to spend more time at the Samuel Lapp farm and Jed came often to invite Sarah to dinner or supper, or to play games with his family. Nothing was said about Sarah's presence; no one seemed to care whether or not they were courting, or that it might seem unusual for her to be with the Lapps almost as much as she was at William and Josie's.

"Sarah." Jed's soft voice interrupted her thoughts. He was driving her home after a shared meal with his family. "I thought we'd spend time with your cousins tomorrow."

Sarah looked at him. "That sounds like a *gut* idea. You don't mind?"

Jed frowned. "Why should I mind? They are your family. I want to spend time with them. We've been spending more time with my family lately. I don't want Josie and William to feel slighted that we haven't spent as much time with them."

"I don't think Josie feels slighted," she said. In fact, Sarah knew differently. Josie was always eager to hear what activity she and Jed had engaged in that day. Sarah, eager to share her happiness, obliged by telling her cousin about her time with Jed—at least, the things she felt she could tell. She didn't tell her how they held hands as they took a stroll, how they sat close in the buggy with shoulders touching but nothing else. The contact of shoulder against shoulder was Sarah's greatest delight next to simply being in Jed's company.

After two and a half weeks of pure bliss for Sarah, a letter arrived. Jedidiah, who had come to visit, was there when the mailman stopped to drop off the mail. Thinking that he would save the Masts a hike to the box, he had carried the stack of mail directly to the house. He'd had no idea that there was a letter among them for Sarah from Kent County, Delaware—from her father.

Josie flipped through the pile of mail and handed the envelope to Sarah. Her brow furrowed with concern when Sarah paled as she accepted the letter and tore open the seal.

Sarah unfolded the page. Her heart thumped hard as she read her father's script. Her eyes begin to sting with the fresh onslaught of tears. She looked up, closed her eyelids and whispered, *"Nay."*

"What's wrong?" Jed studied the woman he loved and was immediately concerned. She looked unhappy and almost physically ill. "Is it your *mam?*"

"'Tis from *Dat,*" she said. "He wants me to come home." With letter in hand, she hugged herself with her arms.

"Sarah—" Josie began and then stopped. "Jed, why don't you take Sarah outside? The boys aren't about. You can sit on the front porch and talk."

Jed nodded. He needed to know what the letter said. He'd promised to go with her when she had to leave, but he had work to finish first; he would have to follow her as soon as he was able.

He led Sarah onto the front porch and saw her comfortably seated in a rocking chair. "May I see?" he asked her gently. He extended a hand toward her.

Silently, she handed him the letter. He began to read and felt a crushing blow that the time had come for Sarah to go home when he couldn't immediately accompany her.

"Sarah, I have this job to finish, but I'll come as soon as I can."

She looked at him, her expression bleak. "Jed, I understand if you don't want to come—"

"Sarah Jane Mast," he said, having recently learned her middle name, "I'm coming to Delaware whether you believe it or not. I love you and I'm not about to lose you."

Sarah's lips quivered. "I love you, too." She stared out into the yard. "What if *Mam* has taken a turn for the worse? What if she needs me? What if something has happened and we can't be together—ever?"

Jed stood before her and gazed lovingly into her eyes. "I will come, and nothing will keep us apart. We will face whatever we need to face—together. *I love you.* Do you understand?"

Sarah nodded and her gaze brightened while a tiny smile curved her sweet lips. "*Ja,* Jed. I understand."

Chapter Nineteen

Mid-August, Kent County, Delaware

The sight of her parents' home warmed her, then gave her a little chill. She climbed from the car, grabbed her valise and thanked the hired *Englischer* driver for the ride. Ervin and *Dat* came out of the house as she approached.

"Sarah!" The cry came from her father, who hurried down the porch steps.

Sarah met him halfway and launched herself into her father's arms. "*Dat!* It's been so long."

"Over two months." He hugged her tightly and she closed her eyes, recalling all those times he'd held her when she was a little girl.

Ervin stood behind their father, waiting to greet his sister. "Sissy," he said. "You're looking well. Happiness seems to have agreed with you."

Sarah gave her brother a hug and then stepped back and regarded them both worriedly. "How's *Mam?*" She trembled at the thought that her mother had become ill again.

"Why don't *ya* go inside and see for yourself?" *Dat* picked up her suitcase, and following her hurried steps, he carried it into the house.

Ervin lagged behind until he saw his brother Tobias exiting the barn.

"Sarah's home," she heard him call out as she entered the house.

She heard Toby ask, "Where is she?"

"Gone inside to see *Mam*."

Aware of her brothers as they entered the house behind her, Sarah rushed toward the room her parents had used as their bedroom since *Mam* became too ill to climb stairs.

"Daughter," Daniel said. "Where are *ya* going?"

Sarah frowned as she turned toward her father. "To see *Mam*."

"Well, you'd be going the wrong way. Your mother is upstairs. I imagine she's waiting to see you."

Sarah raced up the steps and into the room that originally had been her parents' bedroom. She entered the chamber, expecting to see her mother in bed with her face pale, her hair dull and her eyes listless. Stunned by what she saw, she paused on the threshold, unable to believe her gaze. Her mother looked the perfect image of good health. She stood near the bed, sorting and folding laundry. She didn't seem to notice Sarah's arrival.

"Mam."

Her mother turned, her eyes clear and bright, her color good, looking ten years younger than when Sarah had last seen her. Sarah stopped and stared. *"Mam?"*

"*Ja,* Sarah." She opened her arms, and suddenly Sarah was being held. Her mother's hug was firm and strong, and Sarah could scarcely believe it as she stepped back and examined her mother carefully.

"You look wonderful," she whispered.

"I feel it," *Mam* admitted.

Sarah was glad to see her mother looking so well, but she wondered with some guilt why *Dat* sent the urgent message to come home.

"Are the twins home yet?"

"*Nay,*" her mother said. "They will be home later in the week. I wanted this special time with you."

Sarah grinned; she was glad to see her mother even if she missed Jed with every fiber of her being.

Sarah thoroughly enjoyed her mother's company as a week went by, after which her twin brothers finally returned home. Thomas and Timothy burst into the house like a whirlwind of boyish energy.

"*Mam!* Sissy!" they cried early one morning after they'd run out to the barn. "We've got a new calf!" They were happy to be home to see their mother back to her former self. "Please come see!"

Together Sarah and her mother hurried out to the barn to witness the miracle that had occurred during the night.

"She looks like a fine young heifer," her mother proclaimed upon studying the newborn.

"She?" Thomas eyed the animal with a scowl. "How come Betsy didn't have a boy cow?"

"Don't *ya* mean a baby bull?" Timothy said with a grimace at his brother.

"Any calf is a miracle of life," their mother told them gently. "I'm sure this young one won't be the only off-spring Betsy gives us."

"*Ja,* Thomas," Timothy told his brother. "Look how many offspring *Mam* had."

Sarah tried to control her amusement, but she couldn't hold back a chuckle. "You're absolutely correct, Timothy," she said after she managed to become serious again. "*Mam* had six of us."

"*Mam?*" Thomas asked. "Do you think Betsy will give us six calves next time?"

"*Nay,* son," Ruth said. "Just one at a time."

A week passed and then two without a phone message or a letter from Jed. Sarah began to worry that Jed had changed his mind about coming to Delaware. Had he decided that he didn't want her?

Sarah recalled their moments together, the laughter they'd shared, Jed's smiling eyes, his profession of love for her.

Please, Lord, don't let him stop loving me!

She went about her day, trying to be cheerful, and she must have succeeded, as no one said a word. No one seemed to realize that while she was smiling on the outside, she was crying inside. Every morning and afternoon she stood at her bedroom window and stared out toward the road, praying for him to appear.

But he didn't. Finally she headed downstairs to keep her mind busy by doing chores. She worked harder and took on more chores than she did when *Mam* was ill, until one morning, her mother called Sarah into her parents' bedroom.

"Sarah," *Mam* urged softly, "sit down here on the bed by me."

Sarah obeyed and looked at her mother in question.

"Something is wrong," *Mam* said. "What is it, child? What's bothering you?"

Sarah remained silent, as she suddenly had to fight back tears. "I love you, and I love being home, but…"

"But what?" Ruth encouraged softly.

"I miss Happiness, *Mam,*" she admitted, looking away. "I miss him."

"Jed?" Her mother's soft query gave Sarah a jolt as she spun to meet Ruth's gaze.

"You know about Jed?"

"I may have heard about him from Emma and Josie, but mostly, I suspected that there was something special between you from the first moment I saw the two of you here in Delaware before he went home. I couldn't know that he lived in Happiness or that you'd see him again, but when I heard that he did and that you were spending time with him, I knew."

"Oh, *Mam*…" Sarah allowed her tears to fall. "It's been over two weeks, and I haven't heard a word from him. He said he would come, but he hasn't. I thought he would call or write, but I've had no message and received no letter."

Ruth smiled and stood. "Stay there, Sarah." She knelt by the bed and rummaged beneath until she withdrew a large white cardboard box. Setting the box on the bed, she sat and shifted it to rest between them.

Sarah gasped as she saw the powder-blue dress inside the box.

"Your wedding dress." Ruth smiled as she lifted the

garment for Sarah to see. There was also a cape and apron and a new prayer *kapp.*

Tears filled Sarah's eyes as she gazed at it. *"Mam..."*

"I made it while I was recovering." Ruth laid the dress across the bed quilt.

"I wonder if I'll ever get to wear it." Sarah touched the fabric. It was a dress that any young bride would love to wear.

"You'll wear it," *Mam* assured her.

Sarah hoped her mother was right and that some-day she'd wear the dress. She wanted to wear it for Jed.

That afternoon, a dark car pulled into the barnyard. Sarah exited the house in time to see Jedidiah step out of the front seat of the vehicle.

"Jed!" Sarah rushed to his side. She studied him, drinking her fill of the wonderful sight of him.

Jed grinned. "Sarah. I told you I would come."

And Sarah felt her world brighten. Suddenly, *Mam, Dat* and her older brothers exited the house and sur-rounded her and Jed.

"Jed! 'Tis *gut* to see you again. Welcome!" *Dat* beamed at him.

"Sarah was just saying how much she loves and misses you," her mother said, and Sarah blushed.

"She did?" Jed's expression softened as he looked at Sarah with love.

"Jedidiah!" a young voice cried, echoed by another, as the twins ran from the back of the house.

A car door opened, drawing everyone's attention, and Katie and Samuel Lapp stepped out from the back-seat.

"Ruth. Daniel. I'd like you to meet my *vadder* and

mudder—Katie and Samuel Lapp. *Mam. Dat.* Meet Ruth and Daniel Mast, Sarah's parents."

"We're pleased to finally meet you," Samuel said.

"I wondered if this day would ever come," Katie said with a teasing twinkle as she met Ruth's gaze. "My poor son has been miserable without her."

"*Ja,* Sarah, too, has been unhappy without Jed."

Jed edged toward Sarah and captured her hand, despite being surrounded by family. Sarah was too happy to be embarrassed. Jed had come, which meant that he still loved her. *Thank the Lord!*

Sarah left Jed's side to hug Katie and then Samuel, who looked pleased by the attention.

"Welcome to our home." Ruth smiled and gestured for all to come inside.

Sarah studied *Mam* and Jed's mother, noting how comfortable they were with each other, as if they hadn't just met, but were lifelong friends. Everyone took a seat at the long kitchen trestle table, and with Sarah's help, Ruth began to pull muffins and cookies from a shelf in the pantry. Katie put on a pot of water for tea. Sarah smiled to see her moving about her mother's kitchen, looking as if she were at home.

"Sarah, the reason my parents are here is to meet yours. I wanted your family to know mine, since we'll all be family soon." Jed paused. "I spoke with Ruth and Daniel," he continued. "I asked permission to marry you, and—"

"We happily gave it," Ruth finished for him. "Josie wrote me often while you were in Happiness, telling us how she thought it was between the two of you. Your sister, Emma, confirmed it."

Daniel rubbed his bearded chin. "Learning how much you mean to each other made giving our blessing an easy decision for us."

"Jed was unhappy during the weeks after you left. We could see how much he loves you," Katie told Sarah. "We knew you were the woman God has chosen for him."

"It was plain how much Sarah loves Jedidiah," Daniel said.

Samuel smiled. "So it looks like there will be a wedding."

Sarah beamed at everyone happily. Suddenly, she grew quiet. "But where will we live?"

"Jed has land in Happiness. A bride should reside in the house her husband provides for her." Ruth poured a cup of tea for Katie. "You and Jed can come for visits. We want you to be happy, and if that means living with Jed in Happiness, Pennsylvania, then we are content."

Ruth and Daniel exchanged meaningful glances. "Now that I am well again, I'm allowed to travel," her mother went on. "There is no reason why we can't come to visit you."

Sarah was moved to happy tears.

"Now that is settled." Jed rose and extended a hand to her. Sarah took hold of his hand and allowed him to lead her outside.

"This is real," Sarah breathed when they stopped and gazed into each other's eyes. "'Tis truly happening."

"*Ja,* this is real," Jed murmured. The adoring look he gave her made Sarah inhale sharply. His smile was tender. "I love you, Sarah."

"I love you, Jedidiah. I was so afraid that you wouldn't come—that you'd changed your mind about me."

"Never," Jed said huskily. "I will love you until my last breath and beyond. We are meant to be together. I prayed for a forever love, and the Lord gave me you."

"It began with twin boys who ran out into the parking lot and a handsome young man who saved them," Sarah said. "And then I was blessed by God again when I visited my cousins in Happiness, Pennsylvania, and found him...*you*."

Jed reached out, drew Sarah into his arms and simply held her. Sarah could hear the soft inhalation and exhalation of his breath. His nearness, his scent and the strength of his presence were all she'd ever wanted and more.

It seemed that Jed didn't want to let her go, and Sarah loved being within the circle of his arms. But then he released her and gazed into her eyes. He ran a finger along the front edge of her prayer *kapp*. "I've never felt this happy." His voice was low, husky.

"I feel the same way." Sarah gazed up at him, stared at his mouth, his nose, the warmth of his beautiful light brown eyes.

"Let's go inside. Our families are waiting for us."

And holding hands until they reached the front porch, they entered the house and noisy kitchen where their families talked of wedding plans and of joyous things to come.

Epilogue

Six months later...

Jed and Sarah prepared for company. They'd moved into their new home two months ago after marrying in Kent County, Delaware, during the first part of November, with another wedding celebration with their Happiness community a week later. Soon after, their Happiness church community came together to construct the newlyweds' house on the land that Jed had purchased from William and Josie Mast and had paid for in full.

Katie, Samuel and their other children, including Noah and Rachel, who was beginning to get large with child, arrived in time for supper. Moments later, a car drove up, bringing the Daniel Masts from Delaware for a visit.

Sarah felt Jed's hand on her shoulder as she opened the door to her family. *"Mam! Dat!"* She grinned at her brothers—all four of them. "Welcome to Happiness, Pennsylvania!"

"Did you have a *gut* trip?" Jed asked.

"*Ja,* the travel was fine," Daniel said.

"Come in!" Sarah urged. "Come in!"

As the Daniel Mast family entered the house and greeted the Samuel Lapps, Jed and Sarah exchanged loving glances.

"I thank the Lord for the day that He brought me to Happiness—and to you," Sarah whispered.

Jed bent his head, kissed his wife, and then with his arm around her shoulders, he moved inside and into the noisy household filled with family.

He paused in the hallway to touch Sarah's face, and then with his wife close to his side, he shut the door, locking in the warmth and love, and embracing the wonder of God's many blessings as they returned to enjoy the gift of their extended family.

* * * * *

PLAIN THREATS

Alison Stone

To my son Alex, as you embark on your senior year of high school. May you continue to be fearless and intelligent in your choices. You have the world at your feet, Buddy. I can't wait to see what you decide to do in life. I'm so proud of you. Love you. To my editor, Allison Lyons, who continues to believe in me. Thanks for your keen editorial input. My books are the best they can be because of you. To my husband, Scott, and the rest of my kids, Scotty, Kelsey and Leah. Love you guys, always and forever.

God is our refuge and strength,
always ready to help in times of trouble.
—*Psalms* 46:1

Chapter One

❧

"I won't be long." Rebecca Fisher scooted forward on the vinyl seat in the van and raised her voice over the swoosh, swoosh, swoosh of the worn wipers scraping against the windshield.

"I have another pickup." The driver's words were clipped, as if a return ride hadn't been understood. He pulled back the sleeve of his jacket and checked his wristwatch. "Meet you back here in thirty minutes?"

"Yah." Gathering the folds of her skirt and her tote bag, Rebecca climbed out of the van, popped up her umbrella and slammed the van door closed. She cast one last glance at the driver, who seemed oblivious to her indecision. Not as chatty as some, the young driver was one of several employed in the heavily Amish community of Apple Creek, New York, to cart the Amish around when they didn't want to be bothered with a horse and buggy.

Standing on the sidewalk under her black umbrella next to the brick building, Rebecca watched the red brake lights of the van as it slowed, then disappeared around the corner. She tugged on her black bonnet, trying to shut out the brisk wind and the whipping rain. It was late September, too early for snow, but the cold and rain were a hint of the winter to come in western New York.

Rebecca checked the address for Professor Jacob Burke on the slip of paper in her hand. Then she squinted at the name of the building carved into the stone above the nearest doorway. Her heart sank. It wasn't the building she was looking for and all the buildings looked the same.

If Rebecca didn't hurry, she might miss the professor. The college student she had talked to at the Apple Creek Diner where Rebecca worked as a waitress had assured her that Professor Burke had office hours on Monday and Wednesday from four until six-thirty.

Rebecca clutched the collar of her coat and turned down the first brick path leading between a row of buildings. *Oh, so many buildings.* A male college student strode toward her, his hands stuffed in his coat pockets, his hood pulled up against the rain and his eyes straight ahead.

"Excuse me. Do you know where…?"

The young man continued past without as much as a sideways glance.

She squeezed the handle of the umbrella tighter and looked down at the piece of paper as it flapped in the wind, the writing smeared from the rain.

"Can I help you?" An older woman stopped and gestured with her umbrella toward the young man who hadn't bothered to stop. "Don't take it personally, dear. The young people today walk around with those thingies—" she pointed to the side of her head "—in their ears. They don't hear anything except whatever it is they're listening to on their phones."

"Oh," Rebecca said, feeling completely out of her element on the college campus. "I'm looking for the Stevenson Building. Room 214. Professor Jacob Burke's office."

"The anthropology building," the woman said, as if suddenly everything made sense. It was no secret the professor of anthropology studied the local Amish. Perhaps the woman thought Rebecca was availing herself to his research, but that was the furthest thing from her mind.

Smiling, the woman spun around and pointed across a wide courtyard with her free hand. "You're close. It's right over there."

"Thank you." Rebecca tucked the piece of paper into the tote she had draped over her arm. Drawing in a deep breath, she pulled back her shoulders and strode across the courtyard to the arched doorway of the brick building. Her pulse whooshed in her ears in competition with the drops pelting her umbrella.

Rebecca pulled open the heavy wooden door and held it for a second with her foot. After wrestling to close her umbrella, she stepped into the marble entryway. The door slammed, echoing in the cavernous space, startling her. She adjusted her wind-whipped bonnet and smoothed what little hair was visible near the crown of her head.

Dragging her fingers along the cool metal railing, she climbed the stairs and walked down the empty hallway until she found room 214. Professor Burke's office.

Slowing her pace, she fumbled with the hook and eye on her coat, feeling the heat gathering. Finally, her trembling fingers released the hook and she slipped off her coat and draped it over her arm. Through the narrow window on the office door, she noticed a young man sitting at the desk and talking on the phone.

Rebecca turned and looked down the hallway; a trail of water had dripped from her umbrella. If she lost her nerve now and left, she'd have to stand in the rain for close to thirty minutes waiting for the driver.

You've come this far.

When Rebecca finally turned the handle and stepped into the narrow entryway, the young man was watching her with a curious expression, something Rebecca would never get used to. Sometimes she wished she never had to leave the farm. She missed the quiet life she'd led before her deceased husband's actions had drawn her into the limelight.

Now most every day she had to venture away from the solitude of farm life to work at the diner, where she often felt like a character in a play, expected to act out a role when the tourists stopped in for a meal. Some even had the nerve to talk really loud to her, as if she were deaf.

However, the end of summer had meant the departure of the bulk of the tourists and their curious gazes. They had been replaced primarily by less generous college students; vacationers tended to leave her an extra dollar or two at the diner after they had tasted her shoofly pie. Money she could ill afford to lose now that she was a single mother.

"Hello?" the dark haired young man said, his lilting voice making it more a question than a genuine greeting.

Rebecca worked her bottom lip. "I'm looking for Professor Burke."

The boy at the desk, who couldn't be much older than

her Samuel, turned toward the open door a few feet away. "Is Professor Burke expecting you?"

Under her bonnet her scalp tingled. She had obviously made a misstep. She should have found a way to reach the professor before showing up unannounced.

"I…um…" She smoothed her hand across the coat draped over her arm. The umbrella bounced against her leg when she took a step backward.

"Hello, I'm Professor Burke." A tall, clean-shaven man appeared in the doorway, an inquisitive smile in his warm brown eyes.

Rebecca took a confident step forward but kept her hands securely wrapped around the coat she was carrying, her tote and umbrella clasped underneath. "I'm Rebecca Fisher. I'm Samuel Fisher's *mem*…" She let her voice trail off, hoping he'd acknowledge that he knew Samuel before she went on much longer.

Professor Burke's eyebrows raised and his eyes darkened. "Yes, I know Samuel well. Is something wrong?"

Rebecca felt the young man's eyes on them. "Perhaps we can talk in private?"

"Of course." Professor Burke held out his arm, gesturing to his inner office. When she hesitated, the professor entered his office first and sat behind the large desk.

Rebecca followed him and sat at one of two chairs on the opposite side of the desk. She would have felt claustrophobic in the small space if it hadn't been for the large windows overlooking the courtyard.

The young man appeared in the doorway. "I finished collating the test papers. If there's nothing else, I'm going to blow this joint." His gaze traveled the length of her.

Rebecca dropped her umbrella, then she bent over to snap it up, happy for the distraction.

"Thanks, Tommy. Have a good night."

"Night."

The door to the main hallway clicked shut. Rebecca shifted in her seat, relieved to not have an audience. "I'm sorry to bother you this late, but I'm worried about my son. Actually, he was my husband's son, but I claim him as my own." She was telling this man information he already knew.

Professor Burke threaded his fingers and rested his elbows on the desk. She felt as if he was studying her like a farmer inspects a calf before making his bid at the auction.

"I'm very curious why you've come to me, Mrs. Fisher."

"Because I have nowhere else to go."

"Nowhere else to go?" Jake stood, then walked around to Mrs. Fisher's side of the desk. When he sat next to the young Amish woman, she angled her knees away from him, creating as much distance between them as possible. He looked down and stifled a smile.

"I need to talk to you about Samuel." Mrs. Fisher placed her tote and umbrella on the floor and folded her coat over them. She straightened her back and hiked her chin in a gesture that seemed forced. "I may come across as—" she seemed to be searching for the right word "—*backwoods* to you, but I know you spend time researching the Amish and you know a lot of the *youngie*. You knew Elmer King. And you know my son."

Jake's heartbeat slowed as he remembered Elmer, the

outgoing young Amish boy who had died in a car wreck over the summer. The image on the front page of the small-town paper of Elmer King's old red Chevy Camaro wrapped around a tree and his straw hat on the pavement said far more than a tidy quote the journalist had tried to elicit from the professor who studied the Amish. Jake was suspicious that some opportunist had placed the straw hat there for added effect.

A picture is worth a thousand words.

Jake tried to shake the image, but his stomach pitched at his guilt for not having known how to help the boy. Elmer had been one of the youth he had gotten to know over the past three years as a professor at Genwego State. Jake felt strongly that his missteps had led to Elmer racing off in a rage that fateful night.

Dragging a hand across his hair, Jake let out a long sigh, buying time to formulate his thoughts. "Yes, I knew Elmer. What does this have to do with your son?"

"Samuel and Elmer were friends. My son is not the same young man he was before Elmer's death."

"Samuel's had a rough go of it."

Rebecca nodded slowly and wrung her hands in her lap, seemingly growing more agitated. When she didn't seem as though she was going to speak, Jake asked, "How can I help you?"

She gave him a measured stare before dropping her gaze to her hands clutched in her lap. "Professor Burke, I'm worried about Samuel."

Jake rested his elbow on the armrest. He waited for her to continue. As a researcher, he often went into the Amish community and performed a delicate balancing act between developing authentic friendships and fostering relationships in the name of research. It was unusual for an Amish person to stroll into his office, never mind a young Amish woman.

"You've become friends with Samuel and his gang, *yah*?" The Amish referred to the groups of somewhat like-minded young adults who hung around together as gangs. The term lacked the negative connotation that it held in the English world.

"Yes, I've gotten to know your son."

"Is he…" Again, she seemed to be searching for the right word. "Is he okay?"

He studied her face. Myriad emotions played on her features.

"He seems to be okay. I know you both have experienced some backlash from the community after Willard was arrested." Rebecca's husband, now deceased, had been convicted for killing two of his Amish neighbors.

"Backlash." Rebecca seemed to be trying on the word. "*Yah*, we have had issues from graffiti on the barn to smashed eggs on our windows. The sheriff never made any arrests."

"Samuel told me it had stopped." He studied the woman, estimating her to be in her late twenties, early thirties at the most.

"It had. Then more recently, it started up again. Someone took all four wheels off Samuel's wagon…" Her voice trailed off. "I am grateful they took them off and didn't just loosen them. I hate to think—"

"It sounds like a police matter," Jake interrupted. "I'm not sure why you're here… I'm a professor."

Rebecca rubbed her flattened palms together. "It's twofold, really. I called Sheriff Maxwell once… I'm friends with his wife. We grew up together." She waved her hand, as if that part of the story was inconsequential. But any time someone left the Amish community, it scarred those that remained.

Rebecca drew in a deep breath and continued. "Samuel became very agitated when I called the sheriff. He holds himself partially responsible for his father's arrest, even though we all know…well, we all know what his father did."

"Yes, I'm sorry. Sorry for your troubles. Sorry for your loss."

"Me, too. This is not the life I imagined for me or for my children."

"It took a lot of courage for Samuel to work with law enforcement to aid in his father's arrest."

Rebecca ran a shaky hand across her lips. "Maybe he wouldn't be taking this all so hard if his father was simply in prison." Her shoulders rose and fell on a heavy sigh. "When Willard was killed in prison, I think something inside Samuel broke. I don't know how to reach him anymore."

"I'm not sure how I can help, Mrs. Fisher."

"Please, call me Rebecca. I no longer feel like *Mrs.* Fisher."

"Okay…" He hesitated, waiting for her to continue.

"I've watched my son talk to you at the diner. He's confided in you. I need…" She closed her eyes briefly. "…I need to know what you know about my son so I can reach him before I lose him for *gut*. Like the Kings lost their son, Elmer."

Jake ran a hand across his chin. "What is it you're

worried about?" A niggling suspicion told him why she was here, but he didn't dare say.

Rebecca's gaze lingered on his. "I need to know if Samuel's involved with drugs like his friend was." Her voice was strained, as if it took every effort to get out the words.

"Samuel's a young adult." Jake measured his response, trying to distance himself from the pain on Rebecca's face. Her son—her stepson, actually—was enjoying his running around years with the usual bending of Amish rules. If Jake broke the young man's confidence, the young Amish men wouldn't talk to him. On the surface, it would jeopardize his research at the college.

"Samuel needs to find his own way," Jake said.

"He needs guidance. He has no father."

Jake didn't know if Samuel was into drugs, but if he was, Jake wanted to be there for him without the interference of his mother. He needed to foster Samuel's trust.

Jake had learned that the hard way.

Rumors spread after Elmer's tragic death. Apparently, Elmer's father had kicked him out of the house after he had learned of his son's drug use. Jake tapped his fingers on his thigh and tried to ignore the familiar ache of guilt eating away at him. Jake had encouraged—no *forced*—the young man to confide in his family believing they would provide the support system the young man needed to straighten up. Instead, his father threw his son out of the house. Elmer fell into a downward spiral. All because of Jake's advice.

"Professor Burke," Rebecca bit out when the silence stretched a little too long. "My son is at a vulnerable time in his life." She lifted a shaky hand to her mouth, then let it drop. "I'm afraid I'm going to lose him."

Jake thought long and hard on how he was going to phrase this. Finally, he said, "I don't know what you want me to do. I thought the point of adult baptism was to allow the young adults in the community to make their own choices."

"It is…" She paused. "It is. But this is far beyond that. Samuel is a different person since his friend Elmer died. He has become withdrawn. He won't even let me in his room."

"Samuel has suffered tremendous loss." Jake leaned his elbow on the arm of the chair. "Be there for him when he comes around."

Nodding, Rebecca reached down and picked up her coat, tote bag and umbrella from the floor and balanced them on her lap, as if ready to spring out of his office. She glanced toward the door. "I hear a lot of things at the diner. About both college students and the Amish doing drugs." She traced the handle of the umbrella. "I fear I'm going to lose him, too."

"Have you asked Samuel if he's into drugs?" Jake angled his head, trying to meet her eye. He found himself fascinated by her wide brown eyes and full lips, sweet and innocent without any hint of makeup.

"Yes." She finally lifted her eyes, deep with worry. "He told me no, but I don't know if I can trust him to be truthful."

Jake settled back in his chair, weighing how much to say. "Drugs and alcohol are an issue in the Amish community, but I don't know if Samuel is involved. You need to talk to your son and keep talking. It's a rough time in a young Amish man's life. He has a tough decision looming ahead of him. He needs your support."

A look akin to disgust wrinkled her nose. "Are you lecturing me in the Amish ways?"

"I'm trying to…" What exactly was he trying to do? Avoid helping her for fear of alienating Samuel? For fear of giving her the wrong advice?

Rebecca held up her hand, stood and took a step toward the door, her frustration evident by her pinched mouth. "I don't know why I thought you'd understand. I'm sorry I wasted your time." Did she suspect he was holding something back?

"Would you have been satisfied if I had told you your son's a drug addict?"

Rebecca eyes flared wide, an emotion straddling fear and my-worst-nightmare-come-true flickered in their depths. "Is he?"

"I have no reason to suspect he is."

"Can you find out and tell me? Maybe he'll confide in you. I have lost much in my life—I can't bear to lose Samuel, too. If he's made a bad choice, I need to help him before it's too late. But I want to do it without getting law enforcement involved. If he ended up in prison…" She shook her head. "I'm holding on dearly to all that I have left."

"I don't want to lose Samuel's trust. I can only encourage you to keep trying to reach him." Jake already knew the devastation of his meddling in Elmer's life.

"Thanks for your time." Rebecca's words came out clipped. She spun around and stormed out of the office.

Jake sat for a moment, replaying the conversation in his head. A subtle thump started behind his eyes. He stood and returned to his chair behind the desk and dialed his assistant's cell phone number. Tommy picked up on the first ring, his voice hushed. "What's up?"

"How much do you know about Samuel Fisher? Is he big into the drug or alcohol scene?" His assistant had grown up in the Amish community and had left to earn his GED and eventually go to college. His background gave Tommy an "in" to the sometimes rowdy *youngie* scene and made him a valuable asset to Jake and his research.

A long pause stretched across the line. For a minute, Jake had thought he'd lost the connection. "Is that who that Amish lady was? Samuel's *mom*?"

"Yes."

"And his *mem*—" the word sounded foreign on Tommy's lips, mocking almost "—thinks he's into drugs and alcohol? Is that why she stopped by?"

"She's worried about him." Jake absentmindedly doodled an *R* on the piece of paper in front of him and traced over and over it. "She wants to know what I know about him."

Tommy laughed. "Far as I know, Samuel's a good kid. I'd vote him most likely to bend a knee before he's twenty-one."

"Yeah? You really think he'll choose to be baptized into the Amish community?" Jake felt reassured. "Rebecca Fisher seems to think he might be in some kind of trouble."

"Nah, not Samuel." A rustling sounded over the line, like from a gust of wind as if he were still walking.

"Aren't you home yet?"

Tommy laughed. "What? Are you my keeper? I had

some errands to run." Wind muffled his words again. "Let Mrs. Fisher know Samuel's a good kid. He's not into drugs or anything. Not as far as I know."

"She'll be relieved."

"Hey, anything else?" Tommy asked. "I have to run."

"No. Thanks." Jake ended the call and tossed aside the pencil. He stood and grabbed his coat from the hook. If he hurried, he might catch up with Rebecca.

Give her some good news for once.

Rebecca ran down the hall and out the door. Behind her, the heavy door slammed shut, like all her hopes of reaching her son. She stopped short and blinked against the soft mist of rain as she fumbled to open her umbrella. She strode forward, deciding getting wet was the least of her problems.

She had tried everything. Absolutely everything. The professor had been her last hope to uncover what was bothering her son. At the diner, she had noticed how comfortable Samuel seemed chatting with the professor. She had hoped he knew something that would help her reconnect with her son or at least intervene if the professor could pinpoint her son's troubles.

But this not knowing… This was more painful.

Maybe the professor did know something and he wasn't sharing.

Even if he did, what could she do with the information? Samuel paid her no mind.

A strong wind whipped around her long dress and her thick stockings underneath. Not for the first time, she muttered evil thoughts about Willard. He was destroying his family long after his death. The leaves on the trees rustled in the wind, setting her nerves on edge. She released her coat from her tight hold and stuffed one arm, then the other, into the sleeves, juggling her tote bag and umbrella. She ran, fighting back the tears.

She couldn't lose Samuel. His little sisters would be devastated. *She* would be devastated.

She swiped at the tears.

She hadn't realized how tightly she had clung to this last measure. To the notion that Professor Burke would help her.

As a young married woman, Willard had isolated Rebecca and she had felt increasingly alone. She had been ruined when she realized the father of her children was a murderer. But she had never felt more alone, more wrecked, than she felt right now. She could never reclaim her place in the Amish community if she lost both her husband and son to the evils of the outside world.

Her family would never be *gut oh tzene*. No one would ever respect the Fishers again.

Rebecca had heard rumblings at the diner that someone was dealing drugs in town and it might be one of the Amish *youngie*. Her insides ached every time she thought of it. She had no proof that Samuel would do such a thing, but his complete change in character made her imagine the worst. Sure, he had lost his friend, Elmer, but Samuel had been through far worse. Or maybe it was the culmination of everything he had been through that had put him in the pit of despair.

Would the professor have told her if he had heard Samuel was dealing drugs? She hadn't dared to ask him *that* question. She was fiercely protective of her son.

Rebecca stopped to catch her breath and her bearings. Her chest heaved. Blinking, she looked around. She didn't know how long she had been in Professor Burke's office. She only hoped the driver she had hired was waiting for her.

The building in front of her looked unfamiliar. Long shadows darkened her path. Suddenly, she realized the country college campus was deserted except for a couple girls walking away from her, their heads angled close in conversation. A hollow feeling expanded inside Rebecca. She missed her friends. Willard had seen to it that she didn't have any, both before and after his death.

And here she was alone and…lost. In the rain. Where had the van dropped her off? She had been in such a tizzy when she'd left the professor's building, she hadn't paid attention to her surroundings.

Stupid woman! Willard's voice rang in her head. She shook it away. Willard couldn't control her anymore.

Rebecca strained to see if she could hear the idling of a motor, but all she could hear was the wind whistling through the leaves clinging to the branches.

Rebecca turned on her heel and strode back the way she had come, then made a sharp right near the professor's building. Now that she had calmed down, she recognized the bench next to a brick memorial.

Yes, she had passed this way.

Only a little farther to the main road where her driver should be waiting.

Her heartbeat returned to normal.

The shadowed brick path wandered between campus buildings.

Just a little bit farther.

Crash. The sound of exploding glass sounded over

her head. Instinctively Rebecca ducked against the rain of glass fragments.

Squinting, she lifted her head. Someone was running toward her. A dark shape. Adrenaline made her blood run cold.

Dear Lord, watch over me.

The person stopped near her, the face impossible to make out in the heavy shadows under a large hood. When the person lifted an arm as if to strike her, Rebecca cowered and tiny explosions of light danced in her line of vision. Her eyes darted around, searching for an escape.

"Leave me alone," she said, her voice squeaky with fear. Instinctively she held up her umbrella in a defensive gesture.

Get to the van!

"Rebecca!" She glanced over her shoulder, a wave of relief slamming into her. *The professor.*

She spun back around and the mysterious person had slipped down a dark alley between two buildings.

Professor Burke caught up to her. "Did you know that person?"

She shook her head, unable to find the words. She held the umbrella down by her side as the rain hit her fiery cheeks.

"Are you okay?" He placed his hand at the small of her back and gently guided her toward his building. Once inside the doorway, he closed her umbrella, then helped her out of her coat. He stepped outside and shook the glass off it over a trash can.

When he stepped back inside, Rebecca finally found her voice. "I think he intended to strike me. He raised his hand. If you hadn't called my name…"

Compassion shone in his warm brown eyes. Rebecca lowered her gaze. The professor touched her shoulder. "Wait here."

Rebecca put her coat back on, then stood inside the entryway for what seemed an eternity while the professor ran back outside. When he returned he shook his head as concern creased the corners of his eyes. "Someone smashed the light."

"Why?"

The professor rubbed the back of his neck. "You've been harassed before. Because of Willard."

Cold fear rained down on Rebecca. "W-w-we've had the incidents at the farm. The graffiti on the barn. The eggs smashed on the window. Nothing physical. The community was lashing out after what my...what Willard Fisher did."

The professor scratched his head. "Did anyone know you were coming here to see me?"

Rebecca struggled to keep the threatening tears at bay. "I was talking about it at the diner. I suppose anyone could have overheard me." A chill skittered down her spine. "I thought time would make things better. Not worse." She hugged her coat around her midsection. "Do you think that's what all this is about? Willard?"

"I wish I knew." The compassion in the professor's voice warmed her heart. He held out his arm, drawing her farther into the building. "Let's call the sheriff." The professor pulled his cell phone out of his pocket.

Her mouth went dry and she shook her head briskly. "No. I'm not hurt. I don't want to complicate things. I want to go home."

The professor hesitated a moment, then much to her

relief put the phone away. He seemed to regard her a moment. "I came looking for you to tell you my assistant believes Samuel's a good kid."

She studied his face. "What does that mean?"

"My assistant is former Amish. He hangs out with the young men. More than I do, even. He thinks your son is a good kid and likely to be baptized."

Her eyes flared wide and hope sparked in her heart. Had she heard him correctly?

"Some of the men in his gang are a little wild. I've seen it firsthand, but that's not unusual," Professor Burke added.

"Maybe I can get him to switch gangs." Samuel had picked his current buddy bunch when he'd turned sixteen. His group of friends was mostly composed of youth his age. But maybe…

"Maybe." The doubt in the professor's eyes unnerved her.

"Uri and Jonas, the brothers helping out on my farm, are in his gang. Maybe I should question them." She hadn't done this for fear of embarrassing Samuel in front of his friends and pushing him further away. "Samuel is not himself. I don't care what your assistant says."

Silence stretched between them.

"Let me drive you home," the professor offered.

"But my driver…" She didn't feel much like arguing; her nerves were too frazzled.

"Do you have his cell phone number? I'll call him."

She handed him her hired driver's business card. She'd call him from the diner whenever she needed a ride. The professor paused a moment when she handed him the card.

Rebecca wanted to cling desperately to the hope the professor had offered her. *Samuel is likely to be baptized.* But deep in her heart she knew something was wrong. Very, very wrong. She had once heard her friend Hannah describe it as a mother's intuition.

Rebecca feared Samuel was being consumed by the dark shadow his father had cast upon his family.

Rebecca shuddered. She feared that she, too, would forever stand in the dark.

Chapter Two

The wheels of Jake's truck made a rhythmic thrum-thrum-thrum noise on the road. He usually cranked tunes whenever he was in the car, a surefire method to drown out his thoughts. However, he doubted Rebecca would appreciate his penchant for classic rock. And singing along.

Rebecca shifted in her seat, partially facing him. "I appreciate your kindness in driving me home." She tapped her fingers on the seat next to her, as if working up the nerve to say something. "I'd appreciate if you left any mention of our conversation out of any publications."

A sharp dagger twisted in his gut. Jake had prided himself on respecting the Amish and portraying them in the best possible light. But as a professor, he always built off the facts. He never twisted his findings to suit his hypothesis.

"The newspaper quoted you in the paper after Willard's arrest," she said accusingly when he didn't answer. "You shouldn't have mentioned me or my children."

"I only mentioned your family in brief. I focused on

Willard. You have to appreciate how curious outsiders would be."

"All too well. Unfortunately, curiosity didn't stop with the outsiders," Rebecca muttered.

A muscle ticked in Jake's jaw. "Please forgive me for being blunt, but that was a fascinating case. It rarely happens that an Amish person commits murder." He had respected her privacy. He had seen the sadness in her eyes and he would have felt like a vulture—like nothing more than a bloodthirsty journalist hot on the trail of a story— if he had approached her for an interview. Instead, he was careful to feed the news media facts regarding the Amish. It was only logical considering his position at the university and his proximity to Apple Creek.

"While you hide behind your fancy job at the university, I'm stuck living the life of a murderer's widow. How do you think people look at me in town? It's not like I can avoid their curious stares. I had to get a job at the diner to make ends meet."

"The Amish community is known for their forgiveness." Here he was spouting out his Amish research to her, an Amish woman. He did realize the ridiculousness of it, but he was struggling for something to say.

"Many have been kind, but I see the looks of pity in their eyes. It's painful. A few have acted out...like perhaps tonight."

"The sheriff wasn't able to get any leads on the previous incidents?"

"No," Rebecca whispered, "but once we stopped calling the sheriff, the number of incidents died down. I thought we were in the clear."

"Do you suspect your Amish neighbors?"

She shrugged. "It's hard to imagine…any of this, really."

"Now you fear if Samuel leaves the Amish community, the judgment from your neighbors will be unbearable."

"The look when I gaze into a mirror will be unbearable. I want my old life back. Before Willard lost his way."

Jake adjusted his grip on the steering wheel. "I'll be there for Samuel as much as he allows me to be." Samuel had grown quieter of late with him, too. "Maybe he's struggling with his decision to remain Amish."

"He is acting out. Hanging around with boys who drive cars, skipping out early on church service, listening to loud music…" She let her words trail off, perhaps hoping he'd confirm the list or perhaps add to it. "Maybe his friends are leading him astray."

"Perhaps."

Rebecca huffed her frustration. "Samuel has not had the typical Amish upbringing. His mother died when he was a young boy. He had an overly strict father who was killed in jail after his murder conviction. That, I fear, has shaped him more than anything. More than any positive influence on my part."

"My interviews with Samuel show he was confident that testifying against his father was the right thing to do."

"After his father's death…" She stopped to compose herself, then continued, "…Samuel retreated away from everyone. Then this summer, after Elmer's death, he got worse. Far worse. I'm afraid soon I'll have lost him for *gut*."

She faced him squarely. "Perhaps you can talk to him about his father? I can't bear to do it. You could convince Samuel that he did the right thing. By stopping his father, he undoubtedly saved lives." Hope laced her soft voice.

"I can." Jake turned up her driveway as dusk gathered. He thought he saw a light go off in the basement. Maybe it was the reflection of his headlights in the uneven glass of the narrow basement windows.

"I have built a solid relationship with Samuel and a group of other young Amish men. I can talk to them. I'll encourage him to come to you. But I must be cautious about how much I reveal. They are young adults. He's at the age where he needs to be making his own decisions. Living his own life. And dealing with consequences on his own."

Rebecca unbuckled her seat belt and pushed the door open a fraction. She bowed her head, leaving him studying the top of her bonnet. "Thank you." She twisted to get out of the car.

"Let me walk you to the door."

She held up her hand in refusal.

"The house is dark." Now he was second-guessing himself. Had he seen a light snap off in the basement?

"Samuel is…out." The statement seemed more a question. "My daughters are visiting my brother, Mark, spending the night. I'll turn on a lamp once I get inside. I'll be fine."

"Are you sure? The incident on campus must have rattled you. I think we should've called the sheriff."

"*Neh*, I want to put the night behind me. We've had enough trouble out here."

Jake pushed his truck door open. "I'm escorting you to the door."

"Neh." Rebecca shook her head for emphasis. "I've been on my own for well over a year now. I don't need a man to walk me to the door. I'm not looking to bring more trouble into my life. If Samuel trusts you and is talking to you, I want that to continue. You're right. I shouldn't have interfered. And—" a shy smile tilted the corners of her mouth "—I don't want to give my neighbors another reason to gossip." Rebecca ran her fingers down the ties of her bonnet. "You can find me at the diner if there's anything about Samuel you feel you can share."

Jake stared at her for a long moment, then pulled his door closed. "Okay." Her dismissal had been unmistakable. "Please turn on a light once you get inside. I'm not leaving until you do."

Without saying another word, Rebecca climbed out of the car. In the growing darkness, he watched her move toward the farmhouse, her full skirt swinging around her legs. He had spent three years studying the Amish youth, but he had never had a conversation like he'd experienced tonight.

Rebecca's dark hair and dark eyes would stay in his memory long after her clean scent left the cab of his dirty old pickup truck. Completely against his nature, he waited in his truck drumming his fingers on the steering wheel, while Rebecca let herself in.

He watched as she disappeared into the house and he waited.

And waited.

As time stretched, his pulse thudded in his ears. No light.

"Come on, Rebecca."

He angled his head and leaned closer to the windshield, as if that would make the light appear sooner. He glanced at the digital clock on the dash. Three minutes had passed.

Shaking his head, he pushed open the car door.

Something was wrong.

Rebecca unlocked the front door and stepped inside. She locked the door and placed the keys on the small shelf next to the door. The scent from last night's fire in the woodstove still hung in the air. Growing up, the smell always had made her feel warm and cozy, the sign of an inviting home in the cold of winter. That had been a long time ago. Too much in her life had changed since the tranquil days of her childhood.

Back sore, she set her tote bag and umbrella down on the bench inside the door.

When she had met Professor Burke she hadn't expected such a warm gentleman. Some of the Amish elders, although polite, had complained about the so-called professor meeting with their youth and filling their heads with worldly ideas.

However, Rebecca wasn't sure. She thought the professor was truly interested in studying their way of life, not inserting himself into it. However, she couldn't hide her disappointment that he couldn't give her any new information about her son. She had hoped to find a way to reach Samuel because she had failed at all her attempts and Samuel only seemed to be growing more distant with time.

She took off her coat and hung it on a hook. Maybe it was the nature of being a young man on the cusp of making a pivotal decision in his life.

Oh, she wouldn't be able to bear it if he left Apple Creek. She feared for his soul if he did.

A rattling sounded at the back of the house. Maybe it was Samuel. What if it wasn't? A quiet yelp sounded in her throat and she almost called out to him when something made her pause.

Holding her breath, she walked through her home toward the kitchen. The floorboards creaked under her deliberate steps. The back door yawned open and a stiff wind sent it crashing against the wall.

A dark shadow bolted across the yard. Tingles of panic bit at her fingertips.

Someone had been in her house.

Rebecca slammed the back door shut and turned the key in the lock. How had they gotten in?

Her raspy breaths sounded in her ears. A pounding at the front door startled her. She spun around and stared, uncertain what to do. She was out here. Alone.

Slowly, she walked to the front door. Her mouth grew dry and a weight bore down on her chest, making it difficult to breathe. She reached the front door and flattened her hands on the cool wood.

"Who is it?" The words came out as a croak.

"It's Jake. Are you okay?"

Relief washed over her. With a shaky hand, Rebecca grabbed the keys and opened the door. All her limbs went numb. Her lips couldn't form any words.

"I got worried when you didn't turn on a light." The professor's gaze swept across the sparsely furnished room cloaked in heavy shadows. Rebecca wondered if he saw something she hadn't. Rockers sat in the middle of the room. A table with her knitting sat between the chairs. The familiar setting seemed foreign now.

An intruder had been in her home.

Rebecca crossed the room and turned the switch on the kerosene lamp, casting the room in a warm yellow glow. She couldn't stop shaking. "Someone was in my house. They ran out the back door when I came in."

The professor stepped back, the surprise evident on his face. "Are you sure they're gone?"

Rebecca's eyes drifted to the back of her house. "I s-s-saw s-s-someone running across the yard." She clamped her jaw to get it to stop shaking.

"I need to check the house. Make sure no one else is here."

Her stomach dropped to her boots. Why hadn't she thought of that? She grabbed the arm of the rocker and lowered herself into it, suddenly feeling sick.

"Stay close to me while I check the house." The professor held out his hand and she studied it a minute before rising to her feet and taking it. A knot of emotions trapped her words. "Do you have a flashlight?"

Nodding, she dropped his hand and led him to the kitchen. She grabbed the cool handle of the solid flashlight sitting on the counter and handed it to him.

Its beam made everything not in its path seem even darker. The professor must have sensed her discomfort. "I'll make sure you're safe."

A nervous giggle escaped her lips. "Yeah, the professor protecting an Amish woman."

The professor moved toward the basement door. "Don't underestimate me. Before I went back to college for my PhD, I was an army ranger."

"I suppose that makes you tough?" She had heard of the army, of course, but she didn't know what a ranger was. The Amish were conscientious objectors and didn't believe in fighting in wars.

The professor opened the basement door and cast the beam of light down the stairs. "Tougher than most." He gently squeezed her hand. "Stay right here. I'm going to check the basement."

After a few long, tense-filled minutes, he emerged from the basement. "No one's down there. Let's check upstairs."

She nodded, nerves getting the best of her.

As she skulked behind the professor, afraid to walk through her own home, she could already hear the church elders tsk-tsking over a man who wasn't her husband going upstairs. Surely they'd understand. *If* they ever found out. Right now, the elders weren't her biggest concern. Someone hiding under her bed or lurking in a dark corner was.

Fear knotted her stomach. She'd never be able to sleep tonight.

The professor pointed his chin toward the door at the top of the stairs. "Is this your bedroom?"

She nodded and emitted an indecipherable sound that she hoped he took as yes. She lingered in the doorway as the professor made a sweep of the room. *Empty*. He did the same in the room Grace and Katie, her young daughters, shared. She was grateful she had left them with her brother, Mark, and his family for the night. They were only six and eight and Rebecca wanted to provide as much consistency for them after everything they had been through in their young lives.

The last upstairs bedroom was Samuel's. He kept the door shut. He had been doing that for the past few months, ever since Elmer had died. Rebecca immediately felt traitorous for letting this stranger into her son's room. A room her son didn't even allow her access to.

The professor gave her a quick nod, his face heavily shadowed in the hallway. He turned the handle and pushed the door open.

Rebecca skirted around the professor and turned on the kerosene lamp on the bedside table. She sucked in a gasp. The room was a mess. The quilt she had personally made for Samuel was askew on the bed. Papers littered the floor.

"Samuel hasn't allowed me in here for months."

A battery-powered radio sat in the corner, and an assortment of silver disks littered the floor around it. She walked over to the closet and picked up a thin laptop and turned it over in her hands. She willed away her nausea as she met the professor's gaze. "I had no idea he had this." She held up the computer in her hand. Before her job at the diner, where people came in to work for hours on these things at some of the best tables near the windows, she wouldn't have known what it was. "I have no idea how he'd afford a laptop. Why would he need this?"

The professor slowly strolled the perimeter of the room. Was he mentally cataloging her son's belongings as if his room were an exhibit in a museum? Her mouth grew dry. Feelings of betrayal welled up again. Why had she allowed this man who made a living studying the Amish into her son's bedroom?

"Please don't use this in your research. This is my family's private business." She didn't want to give the church elders reason to not allow her son into the preparation classes for baptism next summer.

Her heart filled with self-recrimination. She should have never brought an outsider into her life. *Their* lives.

The professor finally spoke. "You didn't know he had all these things?"

Rebecca shrugged. "I didn't want to know." She lowered herself onto the corner of the bed. "It's not uncommon for the *youngie* to explore worldly things. I hoped after his father, he would have been less likely to stray."

"You suspected something was going on. That's why you came to me." She tried to read the question he wasn't asking. Did he now suspect Samuel of dealing drugs? How else would he have earned the money for these things? Slowly blinking, Rebecca wished she hadn't listened to her gut. Wasn't she happier before she knew what her husband was really up to? The same could be said for her son.

What did she really know?

Rebecca smoothed her fingers along the edge of her cap and nodded. "I can't lose him. I can't. My daughters would be devastated."

I would be devastated.

"Do you notice anything missing?"

Rebecca lifted her head and looked around. "In here? I wouldn't know."

"What about in the rest of the house?"

"I don't think so. I have nothing of value."

"Maybe they wanted something your son had."

Rebecca's gaze swept across the room, a room completely foreign to her.

The professor pulled his cell phone out of his pocket. "I have to call the sheriff. Report a break-in."

"You can't." Desperation made her chest tight.

"I don't understand. Someone was in your house." He stopped and turned to face her. "Do you know who it was?"

Rebecca shook her head. "Of course not."

"I'm calling the sheriff."

Rebecca watched as the professor dialed the number, then lifted the phone to his ear. She was helpless to stop him.

Rebecca had made a huge mistake.

Rebecca sat ramrod straight in the rocker across from the professor as they waited in the sitting room for the sheriff to arrive. She was kicking herself for approaching the professor. She should have kept everything in her family private.

Now look what they uncovered in Samuel's bedroom.

And if she hadn't wasted time going to the university, she wouldn't have given the intruder an opportunity to break in.

Willard's cruel, mocking voice scraped across her brain. *Stupid, stupid woman.*

Neh, neh, neh! She was not *that* woman anymore. She was strong. She had to be.

If you are so strong, why is Officer Maxwell on his way over here to nose into your business? The Amish are supposed to stay separate. In this world but not of this world. You're going to screw things up and lose Samuel now. It wonders me how you'll ever be respected by the Amish.

Rebecca squared her shoulders, trying to shake her husband's mocking words free from her brain. She realized her argument was flawed. The intruder could have made his way into her home while she was there. Then what would have happened? She could have been hurt or worse.

The memory of the man advancing on her on campus flashed in her mind. Were these events related? Had graffiti and egg-throwing veered toward more dangerous personal attacks? Would the community never forgive her for Willard's horrid acts?

If this even had to do with Willard.

Rebecca rubbed her temples, hoping her headache would ease. She dropped her hands and frowned. Better to cloak her growing fear in annoyance. Easier to cast the blame of her predicament onto the professor. However unfair.

Rebecca wasn't in the mood to admit it, but calling the sheriff was the practical thing to do, even if unorthodox for the Amish.

Footsteps sounded on the porch, followed by a brisk rap at the door. She started to get up. The professor was faster.

Sheriff Maxwell looked past the professor toward her. "Everything okay out here, Rebecca?"

She sighed softly and shook her head. She and the sheriff weren't strangers. He had been instrumental in making sure her husband was behind bars. Rightfully so, but his presence was a painful reminder of a part of her life she'd rather forget.

The sheriff's gaze slid over to the professor and Rebecca felt foolish for ever believing a stranger in her life was a good idea. "You know Professor Burke."

The sheriff opened his mouth but closed it again. Perhaps he was going to say something that had crossed Rebecca's mind.

Why was he here?

Instead the sheriff held out his hand. "Hello, Jake. What's going on here? You said Rebecca had a break-in?"

The professor nodded. "Rebecca returned home and saw someone running out the back door."

"Anything taken?" the sheriff asked.

"Not that I can see." Rebecca ran her hands down the skirt of her long dress. The professor's watchful gaze unnerved her.

"Where's Samuel?" the sheriff asked, glancing around.

Rebecca's eyes grew wide. "He's not home." She couldn't help but bristle.

"Do you know where your son is?"

"It wasn't Samuel, if that's what you're thinking. He wouldn't have run away from me." Did she know that for sure? Hadn't he been moving away from her for months? She swallowed hard. "Samuel's a young man. I don't need to keep track of his every move." Yet that's exactly what she had hoped to do by contacting the professor.

The sheriff nodded, as if he were considering this. "If nothing has been taken, I'll write up a report and keep an eye out for any suspicious people wandering around tonight. Make sure you keep your doors locked."

Rebecca nodded again, feeling queasy. Many residents

of Apple Creek had added locks to their doors after the tragic murder of her friend and neighbor. The locks had been useless in keeping the murderer out of her home. Rebecca had been married to him.

"There's another thing, Sheriff," the professor said.

Rebecca spun around and glared at him.

"Rebecca was almost attacked on campus. I'm afraid if I hadn't come along when I had, she would have been hurt."

She wanted to deny this, but...she couldn't. Nervous tingles danced up her arms. In one fell swoop, she had brought two outsiders into her life: the professor and the sheriff. She closed her eyes briefly. If Samuel got wind of this, he'd distance himself further.

She'd lose him forever.

"What happened?" Sheriff Maxwell asked.

Rebecca explained the glass on the lamppost exploding above her head and the man advancing on her. Icy dread pumped through her veins as she finished the story.

"Do you think this is tied to the previous harassment?"

Rebecca lowered her gaze and heat infused her cheeks. The sheriff had been out to her farm after the graffiti and egg-throwing incidents, even though Samuel had begged her not to call the police. He claimed it would only aggravate the situation. But Rebecca had feared for her family's safety. Someone had to stop them. But no one had. The perpetrators were never found. So Rebecca had stopped bothering the sheriff. Eventually things died down, until recently.

"Have you had any interactions at the diner that made

you feel uncomfortable?" the sheriff asked, his tone compassionate.

"It's quiet at the diner this time of year, mostly college students and locals." She cut a sideways glance to the professor, wishing she could read his mind.

"You've had some help on the farm?"

Rebecca glanced up to find the sheriff studying her closely.

"Yes, Uri and Jonas Yoder. They've been a tremendous help. We wouldn't be able to farm the land without them."

"Any chance it was either of them in your house tonight?"

"Neh..." Her tone was less than confident, but she hoped the sheriff didn't pick up on it. She needed the Yoder brothers to harvest the crops. They were the sons of a well-respected Amish couple with ten children. They had been happy to offer their sons to help her in her time of need in exchange for minimal pay.

"Rebecca, if you think of anything else, you know where to reach me," the sheriff said.

She nodded.

The sheriff headed toward the door, then turned back again. "Hannah and I would love to have you over to the house for dinner. The girls would love to play with Katie and Grace."

Rebecca folded her hands in front of her. "That would be nice." For her daughters. For her, seeing Hannah brought back painful memories. Rebecca's husband had killed Hannah's sister and brother-in-law, leaving Hannah to care for her two nieces in Apple Creek, separate from the Amish community. Rebecca and Hannah had been dear friends as children, a lifetime ago.

A stomping sound on the porch drew all eyes to the door. Rebecca's heart sank. Samuel burst into the house. Under his broad-brimmed straw hat shadowing his eyes, she had a hard time discerning if he was angry or afraid.

Samuel took off his hat and ran his hand over his blunt-cut hair. "What's going on?"

The more her son hung around with the *youngie*, the more he sounded like an *Englisher*. It was as if the young Amish were all trying to shed their Amish roots.

"When I came home someone was in the house."

Samuel's gaze wandered to the stairs, perhaps thinking of his bedroom.

Oh, Samuel, please talk to me.

"Who was it?" Samuel's words were clipped.

"I don't know. He ran out the back. Did one of your friends stop by?"

Samuel scratched his head, leaving a tuft of hair sticking up. *"Neh."* Glancing at the sheriff, then the professor, he lowered his gaze. "I don't think so."

"I'll stop by the Yoder farm. See if the young men are home," the sheriff said.

Samuel's eyes grew wide. *"Neh. Mem*, why would you bring these outsiders here? Don't we have enough trouble being accepted among our neighbors after what *Willard* did?" He used his father's given name to distance himself. What son wanted to admit his father was a murderer?

Rebecca's knees grew weak. "My son is right. That will only stir up more trouble. The Yoders are *gut* boys."

The sheriff hesitated a fraction, as if he were thinking it over. He then clapped Samuel's shoulder. "Good to see you, son. Keep an eye out for your *mem* here and be sure to call me if you guys see anything suspicious." The sheriff was savvy enough to know most of the *youngie* carried cell phones during Rumspringa. It was frowned upon, but the elders turned a blind eye to it, hoping the young people would bend a knee when the time came.

"Good night, Sheriff," Rebecca said, eager to see him leave.

She closed the door behind him, then rested her backside against it. "Is everything okay, Samuel?"

Her son narrowed his gaze at the professor. "Are you friends with my *mem*?"

The professor seemed to be searching for the right thing to say. "I hope we can be."

Samuel's nose twitched as if he were trying to process the scene. Rebecca's heart pulsed in her ears. She didn't want to push Samuel away by revealing she had gone to the professor to try to exact information out of him.

Apparently sensing this, the professor spoke up. "I gave your mom a ride home." An apologetic smile slanted his lips. He had told a lie of omission, obviously leading her son to believe he had given her a ride home from the diner. "Then all this craziness broke out."

"Oh." Samuel stared straight ahead, skepticism written on his face. "I'm going to bed." He stomped up a few stairs before Rebecca called to him.

"Do you know anything about what happened here tonight?"

Samuel stopped without turning around. "How would I know? I wasn't home."

Rebecca caught the professor's eye. Unease twisted her insides, worrying how far she'd push Samuel.

"You must be tired."

Samuel nodded curtly. "*Yah*, I'm going upstairs." Samuel continued his stomp up the stairs like a petulant child. When he reached his room, he hollered down the stairs. "Who was in my room?" He thudded down the stairs, his chest heaving.

"I was in your room." Rebecca approached the bottom of the stairs. "Where did you get all that stuff?" The walls of the house seemed to sway as she waited for the answer.

Samuel pressed his lips together but didn't say anything.

Rebecca worried about the consequences of talking in front of the professor, but she was overwhelmed. She couldn't let this defiance from her son slide a minute longer. "Where did you get the money for a computer?"

A muscle ticked in Samuel's jaw and suddenly he looked like a man. An angry man. "Stay out of my room," he spat out.

"Samuel, your mother's worried about you." The professor moved next to her, making her feel like for once she wasn't alone.

"*You* don't have to worry." Samuel ran upstairs and slammed the bedroom door.

Rebecca and the professor exchanged worried looks. Samuel was definitely hiding something.

Chapter Three

The next afternoon at the diner, Rebecca grabbed the whipped cream can she could see through the glass door of the refrigerator and yanked off the cap. Lost in thought she squeezed the trigger on the dispenser and watched the white cream ooze out into a hearty dollop on two pieces of apple pie.

Drawing in a deep breath, she picked up the plates and turned her back to push through the swinging door leading to the dining room. The door swung back with a swoosh on its hinge, and she delivered the two pieces of pie to the elderly couple in the booth by the window.

"Can I get you anything else?" Rebecca asked.

"No, dear," the older woman said, "thank you." The couple came in at least once a week and Rebecca couldn't help but envy the easy way they chatted and held hands over dessert.

As Rebecca retreated to the counter, the elderly gentleman muttered something about how delicious the pie was.

Flo, the waitress on duty with her, pulled the filter

basket out of the coffeemaker and turned it upside down over the garbage. With a gentle tap on the edge of the can, the wet coffee filter and used grounds slid into the garbage.

Flo was in her sixties and she was a fixture at the diner as much as shoofly pie and apple butter. People might have thought she was Amish because she wore her long gray hair in a bun at the nape of her neck and her plain gray waitress uniform might have passed for Amish to the average tourist.

But Flo was *not* Amish. She had *English* sensibilities and had raised three boys, now grown. She freely shared advice with Rebecca whether she wanted it or not.

Flo spun around, planted her fist on her hip and smiled. "Still worried about Samuel?"

"I...um..." Rebecca muttered, embarrassed that she had been caught daydreaming and not getting her work done. She grabbed the dishtowel from the back counter and wiped down the already clear countertop. There was usually enough going on in the small diner to keep both waitresses hopping, but now just so happened to be the short lull between lunch and dinner.

"Well, I didn't figure you were staring at me because you forgot how the coffeemaker worked," Flo said with a funny smile. "What's on your mind?"

Rebecca twisted the rag in her hands. "I went to see Professor Burke last night." Rebecca didn't have many Amish friends of late and she appreciated the friendship of the older woman. Rebecca missed her Amish friends, her family. Her parents had long since moved to an Amish community in Florida for health reasons and her friends had disappeared as Rebecca's troubles multiplied.

Flo raised a pale eyebrow and regarded Rebecca for a long moment. She was a solid Christian woman, but she had a wicked sense of humor that could make Rebecca blush. That knowledge, coupled with the glint in her eye, had Rebecca bracing herself for the older woman's reply.

"Professor Burke is a very handsome man." Flo twisted her lips as if considering something. "Too bad he's not Amish or you're not English. You'd make a striking couple."

Rebecca smoothed a hand across the edge of her bonnet, feeling her cheeks heat. None of her Amish friends spoke this boldly. "It has nothing to do with that. I wanted to talk to him about—"

"You know who he reminds me of?" Flo grabbed a fresh filter and used the orange scoop to put fresh coffee grounds in the coffeemaker.

Leaning her hip against the counter, Rebecca didn't bother to answer because she knew Flo would get to it in her own sweet time. Before meeting Flo, she had never been around a woman who said whatever was on her mind. The Amish women Rebecca had grown up with were far more reserved.

The older woman snapped the coffee basket back into place and turned to face Rebecca. "You know who I'm talking about, right? Professor Burke reminds me of that really handsome FBI agent who works with that Bones lady."

Confusion creased Rebecca's brow. "Excuse me?"

Flo's face lit up and she laughed, waving her long fingers in front of her. "Sometimes I forget you don't watch

TV." She shook her head. Flo grew serious and stopped doing busy work, giving Rebecca her full attention. "I'm sorry. Tell me why you went to see Professor Burke."

Rebecca glanced toward the dining area to make sure no new customers had come in. She didn't want anyone to overhear. The only patrons were the elderly couple by the window, and they seemed content to chat over their pie and coffee.

"Samuel and some of the other Amish youth meet with Professor Burke for research purposes. I wanted to see if he could help me understand why Samuel has been withdrawn lately."

"How so? Did he tell you something about Samuel that you didn't want to hear?"

"No, but when he drove me home—"

"He drove you home?"

"He was being nice." Rebecca decided to leave the part about being attacked on campus out of the story. "Someone was in my house when I got home."

"Oh, dear." Flo leaned forward and cupped Rebecca's elbow. "Who was it? Are you okay?"

"I'm fine." Rebecca shook her head. "I don't know who it was. The intruder ran out the back door. Professor Burke called the sheriff."

"The sheriff will track him down, I'm sure of it." Flo tried to buoy Rebecca's mood with her optimism.

"The only problem is that the Amish try to limit their interaction with law enforcement."

Flo squeezed Rebecca's elbow and gave her a reassuring smile. "Sometimes calling the sheriff can't be avoided. You know that."

A guilty heat burned Rebecca's stomach. Would everyone always remind her of her horrible past?

"I'm trying to help Samuel—not get him into more trouble."

The lines around Flo's eyes deepened in confusion. "I don't understand why calling the sheriff would affect Samuel."

Rebecca bowed her head. "I shouldn't be bothering you with all my troubles."

"You need to share or—" Flo lifted her hands to both sides of her head, then flared her fingers "—or your head will explode."

"Well, the professor wasn't able to give me any new information about Samuel's bad mood. When the sheriff arrived last night, Samuel was rude to him. I don't need my son to be on the sheriff's bad side."

Flo's expression softened. "I'm sorry you're having troubles, but maybe it's time you stop smothering that boy." She laughed, a sharp sound. "A boy. Listen to me. He's a man. He could vote if he was so inclined. Stop trying to make him fit into a certain mold." She lifted her finger and tapped the side of her head. "He's got his own ideas."

Rebecca blinked slowly, realizing her English friend wouldn't understand.

As if reading her mind, Flo said, "I'm a mother, too. I raised three boys. My husband was convinced that one of them would become an engineer like him." She rolled her eyes and shook her head. "One became an accountant, another a policeman, and the last—much to my husband's distress—took up creative writing. Poor kid can't afford to pay attention, but my husband, God rest his soul, finally had to realize each of his sons had their own path in this life."

An ache Rebecca couldn't define filled her.

"The Amish are not like the English. We don't seek personal fulfillment. We are community-centered. God-centered."

"Is your son happy?"

Rebecca flinched. "That is not—" She stopped herself, realizing her friendship with Flo was more important than slamming her over the head with how the Amish culture is different from the outside world.

"I realize the Amish march to a different beat, but Samuel is his own person. If he's not happy, something has to change."

Rebecca didn't do well with change.

The bells on the diner door jangled, startling her. Rebecca's friend and the sheriff's wife, Hannah, strolled through the door with her young niece Sarah.

Flo leaned in close and whispered, "Hannah Maxwell seems happy since she left the Amish."

Rebecca walked away without comment because she couldn't find the words.

Hannah lifted her hand and waved. She placed her hand on her niece's bun. "Sarah had ballet class in town and we thought we'd stop by and say hello. How are you?"

Rebecca smiled, feeling a little less lonely. Hannah had stopped by because she was married to the sheriff and she knew Rebecca was struggling right now.

"I'm doing fine." Rebecca smiled at Sarah, admiring her hair, thinking that not that long ago the little girl had been wearing a bonnet and long dress, not a leotard and a pink bow. This was before Hannah had come back to town to care for her deceased sister's children and had fallen in love with the sheriff.

"We're going to start practicing for the Nutcracker," the little girl said. "I'm hoping to be one of the sugar-plum fairies."

"Christmas is still months away." Rebecca met Hannah's gaze.

"They start practicing early." Hannah unzipped the front of her niece's jacket. "Maybe you can color for a few minutes while I talk to my friend Rebecca."

Sarah slid into a nearby booth and Rebecca gave her a child's paper place mat and three crayons. "Hope you like red, blue and green."

"Thank you," Sarah said, picking up the red crayon and following the maze path on the place mat.

Hannah moved toward the counter and Rebecca followed. "Spencer told me he saw you yesterday."

Rebecca's eyes widened. Embarrassment heated her cheeks.

Hannah waved her hand in dismissal. "My husband doesn't bring his work home. He's a good sheriff. He keeps his business confidential, but I sensed that you might need a friend to lean on." She tilted her head to look into Rebecca's eyes. "You okay?"

Rebecca sat on the edge of a stool and crossed her arms. "Don't you sometimes wish we could go back to when we were all little girls? You, me, your sister. Collecting things for our hope chests."

Hannah's eyes grew red-rimmed and she gave Rebecca's arm a squeeze. "I miss my sister every day." She sniffed. "Nothing turned out like we had planned."

Hannah's lips curved into a thin smile. "But that doesn't mean some things can't turn out okay." She glanced in the direction of her niece. "I love my sister's daughters like my own and Spencer is a good man. I found light at the end of a very dark tunnel."

Rebecca feared the light at the end of *her* tunnel was a flickering pinprick in danger of being extinguished.

Rebecca squared her shoulders and pushed off the stool. "I'm going through a rough patch, but we'll be fine."

"I'm here if you need me. Please don't be a stranger."

"Denki." The Amish word for thank you came easily when chatting with her old friend.

"Well, we need to pick up Emma from her friend's house and get home." She reached out and patted Rebecca's hand.

"Come on, sweetheart," Hannah said to her niece. Sarah scooted out of the booth clutching the place mat.

Rebecca watched Hannah and Sarah walk hand in hand toward the exit. Hannah glanced over her shoulder. "Don't hesitate to call." She jerked her head toward the phone mounted on the wall, indicating Rebecca could call her from the diner if she needed her. "You don't have to go through any of this alone."

Rebecca nodded. Hannah seemed happy outside the Amish, so why did the thought of her son leaving the Amish fill her with unbearable sadness?

Because leaving meant walking away from everything Rebecca firmly believed. It wasn't about happiness in the moment; it was about faith and God and heaven.

What would happen if Samuel left?

Rebecca ran a hand over her forehead. The beginning of a headache was pulsing behind her eyes.

"Excuse me." The elderly lady seated at the window booth snapped Rebecca out of her reverie. "Could we have more coffee, please?"

Rebecca tugged at the edge of her apron, embarrassed that she had been inattentive. "Of course." She spun on her heel and strode toward the coffeemaker.

Flo came out of the back and gave her a sympathetic smile. "You've got the weight of the world on your shoulders, honey. You need to let go and let God."

Rebecca smiled in spite of herself. Flo's outward expressions of faith were contrary to her Amish upbringing, but she appreciated the sentiment all the same.

She had to have faith.

A tiny bit of the weight lifted from her shoulders. She grabbed the coffee and strolled over to her only customers.

A few nights later, Jake pulled his pickup truck—a vehicle that had seen better days—over to the edge of the road in front of the Troyers' farm. The sun had already set and the final remnants of light were making their last stand. An unpainted split rail fence separated the property from the country road. Beyond the house, barn and a few small structures, corn grew for miles.

Jake pushed open his truck's door and climbed out. He flipped up his collar, hunched into his coat and shuddered. He'd grown up in this part of the country, but he'd never get used to how quickly summer's heat turned to fall's cool evenings.

Jake had stopped by the diner this afternoon. He had

been disappointed that he hadn't run into Rebecca, but he had gleaned some useful information. He'd overheard the Troyers had hosted church service this morning, which meant they were hosting the youth singing now. Jake hoped he had timed it correctly to catch some of the *youngie* as they were arriving. He wanted to talk to Samuel, in part to clear up any misunderstanding as to why he was at his home the other night. He didn't want to jeopardize his relationship with the Amish youth. Outwardly, it would hurt his research and his position at the university, but more important, he wanted to be in a position to help Samuel if he had gotten caught up in something. If Samuel pushed him away, he wouldn't be able to help.

Jake's failure to help Elmer would haunt him forever.

Jake wanted to see firsthand why Rebecca was worried about Samuel. To date, the young men he had talked to had not given him cause for major concern apart from the normal shenanigans of an Amish male prior to baptism. But the sheriff's concerns about drugs in the Amish community made him wary.

And Rebecca's plea for help wouldn't allow him to let this go.

The tiny stones on the driveway crunched under his brown loafers. Singing flowed out from the barn. The event must have started earlier than he had thought. As he got closer, he noticed a few Amish boys leaning against a buggy, the red glow of cigarettes lighting up with each puff like fireflies setting the night aglow.

Hands stuffed in his pockets, Jake approached them, scanning their faces. *No Samuel.*

"Ah, it's the professor. So nice to see you," one of

them said. Even with the Pennsylvania Dutch accent, Jake recognized the universal language of sarcasm.

Jake knew the youth. Eli Troyer. Apparently being the host family for the singing didn't mean he felt obligated to sit through song after song from the *Ausbund*.

"Sorry to crash your party," Jake said, trying to sound nonthreatening.

Eli tossed his cigarette on the gravel and snuffed it out with the tip of his boot. Uri and Jonas Yoder, Rebecca's farmhands, watched silently, puffing on their cigarettes. Jake wondered how Eli's father felt about finding all the cigarette butts around the barn after the Amish youth descended upon his home.

"What's up, Professor? You looking to take notes? Count how many cigarettes I've had? Rat me out to my *mem*?" Eli gave him a pointed glare, narrowing his lips and emitting a steady stream of smoke.

Jake ignored the comment. "I'm looking for Samuel."

Eli adjusted his hat farther back on his head, the soft light from the barn lit on the amusement in his eyes. "Didn't you get enough information from his *mem*?"

One of the Yoder brothers laughed, a monotone sound that lacked amusement.

"I told you my research was private. That I protect your identities unless you give me permission to use your names."

Eli tapped out another cigarette and put it between his lips without lighting it. The crunching sound of footsteps on gravel grew closer. Samuel strolled around the corner. His eyes widened a fraction at seeing Jake, but he quickly composed himself, shoved his hands under his armpits and exuded an air of aloofness. "What are *you* doing here?"

"I wanted to talk to you."

"I'm done talking."

"Because I talked to your mother?"

Samuel pushed the gravel around with the toe of his boot. "Exactly. You didn't keep your end of the bargain. I talked to you for research for some stupid paper you had to write on the wild Amish youth." In the heavy shadows, Jake couldn't see it, but he sensed an eye roll accompanying the word *stupid*.

"My research is important." But not as important as the welfare of this young man.

"Not to me."

Uri, Jonas and Eli laughed at their friend's witty comeback. It was as Jake feared. However, securing his research subjects was only part of the reason he had driven out here tonight. The other was concern for Rebecca's safety. Someone obviously had something against her and wasn't ready to let it go. He had heard rumblings throughout the Amish community that not everyone believed Rebecca was blameless. He had heard one young man repeat the ramblings of his father. "It wonders me how a wife couldn't know what her husband was up to. She's just as guilty, I tell you."

Then there was the issue of drugs in Apple Creek and Rebecca's concerns that perhaps Samuel had gotten himself involved.

How had he paid for all the electronics in his room?

Like a research puzzle, Jake wanted to snap all the pieces into place in hopes of discovering what was going on here before any more lives were ruined.

"Can you give me a few minutes, Samuel?" Jake tipped his head toward his truck parked on the side of the road. "I can give you a ride home. It'll be a lot warmer than riding in a friend's buggy. Unless, of course, you brought your own buggy." Jake glanced around but couldn't determine how Samuel had gotten here.

Samuel glanced down, studying the gravel. "I'm going to the singing."

"We both know you have no plans to join the group."

"The professor got one thing right." Uri playfully punched Samuel in the arm. "But my friend here ain't going with an *Englisher*."

Jake caught Samuel's eye; a mix of defiance and fear flashed in their depths.

Jake pulled the zipper on his jacket up to his neck, blocking the brisk fall breeze. "Can I ask you guys something?"

Eli leaned back on the buggy and rested the heel of his boot on the wheel. The other three youth looked at him with apparent disinterest.

"The sheriff told me there are a lot of drugs flowing through Apple Creek."

Eli grunted and crossed his arms over his chest.

"You guys know anything about that? Heard about anyone dealing?" Jake jerked his chin toward the crops. "Heard of anyone growing marijuana?"

Uri laughed. "Yeah, we'll be selling marijuana at the roadside stand next to corn and pumpkins."

Jake turned to Samuel. "How about you?"

Samuel kept his expression neutral. "The only drug stories I hear are the ones that make the papers." *Like*

Elmer's tragic accident. "Sorry…" He shrugged. "Can't help you."

They stood staring at one another, silent save for the youth singing in four-part harmony in the barn.

Eli pushed off the wagon wheel. "Let's get out of here. This singing is a drag tonight." Eli gestured to what Jake thought was the buggy with an overabundance of reflector decals, but actually, he was looking past the Amish form of transportation to a ten-year-old beater car Jake hadn't noticed before. "Let's leave before my *mem* brings out snacks. Then we'll be forced to join the group."

"Samuel?" Jake asked, a hopeful note in his voice.

"I gotta go, man." Samuel turned his back to Jake and followed his friends. The four of them got into the car, Uri behind the wheel. The engine roared to life and the worn tires spit out gravel before the treads finally gained purchase and the car tore out of the yard.

A couple horses lifted their heads and snorted in protest. Jake watched the red taillights disappear into the dark night.

Jake wondered if his father had been this rebellious before he convinced Jake's mother to pack it up and leave everything that she'd ever known for a life on the outside.

Stuffing his hands in his pockets, he hunched his shoulders and strolled slowly to his truck. The sweet, dry scent of corn reached his nose, making him feel nostalgic for a life he had never known. Maybe it was simply because it was in his roots. His genes. Would studying the Amish and teaching a new group of students an Intro to the Amish course each semester ever satisfy his need to connect with his ancestors?

"Whoa!" An Amish boy hollered to his horse as he

tugged on the reins, quickly swerving around a distracted Jake.

Jake jumped out of the way and waved a hand in apology.

The buggy came to a stop in the gravel lot. "Hey, Professor, if you're not careful, you'll end up in one of those research papers of yours. How the Professor Got Run Over by an Amish buggy."

Jake rolled his eyes and laughed. "I'll pay more attention next time."

"It's best that you do." The young man hopped off his buggy and walked around to tend to his horse.

Jake nodded and strode to his truck. He feared he had ticked off a few of his research subjects tonight. His gut told him that was the least of his concerns.

After church service Rebecca had spent the day visiting her brother, Mark, and his family at their farm about a mile from her home. She always had a hard time around her brother, his wife and their five children. *That* was supposed to be her life, too.

She had never anticipated leading the life she did.

Rebecca had spent longer than she had planned at Mark and Gloria's house because her daughters were enjoying the company of their cousins. She hated to pull them away too soon. It warmed her heart to see them laughing, carefree...belonging.

After the girls climbed into the buggy, Rebecca wrapped a buggy blanket around Katie, then helped Grace pull hers up around her shoulders. Her youngest smiled and shuddered, her breath turned into a puff of white. "It's too cold. Can't we sleep at *Aenti* Gloria's house tonight?"

"You have school tomorrow."

Her sister-in-law, Gloria, danced on the balls of her feet, white breath forming on a sigh. "Oh, let them stay. We can get them to school in the morning with my children. What's two more?"

Rebecca hesitated. "You've been too kind to me. They've been here much too often." It would be easier to leave the girls here in her brother's warm house. She felt her resolve slipping.

"The cousins enjoy each other. Let them stay," Gloria said.

"*Yah*, you're right." Rebecca turned to her daughters. "Girls, would you both like to stay?"

Katie and Grace scrambled out of the back of the buggy and jumped one at a time onto the ground while holding Rebecca's hand. She planted a kiss on each of their foreheads. "Now mind your *aenti* Gloria." She lifted her gaze to her sister-in-law. "I'll pick them up after my shift at the diner tomorrow evening?"

"Perfect." Gloria turned around and, with a hand to each of their backs, she guided Rebecca's daughters into the warm, cozy house.

Something about watching her daughters walk away made a cloak of sadness settle around her shoulders. She let out another breath and climbed into the buggy. A stiff wind whipped up, refocusing her attention to the mile-long journey. Alone in the dark.

Rebecca had been foolish to stay late. She flicked her wrists and Buttercup lurched forward. She'd be home in no time, she reassured herself.

Buttercup trotted down the country road. The lamp-posts cast lonely rings of light every couple hundred feet or so. If Rebecca wasn't careful she would doze off behind the reins. Buttercup had traveled this road enough; she could easily make it back to the farm without much guidance from her.

Rebecca didn't care for traveling at night, but it did have one advantage—there weren't many cars on the road.

As if to prove her wrong, a car crested the hill and whizzed past her traveling in the opposite direction. That was always preferable to cars driving too close on the same side of the road.

With the car gone, Rebecca let her mind drift to what she'd do when she got home. Without the girls at the house, it would be lonely. Maybe she'd go into Samuel's room while he was at the Sunday-night singing. She hated to snoop, but she had been shocked to see his stash of electronics. Radio. Laptop. And she knew he had a cell phone. She feared she had already lost him and that his presence at the house was merely out of necessity because he had nowhere else to go.

She wondered how Willard would have reined in his son, then she quickly dismissed the thought. A year had passed since his arrest and she still shuddered at the thought of her husband's cruelty.

Buttercup neighed and Rebecca's attention snapped back to the road. Sensing a car coming up behind them before Rebecca did, the horse instinctively pulled over closer to the edge of the road into the buggy lane. The car sped past them, too close. Rebecca squinted after the red taillights, suspecting it was the same car she had seen going in the other direction only moments before. Her nerves buzzed. A young woman out here alone on a backcountry road was vulnerable.

Stories of buggies colliding with cars made the local paper all the time. She gave the reins a gentle flick and Buttercup picked up her pace.

I'm almost home. Dear Lord, keep me safe.

When the bright red brake lights of the car came on, the tips of her fingers tingled as she tightened her grip on the straps. She made a noise with her lips and snapped the reins. The horse picked up her trot.

The car slowed and made a wide U-turn, its wheels crunching on the berm of the road. Rebecca shielded her eyes against the bright headlights as the car raced back in her direction. A knot twisted her insides, much like it had every time Willard returned home and she'd feared his mood, his outbursts, his angry demands.

Let them drive by. Please, let them drive by.

She flicked the reins again, her eyes locked on the approaching car. At the last minute, the driver swerved into her lane, playing a deadly game of chicken.

Buttercup spooked and took off like a shot, veering closer to the ditch. The buggy's wheel dipped into the deep ditch lining the country road. The sharp motion tossed Rebecca out of her buggy.

A yelp escaped her lips.

It seemed like an eternity as she flew through the air. She landed on her side with an oomph. Her hip and shoulder sank into a few inches of cold, mucky water. Panic made a flush of goose bumps race across her skin. She groaned and struggled to her feet, the wet folds of her dress weighing her down.

Buttercup stopped a ways down the road and neighed his protest. Somehow the buggy had stayed out of the ditch and rested on the side of the road, seemingly no worse for wear.

Thank you, Lord.

Searching her dark surroundings, Rebecca paused and listened. The hum of the vehicle grew distant. Relief, mixed with fear and anger, created a steady pounding behind her eyes. She planted her hands on the cold, hard-packed dirt on the edge of the ditch.

She wiggled her toes in her wet boots.

She struggled to pull herself up but couldn't gain traction. She feared whoever stumbled across her in the light of day would find her, feet frozen in the icy water.

Gravel crunching under tires made the fine hairs on the back of her neck stand on edge.

Had they come back for her?

Rebecca leaned against the edge of the ditch, her palms pushing into the dirt, hoping her black coat in the black of night made her invisible.

Still hitched to the wagon, Buttercup neighed, obviously stressed over the near miss.

A car's engine idled behind her buggy. A door opened. Closed. Rebecca's entire body trembled from the cold. If whoever had returned didn't kill her, hypothermia would.

Footsteps sounded on the gravel. Growing closer. Closer.

Adrenaline surged through her veins. She had nowhere to hide.

She pressed her cheek to the ditch's edge, trying to

make herself small. Invisible. The smell of earth and moisture filled her nostrils.

A man loomed above her and Rebecca bit back a scream.

Chapter Four

"Are you okay, ma'am?" Jake couldn't keep the alarm from his voice. He crouched on the side of the road and stretched his hand out to the woman in the ditch. "Let me help you."

The woman tilted her face up and the moonlight glinted in her worried eyes. "Rebecca! What in the world happened?"

Rebecca squinted up at him, her lower lip trembling. "S-s-someone spooked Buttercup and she dumped me out of the buggy."

Jake twisted and looked down the road. No one in sight. He wrapped his hand around her chilly fingers. "Let's get you out of there and warmed up before you freeze to death."

He immediately regretted his choice of words.

Rebecca gathered up the wet folds of her skirt in one hand and tightened her grip on his hand with the other.

He pulled, but instead of tugging Rebecca out of the ditch, he found himself losing his footing on the muddy edge of the ditch. Rebecca's wet hand slid out of his and she flailed back and landed with a whoosh on her back-side in the water. She closed her eyes, briefly stifling the words to match the look of disgust on her face. "*This* is your plan? Hmm…"

"Whoa…hold on. Step back." The water swooshed around her boots as she stepped out of the way. "I'm going to have to try something else."

Before he had a chance to overthink it, Jake jumped into the ditch next to her. The shock of the cold water shot through him. His leather loafers weren't exactly traipsing-in-icy-water gear. He looked down at her and thought he detected a smile on her lips in the moonlight.

Jake assessed the situation. "I'm going to have to hoist you out of here from behind."

Her lips slanted, indicating her skepticism. "Behind?"

"Trust me," Jake said, grimacing as the cold water sloshed around his loafers.

"I dare say you haven't given me *gut* reason to trust you yet."

"Rebecca," Jake said, feeling more than a little out of his element. "You're going to have to work with me on this before we both catch hypothermia out here." He lifted one foot, then the other, unable to escape the frosty pain.

Rebecca nodded, her lower lip trembling.

"On the count of three, I'm going to give you a shove partway out of the ditch. You'll have to pull yourself up the rest of the way."

Rebecca nodded, her bonnet askew on her head; a long strand of silky brown hair had escaped her bun. He bent over and threaded his fingers together. Put your foot here and I'll boost you up and over the side."

Rebecca gave his hands a you've-got-to-be-kidding look, but she lifted a small foot and stepped into his clasped hands. With one quick push-shove-hoist from Jake, Rebecca was able to grab hold and get to her feet on the side of the road.

"How are you going to get out?" Rebecca wrapped her arms around her middle and loomed over him, the moon haloing her bonneted head.

Jake had maintained his physical fitness since retiring from the army by working out at the campus gym. Now was when all that exercise would pay off. He hoped. He found a foothold on the wall of the ditch and was able to pull himself out rather quickly.

Jake followed Rebecca over to Buttercup. She smoothed her hand down the horse's mane and whispered soothing words to the animal.

Rebecca finally turned to him, a look of fear in her eyes. "The car intentionally swerved in front of me. They spooked Buttercup." Her lips trembled. "I…" She patted Buttercup's mane. "We could have been killed."

"Could you describe the car?"

Rebecca shook her head slowly. "It passed a few times before it came at me."

"Any chance it was an older car? Three or four guys in it?" He thought of the vehicle Samuel, Eli and the Yoder brothers had hopped into.

"I don't know. The lights blinded me. But it was a car, not a truck like you have and not a van."

"Do you think it was random?"

Rebecca shook her head. "No, I think the driver knew exactly who I was. That's why he drove past a few times first. He wanted to scare me." She slurred her words, her lips numb.

Would Samuel really allow his friends to harass his mother? Risk seriously injuring her and her horse? Or worse?

Samuel didn't strike him as that kind of kid. Jake shoved a hand through his hair. The last conversation he'd had with the young men crossed his mind.

"Come on. You can't stand out here. I need to get you home." Jake gently took her by the elbow and led her to his truck. "You need to get inside. Warm up."

Rebecca pulled away. "I can't leave Buttercup here."

"No, no, of course not. I'll call my assistant. Tommy's comfortable with horses."

"No, I don't live far. I'll get her home." She strode back to the buggy, the folds of her wet dress slapping her legs.

Jake followed her. He reached into the backseat and grabbed a thick blanket. As he wrapped it around her shoulders and pulled it tight at her neck, his knuckles brushed against the cool, smooth skin of her jaw. She looked up at him with something in her eyes he couldn't quite define.

Rebecca clutched the blanket and climbed into the buggy. "I'm happy you happened along. Thank you for s-s-saving me." She nodded to him dismissively.

Jake laughed. "You really think I'm going to let you ride off alone? You're freezing. I need to see you safely home."

A look of confusion swept across her features. Jake hopped into the buggy and nudged her aside with his hip. "Give me the reins."

Silently, Rebecca handed him the leather straps. "What about your truck?"

"I'll pick it up later."

"Do you know what you're doing? Have you ever done this?"

"I'm an army ranger—I'll figure it out. If I get it wrong, you can tell me."

Even though he knew that wouldn't mean much to Rebecca, he thought he detected a smile on her quivering lips.

"S-S-Samuel won't be too happy to see you and me together again."

Jake raised his eyebrows but didn't say anything. Samuel was exactly who *he* wanted to see.

When the professor flicked the reins, Buttercup lifted her head and neighed, jolting forward and stopping.

"I think she's still a little spooked from the run-in with the car." Instinctively, Rebecca reached out, her hand brushing his hand as he held the reins a little too tightly. "Let me."

The professor hesitated a minute, then scooted over a bit, making it easier for her to take control of the horse. "I guess I'm more an 'insert key and turn, press gas pedal' kinda guy."

She cut a quick glance to this man, a stranger, really, who spent his time studying her community. Her neighbors. Her son.

The brisk autumn breeze ruffled the edge of the blanket draped over her shoulders. One side slid down behind her back. The cold from her wet skirt seeped into her undergarments. She stifled a shudder. Soon she'd be home and she could light the fire. Put this dreadful night behind her.

Buttercup trotted down the road, the steady, familiar clip-clop-clip calming her nerves.

"This is the first time I've been in a buggy," the professor said.

"Really? I thought with all your research, you would have had the opportunity before now."

He shrugged. "No. Maybe someday when we're not all wet and cold you can show me how to do it."

"Do what?"

"Show me how to get Buttercup to follow my commands."

"There's nothing to it, really," Rebecca said, heat warming her cheeks. "It's a matter of trust. Buttercup has been a wonderful horse." She had taken the animal in when Hannah had moved away from the farm with Sheriff Maxwell.

Rebecca tightened her grip on the reins. "In my world, I don't have the option of 'insert key and turn, press gas pedal,'" she said, mimicking him.

He laughed, the sound pleasant after such a rough evening.

"I remember the first time I saw an Amish buggy." The professor's voice seemed nostalgic. She waited for him to continue.

"I was traveling through Lancaster County, Pennsylvania, with my parents and there they were, one buggy after another traveling on the side of the road. I couldn't believe it."

"What couldn't you believe?"

"That people would actually choose to live without..."

He seemed to be searching for the right word so as not to offend her. "...All the modern conveniences."

"You can't miss what you never had." She gently tugged the reins to direct Buttercup toward her barn. The buggy bobbled over the ruts in the mud.

"At the time, I must have been around ten, I was fascinated with a certain TV show and I couldn't imagine not being able to catch the next episode."

Rebecca smiled to herself. Just the other day Flo had told her how the professor had reminded her of a character on one of her TV shows. Who was it? She wondered if he'd find it flattering.

The professor hopped off the buggy and jogged around to help her down. She had plenty of practice doing it all on her own, but it was nice to have a helping hand. Willard had been gone a long time now.

On the second floor of her house, she noticed a soft light glowing in Samuel's bedroom. A mix of relief and fear tangled in her belly.

Samuel spent far too much time in his room. What was he doing?

"I'll get Samuel to settle Buttercup for the night." Rebecca stopped by the porch steps, a little unnerved that Professor Burke seemed insistent on seeing her to the door. "Thank you for coming to my rescue." She gripped the railing tighter.

"I'll have Samuel take you back to your truck," she said, eager to go inside.

The professor glanced down the road. "No, I can jog back. It's not that far."

"But you must be cold, too." She noticed the bottom

of his wet pants. The leather on his shoes was discolored from the water. "Those don't look like running shoes."

He shrugged. "Actually, I would like to talk to Samuel before I left."

Rebecca bowed her bonneted head and looked up at him shyly. "Can I ask you a question?"

"Shoot."

"Why are we so fascinating to you?" She grabbed the blanket and pulled it tighter around her shoulders.

"The Amish?"

She nodded.

The professor ran his hand over his close-cropped hair. "My parents grew up in an Amish community. They were Amish."

She jerked her head back. "Really? How interesting. They left the Amish community." It was more a statement than a question.

"It was my father's idea and since my mother loved him, she followed him." He lifted his eyes, the moonlight glinting in them, making it hard to read the emotion there. "My father always joked, calling them fence jumpers. My mother always bristled at the comment." There was something sad about his tone.

"So, Professor, is this why you study the Amish?"

He smiled that warm familiar smile. "Partly." His answer came out clipped and she felt as if she had stepped out of bounds. "I think it's time you called me Jake. We've spent a lot of time together."

A smile tugged on her lips, but her feelings of fondness were fleeting. An empty road stretched behind him. And beyond that, her Amish neighbors.

The line of connection snapped as reality slammed

into her. The last thing she needed was the neighbors chatting about poor widowed Rebecca Fisher entertaining the English professor. Her Amish neighbors would be requesting not to sit in her section at the diner in a silent form of protest. A shunning of sorts. The Amish's unique way of guilting a person back into the fold. Back into following the church's rules.

"I'd rather call you Professor." The ever-present uneasiness tightened its grip on her chest. Would she ever be able to move past the shame her deceased husband had created? It was a physical pain she doubted she'd ever be rid of. If only she and Samuel could find acceptance in their own community. If only the Amish could dig deep into their vast well of forgiveness and bestow it on her.

"I don't mean to cause you any grief," Jake said, tilting his head. There was a kindness in his eyes she wasn't used to seeing in a man. Willard had been cruel.

She blinked at him. Flo was right. He was pleasing to the eye. Inwardly, she shook the thought away. She had no business thinking in those terms.

"I'm not looking for your friendship." She didn't try to hide the exhaustion in her voice. "My coming to your office the other night was misguided. I was desperate. I thought you could help me understand what's going on with my son." Rebecca tapped the railing, a nervous gesture. "But I suppose that's something I have to work out with Samuel."

The professor put his hand on the railing near hers. For the briefest moment, she thought he was going to cover her hand with his, warming it. She ignored the disappointment that swelled inside her when he didn't.

She had experienced a riot of emotions tonight and suddenly she felt extremely tired. And cold. So very cold.

"I can respect that," the professor said, a gentleness to his voice. "However, I'd still like to talk to Samuel tonight before I go."

Rebecca glanced toward the door of her house. "I don't know." Her meddling seemed to only cause more problems.

The professor bowed his head, then looked up and met her gaze. Apprehension settled in his eyes. "I know you don't want to hear this, but I think Samuel might have been in the car that ran your buggy off the road."

The blanket fell from her shoulders and her body swayed. *"Neh."*

Rebecca's face grew white and her lower lip trembled. Jake grabbed her elbow to steady her. "Let's get you inside. Where it's warm."

She yanked away her elbow. *"Neh*, I'm fine." He understood her anger, but he wasn't going to let it stop him.

"What's…what's going on?" Samuel stepped onto the wide porch and rushed to his mother's side. "Are you okay?"

She spun around and pointed at her son. "Go inside, Samuel. Professor Burke is leaving."

Then Rebecca straightened her shoulders. "Please." She softened her tone. "Go inside. It's been a long night."

Samuel's gaze implored her. "Did something happen?"

"Do you know what happened?" Jake watched the young man closely. In the year since he'd been meeting with Samuel, the boy had gone from quiet and reserved to angry and fearful. He had assumed Samuel's attitude change had to do with his friend Elmer's death. However, as the harassment on the farm and toward Rebecca continued, Jake began to wonder if something else was at play.

Samuel looked everywhere but at Jake.

"Do you know something?" Jake asked again.

Samuel ran his hand up and down one suspender and stared at his boots for a moment too long. "I have no idea what you're talking about." Samuel turned to his mother. "What happened? Did you have an accident?" His gaze ran the length of his mother's dress, no doubt searching for assurances that she was all right.

"A car spooked Buttercup. I was thrown from the buggy."

Samuel shed his defensiveness and a worried expression crossed his features. He looked much younger than his eighteen years. His gaze drifted to the street, then he seemed to school his expression. "You shouldn't have been out this late." He glanced around; renewed fear pinched his mouth. "Where're Katie and Grace?"

Rebecca touched her son's arm. "They're fine. They stayed with *Aenti* Gloria."

"Were you in the car that spooked the horse?" Jake asked, carefully studying Samuel's expression.

Worry settled in Samuel's wide eyes. He pushed his straw hat back farther on his head. "No. No, I wasn't," he said adamantly.

Rebecca stepped closer to her son. "I know you weren't in the car with them, but you need to be careful. You know the community is still watching us after—"

"After my *dat*." Samuel pulled away from his mother. "Don't you think I know that?" His eyes narrowed. "Is

Alison Stone

that all you care about—what other people think?" He
held out his open palm. "You were tossed in a ditch and
yet you're still yelling at me for riding in a car.

"The elders look the other way when the *youngie*
drive. It's not fair that I'd be treated any differently."
Samuel stormed toward the house, but stopped with his
hand on the doorknob.

"We are different," Rebecca said, her voice quiet. "We
are. We have to try harder."

Jake resisted the urge to reach out and touch Rebecca's arm in a gesture of comfort but he feared it
wouldn't be accepted.

"What ever happened to forgiveness? Why can't they
forgive and move on?" Samuel pounded his fist on the
door.

Rebecca climbed a step and stopped. "I'm saddened
that some people can't seem to forgive. It will take time."

"Were you dropped off without incident tonight?"
Jake had to ask, bringing the conversation full circle.
Last time he saw Samuel, he was hopping into a car
with his friends.

"Yes, Uri dropped me off. He's a good driver, *mem*."
Samuel took off his hat and scratched his head, leaving
it in unkempt tufts.

"Uri was driving?"

"*Yah*, what does it matter?" Samuel crossed his arms
over his chest, not waiting for an answer. "It doesn't help
when you and the professor are asking questions and
snooping around." His voice grew harsh. "I'll never be
accepted by my friends. Professor Burke here accused
us of selling drugs."

"You what? I…" Rebecca lifted a shaky hand to her lips.

Jake glanced at Rebecca. "We need to talk this through." The look of distrust in her eyes tore at his heart. "But for now, I need you to trust me. Please go inside. Warm up."

Rebecca slowly nodded, the defeat evident on her face. Samuel turned to go with her, too, when Jake called out, "Hold up."

The young man slowly turned around but didn't say anything. Rebecca went inside and closed the door.

"Your mother is worried about you."

"I don't know why."

"You're an adult. I'm not sharing anything that you confided in me. So, if you need to talk…"

Jake's mind flashed to Samuel's friend Elmer, the young Amish man who had been in a lot of pain and had turned to drugs. Jake had pushed Elmer to go to his parents with his *issues*. A memory stabbed his gut. Maybe if Jake hadn't forced Elmer, the young man would still be walking God's green earth.

"I don't have anything to tell you." Samuel shuffled his feet and kept sneaking glances over his shoulder.

"If there's something going on, you can tell me. You're not alone. I can help you."

Samuel laughed, a harsh sound void of humor.

"You're just interested in your research. A good research paper. That's all we are to you. You don't really care."

Jake furrowed his brow. Was that what Samuel really thought? "I'm here if you need someone to talk to."

"Night, *Professor* Burke." Samuel disappeared inside.

Jake stood on the bottom step for a long moment. He turned toward the house when he heard the door handle click. Rebecca stood there, looking hesitant. "I'll ask Samuel to take you to your truck."

Jake shook his head slowly. "I'll be fine."

Rebecca nodded and closed the door. Jake strode down the drive to the road, to his truck parked down the way. He prayed the fresh air would clear his mind.

Chapter Five

Rebecca stood at the window and watched the professor until the darkness swallowed up his profile as he jogged toward his truck parked down the street. She hated to think what she would have done if he hadn't happened by. She probably would have had to claw her way out of the ditch.

Something niggled at her brain. *How was it that he had just come by?* She shook away her misgivings and stepped back from the window. The wet fabric of her skirt clung to her legs. *Yuck.*

She jogged up the stairs, stopping outside her son's bedroom. A thin line of light leaked from the bottom of his door. She lifted her hand to knock, then something inside her said to wait. A rational conversation wasn't going to be had while she shivered in her wet dress.

Samuel needed time to cool down, too.

Decision made, she retreated to her bedroom and changed into warm sleep clothes. After she brushed her teeth and washed her face, she climbed into her bed. Pulling the covers up, she said a quiet prayer for wisdom on how to reach her son. She couldn't bear to lose him. Not him, too.

Creak.

The house must be settling, Rebecca reasoned to herself. She rolled over and pulled the covers up over her shoulder. The nights were getting cooler. She took long breaths in and out but couldn't slow the thoughts racing through her head.

Harvest time was coming. She wondered how much longer she'd be able to manage the farm while she spent long hours at the diner.

The girls were spending more and more time with their aunt and uncle.

Everything that was important to her was slipping through her fingers.

Creak. Creak. Bang.

Rebecca froze and the sound of her shaky breath filled her ears. The noise had come from downstairs. She sprung up in bed and tossed the covers back in one swift motion. "Samuel!" she called. "Samuel, are you okay?"

When he didn't answer, a flush of dread heated her skin and made her dizzy. For once in her life, she wished she had a phone—one of the portable ones—to call for help.

She swung her legs out from under the covers and her toes hit the cool hardwood floor. She grabbed her robe from the hook and stuffed her arms into the sleeves. After hesitating at the bedroom door, she finally mustered the nerve to step into the dark hallway.

The house was quiet save for the ticking of a battery-powered clock downstairs in the kitchen, the sound traveling through the house.

Samuel's bedroom door yawned open revealing a dark space.

Her mouth went dry. "Samuel?"

Tick-tock-tick-tock mingled with her shaky breath.

Rebecca stepped into his room. Samuel's bed was empty. In the dark, she made out some of the shadows. The radio. The open laptop. The shock of seeing the forbidden items had worn off a bit, but still they taunted her. He had to get this worldliness out of his system. Come to realize that the Amish way of life was the only way.

Biting her lower lip, she left his room and descended the stairs. At that exact moment, the front door flew open and slammed against the wall. She couldn't make out his expression in the dark, but she knew it was her son. He pulled on something stuck in the wood of the door, then slammed the door shut.

She moved to the sitting room and turned on the kerosene lamp. Her growing unease swelled up, making her shudder. Rebecca tightened the tie on her robe around her waist. "Samuel, what is it? What's wrong?" Her gaze dropped to his hand. A silver blade glistened in the dim light. "What is that?" A lump of emotion clogged her throat.

Samuel glanced at the blade in his hand, as if he didn't know how it had gotten there. With a tight set of his mouth, he moved his other hand behind him. "You've got to leave things alone."

Rebecca took a step toward him, the wood creaking beneath her.

"Samuel," she pleaded, "please tell me what's going on. Did someone stick a knife in our front door?" A chill raced down her spine.

"Looks that way." His clipped words seemed forced. A cover for his own fear.

"Who would do such a thing? Did they leave a note under the blade?" Had she seen a piece of paper in his other hand?

The soft moonlight slanting through the window caught the naked fear in his eyes. He bowed his head, looking as if he wanted to say something.

"I want to help you," she pleaded. "Tell me."

He straightened. A hard expression darkened his eyes. "Stop asking questions. You're only making matters worse."

Rebecca hugged her arms around her middle. Suddenly, she felt sick. "What am I making worse?"

His stance widened and he pushed back his shoulders. Confident. Strong. Defiant. Her stomach twisted. So much like his father. "Isn't Rumspringa supposed to be a time of freedom for me? Time for me to explore on my own?"

"Is that what this is all about?" She shook her head. She couldn't believe it. "There has to be more to it. We're being harassed. Are people still angry about Willard?"

A muscle worked in his jaw, as if he couldn't find the words.

"Something else is going on. Tell me." She stepped forward and placed her hand gently on his arm, hoping to give him an opening. "Does it have to do with Elmer's death? I know you and he were good friends."

"You're worse than *Dat* in trying to control me."

Rebecca flattened her hands over her heart, feeling as if she had been stabbed. "I know you're hurting, but how could you compare me to your father? He was an evil man." The sting of tears burned the back of her eyes. "You need to apologize."

Samuel's lips thinned into a straight line. This was not the young man she'd raised. *Had Willard damaged him this much?*

A cold realization washed over her. She reached out to touch his arm and then thought better of it. "You are not your father's son. You are not Willard Fisher. You are Samuel. You are growing into a *gut* man." A million thoughts swirled in her brain. "Whatever is going on, I can help you. But you have to confide in me."

Samuel placed the knife on the table, crossed his arms and glared at her.

"If you can't confide in me, confide in Professor Burke."

"So he can tell you?" Samuel bit out the angry words.

"The professor hasn't told me anything. He said he didn't want to betray your trust." She angled her head, trying to get him to meet her eyes, but he seemed more interested in the dark ledge of the first stair. "Please, I want to help you."

Samuel rubbed his hand across his mussed hair. "Elmer lived in our barn after his father kicked him out for doing drugs."

Rebecca held her breath, waiting. "You should have told me. Perhaps I could have talked to his *dat* for him."

Samuel shook his head. "Mr. King was so angry. It wouldn't have mattered." The look of regret, sadness, guilt on her son's face hurt her deeply.

Rebecca softened her voice, longing to ease Samuel's guilt. "*Yah*, you were a *gut* friend. You did what you thought was right." It wasn't unheard of for people to take in their friends by providing a blanket and a soft spot to lay their head. Her son was no different.

Samuel ran a finger under his nose, then pointed upstairs. "All that stuff. The laptop. Everything. It was Elmer's. He asked me to hold it for him until he figured out what he was going to do next."

Relief and shame weighed heavy on her chest.

"You were a *gut* friend," she said again, determined to ease whatever was bothering him.

"No, I wasn't. I knew he was smoking weed the night he got into his car and drove away. It's all my fault."

Rebecca pointed to the knife with its sinister blade resting on the small table. "Is someone threatening you because of Elmer's death?"

"I—I think that's what this is about. Some of the guys have been harassing me. Telling me I should have stopped him from driving." He plowed his hand through his hair again. "But I left him in the barn and came inside. How was I to know he was going to get in the car?"

"You didn't." Rebecca wanted desperately to console him, but she knew he'd pull away. She was just happy he was finally opening up.

"Either way, I think you need to stop asking questions. It's only causing us more problems. People are also still mad about Willard. We have to let it go and then things will die down."

"We can't let people get away with harassing us. When will it stop?"

"Leave it alone, and it will stop." Samuel turned the key on the door, then picked up the knife and carried it into the kitchen. The metal blade clattered against the porcelain sink.

Was Samuel right? If she stopped asking questions, if she ignored the harassment, would whoever was doing this get bored and finally leave her family alone?

She closed her eyes and looked up at the night sky. Her wish was a foolish one.

Jake didn't have to teach his Intro to the Amish class until noon, so he drove out to the Fishers' farm early the next morning, hoping to catch the Yoder brothers and see what they'd been up to last night after they'd raced away from the Sunday singing in a car. He hoped the young Amish men he had gotten to know weren't involved in the horseplay that had gotten Rebecca thrown off her buggy.

A dark foreboding knotted his gut. What if it hadn't been horseplay and they had intentionally tried to hurt Rebecca?

Jake had called Sheriff Maxwell last night to ask if there had been any incidents, car accidents, things along that line, with the Amish last night. The sheriff claimed they hadn't had any calls. It had been a quiet night for the most part. The sheriff said he'd send additional patrols by the Fisher farm. Jake hoped that wouldn't cause more problems between Samuel and Rebecca.

Something about Samuel's evasive answers had kept Jake awake most of the night. The young man was either up to something or afraid of something. Or both. Jake had to get Samuel to trust him enough to open up. But he had to be careful not to alienate him like he had Elmer.

Jake parked on the dirt driveway. When he pushed open his car door, he heard angry voices coming from the barn. Jake couldn't make out the words, just the hostile tone. He broke into a jog and slowed at the doorway. Through the opening, he saw Samuel and Uri Yoder standing inches apart. Samuel had his arm up, ready to strike.

"Hey, hey, hey…" Jake yelled as he stormed into the barn. "What's going on?"

The two young men spun around to face him. Samuel lowered his fist and his shoulders immediately sagged. He crossed his arms and huffed, as if struggling to contain his anger.

"What's going on?" Jake repeated.

An aw-shucks smile spread across Uri's face. He took off his straw hat and rubbed the back of his hand across his forehead. "I mucked out the stalls yesterday and I was trying to get Samuel to take his turn."

Samuel's head snapped up, to call him a liar or perhaps surprised at the comment as if that wasn't what they had been arguing over.

Jake strolled in closer and dared put a hand on both men's shoulders. "What's really going on here?"

Samuel squirmed, stepping away from Jake's touch. "What Uri said. But since we're paying him to work here, he doesn't get to decide what *I* do." He hiked up his chin, daring Uri to defy him. "He and his brother are hired farmhands. We tell them what to do."

Uri pulled away with a hard set of his jaw. He grabbed the pitchfork leaning against the stall. "Yeah, whatever. I thought we were friends."

"Wait up," Jake said to Uri. "Did you hear what happened last night?"

The two young men shared a quick glance that might

have gone unnoticed if Jake hadn't been watching them closely.

"I told him this morning." Samuel glanced at the hay strewn on the barn floor and kicked it around with his boot.

"Is that the first you'd heard of it?" Jake watched Uri's expression carefully.

The young man's eyes narrowed into slits. "Are you accusing me of something? As if this day couldn't get any worse…" Without waiting for an answer, Uri stomped into the horse's stall and lifted a manure pile with the fork and dumped it into a nearby wheelbarrow.

Jake rubbed his jawline, realizing that antagonizing these young men wasn't going to help him and his research or, more important, Rebecca. She needed these young men to harvest the crops or she'd be in serious financial trouble.

Uri swiped his brow with the sleeve of his blue shirt. "I only learned of Mrs. Fisher's accident this morning." He lifted another load into the wheelbarrow.

Jake held his breath against the pungent smell.

"Are you both going to stand there and watch me? I have plenty of work to do and I don't appreciate an audience."

Determined to lighten the mood, Jake said, "You guys free to meet for dinner at the diner? Tonight maybe?"

Samuel lifted a shoulder, then let it drop. "Sure."

Uri set the pitchfork down and rested his elbow on the handle. "Food?" He smiled slyly. "I'm in."

Uri went back to work and Jake led Samuel toward the barn door. "Everything okay here, for real?"

Samuel rolled his eyes. "Yeah, everything's fine."

Jake nodded slowly. "Your *mem* home?"

"Inside making breakfast."

Jake didn't want to get all sentimental and scare the young man away, but he had to keep reminding Samuel that he was available if he needed anything.

Samuel's lips flattened into a thin line. He had re-acted negatively when Jake first told him this. Perhaps the young man didn't want to be reminded that he didn't have a father. Even when he'd had one, the guy wasn't much of a role model.

The delicious scent of bacon filled the small space of Rebecca's kitchen. She lined the strips on a plate, care-ful not to let the grease splash.

Every muscle in her legs, arms and back ached from being thrown from the buggy last night. She was grate-ful the accident hadn't been worse than it had been, but she couldn't forget the angry exchange with Samuel in the middle of the night. Someone had stuck a blade in their front door.

Did it really have to do with Elmer's death? Some-thing niggled at her. What more was Samuel hiding?

She wondered if it was time to call the sheriff, but she was caught between a rock and a hard place. Would Samuel be held responsible because he knew Elmer had been doing drugs before his death? Would Samuel shut down for good if she betrayed his confidence? She drew in a deep breath and let it out.

She couldn't think clearly. She had already lost so much. She tossed the tongs in the sink and glanced out the window. Her heart stuttered in her chest. Dressed in a handsome sport coat and clean shaven, the professor walked across the yard toward the house.

Instinctively, she smoothed what little hair wasn't hidden under her bonnet. She ran a hand down her skirt. When she reached the front door, he was already on the porch.

He tilted his head and a half smile slanted his lips.

Exactly what she didn't need.

"I didn't expect you this morning." She hoped her expression was inscrutable.

"How are you?"

Rebecca moved her arms as if to remind herself that her muscles did indeed still ache. "A little sore. But at least I'm in one piece…and dry." She ran a finger under her chin. "Were you in the barn?"

The professor nodded. "I paid a visit to Samuel and Uri. They seemed to be having a disagreement over chores."

"Hmm? That's unusual." Her mind went to Samuel's sour mood last night.

He took a step forward, the wood creaking under his weight. "What's on your mind?"

Rebecca worried her lower lip. "Someone stuck a knife in the door last night." She turned and ran her fingers over the small scar the knife had left.

Worry creased the corner of his eyes. "That's odd."

"I thought so, too." Rebecca nodded toward the inside. "Come in. I don't want Samuel to overhear."

They walked into the kitchen, and she encouraged the professor to sit while she started the coffee. The smell of freshly cooked bacon and eggs hung in the air.

"Samuel finally opened up to me and I need someone

objective to help me decide how to handle this." She had never expected to be a single parent.

She paused and pressed her lips into a thin line. "You have to promise me to keep this in confidence."

The professor gave her a quick nod.

"Samuel feels guilty because Elmer was living in our barn after his father kicked him out. He knew Elmer was on drugs the night he died."

"You had no idea Elmer was staying in your barn?"

"*Neh*. None. And Samuel claims all the electronics in his room belonged to Elmer."

"Did Samuel have an explanation for the knife in the door?"

"He thinks people are blaming him for Elmer's death with some residual anger about Willard. That if I stop asking questions, things will quietly go back to normal."

The professor got a faraway look in his eyes, as if he were processing all the information. "Samuel must think it's one of the *youngie* harassing you. Why else would he tell you to stop asking questions? Your questions led me to go to the Sunday singing."

A headache started behind her eyes. "What are they trying to hide?"

"Drug use? Or are they just angry and lashing out?"

She lifted a shaky hand to her collar, suddenly feeling very hot in her small kitchen. "I don't know. I don't know anything anymore."

"Do *you* think Samuel is into drugs?"

All the color drained from her already pale face. Isn't that why she had gone to the professor initially? To find out what was going on with Samuel, even if it included drugs.

"I don't know. I pray he isn't," she whispered.

The sound of footsteps on the back porch had Rebecca swiping at unseen tears. Uri and Samuel burst through the back door.

"Breakfast is ready." She glanced at Uri and Samuel. "Where's Jonas?"

"He'll be in shortly," Uri said. He smiled at Rebecca, and washed his hands at the sink. "Everything looks great, Mrs. Fisher."

"Eat up. I know you boys have more work once you get home to your own farm."

The boys filled their plates and sat down.

"Working the land is *gut*. I feel close to *Gott*." Uri rubbed his hands together before picking up a piece of bacon and biting into it.

"Would you like to eat, Professor?"

He smiled at her and nodded. "Thank you." He filled a plate and took a seat at the head of the table. No one had sat in Willard's chair since he had left. The sensation that rolled over her was a strange one. She turned toward the counter and collected herself before joining everyone at the table.

They bowed their heads in silent prayer. A few minutes later, Jonas walked through the back door. "Sorry, my chores took a little bit longer this morning." He washed his hands, then sat to eat, too.

"Where are the little ones?" Jonas asked, curiosity in his eyes.

"They spent the night with their cousins."

"Oh."

The empty chairs at the table emphasized her daughters' absence. She missed her little girls. She hoped the day at the diner went quickly so she could pick up her daughters and bring them home. She felt out of sorts with her family scattered. She looked at Samuel who ate silently, a forlorn expression on his face.

And the one who was here seemed the farthest away.

Chapter Six

"I was hoping I'd see you here." Hannah Spencer strolled into the diner midafternoon. She had a shopping bag in each hand.

"Nice to see you." Rebecca always felt a sense of loss when she saw her old friend. They were still friendly, but not like they had been while growing up. How could they be? Rebecca's husband had killed Hannah's sister and brother-in-law. No amount of time would allow either of them to forget that.

Hannah sat down at the counter and glanced around. "Place is quiet."

"Usually is around now. It's the lull between lunch and dinner." Rebecca grabbed a mug and poured a cup of coffee for her friend.

Hannah took a long sip. "Ahh...just how I like it."

Rebecca wiped the counter, mostly for something to do.

Flo grabbed a couple empty mugs from the other side of the counter and lifted them in greeting. "I'm going to take a short break before the dinner crowd starts rolling in." She turned and pushed open the door into the kitchen with her shoulder. As it swung back, the hinges creaked until the door finally stopped.

Hannah caught Rebecca's hand and squeezed it. "You seem…tired, sad." She tilted her head. "Is there anything I can do to help?"

Rebecca glanced over her shoulder, trying to hide her emotions. Hannah was such a dear friend and she really missed her. Had missed her long before she'd left to marry Spencer. Hannah had run away from the Amish as a teenager only to return when her sister Ruth had been killed. By then, Willard had made it nearly impossible for Rebecca to have friends.

"I'll be okay." Rebecca fidgeted with the metal napkin holder, grabbing a stack of napkins from under the counter and refilling it.

Would she ever shake this guilt?

Rebecca looked at her friend, who was studying her. "How are things with you? Are you happy?" The question flew out of her mouth before she had a chance to call it back.

Hannah's brow creased. She tucked a strand of her neatly bobbed hair behind her ear and leaned forward. Probably a throwback to her Amish days, she didn't wear any makeup, yet she was one of the prettiest women Rebecca knew. Or maybe it was her personality Rebecca had always been drawn to.

"Yes, I'm very happy. I'd worried about the girls adjusting, but they seem to be doing well."

Rebecca ran her hand along the molded edge of the countertop. "Everyone has been through so much. I feel selfish for only thinking of my own problems." It wasn't the Amish way. The Amish considered community and not individuality.

Rebecca noticed a puddle of water on the counter, so she picked up the dishtowel and wiped it up. Then, twisting the towel in her hands, she said, "Maybe I should leave Apple Creek. Take the girls—Samuel if he'll go—and make a fresh start in another Amish community." She stared off into the middle distance, not really aware of her surroundings. "I could move closer to Rochester. There are a few Amish church districts that are in fellowship with Apple Creek."

Hannah reached out and clutched her friend's hand. "Oh, you can't run away. We'd miss you too much. Apple Creek is your home."

Hannah's voice grew soft. "This *is* your home."

Rebecca's friend's face grew blurry. "It doesn't feel like home anymore."

Jake smiled as Rebecca approached their table that evening. She handed a menu to him and Samuel. "Are you expecting anyone else?" she asked, all business.

"Yes." Jake held up three fingers. "Three more."

She set three extra plastic menus at the edge of the table. "I'll be right back with the silverware and water."

"Thank you," both men said in unison.

Rebecca turned and walked away.

Resting his forearms on the edge of the table, Jake leaned toward Samuel and lowered his voice. "You have no reason to feel guilty over Elmer's death."

Samuel's mouth fell open, then his posture sagged. "Of course my *mem* told you everything."

"She's worried about you."

The young man rolled his eyes.

Jake tapped his fingers on the table, trying to figure out how to broach the subject. *Be direct.*

"If anyone should feel guilty, it's me."

Samuel slowly met Jake's gaze but didn't say anything.

"During one of our meetings, I sensed Elmer was high. I confronted him. At first Elmer denied it, but then he finally told me he was just—" Jake lifted his hands to use air quotes "—smoking a little pot. No biggie."

Jake ran a hand across his face, then glanced over his shoulder to make sure Rebecca wasn't coming. "I forced him to tell his father."

Samuel tucked his chin closer to his chest and a deep line furrowed his brow in disbelief. "Why would you do that?"

"I watched my own father die from addiction. Alcohol." Jake slowly shook his head, reliving every misstep he had taken with Elmer. "I thought I was doing the right thing." He shrugged, hoping the nonchalant gesture would ease the weight bearing down on his chest. "But as you know, his father kicked him out. He spiraled downward from there." He studied the palm of his hand, unable to look into Samuel's eyes. "If anyone's to blame, it's me."

Samuel let out a long breath.

Jake finally lifted his head and pinned the young man across from him with his gaze. "I want you to know that if you need someone to talk to I'm here. Guilt is an unrelenting companion."

The young man snorted. "You'll tell my *mem*."

Jake shook his head. "Not if you don't want me to."

He set his clasped hands in front of him on the table. "If you're caught up in drugs, I want to help you."

"Wait a minute—" Samuel stopped whatever he was about to say. Jake glanced over his shoulder and saw Rebecca returning with a tray of glasses filled with ice water.

Just then the door opened and Tommy, Jake's teaching assistant, strolled into the diner and slipped into the seat next to Samuel.

Rebecca smiled. "I'll give you a few minutes to read the menu." Jake suspected that no one who frequented the Apple Creek Diner actually needed to consult the menu.

A muscle ticked in Samuel's jaw and Jake regretted that they hadn't had a couple more minutes to talk in private.

Fidgeting in his seat as if he had somewhere else to go, Tommy drummed his fingers on the plastic menu. "Uri called me a few minutes ago. He and Jonas can't make it. They had some chores at home."

"Maybe we should meet another time." Samuel suddenly seemed agitated, glancing over his shoulder at the window.

Jake smiled. "You need to eat anyway, right? We'll meet again when the Yoder brothers are free."

Samuel slumped back in the booth and crossed his arms over his chest. "Yeah, I guess."

Rebecca approached the table, holding a pen and pad in her hands. "Ready to order or are you still waiting for more guests?"

"Change of plans. It'll be just us."

The three men placed their orders. Rebecca caught Jake's eye and he smiled. "Thank you."

Her pale cheeks flushed before she turned to put the orders in.

Jake took a sip of his water and watched Samuel over the rim of his glass. He wondered if they'd ever get to finish that conversation. Had Samuel been about to open up to him?

At a nearby table, a college student waved his hand eagerly, trying to get Rebecca's attention. "Um, we'd like to order, like, sometime this week."

"I hate that my *mem* has to work here," Samuel said. "She shouldn't have to. My father ruined everything."

"You have to forgive him. Move on," Jake suggested.

Samuel furrowed his brows. "Maybe it's time I jumped the fence," he said, using the term the Amish had for leaving the community. The distant look in his brown eyes suggested he was already envisioning it.

Jake watched Rebecca lift a hold-on-a-minute finger to the college student before tacking their order onto the silver wheel above the window leading into the kitchen of the old-fashioned diner. She then refilled the coffee mug of a gentleman sitting at the counter. She smiled and made small talk with the man before making her way over to the table of college students.

Jake smiled inwardly. She'd handled the rude customer with quiet aplomb.

He turned his attention back to Samuel. "Your *mem* would be devastated if you left." Jake hated to heap guilt on this young man, but he needed to know. "Make sure your decisions are for the right reasons. Give it some time. You're still grieving over your friend."

"Leaving isn't always the best answer." Tommy tore off the wrapper to the straw, leaving the tip in place. "I mean," he said, then blew the last bit of paper off his straw, "the grass ain't always greener on the other side. I've had to work my butt off to make money to pay for college."

Jake was ready to quip that he didn't work Tommy *that* hard but decided to let it go. He wanted to hear what Tommy had to say as someone who had walked away from the Amish way of life.

Tommy took a sip of his water through the straw, watching Samuel carefully. "You have an eighth-grade education. What kind of job do you think you're going to get—" he gestured with his chin toward the window "—out there? Do you know how hard it is to get a job? A good paying job?" He stabbed the ice with the straw. The ice clattered against the glass. "Even if you get a job, do you think you can support yourself and a family?" He laughed and shook his head.

"I can work with my hands," Samuel said. "There are several successful Amish businesses in town."

"But you won't be Amish anymore," Tommy said, twisting his lips. "Once you leave small-town Apple Creek, you'd be surprised at how many businesses require a four-year degree to allow you to work with your hands."

Samuel groaned.

This was exactly the complaint Jake's father had had after leaving the Amish. He hadn't been able to get a decent job and what little money he had managed to make he spent on liquor.

"It was a lot of work for me to get my GED and then

get into college. Do you think college is cheap?" Tommy shook his head dramatically. "Nope, now I gotta pay for college. Sure, I'll be done in June, but it's been a long road. Now I got loans to pay back. Don't go thinking running away from home is going to solve your problems."

Silence settled over the table. Jake was surprised to hear his assistant talk this bluntly. Normally, Tommy talked fondly about his experiences as an *Englisher.* How he was happy to escape the mind-numbing tedium of life on a farm.

To each his own, Jake supposed. Letting Samuel know the stark reality of leaving was a good idea.

Rebecca returned with their food and left just as quickly. Perhaps she was hoping her son was confiding in Jake so he could help him.

"How long have you been gone?" Samuel asked Tommy, genuine curiosity in his tone.

Tommy squirted ketchup onto his plate, picked up a French fry and swirled it in the red blob. "I left when I was eighteen. Had to work a bunch of meaningless jobs to pay the rent, buy food…" He took a bite out of his French fry "I studied for two years to get my high school GED. Another year to get accepted to Genwego State University. Now I'm a senior." He exhaled. "It's been a long road."

"If *you* can do it, I can…" Samuel started. The desperation in his voice caught Jake off guard.

Tommy lifted his eyes to Rebecca, who was hustling from table to table in the busy dining room. "Like Professor Burke said, your *mem* would be devastated. Why don't you lay low for a while? *Really* think about it. Like I said, the grass isn't always greener."

Samuel slouched into the booth again, seemingly agitated. "I need to get away. To protect my *mem*. My little sisters." He lifted his backside off the bench and handed a wadded piece of paper to Jake. "Last night, someone stuck a knife into the front door."

"Your *mem* told me," Jake said.

Samuel nodded, as if this didn't surprise him.

"This was left under the knife. I didn't show her."

Jake met the young man's gaze, then smoothed out the piece of paper.

Keep your mouth shut.

Samuel bit his lower lip, struggling to contain his emotions.

"Are they referring to you or your mother?"

"I… I think me," Samuel said. "I believe it was one of the Yoder brothers."

Jake tugged on the collar of his shirt. "Is that why you were fighting this morning in the barn?"

Samuel nodded. "Uri denied he left the note. Told me I was crazy."

Tommy's expression remained placid.

"Why would the Yoder brothers want you to keep your mouth shut?" Jake watched Samuel carefully.

"They're…" Samuel's voice wavered as if he was having second thoughts. "…They're growing marijuana on our farm."

A loud crash made Jake spin around.

Rebecca's scalp tingled as she stared down at the white shards of what had once been ceramic plates, mingled with French fries, buns and hamburger patties.

She bent over and scrambled to pick up the mess, her

thoughts all jumbled. "I'm sorry. So, sorry," she muttered to the patrons at the booth next to her son's. The voices and sounds of the diner swirled around her, growing more distant and fuzzy. Blinking did nothing to tamp down the dizziness.

She glanced toward the kitchen, waiting for her boss to storm out in full rant mode. She had never dropped a platter of dishes before.

Had she misheard? Uri and Jonas were growing marijuana on her farm?

The few French fries she had snacked on earlier revolted in her stomach.

A solid hand cupped her elbow. Rebecca looked up into the professor's warm brown eyes. "Come on." He eased her to a standing position. "Come over here. Sit down."

"I can't. I have to clean up this mess." She stared at the broken plate in one hand and the leaf of lettuce in the other. A throbbing pain started behind her eyes.

The professor took the piece of ceramic out of her hand. "It can wait." He guided her to the seat he had vacated. She dropped the lettuce on a napkin and lifted her gaze to her son.

Rebecca threaded her fingers, leaned forward and whispered. "What did you say?" She fought the hysteria welling up inside her, unwilling to make more of a spectacle of herself. She was tired of being a spectacle.

Samuel leaned across the table, desperation in his voice. "Uri and Jonas are growing marijuana plants on our land." He lowered his head and furtively glanced around the diner.

Rebecca did the same. Several diners were staring at

their table. A busboy was cleaning up the mess she had made. Rebecca leaned past the professor and touched the young man's shoulder. "Thank you, Jason. I was clumsy."

The young man smiled. "No problem, Mrs. Fisher. I got it." He put the last remnant of the ruined dinner in a large gray bus tub. "I'll sweep up the rest."

Rebecca looked up, confusion swirling around her head. "Oh, I need to apologize to the table for dropping their food. I need—"

He touched her hand. "Hold on."

She stared at him, but couldn't really see him. Her mind was reeling.

Flo strolled over and smiled. "I'll take care of the table. Don't worry."

Tears stung the back of Rebecca's nose. "Thank you."

As the other diners seemed to go back to their meals and the din in the diner returned to its normal level, Rebecca kept her voice low, confident no one would overhear her. "Why did you let them?" she asked Samuel.

Hurt lingered in her son's eyes. "I didn't. I only figured out what they were doing a few months ago. Shortly before Elmer's accident." He bowed his head, then looked back up. "That's why I felt bad about Elmer. It wasn't simply because I knew he was doing drugs. It was because I didn't stop Uri and Jonas for providing him with drugs."

All the color seemed to have drained out of Samuel's face. "I'm sorry I wasn't completely honest with you, *Mem*."

"How did you figure out they were growing marijuana?" Tommy spoke for the first time.

"Elmer was living in our barn and he asked me for drugs."

Rebecca pressed her fingers into her temples.

"I had no idea what he was talking about. Elmer told me the plants weren't ready yet, but Uri had some drugs on him to sell," Samuel continued. "I don't know where he got them. Maybe they used someone else's land before ours."

"I don't understand any of this."

"I should have told someone. Maybe Elmer wouldn't have died."

"And you saw the plants?" Tommy asked.

Samuel scrubbed a hand across his face and frowned. "Elmer showed me. He led me through the cornfields. In the far back corner of the field, I found them. There were these plants, plants like I had never seen."

"How did you know what they were?" Tommy asked, pushing his empty plate to the center of the table.

Samuel's cheeks flushed. "I took a picture of them with my phone and then did a Google search."

Rebecca ran a hand across her forehead. She had no idea what he was talking about. Her mouth grew dry. "Why didn't you tell me?"

"They told me they wouldn't do it again. I had to keep quiet through harvest season.

"Then, a few days later Elmer died. They warned me if I told anyone about the marijuana, people would blame me for Elmer's death. That law enforcement would take away our land."

"Did you threaten you to keep you quiet?" the professor asked.

"They bribed me by giving me things." Deep lines

marred his forehead. "Like the laptop. My cell phone." He averted his gaze. "They weren't Elmer's things. I wasn't truthful last night, *Mem*. I just wanted all this to stop."

Rebecca's pulse beat loudly in her ears.

"I should have told you, but I got caught up in the lies and I was afraid. I'm sorry." He pushed his hand through his hair, leaving it standing up, reminding Rebecca of the little boy who used to come downstairs in his night clothes asking for apple biscuits. What she wouldn't do to go back to those days.

"But my conscience started to bother me. I thought I'd be no better than my…than Willard. I didn't want to get Jonas and Uri in trouble. I told them they had to destroy the crops. Get them off our property."

"How did they respond?" Tommy asked, pulling his cell phone out and checking the screen.

Samuel bowed his head. "They threatened *Mem* if I didn't allow the plants to come to harvest. When you started asking around, they started scaring you. I fear they ran you off the road last night, but I promise you, I wasn't in the car."

How could these boys she'd welcomed into her home try to hurt her?

Rebecca closed her eyes briefly. Fear and confusion gave way to a strange sense of relief. "You did the right thing. Now I can go to Mr. and Mrs. Yoder. They're good people. They'll get their sons to listen. Get them to obey."

Samuel looked up, an air of disbelief in his expression. "That's not going to work."

"We have to do something," Rebecca said in a soft voice.

"We should call the sheriff," the professor said.

Rebecca shook her head adamantly. "*Neh*. We can't call the sheriff. I don't want to get the boys in trouble with law enforcement. It's not the Amish way."

"What they did is illegal," the professor said.

"We need to approach their parents first. Mr. Yoder will rein his sons in. I know it."

The professor stared at her for a minute before nodding. "We'll start with the parents, but I can't promise you we won't call the sheriff."

Chapter Seven

Jake climbed into his truck and looked in the rearview mirror. He could see Samuel in the backseat of the extended cab, staring out the window, an unreadable expression on his face.

"It's going to be okay, Samuel." Rebecca buckled her seat belt and slumped into the seat next to Jake. The smell of French fries clung to her clothes. "You did the right thing by telling us. Everything is going to be okay." Her statement sounded more like a question, suggesting she had no idea if everything was going to be okay. If only Jake could give her assurances.

Rebecca turned to Jake. "Thanks for the ride. It saves me paying the hired driver. Are you sure it's not too much trouble to pick up my daughters after we speak to Mr. Yoder?"

"No trouble at all."

When Tommy came out of the diner after paying the bill with Jake's credit card, Jake lowered the driver's side window. Tommy handed the card to him and said, "I'm going to bum a ride from one of my friends back to the university." Tommy leaned in and smiled weakly at Samuel in the backseat. He lowered his voice. "I'd rather not get caught up in all this… I think if I keep some distance, we won't jeopardize my association with the Amish."

"Have a good night, then." Jake watched Tommy, dressed in jeans and a university sweatshirt, stroll away. Jake had a hard time imagining Tommy growing up Amish. He had a worldly way about him.

Jake rolled up the window and pulled out onto Main Street. The silence in the truck was like a fourth occupant who couldn't be ignored.

When his truck crested the country road, Jake glanced in the rearview mirror and studied an unsuspecting Samuel. The young Amish man took off his hat and scrubbed a hand over his hair. The lines around his eyes revealed his stress.

"I'm not sure I'm ready to talk to the Yoders. Are we doing the right thing?" Rebecca asked in a soft voice laced with concern and worry.

Jake wanted to reassure her, tell her everything was going to be fine, but he knew they had a rough road ahead of them. "It's a start, but I'd feel better if we had called the sheriff."

"Not yet. Let's keep this matter among the Amish." She gave Jake a pointed glare. Jake, who was clearly not Amish.

Samuel made a disagreeable noise. "What have I done?" he muttered. "I should have kept quiet."

"You couldn't keep going on this way. You haven't been yourself. You've done the right thing. We'll help you straighten out this mess. *Without* the sheriff," Rebecca added for emphasis.

Jake parked in front of the Yoders' farm. "You can wait here." Jake felt strangely protective of Rebecca.

"No, I need to talk to the Yoders myself. I've known them for a long time. They've known my family."

Samuel didn't say anything as he climbed out of the truck.

A soft light glowed in the front window. Jake smiled at Samuel, trying to reassure him.

Jake knocked, and a few seconds later an older gentleman opened the door. "*Yah?* How can I help you?" The line between his eyes eased when he noticed Rebecca. "Rebecca, is something wrong?"

"Are Uri and Jonas home?" she asked, a hint of apology in her tone.

Mr. Yoder fingered his unkempt beard. "*Yah*, we're finishing our meal." He turned away from the door without inviting them in. From inside, Jake heard a lot of commotion, perhaps standard when a family had ten children.

Jake's stomach pitched. It had been a little over three months ago when he pushed Elmer to go to his father regarding his drug use. Jake never could have imagined the series of events that would follow, ending in tragedy. And here he was, an outsider standing on his Amish neighbor's stoop.

Uri appeared at the door with an innocent-looking expression. "What's going on?"

"Where's your brother?"

Uri grabbed the door and opened it wider. Jonas stood next to his father. His expression was less cocky than his brother's.

"What's going on?" Mr. Yoder asked with a strong Pennsylvania Dutch accent.

"We believe your sons have been growing marijuana on Rebecca's farm."

Mr. Yoder pulled his head back. A look of confusion and fear crossed his dark eyes. "Growing what?"

"Marijuana," Samuel spoke up for the first time. "They plan on selling it and making a lot of money."

A muscle ticked in Uri's jaw and Jonas gave his brother a sideways glance.

Mr. Yoder turned to face his sons. "Is this true?" Without waiting for an answer, he turned back to Rebecca. "Who told you my sons planted this marijuana?"

"*My* son." Rebecca played with the folds of her gown.

"*Dat*, me and Jonas had nothing to do with those crops."

"You knew about the marijuana?" his father asked accusingly.

"I didn't know what it was until Samuel told me."

"That's not true," Samuel bit out. "That's not true at all."

Uri turned to his father, a dark look in his eyes. "*Dat*, I have never lied to you. I was afraid to say anything for fear we'd be fired. Jonas and I know how much this family needs the extra money from our work as farmhands."

Mr. Yoder flinched.

Uri bowed his head contritely. "Who are you going to believe? Me or Samuel, *Willard Fisher's* son?"

Rebecca stumbled backward and Jake grabbed her arm to steady her. "Keep calm," he whispered close to her ear.

Mr. Yoder ran his hand down his beard again. "The

crops are on *your farm*, Rebecca. Don't come here and accuse my boys of these things. They are *gut* boys." Mr. Yoder hiked his chin. "I think it's time you left."

Mr. Yoder stepped out onto the porch and pulled the door closed behind him, leaving his sons inside.

"My son isn't lying," Rebecca said. "Your sons have taken advantage of my situation and used my land to grow marijuana."

Mr. Yoder pinched his lips together and shook his head. "I suggest you leave before I call the sheriff."

Jake squeezed Rebecca's elbow. "Let's go."

She yanked her elbow away. "Mr. Yoder," she pleaded.

Mr. Yoder stood his ground. "Sounds like a convenient excuse. How do you know Samuel's not looking for a way out?" The anger flashed in the older man's eyes.

"*Mem*, I had nothing to do with those crops."

"I suggest you get your son under control." Mr. Yoder paused a long few seconds. "My sons won't be working on your farm any longer. It seems your family is a bad influence." And with that, he shut the door on the conversation.

With a firm hand to the small of her back, Jake led Rebecca to his truck. When Samuel didn't follow, Jake called to him over his shoulder. *"Let's go."* Jake didn't want any more trouble tonight that would require either him or the Yoders to call the sheriff. "We have to pick up your sisters."

Right now it was their word against Samuel's, and after recent events, the sheriff might be more likely to believe the Yoders.

That night in bed, Rebecca tossed and turned, a million things going through her mind. What if Samuel was lying? What if he had been looking for a way out and decided to pin his mistake on the Yoders? What if he was growing the marijuana?

Willard had committed murder under her watch and she'd had no idea.

Rebecca rolled over and punched her pillow. She felt sick.

After everything Willard had done to put her family in a bad light, how could she and Samuel convince anyone he was telling the truth? *If* he was telling the truth. Her family wasn't exactly well respected in the Amish community.

Feeling queasy, Rebecca propped up her pillows, hoping that would help. She took a deep breath.

Nothing would help.

Rebecca had hoped Samuel would confide in her once she put her daughters to bed, but he had retreated to his room and slammed the door.

Nothing—yet everything—had changed.

A tear slid down her cheek and plopped on the pillow. She felt as if her relationship with Samuel was beyond repair.

Could she ever reach him now?

Closing her eyes, she tried to relax and think of her blessings: Katie and Grace. Rebecca wanted to hold everyone she loved close. As if that could stop her world from spinning out of control.

The fierce protectiveness she felt for her family was also reminiscent of the days after Willard's arrest. Yet, after her husband had been arrested, Rebecca also had felt a strange sense of freedom, unlike she'd ever had.

Had this freedom ruined Samuel?

Rebecca pulled her quilt up to her chin and smoothed the fabric, running her fingers along the careful stitching she and her mother had done back when Rebecca still had dreams of a happy marriage and a quiet life in Apple Creek.

Her life had turned out nothing like she had planned.

No one planned to marry a murderer.

Rebecca closed her eyes. Sweet, handsome Jake filled her mind. *The professor.* She didn't know if she'd ever be able to call him anything else. She felt that she'd be breaching the social norms if she called him Jake.

Jake. Jacob.

Nervousness tingled across her skin. The professor had told her he'd be back tomorrow between the classes he taught at the university. They could plan their next steps then. He promised he wouldn't call the sheriff, and she only prayed the Yoders didn't either. It was unlikely; the Amish preferred to handle things on their own.

A new surge of adrenaline made her restless. Rebecca tossed back the covers and swung her legs over the edge. She hated that she doubted her son. She closed her eyes and prayed for God's guidance. And for help in believing in a young man she had grown to consider her son.

Maybe her influence had come too late.

Pacing the hardwood floor, she suddenly had the urge to do something. She could no longer lead a passive life waiting for her world to implode. Waiting for someone to help her. She had to help herself.

Help her family.

She pulled back the curtain on the window. A bright moon and a million stars dotted the night sky. Besides the barn and a few outbuildings, all she could see were the crops. Acres and acres of corn.

And marijuana.

Dressed in her nightclothes, she slipped into her young daughters' bedroom and kissed each of them on the forehead, breathing in their fresh scent. Her daughters consistently brought her joy and she'd do whatever it took to protect them from further hurt.

She passed Samuel's closed door, lingering long enough to drag her fingers along the cool wood.

Oh, Samuel, I wish you'd come to me a long time ago. Now I don't know what to believe...

The wood on the stairs creaked under her weight as she descended to the first floor, her hand gliding along the smooth banister, the one her children's great-grandfather had carved. The rock solidness of her life, the one built on the foundation of her family's Amish ancestors, was crumbling around her.

Rebecca yanked her coat from the hook by the back door, slipped her bare feet into her cold boots and stepped out onto the back porch. The fall air smelled crisp. Fresh. Refreshing.

She'd never be happy anywhere but here. On a farm. Close to God's creation. The moonlight glowed brightly in the night sky, casting the crops in a white glow.

Before she lost her nerve, she strode to the barn. She pulled back the heavy door and stepped inside, slivers of moonlight glinting in between the wood slats. Buttercup neighed at her intrusion before settling back in.

Crossing to the back of the barn where Willard had kept his tools, she grabbed a sickle from its hook. She wondered if there was a better tool, but decided this would have to do. Growing up on a farm, she wasn't un-familiar with the tools, she just wasn't as experienced with using them as her older brothers had been.

Gripping the wood handle tightly in her right hand, she trudged toward the cornfields. Based on Samuel's description, the evil drugs should be hidden in the far corner of the field where her property ended and a thick lot of trees started.

Holding the sickle by her side, she held her left hand out to push aside the stalks as she strode deeper into the fields. The earth shifted under her footsteps, adding to her sense of unsteadiness. Somewhere in the distance, she heard the *hoot-hoot-hoot* of an owl.

Goose bumps raced across her flesh. She slowed her pace and turned around, unsure if the sounds she heard were of her own making or if they were out of place.

A giggle bubbled up. *Out of place?* There was nothing about this entire scene that made sense. Nerves implored her to go back home. Crawl into bed and cover her head. To never get out of bed again.

"No, I'm going to do this," she muttered. "I'm going to protect my family."

Tightening her grip on the sickle, she turned and walked forward. Her sense of hopelessness had been replaced by something else. Confidence. Assuredness. Determination.

She could do something. Help Samuel.

Just as Samuel had said, tall bushy plants grew where the corn stopped. *This must be the marijuana.* Feeling their soft leaves, a hint of citrus tickled her nose. How dare the Yoder boys betray her trust and use her land to grow drugs.

The tired, weary face of Mrs. King slammed into her memory. Poor Elmer had been high on drugs when he'd crashed his car into a tree.

Rebecca feared she was going to be sick. She focused all her attention on calming breaths until her stomach settled.

A new emotion, one she hadn't allowed herself to feel when Willard was arrested, washed over her. *Rage*.

She lifted the solid sickle and whacked at the thick stem of the unfamiliar plants. The sharp blade sliced through the stem, felling the plant. She lifted her hand again and again.

Thwack. Thwack. Thwack.

The plants rustled as they fell.

The muscles in her shoulders and arms began to ache. Tears streaming down her cheeks, she tossed the sickle aside. Hands planted on her hips, she studied her destruction. She had barely made a dent in the illegal crops.

Rebecca pressed her lips together and lifted her eyes. The first hint of a new dawn touched the sky. She rolled her shoulders back, trying to ease the tension.

A strangled cry sounded behind her. Slowly she turned and a dark figure advanced on her.

"Samuel?"

A scream got trapped in her throat. The figure lifted his hand.

Rebecca lifted her arms to defend against the blow.

She was no match.

The pain on the top of her head was the last thing she remembered as her knees buckled and the earth rushed up to meet her.

* * *

Jake jumped into his truck as soon as he had gotten the phone call from Samuel. Rebecca's son had woken up to his little sisters' tears because they couldn't find their mother.

Jake exceeded the speed limit, the engine in his old truck straining to keep pace. He offered a prayer, the first he could remember since childhood, that Rebecca was safe. Perhaps Samuel had been lax in his search for his mother and she was safe. The knot twisted in his gut. Or had someone retaliated against her because of her inquiries?

He shook his head. He couldn't think the worst.

Once he arrived at Rebecca's home, he ran up to the porch. Samuel opened the door before Jake had a chance to knock.

"Has your mom returned?"

Samuel had his hand on Grace's shoulder. Katie hung back, her face stained with tears.

"No. I checked the barn, but I didn't want to leave my sisters for too long. It's unlike *Mem* to leave the girls without asking me to watch them. They're only six and eight."

Jake turned and gazed out over the land. Sun peaked over the horizon. The promise of a beautiful new day was at odds with this horrible sense of foreboding.

Really, she could be anywhere: the barn, the fields, or maybe she *had* gone out. But a tiny whisper in his brain grew louder by the second. *Something's happened to Rebecca!*

Jake clamped his jaw, not wanting to alarm the young girls. "When was the last time you saw your mother?"

After they all came to the consensus that they hadn't seen their mother since they had gone to bed last night, Jake told Samuel to stay inside the house with his little sisters while he went outside to look for her.

"Maybe you missed her when you checked the barn earlier. Could she be milking a cow?"

Katie, the older of the two girls, tilted her head and scrunched up her nose. "We don't have a cow. *Mem* brings milk home from the market now. It's easier. We have an icebox."

"Well, maybe she's checking on Buttercup."

The younger of the two took a step forward, eager for an adventure. "Let me come with you. I like to give Buttercup carrots."

Jake reached out and touched the top of the young girl's soft hair and smiled. "Later, okay."

Grace pouted and spun on her heels, her loose curls flying out behind her.

"Stay here." Jake locked gazes with Samuel. "I'll be right back."

Jake jogged down the steps and toward the barn, calling Rebecca's name. Disquiet crept into his bones and he worried he hadn't done enough to keep Rebecca safe. He also began to wonder how he had allowed himself to become so involved with his Amish neighbors when his intent had been to learn about them, not become entangled in their lives.

He supposed his mission was irrevocably intertwined.

Jake wiped a bead of sweat trickling down his forehead.

Where would she have gone?

"I'm sick of doing nothing." Rebecca's words from

last night pinged around his brain. "I'm tired of feeling hopeless. Of not being able to keep my family together."

Jake knew she wouldn't hurt herself, but the worry kept resurfacing. He thought of his own father, who drank himself to death after Jake's mother died. Some people couldn't see past their own grief.

Scrubbing a hand across his face, he had an inkling she might have gone in search of the marijuana crops. He jogged toward the cornstalks. To the far corner of the lot. To where Samuel had claimed the Yoder brothers had planted the marijuana.

Something was drawing him there.

Still calling her name, Jake ran through the stalks, the smell of earth and dried corn filling his nose. Then, suddenly the corn ended and a different kind of plant started.

A rock solidified in his gut. It looked as if someone had been hacking away at the plants.

"Rebecca?" he called again, the frantic whoosh of his pulse drowning out any possible answer.

Jake took a few more cautious steps.

"God, help me find her," he finally muttered, the words feeling foreign on his lips. "Rebecca, where are you?"

As Jake pushed through the plants, he heard a soft moan.

He stopped, his heart pounding against his chest. "Rebecca?"

He strained to hear. The moan came again. He spun around and ran to the pile of felled marijuana plants. He found Rebecca lying there, her face covered in blood.

In a frenzy, he tossed aside the plants and knelt down beside a battered and bloodied Rebecca.

Gingerly, he swept her hair out of her eyes, tugging it away from the dried blood. "Can you hear me?"

Her eyes fluttered but didn't open. *She's not dead. There's hope. Thank you, God.*

Jake reached down and grabbed her hand and squeezed. "I'm here. You're going to be okay." With his other hand, he reached into his back pocket. "I'm going to call an ambulance."

Chapter Eight

A persistent tugging near Rebecca's forehead nudged her out of the blackness. She focused all her energy on opening her eyes, but they wouldn't budge. A strong citrusy-grass smell clogged her nose.

Why can't I open my eyes?

She craned her neck and a horrible pain sliced through her head. She tried to lift her hand to touch it, but her limbs didn't want to cooperate.

A familiar soothing voice threaded into her subconscious. *I'm here... You're going to be okay...*

She finally pried her eyes open a sliver and the line of light made her brain explode. Instinctively, she snapped her eyes shut again and groaned.

A warm hand squeezed hers. "Take it easy. Don't try to move. I've called for an ambulance."

Dread squirmed its way in to keep her fear and queasiness company.

Rebecca's mouth grew dry. *"Neh..."*

"Don't try to talk."

She shook her head slowly and immediately realized

her mistake. She pressed her lips together against the nausea.

"No ambulance," she finally whispered, her voice raspy. "No police."

The professor dragged his warm thumb gently across her cheek. The small gesture provided comfort. She couldn't remember what happened. One minute she was hacking away at the marijuana plants and then...

Closing her eyes, flashes of memory assaulted her. Standing in the field admiring the first hint of early morning sky. Turning around. A dark shadow.

Samuel?

Her stomach revolted at the thought of her own son striking her.

Neh, neh. Rebecca refused to believe that.

She covered her mouth, as if she feared his name might slip past her lips.

"What is it?" the professor said in a soothing voice. "Do you know who did this to you?"

"*Neh.* Please..." She tried to sit up again and he touched her shoulder.

"You have to wait for the ambulance. It's not safe to move since I don't know if anything's broken."

"Don't you understand?" Her voice came out raspy. "You can't call an ambulance...the sheriff will come. The plants."

"Your well-being is more important," the professor said.

"Help me get to the house so the sheriff won't see what's back here." Her brain hurt with the effort of every word.

Kneeling over her, the professor shook his head. "I can't do that."

"Why not?" Anger and nausea competed for her attention.

"I can't risk it. I don't know where you're hurt."

Rebecca struggled to move into a seated position, and the professor seemed to capitulate by offering her a hand, steadying her. "Don't try to stand."

Adrenaline surged in her veins. "Are the girls okay? Samuel?" She tried to push off the ground, but the palm of her hand sank into the earth. "I have to check on my family."

The professor touched her arm in a soothing gesture. "Everyone is okay. Samuel's in the house with the girls. I told them to stay put."

Rebecca lifted her arm to touch her forehead, and the effort made her groan.

"Did you see who attacked you?"

Rebecca caught herself before she shook her poor head. *"Neh."*

"What were you doing out here?"

She squinted up at the professor, trying to minimize the amount of light hitting her brain. "Destroying these crops." She clawed at one of the discarded plants next to her.

"In the middle of the night?" The protectiveness in his voice made her feel like she hadn't felt in a long time.

Too bad the professor was an *Englisher*.

In the distance she heard a siren, and panic raced through her. "You have to tell the children I'm okay. They'll worry when they see the ambulance."

The professor squeezed her hand and smiled. "Are you sure?"

"Please," she begged. "You need to warn them so they don't worry."

Rebecca watched as the professor ran through the cornstalks. Desperate to get away from the marijuana crops, Rebecca struggled to her feet. The world tilted and her empty stomach heaved.

With one hand to her forehead and the other to her belly, she moved one foot in front of the other through the tall cornstalks.

Please help me, Lord.

The sound of the sirens grew closer, adding to the clanging in her head. She paused and leaned over, bracing her hands on her knees. It didn't help.

Dizzy, she straightened and walked shakily forward. Finally, she stepped onto the hard-packed surface of her driveway. The lights on the ambulance caught her eye before her gaze landed on the professor coming out of the house.

Tiny stars danced in her line of vision before darkness consumed her and she collapsed.

With a bouquet of wildflowers in his hand, Jake lingered in the doorway of Rebecca's hospital room while she slept. Her shiny brown hair, usually wound in a bun and hidden under a bonnet, was splayed on the white pillow. A white bandage covered a portion of her forehead, but her cheeks had regained some of their color and her expression was peaceful.

Something inside him shifted.

He stepped into the room, and she must have sensed

him because her eyes fluttered open. A small smile curved her pink lips.

"I didn't mean to wake you." He took a step closer, letting his fingers brush against the cotton blanket on the bed. "How are you?" he asked, his voice low. Something about hospitals made him feel melancholy. Perhaps it had to do with watching his father waste away from liver failure in one.

"I've been better."

Yellow-greenish bruising blossomed under each eye. Anger burned inside him. She could have been killed.

Suddenly aware of the flowers he was holding, he offered them to her. "For you."

Rebecca took the bouquet and brushed it under her nose. A faint smile graced her lips. "They're beautiful."

"Let me find something to put them in." He held up his finger, ran out to the nurses' station and came back with a pitcher. He filled it with water from the bathroom, then plunked the flowers in it, plastic wrap and all.

A smile lit Rebecca's eyes. "Thank you." She lifted her hand and gingerly touched the dressing on her forehead. "The nurse told me Katie and Grace are okay." There was a question in her tone. "Did you take them to my brother's house?"

"Actually," Jake said, sitting down in the pleather chair next to her bed, "Katie and Grace are with Samuel in the waiting room at the end of the hall. The nurse said they could stop in briefly if you felt up to a few visitors."

"I do." She struggled to push herself up with her elbows and winced. She lay back down. "It would make me feel better to see for myself that they're okay."

Jake rested his elbows on the edge of her bed and his

fingers lingered inches from the tubes running into the back of her hand. "I'll get them in a minute, but first we need to talk."

She slowly turned her head on the pillow to fully face him and lifted her eyebrows as if to say, "What?"

"You're going to have to make a statement to the sheriff."

Rebecca pressed her lips together but still didn't say anything.

"Someone tried to kill you."

She stared at him, her eyes lacking both shock and fear.

"Samuel is also going to have to talk to the sheriff. The events this morning won't allow me to have you resolve this through your Amish neighbors. Law enforcement must be involved."

Rebecca tried again to sit up by pushing her elbows under her, but she collapsed back on the mattress. "*You* don't have the authority to tell me anything. This is my life. My family."

The sudden harshness of her words sliced through him. Confused by her anger, he dared touch the back of her hand, cautious of the tubes. "I need to make sure you're safe."

"I imagine this would also make a great research paper for you. A nice—what do they call it?—a feather in your cap? Lots of publicity for you. Professor Burke stumbles upon drugs on an Amish widow's farm." She scrunched up her nose. "Imagine when they connect this all to Willard, the Amish murderer."

Rebecca closed her eyes and pulled her hands over her midsection in a protective gesture.

"I'm sorry. The sheriff needs to talk to you."

A single tear leaked from the corner of her eye.

Jake stood, pushing back the chair, its wooden legs dragging across the worn linoleum. He tamped down the conflicting emotions welling inside him.

Did she really think that little of him? That he'd use this information for a research paper?

"If it's okay with you, I'll bring in the kids now."

Without saying a word, Rebecca nodded.

Katie's chatter floated down the hall to Rebecca. She touched her forehead and wished she could somehow hide her injury. She didn't want to worry the girls.

Rebecca fumbled with the remote the nurse had showed her and she moved the head of the bed up a few more inches. Squaring her shoulders, she hoped she appeared stronger than she felt.

The professor appeared in the doorway, then stepped aside to allow her children to enter the room before him. Samuel held his little sisters' hands. *He's such a good big brother.* Rebecca quickly swiped at a tear, frustrated with how close to the surface her emotions lurked. The reason she had lashed out at the professor.

"Hi, *Mem*," Samuel said sheepishly. Rebecca forced a smile, but suddenly the memory of the dark shadow raising his arm to slam something down on her head came to mind.

An oppressive weight squeezed her lungs and she turned to stare out the window. Soft white clouds floated across the pale blue fall sky. She wanted nothing more than to go home and forget about this mess.

Neh, not her Samuel. He wouldn't have hurt her. Not

this young man who was protectively ushering his little sisters into her hospital room with whispered words of reassurance. She had heard him when they entered the door: *"Mem's* okay. She'll be better and home soon."

Grace broke free from her big brother's grasp and ran over to the bed. *"Mem!"* She threw herself down on the bed and buried her face in Rebecca's knees.

Katie, the quieter of the two, wandered over to stand next to her mother and sister.

"I'm okay, girls. I should be home soon. Is everything okay?"

Grace nodded slowly.

Then Rebecca turned to Samuel, who stood at the end of the bed. "Are you okay with the girls?" She trusted him, she truly did.

He nodded, the look in his eyes hard to read under the shadow of his straw hat.

Muffled voices sounded in the hallway outside her door. The sheriff strolled in, a small smile curving the corners of his mouth. He touched a black unit on his shoulder and the voices stopped.

"Didn't know you had a full house." The sheriff took a step back. "I could come back later."

Rebecca gently brushed her hand across Grace's hair and the little girl lifted her head. Rebecca forced a smile that hurt the inside of her head. "Go with your big brother to the waiting room. Sheriff Maxwell wants to talk to me." She looked up and locked gazes with Samuel.

He bowed his head and reached for Katie's hand, then Grace's.

"There are too many people in this room," a nurse said as she strode in. She stopped short upon seeing the sheriff. Then she hiked her chin and glared pointedly at each of the offenders. "I'm sorry, Sheriff Maxwell, but Mrs. Fisher needs to rest. She has a concussion."

"I'll just be a minute."

"A minute." The nurse turned and left the room.

Rebecca's family said their goodbyes, and Samuel ushered the two girls out, their Amish dresses and bonnets out of place against the sterility of the modern hospital room.

The professor touched Rebecca's arm. "I'll be outside if you need me."

"I'd like you to stay."

The sheriff nodded in assent.

"I have a few questions," Sheriff Maxwell said.

Samuel slowed up at the door with his sisters. "Samuel, please take your sisters to the waiting room." Her daughters didn't need to hear this.

"What do you know about the marijuana crops growing on your land?"

Something about the way the sheriff said *your* land unnerved Rebecca. She folded over the corner of the blanket and ran her pinched fingers along its edge. "I hired Uri and Jonas Yoder to help on the farm. Yesterday, Samuel told us he'd discovered they had been using our land to grow these horrible plants."

The sheriff scratched his jaw. "The Yoder brothers tell me your son was the one who planted the marijuana. They claim they knew nothing about the plants since they were tucked in a back corner of your land."

Rebecca smoothed the folded edge of the blanket. The dull pain in her head grew to an unbearable thump. "I… They…" She crossed her arms over her middle.

"Last night we went to the Yoders' house and the boys claimed my son was involved, but they were using that as an excuse."

The sheriff wrapped his hand around the metal bar of the footboard. "Rebecca you've had a few rough years."

She felt her mouth grow dry.

"Have you considered that Samuel *might be* responsible?" he continued.

She blinked slowly, sensing the professor's watchful gaze. Did everyone think she lacked good judgment? She had, after all, married a murderer.

Rebecca couldn't squeeze out any words, fearing her emotions would get the best of her.

"Samuel's a good kid," the professor said. Relief swept over her. *Yes, yes he is.*

"I don't think he'd get mixed up with drugs," the professor continued. "From my experience, I've had no indication he's been involved with the drugs in Apple Creek."

"What are your impressions of Uri and Jonas Yoder?" The sheriff tapped his fingers on his thigh.

The professor stuffed his hands into his pockets and shook his head. "I had no indication that they were involved with drugs either. But my time with any of the Amish youth is limited."

The sheriff nodded his head slowly, as if considering all this. "I'm sending a crew over to the farm to destroy the crops."

Rebecca nodded quickly, immediately regretting the motion as a new wave of pain crashed over her. "That's what I was trying to do when I was attacked."

"You didn't see your attacker?"

"No." She threaded her fingers together, unease tickling her throat.

"Rebecca, I know you've had a tough time of it, but I want you to know that state forfeiture laws state that any property connected to a crime *can* be confiscated."

"Confiscated?" the professor asked, the alarm in his voice setting her nerves on edge.

The sheriff cut a sidelong glance to the professor. "Yes, and if the drugs that led to Elmer's crash can be traced back to illegal activity on your farm, you would also be liable. And there's prison to consider."

If the sheriff had come here to scare her, he could consider his visit a colossal success. She moved to place one hand to her mouth, but the wires on her hand got caught on the side rail. A painful tug reminded her of her injuries, and she dropped her hand. The professor gently untangled the wires and placed her hand by her side. He grazed the skin on the back of her hand softly with the pad of his thumb before releasing her hand.

Rebecca glanced up at the professor through a watery haze. She couldn't talk for fear of having a total meltdown.

"Can this wait until she's feeling better?" the professor asked. "This is all news to Rebecca. She had no knowledge of the crops prior to yesterday."

The sheriff stepped toward the door. "I don't want you to blindly protect Samuel. There's a lot at stake here for you *and* your little girls."

A dull thud pulsed behind her eyes. "I am not *blindly* protecting anyone." Did the sheriff think Samuel had planted the marijuana and tried to stop her this morning? Her mind flashed to the shadow bearing down on her. Samuel couldn't have possibly—

"I did it," Samuel blurted from the doorway, where he must have been secretly listening to their conversation. "My *mem* had nothing to do with this. She didn't even know about the crops until I told the professor last night. I'm the *only* one responsible."

With a trembling hand, Rebecca peeled back the white covers of her hospital bed. She swung her feet around and shook her head, refusing the professor's assistance.

Standing on shaky legs, Rebecca held out her arm to Samuel. "You need to forgive yourself."

Her son bowed his head and tapped the frame of the door with the tip of his boot. The image of the little boy she had first come to know haunted her memory. She loved him as her own. Her heart ached for him.

She moved slowly across the cold hospital floor that seemed to tilt with each step. She was aware of the professor hovering next to her.

"You need to forgive yourself for whatever you feel you did wrong when it came to your father," she repeated. "Your *dat* was a bad man. Not you."

Samuel hung his head, unwilling to look her in the eyes.

"You saved lives by helping law enforcement get him off the street." She reached up to touch Samuel, but her arm dropped to her side. "Forgive yourself. Move on. Don't try to ease your guilt by taking blame for the marijuana crops in some misguided attempt to protect me. It's not going to solve anything."

Samuel sniffed and his shoulders shook.

"I know you would never hurt me." She touched the

bandage on her head. "I know it wasn't your idea to plant the marijuana on the farm." She shook her head and immediately regretted it. "I know that's not you. *Elmer* made his own bad choices. *Not* you. Forgive yourself."

Little footsteps sounded and Katie and Grace ran into the room, then hung back, as if sensing something intense was going on.

"Son," the sheriff finally spoke up, "are you confessing to growing the marijuana?"

Her son's eyes moved to his little sisters, then to his *mem*. Samuel nodded. "Yes, I'm responsible. My *mem* had nothing to do with it."

"*Neh*, Samuel. Stop this foolishness," Rebecca pleaded.

"I'm guilty." Samuel stepped forward.

The sheriff grabbed Samuel's arm. "I'm going to have to take you down to the station." The sheriff started rattling off something about a right to an attorney, but all Rebecca could focus on was the metal handcuffs binding Samuel's wrists.

The world suddenly grew very dark. Rebecca sensed the professor's hand on her elbow as she backed up until the back of her legs connected with the bed. She planted a hand on the mattress to steady herself. "Don't do this."

The sheriff glanced her way, a look of contrition in his eyes. "I'll call Jake to let you know what's going on. Okay?"

When she didn't answer—couldn't answer—the sheriff added, "I'll make sure he's okay in lockup."

Rebecca heard soothing words from the professor but couldn't make heads or tails of them. Didn't the sheriff know that nothing would ever be okay again?

Chapter Nine

Jake swiped the back of his hand across his forehead and squinted up at the sun hanging low in the sky. A few days had passed since Samuel's arrest and subsequent release on bail. The Fisher family had a lot on their minds. Fortunately, Rebecca had been released from the hospital. She dismissed the doctor's orders to rest, insisting that farm life went on.

With aching muscles, Jake maneuvered the wagon into place behind the barn with Samuel's help. Then Samuel rode the tractor—without rubber on its tires—into the far corner of the barn. The two men had worked in relative silence most of the day, both in tune with the work at hand. Jake had done some gardening as a kid, but he had no idea he'd enjoy working the land so much.

When Samuel emerged from the barn, he made a straight line for the house. Jake called out to him. "We need to talk."

Samuel kept walking.

"You can't ignore the situation. The Amish might like

to keep the law separate, but you're caught in the legal system now. It will *not* go away."

Samuel spun around and adjusted his straw hat low on his forehead to hide his eyes. "Who says I'm ignoring it? I promised you wouldn't lose your bail money. I'll be there on the court date." He rubbed a hand across the back of his neck. "Any idea when that will be?"

"It hasn't been set yet. The lawyer I hired will let us know."

Samuel slowly shook his head. "Why are you doing all this for us? It's not your problem."

"I don't think you're guilty. I think you're trying to protect your mother by taking the blame. Confessing to something you didn't do is not going to help you or your mother. The right people need to be punished."

Samuel clenched his jaw.

"Someone's been threatening you and your mom."

"You think you're so smart?" Samuel's words came out clipped with frustration and anger. "If you're so smart, you'd stay away from here, too. How do you think having an *Englisher* work the farm appears to our Amish neighbors?"

"Your *mother* needed help. I'm helping you guys harvest the crops now that you've lost the farmhands."

The young man pressed his lips together and shook his head. He had obviously said his piece.

Jake rolled his aching shoulders and decided to change the subject. "I haven't had this much physical exertion since my army days."

Samuel's expression softened. "You were in the army?"

"Yes, I wanted to serve my country and it helped pay for college."

"Maybe I could follow that path and go to college. Tommy seems to think I couldn't get a decent job without a college degree."

Jake studied the young man's thoughtful expression. A criminal record would also prove limiting, but he decided not to go there. "Do you agree with the Amish stance on being a conscientious objector?"

Samuel straightened his back and tried to take on an air of nonchalance, but Jake saw through his false bravado.

"I'm not baptized yet. I don't have to follow the Amish rules."

"True, but going into the army would be difficult for someone like you."

"You think I'm weak."

"I didn't say that. It's not a decision to make lightly."

"If I go to jail, the decision will be made for me, right?" Samuel's biting tone was at odds with the fear that flitted in the depths of his eyes. He shrugged and said, "I'm going to clean up before dinner." He spun on his heels and marched toward the house.

Jake stood and watched the young man until Rebecca caught his eye. She was walking across the field toward him, wisps of hair loose around the front of her head, like a halo glowing in the soft light from the setting sun. They had all put in a long day in the fields, riding the tractor with rudimentary equipment, harvesting the corn for feed. Rebecca had insisted on helping despite Jake's protests that she rest. The Amish were apparently made of hearty stock.

When she reached him, she smiled shyly. "You're a natural." She fingered the strings of her bonnet, then dropped her hand.

"Maybe it's in my blood." Both his parents were Amish, after all.

"I can't thank you enough. Will you stay for dinner?"

He scrunched up his face, realizing how hungry he was. He had been too busy to think about it earlier. "I would hate to intrude."

Rebecca waved her hand in dismissal.

"When did you have time to make dinner?"

"I made a shepherd's pie from some leftovers in the icebox. I hope that's okay."

"Sounds great."

He followed Rebecca up the worn path to the house. She slowed before they reached the porch. "You were talking to Samuel. How does he seem? He hardly speaks to me."

Jake wanted to take her hands in his, to reassure her, but he resisted. "He's sticking to the same story. I hope he changes it before the court date."

Rebecca lowered her eyes and nodded. "I can't thank you enough for intervening on his behalf. If not for you, I fear he would have been overwhelmed by the *English* legal system." She let out a mirthless laugh. "For an Amish woman, I've had my fair share of legal troubles."

This time Jake did reach out and touch her wrist briefly. "I'll help you however I can."

"Denki." The Pennsylvania Dutch word for *thank you* rolled off her pink lips.

"You're very welcome."

When they entered the kitchen, Grace and Katie had

finished setting the table. Grace smiled up at him. "Oh, we'll set another plate." She stretched up and grabbed a white plate from the cabinet.

Rebecca held out her hand. "You can wash up. The bathroom is at the back of the house."

After Jake washed his hands, he joined them at the long pine table. He had been invited to join an Amish family a time or two as part of his studies, but he had always felt as if the family was putting on a show for his benefit. Only when he joined Rebecca and her family did he feel comfortable.

He looked over at Rebecca and she caught him watching her. Well, almost comfortable.

Samuel sat across the table from him. An aura of teenage angst rolled off him. Jake supposed he had gotten all he was going to get from the young man today.

Samuel put his hands in his lap and they all followed suit. They bowed their heads in silent prayer. Samuel was the first to raise his head and pick up his fork, signaling it was time to eat.

"How was school today, girls?" Rebecca asked.

Grace smiled. "We got to play outside at recess. The teacher thinks we might not have many nice days left before it snows."

Her mother laughed. "Did you learn anything?"

"Our teacher Miss Marian is getting married."

Rebecca caught the professor smiling.

"I suppose some things are universal. Kids love recess and their teachers," Jake said.

Rebecca took a scoop of potatoes with her fork and stopped midway to her mouth. "Girls, did you know Professor Burke is a teacher?"

They both looked at him without saying anything.

"*He* doesn't teach little kids. He teaches big people in college."

"Amy's older brother left home and went to college. He's now under the *Bann*," Katie said, her tone ominous, as if at her tender age she already understood the full repercussions of being shunned.

Jake fidgeted with the knife, pushing it under the edge of his plate. Shunning was losing popularity in a number of Amish communities, but some Amish parents still felt it was the only way to encourage baptized members to return to the fold. Some parents used it to encourage their child to be baptized.

Tough love.

Katie swallowed a mouthful of food and asked, "Is being a professor bad?"

Rebecca laughed nervously. "No, it's just something Amish people wouldn't do. We only are allowed an eighth grade education."

"Why?" Grace asked.

"Because that's all we really need. You'll learn everything necessary to be a good wife and *mem* at the Amish schoolhouse."

"*They* want to make sure they can keep us close," Samuel bit out. "*They* want us to have no choice but to stay." He tossed down his fork and pushed back his chair. The legs scraped against the wooden floor, making a sharp squeal.

Rebecca slowly closed her eyes, as if gathering strength. Samuel stomped up the stairs. The young girls stared after their brother with shocked expressions.

"Girls," Rebecca said, "your brother has been rude

and I will deal with him later." She paused, perhaps to quell the shakiness in her voice. "Anyway, the Amish school will teach you everything you need to know." Rebecca watched her daughters with a look of hope and sadness in her eyes. Jake knew how important it was that her daughters stayed in the Amish community, especially with her eldest pushing all the boundaries.

"What if I decide I want to be really smart like the professor? Will you stop talking to me?" Katie said with a hint of what the future teenage Katie might be like.

Rebecca's jaw tightened and she blinked slowly. "My wish for you is that you grow up to love being in Apple Creek as much as I do."

"When Miss Hannah married Sheriff Maxwell, she moved to a house in Apple Creek, but she's not Amish anymore. If you marry Professor Burke, can we get a house near them? We could play with Emma and Sarah every day after school."

Rebecca picked up her fork and stabbed at her mashed potatoes. "Girls, eat before your food gets cold."

Rebecca washed the last plate and handed it to the professor to dry. He placed it in the cabinet and hung the damp dishtowel on the hook.

Rebecca turned around and leaned back, curving her hands around the edge of the counter. "My husband never helped with chores inside the house." She lifted a shoulder to shrug. "I suppose most Amish men know their place is on the farm." She lowered her gaze, suddenly feeling flushed. "Or more and more nowadays at the factory or building swing sets down the road. Things are changing fast." She didn't say more because Willard's nasty words rang in her head. That had been his battle cry. *Things were changing too much. We had to hold on to the old ways.*

The Amish must remain separate.

Her stomach ached. She hated that she agreed with her husband's general premise, yet she'd never resort to Willard's extremes.

The professor smiled and Rebecca worked her lower lip. Her growing feelings of affection were getting difficult to ignore.

"I suppose I should go." He apparently sensed her unease.

"Maybe—" she couldn't believe she was about to say this "—we could sit and talk on the porch for a bit?" Oh, what was she doing? What kind of example was she setting for her daughters? She should escort the professor out the door to go home for the night.

The professor held out his hand. "After you."

She was lonely and longed for adult companionship. The nights were too long with all her racing thoughts about Samuel's future.

Her future.

As Rebecca and the professor passed through the house, she called up the stairs. "Girls, I'll be on the front porch. Get changed and you can read a bit before bed."

Footsteps scampered overhead and she heard the bathroom door slam shut. No doubt Katie had beaten Grace to the bathroom. She smiled at the ordinariness of everyday life. What she wouldn't do to have all of life be that simple.

Rebecca stepped onto the porch and sat in the rocker.

A warm fall breeze swept across her skin and with it the scent of dried hay and freshly harvested crops.

The professor lowered himself into the chair next to hers and sighed contentedly. "I could get used to this."

Rebecca laughed. "The path not chosen."

"At the time, it wasn't for me to choose. My parents left their Amish community and eloped."

"Were they happy?"

The professor settled back in his chair and made an indistinguishable sound in the back of his throat. "I imagine they were happy in the beginning. They were young and free of all the rules of the *Ordnung* for the first time in their lives. They were together."

Rebecca stared over the farm. The bright moon cast the land in a warm glow. A deep but good tired settled around her. Momentary peace, compliments of the man sitting next to her. A man who was completely wrong for her.

She shook away the thought. She could never get together with an *Englisher*. It would go against everything she believed in. Every reason she had worked so hard to bring Samuel back into the fold.

She'd be a hypocrite.

A wistfulness in the professor's tone made her pause. Made her realize something. "Did something happen to make your parents regret their decision to leave the Amish community?"

"I never said…" He shook his head and laughed. "I guess I didn't have to say as much." He sighed heavily. "My father was frustrated because he could never get a decent job. He was stuck working minimum-wage jobs because he—"

"Only had an eighth grade education," Rebecca finished for him, realization dawning. "We talked about that over dinner."

"Exactly."

"Is that why you got all that education and teach at a university?" She swatted away a moth fluttering close to her face.

"Yes, I always equated an education with a happy life. My father would sit down every night with a beer in one hand and a remote in the other in front of the TV and mutter something about 'get an education son, because them people hold all the power.'"

The ever-present emptiness inside Rebecca expanded. She was not the only one with a painful past.

"He pretty much gave up on life. Drank himself stupid right until the end."

She was grateful for the cloak of darkness to hide the tears brimming in her eyes.

"He died of liver failure."

"I'm sorry." Nervously, Rebecca played with the folds in her long gown and tucked her bare feet under the rocker. She hated to ask, but curiosity got the best of her. "What about your mom?"

"My mom died when I was ten. From cancer."

Rebecca gasped. "I didn't mean to pry. How horrible. I'm so, so sorry."

"My parents couldn't afford anything but the basic treatment. I suppose they could have gotten more care if they weren't naive to the system. It was all foreign to them." He scrubbed a hand over his face and his features grew pinched. "My dad's drinking got worse the sicker my mom got…"

He let out a quick breath. "I've never told anyone the story of my life. I guess I never wanted to share my past with anyone before."

"I'm glad you told me. I feel closer to you." She glanced away, suddenly feeling very self-conscious.

He reached out and covered her hand on the arm of the chair and gave it a gentle squeeze. "Life gets complicated sometimes."

Keenly aware of his hand on hers, she glanced over her shoulder at the door. "I know. I hope we can get Samuel out of trouble. I really appreciate your putting up his bail." She slid her hand out from under his and wrapped her arms around her midsection. "The thought of him in jail…"

He leaned toward her. "I'll help you in every way I can." He tilted his head. "But when I said life gets complicated, I wasn't talking about Samuel."

Rebecca glanced up into his warm brown eyes. Her pulse beat steadily in her ears and her skin flushed warm.

Get up. Move away from him.

She couldn't. This gentle man held her heart. She sucked in a breath, waiting for him to continue.

He leaned closer, his breath whispering across her cheek. A smile tilted the corners of his mouth. He hesitated a minute, as if waiting for her reaction. Her permission. A boldness she'd never known surged through her. She reached up and touched his cheek; the scruff of his unshaven jaw felt rough under her palm.

He leaned in closer and brushed a gentle kiss across her lips. Then he pulled back and angled his head, studying her.

Closing her eyes briefly, she dropped her hand into

her lap and wrung her hands. She opened her eyes and met his.

"Should I apologize for kissing you?"

No, no, no.

"We're from two different worlds." Her voice came out in a strained whisper. This entire situation was foreign to her.

A twinkle lit his eyes. "So, that's a no?" He laughed.

Rebecca smiled. She could get used to this man's easygoing ways. His warm heart. His companionship.

Too bad a relationship between them would never happen.

Jake scooted forward in his rocker and curled his hands in an effort to keep them to himself. He was having trouble containing a smile. Rebecca had her hands wrapped around the arms of the chair and looked as if she was ready to bolt. He really should apologize, but if he was truly honest with himself, he wasn't sorry.

The memory of her soft lips on his. Her clean scent. Her soft skin.

Definitely not sorry.

But he hated to see her filled with angst. And he didn't want to risk having her send him away forever.

"Did I overstep my place?" he asked in a husky voice.

Rebecca lifted her fingers and touched her lips. An emotion he couldn't quite define flittered in the depths of her eyes.

"It's my fault."

"Your fault?" Intrigued, Jake leaned back in his rocker and relaxed his hands. "Because you're beautiful?"

She lifted her hand in dismissal. "Please. You're embarrassing me." She turned her face away from him and smoothed a hand along the edge of her bonnet. Slowly she turned to face him, clutching her hands in her lap. "This kiss can't *mean* anything. We have no future together."

She was right. The pain in her eyes cut to his core. "I didn't mean to cause you any more stress."

The thought of encouraging Rebecca to leave the Amish didn't bring him joy any more than saying goodbye to her would. His father had convinced his mother to leave and he had experienced firsthand the sadness that had ensued.

"I hope I didn't destroy our friendship," Jake said, a muscle working in his jaw.

Rebecca bowed her head. "Don't blame yourself. I feel the connection between us, too."

Jake's heartbeat spiked at her admission. Yet, still, he could never ask her to leave the Amish.

Rebecca met his gaze, a look of clarity in her eyes. "I should have never put you in this position, Professor Burke. I came to you because I was worried about Samuel." A tendril of hair that had escaped her bonnet fluttered in the breeze. "I don't want you to feel responsible for me every time something goes wrong. It's not your responsibility."

"I don't mind."

Rebecca shook her head slowly. "You're a good man. But I need to rely on my own community. Not an outsider."

"An outsider, huh?" Jake laughed before giving her a wounded look and covering his midsection as if he had been punched in the gut.

Rebecca's brow furrowed. "Are you not feeling well?"

Jake lifted an eyebrow. "We really are from two different worlds."

"Yes, we are. I don't think it's a good idea for you to keep coming around."

A rustling sounded from the yard and Jake rose to his feet and squinted into the darkness. Lester Lapp, the bishop's son, stepped into the soft light flowing from her house.

Rebecca was slower to her feet. She walked to the railing and wrapped her hands around it. "Hello, Lester. It's late to be calling."

"I have business to discuss."

"Business with me? You haven't come by my farm since before Willard's arrest."

Lester adjusted his hat on his head, as if trying to gather his thoughts. "He killed my brother."

The soft gasp from Rebecca made Jake's hands twitch. He longed to pull her into an embrace. Comfort her.

Lester held up his hand. "I'm sorry. I should have been more sensitive. I have forgiven him, but I still struggle with my loss."

She bowed her head and whispered, "I understand."

Lester gave Jake a pointed look, but turned back to Rebecca. "The bishop hasn't been feeling well. I'm here on his behalf."

"I hope your father is feeling better soon."

Lester nodded. *"Denki."* He took a few steps closer, put his foot on the bottom porch step and rested his elbow on the railing. "The bishop would like Samuel to meet with him and a few of the church elders."

All the color drained out of her face and Jake immediately felt defensive. "I don't believe he's guilty of the things—"

"He's confessed to?" Lester interrupted with a smug quirk of his lips.

Rebecca wrung her hands in front of her. "Samuel's afraid of something. He's trying to protect me." Her words came out rushed and flustered. "And he's not baptized yet. The church elders have been known to overlook transgressions of our *youngie*."

Lester removed his hat and gave her a look Jake could only read as "you've got to be kidding me."

"Growing marijuana on God's land is more than a *little* transgression."

"Rebecca's been through a lot," Jake spoke up. "Now is not a good time."

The Amish man wiped his forehead, then settled his hat back on his head. "Perhaps Mrs. Fisher should remember she *is* a baptized member of this community."

A muscle started ticking in Jake's jaw, but despite the fury racing through his brain, he got hold of his emotions. Blasting this man with a piece of his mind wasn't going to help Rebecca.

"I was telling the professor he needs to find new subjects to study." Rebecca's voice was surprisingly firm.

Lester held up his hand. "Is that all this is?"

Jake slowly descended the steps. "Good night, Rebecca."

"Good night, Professor." She paused a brief moment. "Good night, Lester." Rebecca turned around and went inside, obviously unwilling to discuss this further with either of them.

In the front yard, Lester turned to Jake. "I trust you're not courting Rebecca."

"Courting?" Jake asked noncommittally before changing the subject. "You are the bishop's son." Jake knew who Lester was, but he was buying time to formulate his thoughts…his words.

Lester tipped his hat.

"How often does someone join the Amish community?" From his own research, Jake knew it wasn't often.

Lester's eyes flared wide under the moonlight. "Join the Amish?" He let out a bark of laughter that grated on Jake's nerves. "Are *you* considering joining us?"

Jake didn't trust himself to answer, suspecting that clocking the arrogant man wouldn't win him any favors.

"You don't join the Amish like you're joining a country club. This is our community. A way of life. A serious commitment."

"I am very familiar with the Amish. I have been studying the Amish and teaching at the university for years."

"So," Lester said, the single word dripping with sarcasm, "is this the last step in your research? To join the Amish?" He shook his head and scoffed. "Through your vast research you should have already figured all this out."

Jake blinked slowly, trying to tamp down his emotions. "I know outsiders joining the Amish is unusual, but it has been done."

Lester's eyes locked on the front door of Rebecca's home. "The church elders will look unkindly on a man choosing to join the Amish for the wrong reasons."

Jake kept his thoughts to himself.

"Joining because you want to court the widow Fisher is not valid grounds." Lester took a few steps away, then turned around. "Rebecca was right. You shouldn't keep coming around here."

Jake narrowed his gaze, more than a little annoyed that Lester had obviously been eavesdropping on them before he'd made his presence known.

Chapter Ten

While Jake was driving home, he realized he'd never be able to sleep so he decided to go to his campus office and catch up on some work. He'd had his graduate teaching assistant cover his class today, but he couldn't keep doing that. Not if he still wanted a job.

Jake easily found parking in the nearly empty lot. It was after nine, a few students were crisscrossing the campus on the quiet fall evening.

"Hi, Professor Burke," a young woman said as he strolled across the quad to his office in the Stevenson building. He waved at her as he remembered his first day on campus a few years ago. He thought he had finally made it. He thought he should finally be happy because he had the education, he had the job, all the things that his father lacked.

So why had happiness—real happiness—eluded him until now? Until Rebecca had come into his life? The quiet Amish woman had made him feel content. But was Lester right? Were his motives to join the Amish pure or just a way to remain close to Rebecca?

Jake pulled open the large door to his building. Guilt pinged him. He'd had no right to kiss Rebecca. To take advantage of her. She was vulnerable.

Jake tried but couldn't forget the feel of her soft lips, her quick intake of breath, the fresh smell of windswept hair…

Wrapped in the memory of the kiss, he walked down the long hallway, his footsteps sounding on the marble floor. As he approached room 214, he noticed a light filtering out from under the door. His head jerked back.

Jake turned the handle on the door; it was unlocked. The computer at Tommy's desk was on, but he saw no sign of his assistant. He strolled into the office and heard a voice.

"Yeah, I'll figure something out."

Jake turned the corner and saw Tommy sitting on the floor of his office, leaning against the wall with his legs stretched out in front of him. Tommy looked up when Jake entered the room. "Gotta go," he said into the phone. He ended the call and scrambled to his feet.

"Hey, Professor, what are you doing here?" Tommy moved around to the desk. The chair squeaked when he plopped down into it and leaned back.

"I suppose I could ask you the same thing."

"I come in here to use the computer when the computer lab's too busy." Tommy wiggled the mouse and the screen came to life. Some Word document was on the screen. "My laptop bit the dust and I can't afford a new one."

Jake waved his hand, indicating it wasn't a problem. He stepped into his office and sat behind his big desk.

He moved some of the papers and books around. Once this—all of this—had meant everything to him.

Studying the Amish had made him feel connected, but not in the way that Rebecca made him feel…connected. When he was with Rebecca, he felt as if he was home.

"Professor Burke?"

Jake snapped his attention to the door. Tommy had a look that made Jake think he had called his name a few times.

"What's up, Tommy?"

His assistant jabbed his thumb toward his desk. "I'm going to wrap things up here and call it a night." Tommy leaned across the desk and clicked a few buttons on the computer. "…And sent. Got to love technology. Paper was due by midnight. I submitted it through email."

Jake nodded. He still gave his students the option of handing in a paper or sending him an email.

A slow smile spread across the young man's face. "Everything okay? You look like someone stole your favorite toy."

Jake laughed. "No, just trying to catch up with work here."

"You're spending a lot of time with the Fisher family." It was more a statement than a question. Tommy crossed his arms and leaned his hip on the frame of the doorway. "You're really deep in research mode."

"Mmm" was Jake's only response.

"This whole growing marijuana on the Amish farm will make a great paper. You'll put the Amish Apple Creek community on the map. Kinda like that gunman did with the Amish in Nickel Mines."

Anger started burning deep in Jake's gut, but he didn't

want to lash out at Tommy. He was a kid, not exactly socially savvy.

"I'm not going to write about it."

A smirk slashed across Tommy's thin lips. "Really? I thought it would make an interesting paper."

"I want to be respectful." Jake stood, walked around the front of his desk and perched on its corner. "I've been giving her a hand since the Yoder brothers quit. She needed help with the harvest."

"I'm sure some of their Amish neighbors would step up to the plate." Tommy stuffed something into his backpack and zipped it up. "You're an expert on the Amish. They help one another. You know that."

"The Fishers have felt isolated since Willard Fisher was convicted of murder. Hopefully with time, things will change." *If* Jake stayed away that might help bridge the gap. Rebecca had to learn to rely on her Amish neighbors again. Her Amish neighbors needed time to forgive, even if they never forgot.

Tommy shook his head. "Talk about bad karma with that family. It's like they're a bad-luck magnet. But you know as well as I do that the Amish will eventually find forgiveness in their hearts. Someone will step forward and help them in their time of need."

"One can hope."

Tommy slung his backpack over one shoulder and gave Jake a knowing look. "Forgive me for speaking out of turn, but do you have something for Mrs. Fisher?" He lifted an eyebrow.

Jake couldn't help but laugh. He threaded a hand through his hair. "I enjoy spending time with Rebecca."

Jake waved his hand. "But that's it. I'm just helping a person who's having a rough time."

Tommy levered off the doorframe and nodded slowly. "Guard your heart, Professor. Mrs. Fisher…she's gonna break yours." He turned to leave, then muttered over his shoulder. "They always do."

"We are *not* having this conversation."

Tommy turned around to face him. "I can't see you becoming Amish."

"That's what I call jumping to a conclusion without supporting evidence." Jake kept his voice even.

"You'd never give all this up. You've worked too hard." The young man scrunched up his nose. "You may have a romanticized notion of the Amish from your research, but studying and living it are two different beasts." Tommy adjusted the strap on his shoulder. "Trust me. Been there, done that. Got the T-shirt—or should I say, broad-brimmed hat—to prove it."

The next morning at the diner, Rebecca's head pounded. Not getting enough rest despite her recent injury was bound to do that. Rest was long in coming. After her job at the diner, she still had chores to do on the farm. Samuel had promised to see that his little sisters got to school, and her sister-in-law Gloria would pick them up after school and bring them home after Rebecca's shift.

Rebecca rolled her shoulders, trying to ease out the kinks. She grabbed the milk from the counter, screwed on the lid, then yanked on the lever of the walk-in freezer.

"Hey, hey, hey…" Flo walked up behind her and put a hand on her back. "Dear, unless we plan to plop frozen milk into glasses, we better put that back in the refrigerator."

Rebecca blinked a few times, wondering how she'd ended up standing in front of the freezer with a jug of milk in her hand.

Flo took the milk and put it in the refrigerator. "What's on your mind today? Worried about Samuel?"

Rebecca was *always* worried about Samuel, but something else was pressing on her heart this morning. She looked up, met Flo's warm gaze and smiled.

Flo tilted her head, a pleading look in her eyes. "Dear, if you're gonna spill it, you better do it soon before the breakfast crowd gets here. Then you're going to have to hold your peace until midmorning." She twirled her hand in a get-on-with-it gesture. "And you are *not* going to leave here today without telling me what's on your mind."

Rebecca smoothed a hand across the edge of her bonnet and her mouth went dry. "The professor and I visited for a bit on the porch last night."

Her friend's eyebrows shot up. "You did, did you?"

Rebecca couldn't help but smile at her friend's response. Oh, how she wished it was as simple as Flo thought it was.

Flo crossed her arms and leaned her hip on the silver counter, settling in for all the gossip. "Did something happen?" Flo had a way of pinning her with a penetrating gaze. Flo's hand flew to her mouth. "Oh, something happened. Did he kiss you?"

Rebecca had no plans to kiss and tell.

"I didn't mean to embarrass you, dear. You're young

and pretty and you have your life in front of you." She leaned in close. "I say go for it."

Rebecca laughed. "Go for what? You know how conservative the Amish are. He'd have to become Amish for us to have a future."

Flo ran a finger across her bottom lip. "There is that." Her shoulders sagged. "Poor girl, you have that handsome man paying you visits, yet you're bound to the Amish ways." She bit her lower lip and furrowed her brow. "Are you sure? Maybe a fresh start would be a good thing for you."

Rebecca knew there was no way her friend would understand. "A fresh start would mean leaving everything I've ever known."

The bell on the door jangled, indicating their first breakfast customers, a handful of retired men who stopped in five days out of the week to chat.

"I'll get this table." Flo walked toward the dining room, then glanced over her shoulder. "Considering everything you've been through, would a fresh start be so bad?"

After another long day at the diner and a ride home from Flo, Rebecca hung her coat on the hook and turned to see a horse and buggy come up the driveway. She hustled to the front door and greeted her daughters. Gloria walked them to the door briskly through the steady rain while Mark waved from the buggy.

"Thank you," Rebecca yelled to her brother, then smiled at Gloria. "I can't thank you enough. I appreciate you bringing them home."

Gloria touched each of the girls' bonnets with a tender look on her face.

The two girls ran into the house, shaking off their damp coats.

"Go on up and get into your nightclothes," Rebecca said to her daughters. She missed seeing their sweet faces all day long.

Once the girls had pounded up the stairs, Gloria leaned in close and whispered, "It wonders me if we should let the girls stay at our house during the week. Since you have to work. We'd love to have them."

Rebecca frowned and she cast her glance toward the floor. "I'm their *mem*. They need to stay here."

"*Yah*, well, I know you're their *mem*," Gloria said, compassion in her tone. "It's too much back and forth. The girls might feel more settled. It will be right like they're home."

Rebecca wrung her hands. "Why do you think the girls aren't settled?"

"I can tell I've offended you. I know you're doing the best you can. The girls need stability. With everything going on with Samuel, maybe it's best if they weren't around that."

"Samuel is their brother. Samuel is innocent." Rebecca hesitated a minute. He was innocent, wasn't he? What if he went to jail all the same? Her poor family would be the subject of more finger-pointing.

Rebecca let out a long, slow breath and ran a hand over her face. Her eyes felt gritty from a long day at work. Another day in which she had been away from her family.

Her little girls.

"Maybe they could stay with us until things settle down. I'd hate for something to happen to them," Gloria said.

Suddenly that piece of apple pie with ice cream Rebecca had had before she'd left the diner didn't seem like such a good idea.

"What do you mean, 'something happen to them'?"

Gloria bowed her head and her cheeks turned pink. "Many evil things have surrounded your family."

Rebecca gasped. She struggled to find the words. "You don't think they're safe here?" Apprehension knotted her stomach.

Through the open front door, Rebecca could see her brother sitting in the buggy, his broad-brimmed hat pulled down low on his forehead as he stared straight ahead, squinting against the wind and rain blowing in the open sides. Served him right for taking the coward's way out and leaving his wife to broach this difficult subject.

"Grace asked me if they could still visit if you married the professor."

"What?"

"She's worried that she'll be leaving the Amish community. She's worried she won't get to see her cousins, but she seemed somewhat comforted by the idea she could still play with your friend Hannah's children."

Rebecca blinked slowly, trying to absorb it all. She laughed, a nervous sound. "Kids get silly ideas. The professor has been helping me. There's nothing romantic going on." The little white lie burned on her lips.

"Perhaps things would be less complicated for you if you spent more time with the Amish than with the English."

Little feet sounded on the stairs and Rebecca spun around. Grace descended the stairs with a doll under her arm. "Can I play with my doll before bed?"

Rebecca smiled at her sweet daughter. "Of course. Let me finish talking to *Aenti* Gloria. I'll be right up to hear all about your day."

Rebecca watched her daughter climb the stairs, then when she was satisfied the little girl was out of hearing distance, she turned to Gloria. "I was desperate when I approached the professor."

"Why didn't you come to us?" The hint of accusation in her sister-in-law's question heated Rebecca's skin.

"When was the last time you spent time with Samuel?"

Gloria bristled, but didn't say anything.

"The professor has been meeting with the Amish youth. I thought he could provide insight into Samuel's behavior."

"I've never liked the idea of outsiders coming into our community and studying us."

Rebecca laughed. "Me neither, but the professor is a good man."

Gloria raised a curious eyebrow.

"His parents were Amish."

"Really?"

"They left before they got married."

Gloria lowered her voice. "You're not planning on leaving, are you?" There was an ominous quality to her voice.

Rebecca slowly shook her head. "I'm not leaving. You know that. I've been working hard to guide Samuel on the right path. Why would you ever think I was planning on being a fence jumper?" An iciness sped through her. "Did the church elders come to you? Did they put you up to this?"

Her dear sister-in-law nodded. "Everyone's worried."

"I wish the elders had jumped in to condemn the members who have been harassing us. We've felt all alone."

"I believe those incidents were addressed. The community was devastated by your husband's actions."

Tears bit at the back of Rebecca's eyes. "They were addressed, but not with the tenacity that they have been addressing the issues with Samuel. Lester stopped by and told us the bishop wants to meet with Samuel. I'm reluctant to send him over there for fear Samuel will run away for good."

"You can't ignore the request."

"I don't plan to, but I do plan to go with him. The last thing I want him to feel is ganged up on."

Gloria gave her a sad smile. "You are a much stronger woman than I am. Please be careful not to turn your back on the Amish way, too."

Rebecca furrowed her brow. "Why would you say that? I have no intention of running away. I only plan to protect my son."

"You are a kind and forgiving woman. Just be sure Samuel is worthy of your kindness."

Rebecca clamped her mouth shut, unwilling to lash out on a woman who had shown her and her daughters much kindness. She took a step toward the door. "I've had a long day and I'm tired. Thank you for bringing the girls home."

Gloria stared at her a moment, before smiling tightly and nodding. *"Guten Nacht."*

Rebecca saw her sister-in-law out the door and then dropped down in one of the rockers, her knees weak with the turn of events. Her heart might be confused over her feelings for the professor, but she was steadfast in her determination to live the Amish way. And to set her son on the right path.

She tugged at the straps on her bonnet. She had two daughters to consider. If she had any hope of keeping them on the straight and narrow, she'd have to be stronger. She'd have to ignore the feelings she had for a man who was absolutely wrong for her and she'd have to stand strong against Samuel's misbehavior.

Rebecca prayed she could save her son. But she could no longer be weak. Not if she didn't want to risk her two young daughters watching with impressionable minds and thinking that flaunting the Amish rules would get nothing but more attention and coddling.

No more.

Chapter Eleven

A few days later, Rebecca stood by the back door—her stomach twisted in knots—and waited for Samuel to return from his morning chores. She had sent Katie and Grace out to check on the pumpkins in their small garden. Rebecca couldn't bear to see the look of disappointment in their eyes, too.

When Samuel appeared outside the barn, his head slightly bowed, a bead of sweat popped out on her forehead.

Could she really do this?

Her gaze fell to the suitcase inside the door. Samuel's suitcase. The one she had packed for him while he was outside. Rebecca had met with the bishop without Samuel and through the professor, she had gotten approval from the courts for this next course of action. It was her hope to get Samuel away from the negative influence of his local friends while he awaited a court date.

Rebecca glanced at the wall clock. The ride to the bus depot that she had arranged for Samuel would be here soon. The last thing she wanted was for Flo's son to arrive before she had a chance to tell Samuel what was happening.

When Samuel reached the back porch, he slowed and glanced up at her with a quizzical look on his face. "What's going on?"

"You're going on a trip," Rebecca said, barely able to get the words out of her parched mouth. She pushed open the screen door for her son and he stepped inside.

Samuel's gaze dropped to the worn suitcase on the floor. He took off his hat and tossed it on the hook. A strand of hay in his hair almost broke her heart. She had a flash of meeting Samuel for the first time. He had been a little boy who had lost his mother and had been reluctant to welcome Rebecca into his life. To welcome a second mother.

She immediately second-guessed her bold plan. She was blindsiding him. Maybe she should have warned him.

Samuel brushed past her and into the kitchen to wash his hands. Rebecca followed him.

"I've packed your things for a trip to—"

"You're kicking me out?" His brow furrowed and anger flashed in his eyes. It wrecked her to hurt him like this. She grabbed the back of the chair to steady herself, fearing her weak knees would go out from under her.

She struggled to form the words. She wanted him gone before Grace and Katie came back inside. She didn't want them to witness her sending their big brother away. She wanted time to explain things to her daughters without adding an emotional goodbye scene.

"I've made arrangements for you to stay in an Amish

community in the Rochester area. Their church is in communion with ours."

Samuel's brows drew together. "You're kicking me out of my home? *My* home." His jaw trembled. "You said I was your son, but now I know the truth. You've always considered me *Willard's* son. The son of a convicted murderer. I'm no better than my father and you want me out of the house because I'm such a wicked influence."

"That's not true." Her voice came out shaky as what little resolve she had drained out of her.

What had she done?

Samuel kicked the small suitcase and the buckle released, scattering his plain clothing across the floor. Rebecca dropped to her knees and stuffed everything back into the suitcase, the suitcase she had used when she had been a young woman moving into Willard's house. To take over for his dead wife.

What a miserable job she and Willard had done.

Had she actually fallen so far as to compare her parenting skills to her husband's? A murderer?

Rebecca looked up from a kneeling position on the floor.

She had to remain strong.

"It's not forever," she whispered.

She struggled to her feet, then took a step toward Samuel. He recoiled from her, but she persisted. "I love you, but you need to get away for a little bit. Away from this mess until we figure out what's really going on."

"I already confessed." Samuel bowed his head. "You can't lose this land for my stupidity."

"I don't believe for a minute that you're responsible for planting the marijuana plants. Your only mistake was giving your friends, Uri and Jonas, the benefit of the doubt. I talked to the sheriff. Special arrangements have been made with the courts to allow you to travel as long as we assure them you'll come back when the trial starts."

An uneasy feeling roiled in her gut. Courts, lawyers, law enforcement were all contrary to the Amish culture, but there was no way she was going to let Samuel fend for himself in the *English* world.

Willard would have kicked him out and not lost a night's sleep. She wasn't Willard. She had to protect Samuel. Save him from prison.

A dark memory seeped into her bones.

Willard had been *killed* in prison.

Samuel's rigid posture slackened. He lifted his hands in a supplicating gesture. "Please, *Mem*, don't send me away. I need to be here. To protect you."

Rebecca shook her head slowly, tears forming. "Mr. Yoder has assured me he will make sure his sons stay obedient."

Samuel let out a heavy sigh, as if suggesting Mr. Yoder hadn't had success controlling his sons in the past. Just then, a beeping sounded from the driveway.

"That's your ride. You've met my friend from the diner, Flo. Her son will drive you to the bus depot."

Samuel turned to march up the stairs and Rebecca stood in front of him. "*Neh.* You must leave without any of your electronic things." She closed her eyes briefly, the hollowness expanding inside her. "Please, don't make it harder than it has to be."

Samuel glared at her. He bent over at the waist and

scooped up the suitcase, turned and stormed out of the house.

With a hand to her midsection, Rebecca moved to the window and watched Samuel climb into the pickup truck. She stood at the window long after the tailgate disappeared down the country road.

An ache twisted in her heart. She had lost Samuel. Her worst nightmare had come true.

After Samuel had left, the bishop saw to it that some Amish neighbors came over to help her harvest the remaining crops. Perhaps the Fisher family was one step closer to bridging the gap. Rebecca just prayed Samuel's innocence would be proven in court.

A few long days in the fields and they were done for another season. She was relieved they had finished when they had because a storm front moved in, leaving little Apple Creek under dark clouds and steady rain.

And that was fine with Rebecca. It suited her mood.

Rebecca had worked at the diner today and was happy for the distraction. Working on the farm without Samuel only emphasized his absence. But now, after her diner shift, she was tired and wanted to go home and spend time with her daughters.

But first, Rebecca had to run to the local market to grab milk and a few other basics. Groceries in one hand, she fumbled with the handle of the umbrella as the automatic doors swooshed open. The steady rain pelted her umbrella. With the handle of her tote wrapped around her wrist, she reached up and gathered the collar of her coat. She wished the rain could wash away her feelings of indecision.

Of failure…

The swoosh of a tire in a puddle made her instinctively move closer to the buildings. It wouldn't be unheard of for one of the college students to make sport of splashing pedestrians.

Score extra points for soaking the Amish.

She shook her head and kept walking across the small parking lot toward Main Street, her mind otherwise preoccupied. She was headed back to the diner to meet her ride. Flo had offered to drive her home so she didn't have to spend part of her paltry wages on a ride. She'd have to make some big changes soon. Under the circumstances, she didn't know how much longer she could run the farm, hold down a job at the diner and support her daughters.

"Rebecca."

She stopped in her tracks and turned slowly to face the familiar voice. The professor had pulled his truck up alongside her and had rolled down the passenger window.

"Come on, I'll give you a ride."

Rebecca pointed at the diner. "Flo's going to drive me home. Thanks anyway." The memory of Samuel climbing into the truck and departing for Rochester amplified the emptiness inside her. All her efforts had to mean something. Now she had to do her part, too. Behave like a good Amish woman if she hoped to further patch the tear in her association with the Amish.

"Good night." Rebecca gave her best polite smile, hoping he'd take the hint. She had a lot on her mind, but she hadn't yet figured out how to share it with the professor. She thought she'd have more time.

He reached across the cab of the truck and pushed

open the door. "Come in out of the rain. I'll drive you home."

Rebecca slowly walked toward the door, unable to resist his friendly smile. She muttered something under her breath about his smile. This was not unfolding in the way she had intended.

"I don't want Flo to worry."

He pulled out his phone and held it up. "I'll call the diner. Let her know."

When she angled her head with indecision, he said, "You'll save her a trip." He waved his hand in a come-on gesture and she let out a long sigh before closing her umbrella and climbing into the truck. She rested the wet umbrella against the seat while the professor made a quick phone call.

"Are you okay?" he asked, compassion in his tone.

"Um, yeah…" A slow ticking started in her head. She wasn't ready for this conversation.

"It had to be tough to see Samuel leave."

And there it was. The conversation she was dreading. Not because she was still reeling from Samuel's departure, but because there was something else she had to do.

Rebecca bowed her head and played with the straps of her tote at her feet.

"Rebecca," he said softly, "don't be hard on yourself."

Tears started to build and she feared if she opened up to him she'd crumble with all the emotions she had kept locked inside. She wrapped her hand around the door release but stopped when a lightning bolt exploded nearby.

The professor touched the crook of her arm. "I'll just drive you home. We don't have to talk about Samuel."

She met his compassionate gaze. "I should have at the

very least thanked you for posting bail and for working within the English system to allow him to travel. I understand that's not always allowed."

"I promised I'd help you."

"Well, I've known men not to keep their promises."

"I'd like the opportunity to show you that some men keep their word."

Rebecca tracked a raindrop as it raced down the window in a wild zigzag, much like her thoughts.

The professor pulled out onto the road. "I'm free this weekend to help you with the harvest again."

Rebecca twisted the handles of her tote bag. "Some neighbors have already helped me. You've done more than enough for my family." She hadn't meant to sound so accusatory. She turned to smile at him in apology.

The professor rubbed his jaw and kept his eyes on the road. The worn wipers scraped across the windshield.

Screech-swoosh-screech-swoosh.

"I enjoyed working the land." There was a faraway quality to his voice. "I guess it's in my blood."

"You learned very quickly." She remembered his easy smile as she'd instructed him on how to operate the farming equipment. Not only was he eager to learn, but he also had asked all the right questions.

"I *be* a college graduate."

She frowned, his joke having fallen flat.

Rebecca fingered the strap of her seat belt. "I appreciated your help, but I need to rely on the Amish. I need to be a better example for Samuel and for my daughters." She turned and stared out the window, watching the scenery change outside. Heat pumped out of the vents in the dash and she was grateful she wasn't in a buggy or still out in the rain.

"Well, I'm glad you finally got the help you needed." He sounded hurt, but she had to stick with what she felt was best for her family.

"I should have never gone to an outsider. It's not our way. I should have relied on our community."

The professor slowed at a stop sign and glanced over at her. A muscle ticked in his jaw. With the rain pelting his truck, she felt as if they were all alone. In a cocoon. As if there was no one else in the world.

He reached over and placed his hand over hers. Warm. Protective. Gentle. Qualities she had never seen in her deceased husband. She resisted the urge to pull her hand away. She needed to put distance between them. At the same time, she wanted to savor this connection with the professor one last time.

He brushed his thumb across the back of her hand. "You did nothing wrong by reaching out to me. I've done a lot of research on the *youngie* here. I've gotten to know your son. You weren't wrong in thinking I'd know something that could help you."

"But you didn't. These young men have been doing things and hiding things right under our noses. I should have been harder on Samuel a long time ago."

"You think he'll be better off away from here?"

"He needs to be away from his gang."

The professor nodded. He lifted his hand and touched her cheek briefly. "Don't push me away, too."

A car honked behind them and the professor dropped his hand and turned his attention to the road.

"I have to," she whispered, her voice barely audible over the noisy wipers. "I have to."

Jake's truck bobbled over the puddle-filled ruts in Rebecca's driveway. The rain pelted the roof of his truck, filling the silence with a steady drumming beat.

"When Samuel comes home for the trial, I hope you make him feel welcome. He needs you now more than ever," Jake said.

Rebecca's bonnet was damp from the rain. The look on her face pained him. "You think I was wrong in sending him away." He was surprised by the harshness of her tone. "I'm not the King family. I didn't throw him out on the street, leaving him to fend for himself. I sent him to an Amish home." She drew in a shaky breath and continued, "I can't have all these *worldly* influences around my young daughters." She tucked a stray hair behind her ear and bowed her head. Her cheeks flared pink from the heater vents. He adjusted the knob to moderate the heat.

"I didn't mean to add to your pain." He rubbed his jaw. "I played a part in Elmer getting kicked out of his home. I encouraged him to share his troubles with his father. His father responded by kicking him out of the house."

"And you feel that led to his car accident?"

"Yes." Jake's gut tightened, remembering the fury Mr. King had unleashed on his son. His father hadn't been understanding and had kicked his struggling son out of the house. Before Jake had had a chance to defuse the situation, given Elmer hope for the future, the young man had revolted and gone on a drinking and drugging binge.

Guilt welled up inside him again. He ran a hand across

his forehead, realizing guilt was one of his primary driving forces. It was a horrible way to go through life.

"I'm sure Samuel will be fine," he said, his voice softening.

"I'm doing the best I can to protect my family. My *entire* family."

Did Rebecca think Samuel was guilty? That she had to keep him away from her daughters?

"I wished I could have done more to help you."

"You have. You really have, but I need to learn to rely on my own community. It may or may not be too late for Samuel, but I can't allow him to get away with doing all sorts of worldly things." The lines around her eyes grew tense. "Soon Samuel's case will come to court. Hopefully then we can put this all behind us."

She wrung her hands. "I'm really sorry, Jake."

"Jake? You called me Jake." He couldn't help but smile.

A deep line marred her forehead in confusion.

"You've always called me Professor." He laughed. "Now you finally call me by my given name at the same time that you're brushing me off."

"Brushing you off?" She repeated his words as if she was trying them out, unsure of what they meant. She bowed her head. "I'm sorry. I should have never let you think you could court me."

Jake reached out to touch her cheek, but he pulled his hand back. "Can we still be friends?" He hoped her insular childhood wouldn't allow her to recognize how cliché his comment was.

She pulled the door handle and the dome light clicked on. He studied her. "Can we?"

Rebecca shook her bonneted head. "It would be better if we didn't. I will never leave the Amish and you're not Amish."

"You don't have any non-Amish friends?"

Their gazes lingered. "We aren't friends."

Her words took the wind out of him. "So," he said, his voice hard-edged, "that's it? I don't get a say in this?"

She lifted her brown eyes and stared at him. "We're from two different worlds. It would never work. I could never be happy anywhere but here on the farm."

"Work on the farm is peaceful."

She glanced at him, confused, and suddenly Jake felt as though he wasn't being fair to Rebecca. She was struggling; she didn't need him muddying the waters.

"Give it some time. Wait until Samuel's situation is settled. Don't just…" He let out a long breath. "Don't throw this away."

Rebecca pulled the door closed and the dome light faded to black. She turned to him, her features cast in darkness. "You of all people know how hard it would be for some Amish to leave."

The silence stretched between them as his mother's forlorn face came to mind. Rebecca pushed open the door again and the light revealed a sad smile on her beautiful face.

Jake cupped her cheek. Slowly, she wrapped her fingers around his wrist and pulled his hand away. "Good night, Jake."

He sat back in his seat and watched her run through the rain toward the house, not bothering to stop to open her umbrella. Her tote swung by her side. Once she was inside, a light came on and her shadow paused in front of the window and then disappeared.

He put the car in Reverse and backed out of Rebecca Fisher's driveway.

And out of her life.

Chapter Twelve

"The Amish have moved into New York as land has become more expensive in parts of Ohio and Pennsylvania." Jake paced in front of his Intro to the Amish class. He stopped and scanned the students, mostly composed of freshman and sophomores. He'd never get used to staring at the tops of heads hunched over their laptops, recording his every word. "Others moved here because they had disagreements within their communities."

Or perhaps if they weren't documenting his every word, they were updating their status on whatever social media was popular at the moment with the college set.

He continued, "Many Amish are moving away from farming and into other areas to make a living. They work at local factories or businesses, and some hop into vans and are taken to new neighborhoods to build homes."

As he went on speaking on the subject he knew so well, his mind wandered to the glorious fall afternoon he'd worked on the farm, enjoying every minute with Rebecca.

Jake's heart thudded dully in his chest. Rebecca's request to keep his distance still stung. But it was a request he had to honor.

A young man's hand shot up near the middle of the lecture hall. Jake flattened his palms on the large black marble surface of the long table in the front of the room. "Yes?"

"How come I see all these young Amish guys driving around in cars? Are the buggies simply for show?"

Jake put the cap on the dry erase marker and twisted it. "We'll be talking more about Rumspringa and the youth in the Amish next week. But in short, no, the buggies are not for show. The Amish in this community—the baptized Amish—do not drive cars.

"But they can ride in cars?" A young girl in front with her chin resting on her palm scrunched up her nose.

"Right." Jake glanced at his watch, trying not to show his frustration. "Are you guys also reading the text? It might help you retain some of the information we've gone over in class. You're in college now, so you need to step up your study skills. You're all registered for or have had Study Skills 101, right?"

He heard a few groans and laughed. Not many of these kids appreciated their education and probably thought nothing of the Amish not being allowed to attend school past the eighth grade.

Class was winding down. "Okay, be sure to turn in your papers by 5:00 p.m. tomorrow online. Or if you have them now, I'll take them."

Jake closed his laptop and Tommy approached his desk as the students filed out. "When do you need the papers graded?" Tommy graded the shorter papers and Jake graded the term-length project and their final.

"Next Monday would be great."

Tommy made a noise of dissatisfaction.

"Too much work for you?"

Tommy shook his head. "Not at all."

"If you're unsure, I'll spot-check a few to make sure you're on the right track."

Tommy nodded.

"You finish your applications for grad school?"

"Working on it." The young man drummed his fingers on the table.

"Is something wrong?"

"Nothing I can't work out."

And Jake didn't doubt it. Tommy had left his Amish home at eighteen and worked his way to a GED and then college. He was nothing if not resourceful.

"How's your senior project going?" Jake asked.

"The King family isn't thrilled with me coming around. Samuel and I are friends." He shrugged. "Guilty by association." He lifted his eyebrows. "Jonas and Uri were key to some of my research." Tommy seemed uncharacteristically glum. He was usually pretty easygoing.

"Reach out to other *youngie*. You can be resourceful."

"Perhaps."

"Things will calm down."

"It usually does." Something dark fluttered in the depths of Tommy's eyes. "How's Mrs. Fisher doing? All this had to come as a blow on the heels of the tragedy with her husband."

"Yes, it has." Jake purposely kept his answer short, not wanting Tommy to know that Jake had crossed the professional line with Rebecca. But that was all in the past.

Tommy frowned. "Sounds like we've both alienated

the local Amish. It doesn't bode well for our respective futures."

"Did you hear Samuel left town?"

Tommy arched an eyebrow but didn't acknowledge what he knew.

"Rebecca sent him to live in an Amish community near Rochester. For now."

Tommy tucked his laptop under his arm. "I better start cultivating more Amish friendships."

"Why don't you find some who are a little less worldly? It might give you a different perspective. Some *youngie* actually try to follow the rules."

Tommy rolled his eyes. "What fun would that be, dude? I'd have to tag along on the farm or at those tone-deaf singings for the goody-goodies. Remember, I've already experienced that firsthand."

Jake clapped his teaching assistant's shoulder with the palm of his hand. "Don't let anyone ever tell you that you haven't acclimated to the outside world, *dude*." Jake smiled when he emphasized Tommy's favorite word.

"I am nothing if not adaptable. My life experience up to now has taught me that."

"With your background, your senior project will have a unique perspective. Keep plugging away. Don't let this setback throw you."

Tommy's cell phone dinged and he glanced down at the screen. "Gotta run. I have some things to take care of."

"Night. Contact me if you have any questions once the term papers start coming in."

"Sounds good." Tommy stuffed his laptop into his backpack and hiked the strap up on his shoulder.

"You got your laptop fixed?"

"Yes. Couldn't live without one."

Jake watched the young man stomp up the stairs of the large lecture hall and disappear through the back exit. Was Tommy happy? Could people make huge life changes and not have regrets?

His parents were an example that it couldn't be done.

Could Jake be any different?

After his class ended, Jake decided to drive out to Bishop Lapp's home. When he arrived, he double-checked the time. The dark rain clouds hovering in the distance made it seem later than it was.

Jake climbed out of the truck and strolled to where he'd noticed an older Amish man leading a horse into the barn.

"How can I help you, Professor Burke?" Bishop Lapp asked without looking at him. The elderly gentleman hiked the leather straps from the horse's rigging onto a hook; his arms shook under the weight. Jake stepped forward, ready to help the man, when something made him stop. Perhaps it was the quick sideways look the bishop shot at him. Perhaps an offer of help would be offensive to a man who had spent his life on a farm.

Or perhaps an offer of help from an outsider was unwanted.

Bishop Lapp limped to the back wall and grabbed his cane. He leaned on it, resting one hand on top of the other. "Looking for more information for your study of the Plain people?" His even tone made it difficult for Jake to understand the elderly man's frame of mind.

"Actually, no."

The bishop lifted his chin in understanding. "My son Lester told me you were asking about joining the Amish. Do you think coming to me will yield you different answers?"

"I'm knowledgeable about the Amish. I understand the difficulties of joining the community as an outsider."

"Understanding the difficulties on an intellectual level is different—" the bishop enunciated each word as if to emphasize his point "—than becoming a humble man who lives in a community as a baptized member."

Jake ran a hand across his jaw. "I love Rebecca Fisher."

Did he really say that out loud?

The bishop leaned heavily on his cane and met his gaze. "Your *dat* loved your *mem*?"

"You knew my parents? You know who I am?" His father had changed their last name once they'd left Apple Creek to further distance themselves from their Amish background.

"Your parents were Mary Miller and John Leising, right?"

"Yes." A muscle ticked in his jaw. "How did you know? I've told very few people."

"You have your *mem*'s eyes. But I didn't know for sure until now."

"So, you knew them?"

"I wasn't bishop then, but yes, I knew them. Your mother was a fine woman and your father had a taste for the worldly." The older man pressed his lips together. "How are they?"

Jake glanced down, then back up at the bishop. "They're deceased."

The bishop ran a hand down his unkempt beard. "I'm sorry. Too young."

Nostalgia twisted Jake's insides as long-forgotten memories of his parents crossed his mind.

"But I suppose I remember them as the youth they were."

"My mother did die young. I was only ten. My father died when I was seventeen."

The bishop cleared his throat, as if the subject was too uncomfortable. "Now you believe you want to return to your Amish roots?"

"I have been thinking about it for a long time now. Even before I met Rebecca." The peace he felt in her presence, on her farm, had made the feelings he had buried come to the surface. "I have to continue to pray on it."

"Come with me." The bishop limped with his cane toward the barn door. "I have some information regarding baptismal classes in the house."

Jake followed him and waited outside on the porch for the older gentleman to return. When he did, the bishop handed him a book.

"Whatever you decide, you cannot make this decision lightly."

Yet another rainy day saturated the fields in Apple Creek. Rebecca was beginning to wonder if it was ever going to let up. She sat in the rocker while enjoying a cup of tea and watched Katie and Grace, a luxurious break she rarely afforded herself.

A rumble of thunder rolled over the house and a chill skittered down her spine. Rebecca grabbed two small quilts off the wood stand and put one on each girl's lap.

Katie was reading a Laura Ingalls Wilder book to her little sister. "Are you girls okay?"

Katie put her finger on the page to mark her spot and looked up.

"The storm doesn't bother you, does it?"

They shook their heads in unison. "There's no reason to be afraid," Katie said, sounding older than her eight years. "We're all snug like bugs in our house. Do you know we have a house like in *Little House on the Prairie*?"

A smile tugged at the corners of Rebecca's mouth. She had loved those books and had feared she might never be able to share them with her girls because Willard had been against most every book. She shook away the thought, unwilling to let the past ruin their cozy afternoon.

Another thunderclap rocked the house.

Rebecca looked up at the ceiling and frowned. "Buttercup's not a fan of storms." Her gaze dropped to her daughters snuggled up in the corner of the room. "I'm going to run out to the barn and make sure she's okay. You girls keep reading your book."

"Can I go with you? I can give her carrots." Grace jumped up, the quilt pooling around her feet.

"Oh, but it's yucky out. Why don't you stay inside with your big sister? Keep each other company."

With a huff, Grace plopped down on the rocker her mother had vacated. Rebecca picked up the quilt and tucked it around her daughter, ignoring her little tantrum. "I'll be back in soon and then I'll warm up some soup for dinner. Okay?"

Rebecca put on her raincoat, flipped up the hood and

grabbed a few carrots to put in her pocket. She opened the back door and hustled down the back steps. Her boots squished in the mud as she crossed the yard to the barn.

When will this rain ever stop?

Squinting against the pelting rain, she picked up speed. She clutched her hood to prevent a gust of wind from blowing it down.

When she reached the barn and pushed back the door, another rumble of thunder rolled across the sky. Goose bumps prickled her skin. Sensing someone was watching her, she glanced behind her. Nothing but fields.

A truck barreled down the country road.

Turning her attention back to the task at hand, she entered the dimly lit barn and pulled a carrot out of her pocket.

"Hey, Buttercup. Everything's okay," she said in a soothing voice. "The storm will pass quickly." A part of her felt as if she was trying to convince herself.

The storm in her life would pass quickly. Reaching through the wide spaces in the bars of the stall, she patted the horse. Buttercup neighed. "You've been through a lot, too, huh?"

Buttercup eagerly ate the carrot and then sniffed Rebecca's hand, eager for more. She reached into her pocket and found another carrot. "Here you go."

She rubbed the side of the horse's head until she seemed to calm down. She decided to find a blanket for Buttercup, to comfort her.

She walked to the back of the barn and past a door yawning open to the back fields. Something blue flashed in her periphery and then disappeared behind the outbuilding where Willard had kept a stash of weapons. She often wondered what he had been planning if he hadn't been caught. She hadn't been in the building since before Willard's arrest.

Biting her lower lip, she wondered if she had imagined the movement.

She returned to Buttercup, covered her with a blanket and patted her. "Everything is going to be okay."

Rebecca grabbed the pitchfork and measured the weight of it in her hands. With a fluttery feeling in her chest, she strode out of the barn, glancing toward the house. Her daughters were in there. They were safe. She'd never be able to relax unless she checked the outbuilding and made sure someone wasn't trespassing on her property.

Pulling her hood back over her head, she held her raincoat close at her neck and gripped the pitchfork tightly in the other hand. She'd never be able to use it as a weapon, but what the potential trespasser didn't know might save her.

A long time ago, she had ceased being a quiet Amish wife. She had to be the head of this household. Protect her family.

You're seeing things, silly woman. Willard's voice clashed with the wind and rain and a dull roar of thunder moving off to the east.

Each step seemed harder to take, but she knew if she stopped she'd lose her nerve. When she reached the outbuilding, she pressed her body against the wall and peered toward the open door.

Was someone in there?

A rustle of plastic sounded overhead. She glanced up just in time to see a huge blue tarp dropping out of the sky. She raised her hands to fling it away when something heavy landed on top of her, shoving her down into the wet mud. Her pitchfork useless by her side.

Dear Lord, help me.

Chapter Thirteen

Jake placed the book on the passenger seat of his truck and made a spontaneous decision to drive over to check on Rebecca and the girls. He knew the bishop had seen to it that she had some help with the farm now that Uri and Jonas were prohibited from working for her. But there were always things to be done.

He knew Rebecca wanted him to stay away because their future was predetermined due to their different backgrounds. He tapped the book on the seat next to him. Nervous indecision pressed on his chest. Maybe... just maybe he could change that.

As Jake rounded the curve on the country road, the clouds had turned an ominous steely gray. He adjusted the windshield wiper speed to keep pace with the driving rain. A rumble of thunder sounded overhead. When he turned up Rebecca's driveway, her quaint home came into view beyond his blurry windshield. He really needed to replace his wipers.

Jake climbed out of the vehicle, flipped up his hood and shuddered against the cool rain. Bent forward, he jogged toward the house. He lifted his hand to knock when he heard a cry in the distance. He spun around and squinted toward the sound. Katie and Grace were holding hands, dodging mud puddles and running toward the barn.

Unease twisted around his spine.

Where was their mother?

Perhaps she had been in front of the girls and had reached the barn before the strange muffled cry rang out. *What was that?* Not wanting to waste another moment, he ran after them, muttering his annoyance when his dress shoes sank in the mud with each step.

He also really needed to get some boots.

He caught up with the girls inside the barn's entrance. Katie had her arm around Grace, comforting her. He glanced around the barn. *No Rebecca.*

"Girls, what are you doing out in this weather? Your mother will be worried about you."

The girls turned around as a unit. Grace had red-rimmed eyes and wet cheeks, both from the rain and tears. His heart stuttered.

"What's wrong?"

"*Mem* came out to the barn to check on Buttercup and—" Katie sniffed "—and she didn't come back." Katie squeezed her sister's shoulders. "I thought she couldn't get Buttercup to settle down and that's why it was taking a long time." The corners of her mouth tugged down in a heartbreaking display of emotion. "She's gone."

Tamping down his growing unease, Jake crouched down to the girls' level. "Are you sure she's not in the house?"

"*Neh*, we came from the house."

Grace's big eyes canvased the barn. "She's missing. Maybe she's gone like our big brother."

Jake gently touched Grace's arm. "Your *mem* wouldn't leave you."

"After our *dat* went away," Katie joined in, "Samuel promised us he would never leave. But he did."

A knot formed in Jake's stomach. These poor children had experienced much loss in their young lives.

Jake surreptitiously scanned the barn behind the girls, looking for any signs of mischief. "Your *mem* came out here to check on Buttercup?"

Grace nodded and her chest rose and fell on a sob. "Buttercup doesn't like thunder."

As if on cue, the horse neighed her annoyance at a distant rumble of thunder. Jake strolled over to the horse's stall with the girls and let them pet her. "Buttercup's fine."

His pulse ticked in his ears, like time slipping away. But he didn't want to jump to conclusions or to alarm the girls. "Let me get you both inside, then I'll come back out and find your mom."

"Where can *Mem* be?" Katie asked. The slightly older girl easily slipped into the role of big sister, protector. But even she had a hitch in her voice.

Grace broke away from her big sister and clung to Jake. He wrapped an arm around her and squeezed. "It's going to be okay." A drip of rain plopped down onto her bonnet from a leak in the barn roof. He smiled, trying to lighten the mood. "Let's get you inside where it's dry."

Grace took his hand. The feel of the little girl's cool hand in his caught him off guard. His parents had never been affectionate. It was not a common trait of the Amish. Yet Grace must have been frightened enough to reach up and take his hand. He smiled down and gently squeezed her hand. "Everything will be okay."

Grace nodded.

Katie marched ahead and when they stepped outside the barn, he noticed the rain had turned from a torrential downpour to a gentle shower. In the distance against the gunmetal sky, a streak of lightning flashed. He noticed Katie quietly counting under her breath. Then a crash of thunder. Grace startled next to him.

"Seven," Katie said confidently. "The storm is seven miles away. We're okay."

Jake reached out with his free hand and gently touched Katie's shoulder. "Yes, we are. Let's hurry inside so you don't get too wet."

They pounded up the steps of the porch. The front door stood open and, instinctively, Jake moved the girls behind him.

"Did you girls leave the door open?"

Grace shrugged and Katie looked a little sheepish.

Jake stepped into the room, holding the girls back. He called out for Rebecca, but he was met with only the soft sound of rain on the roof.

"No, Professor, she's outside. I told you," Katie said, her voice edged with youthful exasperation.

"I know, honey. The door was open. I wanted to make sure she hadn't returned while we were in the barn."

Jake made the girls sit in the rockers in the front room while he quickly checked all the rooms in the house, calling Rebecca's name while he did.

As the seconds ticked away, his unease amped up.

Something was wrong.

"Katie, follow me to the door." When she did, he turned and said, "Lock it behind me. I'll be right back with your *mem*."

She nodded. Jake paused on the porch while he listened for the snap of the bolt. He pulled his hood up, stood at the edge of the porch and scanned the yard.

"Rebecca," he called, cupping his mouth. "Rebecca."

His mouth grew dry.

No answer.

The wind kicked up and blew leaves across the yard, some settling against the grate protecting the underside of the porch.

Jake stepped off the porch and ran toward the barn.

Where are you, Rebecca? Where are you?

Planting her palms into the cold, wet mud, Rebecca pushed herself up. The blue tarp crinkled in the wind and the distinct smell of plastic mixed with the earthy scent of mud tickled her nose. She braced herself, fearing whoever had thrown this down over her would jump on top of her to finish her off.

Fear tingled her scalp.

Maybe the wind had blown the tarp down on her. Maybe her imagination was getting the best of her.

Yet the tarp felt weighted at the corners.

Pulse whooshing in her ears, she held out her arm and yanked back a side of the stiff tarp, finally untangling herself from this mess. A cool breeze caressed her damp cheeks as she squinted up at the darkening sky. The shadow of the outbuilding hunkered over her like an ominous threat.

"Is someone there?" Her soft voice shook, barely audible over the stiff winds.

A solid thud and a groan sounded from around the back of the building. Gathering the folds of her dress, she pushed to her feet. She picked up the pitchfork. Pressing against the rough wood of the poorly cared for shed, she shuffled toward the edge, afraid of being detected.

Someone was running across the field. Away from her.

She stood paralyzed, flat against the building. Her grip tightened on the tool.

Was it one of the Yoder brothers?

She couldn't be sure. All she could see was a dark form growing smaller across the field.

A deep voice carried on the wind. Was someone calling her?

"Rebecca."

Glancing toward the barn, she realized the house was out of view, but at least whoever had thrown the tarp on her was running away from the house.

Her girls should be safe.

A tingling started in her fingers and worked its way up her arms. She had to check on them to be sure.

As she stepped away from the shed, she noticed its door yawned open. All her senses went on high alert. The glass on the bottom pane closest to the door handle was broken.

Willard used to keep the outbuilding's door locked. The building was little more than an oversize shed. He'd kept weapons in there. A million memories swirled in her head. Willard's angry voice to stay away from his stuff scraped across her brain.

Willard's gone. He can't hurt me.

Holding her breath, Rebecca pushed the door all the way open. It creaked on its hinges and bounced off a nearby table. Goose bumps raced across her flesh as she stepped into the small structure. The unkempt ten-by-ten space was empty save for branches hanging from the ceiling.

The marijuana? She reached up and touched the drying leaves. A pain started behind her eyes.

How could this be?

Rebecca lifted her hand to her temples and rubbed.

"Rebecca!" The familiar sound of Jake's voice made her spin around.

"I'm here." She ran toward the door and tripped on the lip of the doorway. She caught herself on the doorframe.

Jake came into view and the look of relief on his face caught her off guard and secretly thrilled her. He gripped her shoulders and angled his head. "What happened to you?" He stared at the pitchfork.

Rebecca leaned it against the wall.

"I'm fine. I'm fine." She searched frantically behind him, looking toward the main house. "Are the girls okay?"

"Yes, yes. They're fine. I saw them before I came looking for you. Now tell me. What happened?"

Rebecca pointed up, to the roof of the outbuilding. "Someone threw a tarp down on me. And then he took off. Over there." She pointed across the field.

Jake squinted in the direction she pointed. "I don't see anyone."

"I'm afraid he's gotten away."

Jake turned his attention back to Rebecca. He brushed

his thumb across her cheek. When his thumb came away with dirt, she stepped back and swiped at her face, heat reddening her cheeks. "I landed face-first in the dirt."

"Are you okay?"

She stepped out of the doorway and raised her palm to the contents inside. "Look at this. Tell me what this means."

Jake slipped past her and took in the scene.

"I thought the police destroyed the drugs," she whispered.

"Whoever knocked you out must have grabbed a few plants before they escaped."

"Why are they hanging the plants?"

"I don't know much about marijuana, but I imagine they needed to dry it out and cure it. To get it ready to sell." Jake touched one of the leaves. "It seems too damp in here."

"They probably were trying to put the tarp on the roof to stop it from leaking." A smile pulled at the corners of her mouth.

He smiled, mirroring her, but one of his brows pulled down at the corner as if her sudden change in mood had confused him. He wiped what he suspected was another spot of mud from her cheek. "You are a mysterious woman, Rebecca. Why are you smiling?"

"Don't you see? This—" she held her palm up to the shed that had seen better days "—this proves my son is innocent. Samuel's near Rochester. He couldn't have been responsible for this. He's innocent."

Chapter Fourteen

The hope in Rebecca's eyes crushed Jake. He wanted nothing more than to reassure her. To tell her that Samuel *was* innocent.

What did this incident really mean? Leaning over, he dragged the damp tarp away from the building and saw nothing other than an uneven muddy patch. He held out his hand to the dirt staining the front of her dress. "This is where you fell?"

Rebecca brushed at her dress but it only served to rub it in. "Yes. I didn't see the man until he was running away." A look of disgust flickered across her face. Jake turned and squinted up at the roof of the small outbuilding.

A gust of wind whipped up and brought with it more rain.

"Let's get inside." With a hand gently on the small of her back, Jake guided Rebecca across the uneven earth.

When they reached the house, Rebecca turned the handle and found the door locked. A look of concern creased her smooth forehead.

"I told them to lock it."

Rebecca looked up at him with gratitude in her eyes. "Thank you for looking out for them. I shouldn't have left them alone, but we were all worried about Buttercup in this storm…"

"They're fine. Don't beat yourself up."

"It's so dark out here. Anyone could be out there." Her lips began to tremble. "We're out here all alone. If something more serious had happened to me, who would have…"

Jake leaned in close and resisted the urge to kiss away the tears. "It'll be okay. You have to trust in God."

"I've done nothing *but* trust in God." She plucked at her skirt again. "Look at me."

Jake stared at the top of her bonnet, unsure of how to comfort her. He didn't want to offend her by drawing her into his arms. He didn't want to add to her inner turmoil.

"Are you ready to go in?" he whispered. He knew she wouldn't want to upset the girls by appearing out of sorts.

Rebecca lifted her head and swiped at her cheeks, leaving more mud streaks. Jake felt a smile tugging on the corners of his mouth. "You are a real mess."

"I'm fine. It's not unusual to get a little dirty working the farm."

"In the rain," he added.

"Exactly." A bright light shone in her eyes. A slow smile crept across his face in response to hers. He had done that. He had brought Rebecca a small moment of happiness.

They locked gazes, and then she lifted her hand and knocked. From inside, he heard a fumbling as someone worked the lock. The door eased open and Katie's curious gaze appeared in the crack. When she saw her mother, she pulled the door all the way open.

"Mem," Katie said, her eyes drawn to her mother's dirty clothes. "What happened to your dress?"

Rebecca waved her hand in dismissal. "I fell in the mud." When Katie's eyes opened wide, her mother reassured her. "I'm fine. Nothing a good scrub won't get out."

Katie stepped back and Grace ran up, wrapping her arms around her mother's waist undeterred by the mud. "Don't ever leave us."

Jake read every sorrowful emotion playing out on Rebecca's pretty face. Squaring her shoulders, she said, "Oh honey, I was checking on a few things and got caught in the rain." She ran her hand down her daughter's head. "You're getting all muddy." She took her daughter's hands and held her at arm's length. "I'm here. I'm your *mem*. I'm not going anywhere."

Across the room, Katie stared at Jake with her little mouth set in a pout. Then her steely gaze landed on her mother. "You have dirt on your face."

Rebecca lifted her hand to her cheek. "I know. I'll have to clean up."

"When is Samuel coming home? *He* should have been checking on Buttercup."

Rebecca stepped back and Jake caught her arm to steady her, then quickly dropped his hand. Rebecca met Jake's gaze.

"We'll talk about this later," Rebecca said to her daughter.

"Aenti Gloria said you sent my brother away because he was bad. Now with him gone things would be better." The child sounded much older than her years.

Rebecca slowly sat down on the rocker, playing with the cold, wet, muddy folds of her skirt. "This is a very grown-up conversation. Your brother made some bad decisions. He didn't follow the rules. We must pray that he finds his way."

Katie's lips twitched and she looked up at Jake. "*He* shouldn't keep coming around here. It's not right."

Both he and Rebecca realized Katie had redirected her fear over her missing mother to disappointment over her brother's absence. When that didn't earn her any satisfaction, she channeled her anger toward Jake.

"I wanted to make sure your mom was okay," Jake said.

Rebecca stood and opened the door. "And since I am, Professor Burke is heading home," she said pointedly to Jake. "Thank you for stopping by, but my girls and I are fine." Her eyes projected an apology.

Jake stepped closer to Rebecca and whispered, "Can we talk on the porch?"

Rebecca sighed heavily.

Without waiting for an answer, Jake slipped the quilt from the rack and draped it around her shoulders. *"Please,"* he whispered.

She seemed to take in the room, then stepped out on the porch with him.

She crossed her arms under the quilt. "What is it?"

"I don't want you to get your hopes up."

Her eye twitched. "About Samuel?"

"Yes, just because he's not here doesn't make him innocent. He could have been working with the Yoder brothers. Or someone else. One of them might have thrown the tarp over you today."

Rebecca bit her lower lip. "Call the sheriff. Tell him what happened here. Ask if he'll check on the Yoders. Maybe one of them will…what would you say…crack? Can you do that for me?"

"Yes." He touched her elbow and she stepped back as if it burned. "You need to be careful out here all alone with the girls."

"This is my home." She set her jaw. "And the more I think of it, you shouldn't be here. It doesn't help. I'm trying desperately to be a good influence on my girls. We need stability."

Bowing his head, Jake ran a hand across the back of his neck. He hadn't anticipated sharing his plans, but he needed to reach across the gap. "I've talked to Bishop Lapp."

"About Samuel?" The indignation was evident in her tone. "I don't need—"

"I talked to him about me," he interrupted.

She looked up, curiosity lighting her brown eyes. *"You?"*

Jake leaned on the porch railing and crossed his arms. "I have never felt more at home than I do here. With you."

Rebecca tugged the quilt closer around her neck. "I don't understand."

"I'm exploring being baptized into the Amish community."

Her brows snapped together. "What? Why?" She leaned toward him, then stepped back, flattening herself against the siding of her house. "Is this all part of your research? For some paper?" Her eyes sparked with anger. "We are not…" She bowed her head and grew quiet.

He pushed off the railing and stood in front of her,

careful not to make her feel trapped. "No, it's not for a paper. It's not for my job at the university… It's for you."

His heart pounded in his ears and her face went still. She took a step to the side and yanked open the door. She paused but didn't turn around.

"Despite that fancy education, you have it all wrong about the Amish. All wrong."

She stepped inside and closed the door. He heard the lock click.

"You look exhausted," Flo said, screwing the silver top of the saltshaker back on after refilling it. She placed it in the rack next to the pepper, set it aside, then turned to give her full attention to Rebecca.

"I am. I couldn't sleep." Rebecca blinked her eyes a few times, trying to get rid of the gritty feeling. She grabbed the gray bin of clean silverware and placed it on the counter with a clatter.

Flo laid out a paper napkin and rolled a fork, spoon and steak knife in it. "No need to be lying awake at night. You did the best thing for Samuel right now."

"I have faith Samuel will be okay." Rebecca sounded bleak, unconvincing.

Flo rolled up another napkin with silverware and tossed it into the basket. The older woman tipped her head toward the large bin of silverware. "I've heard busy hands are the best antidote for a worried mind." She arched a brow in amusement.

Rebecca felt her face grow warm. "I'm sorry—I'm distracted." She scooped up a knife, fork and spoon, placed them on a napkin and started rolling. She hated bringing her worries to her friend, but she felt lonely sometimes and she couldn't get the conversation she had had with Jake yesterday out of her mind.

Jake was considering joining the Amish community.

"I have a feeling it's not only Samuel who's distracting you." Flo never missed anything.

"Jake…" She lifted her eyes to meet Flo's. The older woman nodded in understanding.

Rebecca held up her hand to stop her friend before she made a comment that would make her blush. "I have to tell you because you're the only one I can trust not to judge me."

Flo rested her hip against the counter and slipped her hands into her apron. "What is it, honey?"

"Jake told me he's thinking about joining the Amish." Her pale eyebrows shot up. "Really?"

Rebecca nodded slowly, feeling the world close in on her. Heat gathered around her face and she tugged on the collar of her dress.

"Do people do that? I don't think I've ever heard of an outsider joining the Amish community. I usually hear about the heartache when one of the Amish youth runs away." Flo stood straighter, her eyes unfocused as if lost in thought. "*Can* people do that?"

"It's highly unusual, but it has been done."

A light came into Flo's eyes and she lifted her hands and covered her mouth. "Oh dear, he's doing it so he can be with you, isn't he?"

Rebecca bowed her head and shook it. "He must make the decision on his own for reasons more than me." Her mind flashed back to how comfortable Jake seemed working on the farm. His mention of feeling at peace.

She pressed her lips together and sighed. "*Neh*, he can't join the Amish community just because of me."

With her index finger, Flo lifted Rebecca's chin to force her to meet her gaze. "You *are* worth it. Don't underestimate yourself."

Rebecca shook her head again, this time more adamantly. "He should do it because he wants to embrace the Amish ways. No other reason."

"Of course, of course," Flo agreed, "but you would be a nice bonus."

Rebecca was surprised to hear a giggle escape her lips. "You're the best part of this job. I'm grateful for your friendship."

Flo made a dramatic show of looking around the diner. "That's high praise," she said, her words dripping with sarcasm. Then her face grew serious and she pulled Rebecca's hands into hers. "It's time you found happiness."

"It's not the—"

"—Amish way," Flo finished her sentence. "I truly don't think God would mind if you found happiness."

With Flo's words swirling around her head, Rebecca picked up more silverware and set it down on the napkin.

Could she and Jake find happiness together?

The empty space inside her no longer seemed so empty. Dare she hope?

The jangling bell on the door signaled the arrival of a few customers coming in for an early breakfast.

"Have a seat wherever you'd like," Flo hollered to them.

The older woman grabbed the coffee carafe. "I'll get this table."

"Thanks." Rebecca's gratitude was short-lived. The sheriff walked through the door with his keen focus solely on her.

Rebecca filled a mug with coffee. Black. Just how the sheriff liked it. He strolled over to the counter and slipped onto the stool in front of the mug. "Morning, Rebecca. Thanks for the coffee."

"Morning, Sheriff Maxwell."

He took a sip, studying her over the rim. "Have you recovered from last night?"

"I'm fine. No worse for the wear, I suppose. But it'll take some work to get the mud out of my dress." She smiled. "Did you have a chance to talk to the Yoder boys?" Butterflies flitted in her stomach as she waited for the sheriff's response.

"Yeah. I met Jake at their house. Mr. Yoder assured us that both boys had been home all day doing chores on the farm. At the approximate time of the incident, Mrs. Yoder said the family was gathered for dinner."

A sinking feeling weighed on Rebecca. "I see."

"There's always a chance they're mistaken," the sheriff said, setting his spoon on the napkin. A brown spot grew where he had placed it.

"Mr. And Mrs. Yoder are good people. I don't believe they'd lie." Outside the window, the weather was dark and dreary, like her mood.

Flo brushed past her and pinned her order to the wheel above the window leading into the kitchen. "Morning, Sheriff Maxwell. Hungry for some breakfast? Pancakes?"

The sheriff took another sip of his coffee, then pushed

away from the counter and stood. "No, thanks. I have to get on the road."

He turned to Rebecca. "Contact me if you need anything. Please." She must have been wearing a look of concern because the sheriff paused. "Hannah would want you to reach out. To me. *To her.* She loves you and doesn't want anything to happen to you."

"Thank you." Rebecca slowly blinked. "Have a good day, Sheriff."

Flo picked up a small stack of plastic menus and pressed them into Rebecca's hands. "Next table's yours."

"Thanks." Rebecca started to walk away when she heard Flo mumble.

"Professor Burke would look great in suspenders and a straw hat."

Rebecca whirled around and playfully whacked her friend with a menu. "Shush."

"You shush." Flo reached out and squeezed Rebecca's hand. "It's time things turned around for you."

"Go ahead, I'll lock up," Rebecca said to Flo at the end of their shift a few days later. She had sent her girls to stay overnight at Mark and Gloria's house. Even though Rebecca hated to have her daughters away at night, she knew playing with their cousins afforded a wonderful distraction. They needed a stable home environment.

Jake's conversation came to mind again. The girls could use a father in their lives. A loving father.

Neh, neh, neh. If Jake decided to become Amish, it had to be for the right reasons.

"No, no, I'll stay and help." Flo dumped the remainder of the coffee down the drain.

"Go." Rebecca scooted in next to her, took the carafe from her hand and set it on the counter. She'd wash it in a minute. "I know you wanted to get home to watch your TV program. Go."

"Ah, you say that like it's a bad thing." Flo tilted her head and gave Rebecca a sad smile. Rebecca didn't know how to respond anymore. It seemed lately everyone watched her with an air of pity. At least when the tourists came to town in full force next summer, she could go back to playing her stereotypical Amish role. She could at least meet someone's expectations.

Met real-live Amish woman. *Check.*

"Are your girls staying with their aunt and uncle again tonight?"

Rebecca wiped the counter down. *"Yah."* Even though she hated to admit it, she felt safer knowing they were with Mark and his family. Until she cleared Samuel's name and found out who was growing marijuana on her farm, things wouldn't feel safe there.

She scrubbed the carafe a little more vigorously than necessary, trying to hold back her emotions.

Flo gestured with her chin toward the last table. "Want me to tell him it's time to pack it in?" she asked in a protective tone. "I don't know why those college kids have to hog our tables to do their schoolwork when there's a perfectly good library on campus, right?"

Rebecca shrugged. She had only been on the local campus once, and after being attacked she didn't plan on going back anytime soon.

"The customer's fine. I'll give him a few more minutes while I clean up."

"As long as you're sure."

Rebecca watched her friend remove her apron, drape it over her arm and slip out the front door, the bells clacking on the glass.

Rebecca organized things to make startup easier for the first shift. She glanced up and the young man was still sitting there, his back to her, she supposed, to gain a better view out the window.

She flicked off a few lights, figuring he'd take a hint without her having to ask him to leave. Confrontation had never been her strong suit. She tidied up a few more things, then peeked into the dining room through the service window. The young man was no longer sitting in the corner booth. A hint of relief swept through her. Problem solved.

Rebecca strode to the front door and turned the key in the lock. She paused a minute and stared over the darkened street. Her haunted expression stared back at her. Would her life ever calm down? Would she ever find the peace she once enjoyed living on an Amish farm? *Before* she'd married Willard. She longed for it, but she knew she had to be humble and trust in God's plan.

She set the keys on the edge of the counter when she realized she'd forgotten to empty the orange-handled decaf carafe sitting on the warmer in the far corner.

A scraping sound—the sound of someone dragging keys across the counter—made her swing around. Her heart stopped at the strange expression on the young man's face.

"Hello, Mrs. Fisher."

"Hello… Tommy." *Jake's assistant.* Her gaze dropped to the keys in his hand. *Her keys.* "I didn't realize you were still here." She lifted a shaky hand to the corner booth. "I didn't realize that was you in the booth."

"I was in the little boy's room."

She held her hand out for her keys. "I'll let you out."

Tommy pressed the keys between his palms and pulled them close to his chest. "You want me to leave?" His mocking tone sent terror racing through her veins.

"Um, yes…" She drew her elbows in close to her sides. *It's Tommy. Jake's assistant. He's harmless.* Dread tightened like a band around her lungs. "We're closed for the night," she said, a little more forcefully.

Tommy pivoted to look out the front window, then turned back to her, a brazen expression on his face. "Shame. I have more studying to do."

"Where are your books?"

He gestured with his head toward a backpack resting on the floor near a booth.

"I'm sorry. The diner is closed." Rebecca clasped her hands in front of her as she struggled to rein in her frantic emotions. Something was off.

"I know." Tommy made no effort to move toward the front door. "I'm not ready to leave." He tossed the keys from one hand to the other; each time they landed in his hand with a loud jangle of metal.

Rebecca wiped her sweat-slicked palms on her cotton skirt. She held out her hand again, determined to be more forceful. "I need my keys, *please*."

An oily smile slid across Tommy's lips and he made no effort to offer her the keys.

Rebecca forced a shaky smile, trying to hide her nerves. "I need the keys to unlock the door to let you out."

Tommy lifted the keys and tossed them well past her. Rebecca spun round. The keys crashed into a framed football jersey from a long-ago high school state championship team and clunked onto the ground.

The words *why are you doing this?* froze on her lips as a cold chill swept over every inch of her skin.

Rebecca ran around the counter to put a barrier between her and Tommy. She glanced over her shoulder to the kitchen, but the back door to the alley was locked and she needed the key to unlock it. Same went for the front door.

Tommy slowly walked toward her. "I have good news and I have bad news. Which would you like first?"

Rebecca shook her head in disbelief. "You need to leave. I have to close the diner," she repeated.

"Okay, I'll give you the good news." He dragged his hand across his mussed hair. "Samuel was telling the truth. He wasn't involved with the drugs at all." A light lit his eyes in a way that sent terror pumping through her veins. "*I* was the one who recruited your Amish farmhands into helping me grow marijuana on your land."

Rebecca stared at Tommy in disbelief, her vision narrowing and tiny dots dancing in her eyes.

"Don't you want to know the bad news?" His lips thinned into a line and he shook his head slowly. "You won't be able to tell anyone because I'm going to kill you."

Chapter Fifteen

Jake walked across campus to grab a bite to eat before heading home. The school kept the student union open late for hungry students. A half carton of expired milk and a mushy cucumber were probably the only things waiting for him in his refrigerator at home.

When Jake reached the student union, he noticed the news station blaring on the wall TV. He slowed when he saw the news truck on a country road in front of a familiar home.

The laughter of students at a nearby table dulled to a distant din. He moved closer to the television. Jake glanced around the mostly empty dining room. No one except the young woman reading a novel bothered to look up occasionally at the screen.

"...*As you may remember, this is the home of Willard Fisher, the Amish fanatic who killed his Amish neighbors to protect the Amish way of life. Now his son, Samuel Fisher, has been arrested for growing marijuana on this very land.*"

The well-groomed blonde newscaster angled her body and held out her hand to gesture to the land behind her.

"The whole situation is ironic, Jim, considering his father killed *to preserve the Amish ways, yet his own son has turned to what the Amish would call worldly ways."*

Jake plowed his hand through his hair and sagged against the half wall that separated the TV area from the rest of the cafeteria.

"Who alerted the news?" Jake muttered to himself.

A well-coiffed man with shiny black hair filled the screen, a serious look on his face. *"Have you been able to get a comment from his stepmother, Rebecca Fisher?"*

The screen split in two and the reporter appeared again, her fingers pressed to her earpiece. *"No, Jim. Not yet. No one is home at the residence. We hope to catch Mrs. Fisher when she returns."* She smiled brightly and Jake's stomach dropped at the ghoulishness of their voyeurism.

"Excuse me," an annoyed voice came from behind Jake.

Jake glanced over his shoulder at a young woman craning her head to see around him. "Oh, sorry."

Jake checked his watch. It was getting late, but if he hurried, he could catch Rebecca at the diner before she went home for the night. He didn't want her to get a camera in her face in her front yard.

But more important, he wanted to be there for Rebecca. She might not want to admit it, but she was the closest thing to family that he had.

* * *

Tommy was behind the drugs!

Rebecca's pulse thrummed in her ears as she scrambled to find an escape. "*Please*, don't hurt me. I have two young daughters. Without me, they'll be orphans."

Rebecca clamped her jaw, trying to tamp down her rioting emotions. Willard's constant criticism and yelling had taught her to hide her feelings behind a mask of calm. She had been successful *most* of the time. She had learned to be a good Amish wife to keep peace in the home. But she had failed her children miserably.

"Go into the kitchen," Tommy said, grabbing her arm.

Using the backrest of the nearest stool to anchor herself, she shook her head. She wasn't going into the kitchen where no one could see her from the street. "No."

Tommy pulled her arm and she held tightly onto the stool with the other. Craning her neck, Rebecca glanced toward the street and her panic spiked when she realized no one was out there. No one to save her. Her fingers felt numb. She'd have to figure a way out. On her own.

For her daughters' sakes. For Samuel's. If she died, what would happen to them?

A sense of calm and determination settled over her.

"I'm not going anywhere with you."

Tommy grunted and peered around; the dark look in his eyes chipped away at her resolve.

"Tell me why you're doing this."

Tommy narrowed his gaze. "I wouldn't expect an uneducated Amish woman to understand, especially one who was stupid enough to marry the biggest loser in Apple Creek."

Rebecca sucked in a gasp. Even though she had constantly said worse in her own mind, hearing someone say it out loud was like a punch to the gut.

She hiked her chin, trying to muster a confidence she didn't feel. "Willard made his own bad decisions. I had nothing to do with it."

Tommy leaned in closer. The stale smell of coffee on his breath assaulted her nose. "He lived with you, slept in your bed and *you* didn't know what was going on?" He raised an eyebrow, a mocking glint lit his eyes.

"I didn't know what he was up to. I trusted him. Much like Professor Burke trusted you."

"Don't try to manipulate me."

The walls swayed and Rebecca sent up a silent prayer. "You'll go to jail for the rest of your life. You don't want that."

Tommy lifted an eyebrow. "Your murder will be blamed on Samuel. Poor Samuel, the son of the evil Willard Fisher. Then maybe I can put some distance between me and this mess while I figure things out."

"Samuel will tell the police you were involved with the drugs. You won't get away with it."

"*Ha.* Samuel doesn't know I'm behind it. He only knows about the Yoder brothers. And I don't suspect they'll get involved. You know how the Amish feel about law enforcement, right? And they'd have to admit their guilt. Don't see that happening. Besides, Samuel already confessed." He laughed again.

"Samuel's not even in Apple Creek. No one will blame him for this."

"I'll figure something out. I always do."

"No…" Rebecca's vision tunneled and her knees grew weak. Tommy had obviously lost his mind.

Dear Lord, help me. Give me wisdom. Let me get home to my family.

Breathe. In. Out. In. Out.

She closed her eyes briefly and Tommy came into focus. Obviously Tommy needed to be heard, otherwise he would have already hurt her. She had seen the same behavior in her husband. He liked to rant and rave and pace, forcing her to listen to his half-cocked theories. It was when she accidentally looked at him the wrong way or didn't make dinner on time that he'd lash out. He'd belittle her. Point out all her shortcomings, real or imagined.

She clung to the back of the stool tighter. "You've done well for yourself. Why did you get involved with drugs?" She had to keep him talking.

Tommy angled his head, an unreadable expression on his face. A surge of adrenaline coursed through her. Had he sensed she was patronizing him?

"I *was* making something of myself." For a fleeting moment, he seemed smug, then his gaze snapped into focus and landed with an unnerving intensity on her. "And *you* had to ruin that." He reared back and spit in her face.

Wincing, she lifted her shoulder and wiped the spittle from her cheek.

She struggled to swallow around a parched throat. "Did you break into my house, too?"

"I was looking for a dry place for the marijuana plants. Like your basement. But you just kept interfering."

"You were in *my* home," she bit out the words. "I've never done anything to you. I don't understand."

"You wouldn't. You're satisfied with your *small* life

here in Apple Creek. Working at this boring diner. You haven't been able to survive doing what your ancestors have done for years. Farm." His lips grew pinched.

"I have a family. I have young daughters. *Please.* Leave me be." She let go of the stool and ran toward the wall where Tommy had thrown the keys.

The sound of footsteps behind her made her pulse spike.

Please, God, let me escape.

Tommy slammed her against a nearby booth, pinning her body against the cool vinyl. He squeezed her cheeks with his rough hand. She struggled to draw in a breath, yet she bit back the sting of tears. She would *not* let him see her cry.

"You *shouldn't* have done that, crazy woman."

The memory of Willard's harsh rebukes scraped across her brain tangling with Tommy's gruff voice. His rough touch.

"You're *not* going home." Tommy lifted his hand, ready to strike her. "I'll kill you right here." She closed her eyes against the rage playing out across his features. "Your daughters will be better off without you."

The adrenaline spike made her feel both anxious and strong at the same time.

Do something! Save yourself!

Rebecca raised her arm suddenly, pushing his hand away from her face. She hip checked him and he fell on his backside, cursing her in surprise.

Rebecca bolted toward the kitchen. Her only hope now was to get to the phone on the wall next to the swinging door. She just had to dial three numbers: 9-1-1.

Icy fear pumped through her veins. Her sole focus was on the white receiver. She reached out and grabbed it.

"You ain't going anywhere." Tommy flung the phone out of her hand and it dangled by the curly cord. The distant dial tone mocked her.

Rebecca spun around and glared at him. He stopped short of slamming into her. His eyes drew into angry slits. "Because of you, I can't afford tuition. I won't be able to continue my studies. No degree means I'm going to be no better off as an outsider than I was as a Plain person." His face crumbled in rage. He grabbed her arms and squeezed. "Do you understand?"

"I understand that you've been terrorizing me to keep me quiet. To get me to stop asking questions." She thought of all the incidents of late. Her campus scare. Getting run off the road. Getting attacked not once, but twice on the farm. "You have to realize I'd do anything to protect my family. To protect Samuel. Now, *get out*!"

"If Samuel hadn't started acting all weird, you wouldn't have started asking questions." Tommy gripped her tighter and pain shot up her arms. "I want to ruin Samuel's life like he's ruined mine."

Keep me calm, Lord. Help me. When Tommy didn't budge, she blinked back her fear and met his harsh gaze. "Take your hands off me *now*."

Surprisingly, Tommy dropped his hands. He muttered something under his breath she didn't understand. He paced, his movements short and jerky. She eyed the keys on the floor by the wall.

"You destroyed the marijuana crops. *You* destroyed the last bit of hope I had of making money. You ruined everything that I had carefully planned. Do you know how hard it was to find a farm I could do this on? To find Uri and Jonas, who were willing to help me?"

"There have to be other ways to pay for college." Rebecca realized she was trying to reason with a young man who was past the point of reasoning.

"You would know this how?"

Rebecca took a step backward closer to the front door. "You can't do this. You can't hurt me. You'll end up in jail for life."

Tommy let out an obnoxious laugh. "Yeah, right. I'm not going to jail. And if Samuel could have played it cool after he realized the Yoder brothers had planted the marijuana, no one would have been the wiser.

"Uri and Jonas tried to bribe Samuel. Keep him quiet, but—" Tommy snorted "—I think it made him feel worse. He wasn't supposed to have worldly things. They warned him to keep his mouth shut or bad things could happen. He went over the edge after Elmer died. Stupid kid. Then you started in with the questions."

"Tommy, it's over now." Rebecca kept her tone calm. "You must take responsibility."

"No." Rage vibrated off him. "I refuse to be a nobody. Without an education, without a good job, I will be as invisible as all the Plain people in this community."

"You are not invisible," Rebecca pleaded.

Tommy glanced down, then reached for something under the counter. The silverware bin.

Rebecca grew lightheaded.

Tommy reached into the gray container, grabbed a steak knife and held it out to her in a menacing gesture. "Move into the kitchen. *Now.*"

Rebecca slowly shook her head. "Please, I have children. Katie. Grace. You've met them. I'm all they have."

Tommy's face scrunched up and he shook his head quickly, as if he were trying to dismiss a bad taste. His features smoothed over and he held the knife low near her side. "You will *not* use Amish guilt on me. I am not Amish."

A knocking startled her. Tommy snapped his gaze toward the door and fear flashed in his eyes.

"It's Jake," she breathed, relief and fear tangling in her stomach.

Tommy let out a mirthless laugh. "Jake, huh? Figures."

"He's not going away."

Tommy lowered the knife to hide it below the counter. There was a chance Jake hadn't seen Tommy or if he had seen him, he wouldn't realize what was going on.

Jake knocked again, this time more urgently.

"Let me answer it," Rebecca whispered. "It's time we ended this."

Tommy looked discreetly down at the sharp knife pointed at her delicate midsection. "Wave him off. Tell him to go home."

Rebecca did as she was told, waving to Jake to go on home. *I have to finish up here,* she mouthed.

Every movement, every word, every motion shifted into slow motion. Rebecca felt as if she was having an out-of-body experience.

The door rattled as Jake tried to get in. "He's suspicious." Her mind raced. "Let me get the door, please. I'll get rid of him." She decided to change tactics.

"I'm not stupid. You have no reason to get rid of him."

"I love Jake. I don't want him to get hurt."

Tommy's eyes flashed dark and he tilted his chin toward the door. "Answer it. Tell him I'm here interviewing you for a research paper."

Rebecca opened her eyes wide, a spark of hope igniting in her chest. "Okay, I will. But…what if he wants to talk to you?"

Tommy has nothing to lose.

"If you tell him what's going on, I'll kill him, then track down your daughters at your brother's house and kill them, too."

All the blood rushed to her head and heat swept over her. Each tic of the clock was amplified in her ears. "How do you know where my daughters are?"

He lifted a knowing eyebrow. He must have heard her talking to Flo.

"I'll get rid of him." Tears bit at the back of her eyes, but she refused to cry. She cautiously walked over to the floor where her keys had been thrown. She picked them up and moved toward the door. She startled when Tommy came up behind her.

"I'll be right by your side." He put the hand with the knife on her back and they moved as a unit toward the door.

The pressure of the knife at her back made her dizzy with fear. Staring at the lock and not meeting Jake's curious gaze through the glass door, she inserted the key, turned the lock and opened the door a fraction.

When Jake reached the diner, the door was locked but he saw Rebecca and Tommy in what looked like a heated discussion behind the counter. His brow furrowed with curiosity.

What's Tommy doing here?

Something felt…off.

Jake knocked on the glass door and both Tommy and Rebecca jumped. Something was definitely off.

When they continued to talk without coming to the door, he pounded on it. This time harder. He didn't know what was going on, but he knew he had to get in there.

Rebecca waved at him to dismiss him and if he was being honest with himself, it hurt. She wasn't even going to talk to him?

"I need to talk to you." Jake shook the handle of the door. "Please open up."

Rebecca glanced over her shoulder. If Jake hadn't been watching her closely, he might have missed the worry in her brown eyes.

Adrenaline surged through his veins. "Unlock the door, Rebecca!"

Rebecca picked something up off the floor, then walked toward the door with Tommy right behind her. Jake tried to get her attention, but all her focus was on the door lock.

Tommy gave him a half smile, but something in Tommy's eyes made Jake pause.

Rebecca pulled open the door a fraction, but she didn't invite him in.

"Hi, Jake. Did you need something?" The stiff set of her shoulders confirmed his suspicions.

"I'll drive you home." He decided he could tell her about the news crews in front of her home once they got into the car.

"I'll drive her home," Tommy said casually. "Mrs. Fisher is answering some questions for my research paper."

Jake's gaze moved from Tommy to Rebecca and back. "Is everything okay?"

"*Yah.* Tommy promised me it wouldn't take long." Jake thought he detected a shudder in her breath.

"Not long at all. Then I'll make sure she gets home," Tommy said.

"Are you sure?" Jake put his palm on the door.

"*Yah*, it's fine. Please go."

Jake leaned in close. "Are you okay? You look pale." He reached out to touch her arm and she blinked slowly, not answering him.

Jake pushed the door open and Tommy stepped back, a knife in his hand. The knot in Jake's stomach twisted. He reached out to grab Rebecca, to pull her out of the way, but Tommy was faster. He grabbed Rebecca around her neck and held the knife against her cheek.

Jake lifted his hands in a surrender gesture. "Don't hurt her. Whatever's going on, I can help you."

Beads of sweat glistened on Tommy's forehead as he gritted his teeth. "If the two of you hadn't stuck your noses where they didn't belong... I needed to sell the drugs to pay tuition. Who was I hurting?"

Tommy yanked Rebecca's head back and she gasped. Her brown eyes widened with fear. A single tear rolled down her cheek.

Tommy was not going to let her go.

"Hurting Rebecca won't solve your problems." Jake slowly took a step forward while Tommy walked backward.

"Killing Rebecca would have been justice. Justice for everything she took away from me."

Rebecca groaned as Tommy tightened his hold.

"Let her go. It's no longer about Rebecca. I'm here, too. You'll have to kill us both."

Tommy smirked, as if he had already figured that out.

Anger bubbled in Jake's gut. Someone had really messed Tommy up.

"I'm not going to be easy to take down." All of Jake's senses went on high alert.

"I'll take my chances." Tommy continued his backward motion toward the door leading into the kitchen. He gave a quick glance over his shoulder and adjusted his direction. "I'm not going to live as a jobless nobody… And I'm not going to prison."

Jake tried reasoning again. "We could have found ways to pay your college tuition without resorting to drugs. We *can* still find a way."

Tommy's laugh grated across Jake's brain. "Yeah, right. I'm sure the financial aid office—which is already useless—will give *me* a scholarship. Perhaps from the pool of scholarships for convicted felons."

Jake fisted his hands. "You haven't done anything too serious yet. Hurt Rebecca and all bets are off."

"There's no going back." Tommy's voice shook with fury. He pulled Rebecca back with him and she flinched. He reached the swinging door and tripped backward over the lip on the floor.

Rebecca reached out and Jake grabbed her arm, pulling her away from Tommy, who had fallen onto his backside. Jake pushed Rebecca out of the way and swung into action. His army training all coming back to him.

Jake kicked the knife out of Tommy's hand. It spun across the linoleum floor and disappeared under the stove. The young man scrambled to his feet and Jake slammed him into the wall.

"It's over," Jake said. "It's over." He met Rebecca's gaze as she collapsed onto a nearby counter stool and bowed her head.

Chapter Sixteen

Jake held Tommy's arms firmly behind his back while Rebecca called the sheriff. She stood by the doorway to the kitchen, as if she were ready to take flight if Tommy escaped his grasp.

That wasn't going to happen.

"How could you do this?" Jake asked Tommy. "I trusted you. The young Amish men who talked to us trusted you."

"An opportunity to make some easy cash. I couldn't refuse. Tuition is expensive," Tommy said, his tone flat and distant, as if he were replaying the choices he had made over the past year.

"The cash didn't come easily, did it?"

When Tommy didn't answer, Jake pushed Tommy's cheek into the wallpaper that had probably been there since the 1950s. Tommy groaned. Straining his neck to glare at Jake over his shoulder, Tommy said, "What does it matter now? My future's ruined."

"Don't be too rough." At some point Rebecca had moved next to them.

"Yeah, listen to the lady," Tommy said, full of snark and authority.

Rebecca's gaze drifted to the door. "Here's the sheriff."

Sheriff Maxwell strode into the room, curiosity in his gaze. Jake and Rebecca explained what had happened and the sheriff took Tommy away in handcuffs.

Rebecca collapsed onto the stool and put her hand on her forehead.

Jake walked over to her side and grabbed the back of the stool, even though he really wanted to pull her into an embrace. Thank God he'd arrived when he had. He glanced around at the people milling about outside and he knew a hug wouldn't be appropriate.

"Are you okay?" he asked, squeezing the back of the chair. He wanted to push a loose strand of hair behind her ear.

When it came to Rebecca, he was definitely in trouble.

"I am now." She swallowed hard. "What brought you to the diner tonight? If you hadn't come by…" She shivered and wrapped her arms around her middle.

Jake ran a hand across the back of his neck. He hated to bring Rebecca any more bad news.

She must have read it in his eyes. "Tell me. It can't be worse than this."

"The TV was on in the student union on campus. There's a news crew in front of your house. I wanted to make sure you didn't have to face them alone."

Rebecca's forehead furrowed. "News crew? From the television. Why?"

"Someone must have alerted them about Samuel's arrest, so they set up on the road in front of your farm."

"How did they find out?"

"They have ways. They might have seen his name on a police report and wondered if he was related to Willard."

"Fisher is a common Amish name," she said. "It would have been a leap to make the connection."

"Maybe it was Tommy," Jake suggested.

"Yes, it had to have been. He told me he was going to make it look like Samuel had killed me." Rebecca covered her mouth, bowed her head and whispered, "I could have been killed tonight…and my daughters wouldn't have had a *mem*."

"I'll never let anything happen to you." The words came out of his mouth before he had a chance to think how they would affect Rebecca.

She looked up at him with watery eyes. She covered his hand with hers, then quickly pulled it away and placed it in her lap.

"I didn't mean to add to your stress tonight." Jake smiled. "We can discuss our relationship at another time."

Rebecca blinked slowly. "Tommy told me Samuel was innocent. He wanted to rub it in my face that I'd never be able to tell anyone."

Tommy had been willing to kill her.

"Do you think Tommy's confession will be enough to bring Samuel home? To untangle this mess?"

"We can talk to the sheriff. It'll definitely be a good start."

Jake slipped his arm around her back and helped her stand. "I'm going to take you home."

Rebecca looked up at him. "Thank you. I can't thank you enough."

Jake brushed his thumb across her cheek. "Thank God I was here."

Rebecca touched his arm. "Can we pick up Katie and Grace before you drive me home? I need to see them."

"Of course." With a hand to the small of her back, he escorted her to his vehicle parked along the curb out front.

Jake parked his truck sideways in front of her house, blocking the view of the front door from the news truck. Rebecca ran ahead with the girls and unlocked the door while Jake walked down to the street and asked the crew to leave.

Rebecca closed the door behind her and drew in a deep breath. The scent of an old fire in the stove and a hint of peppers from breakfast reached her nose. *Home.* She had never been more grateful to be home than she was tonight.

She bent and drew her daughters into a hug. The Amish weren't big on physical displays of affection, but tonight Rebecca would make an exception. She might have never seen her daughters again if Tommy had had his way.

"Are you girls hungry?" Rebecca asked.

"*Neh,*" Katie answered.

Grace shook her head. "Maybe Katie can read me more of *Little House on the Prairie.*"

"*Yah,*" Katie said without hesitation. "I want to know what happens next."

Rebecca placed her hands on their heads. "Well, okay. But instead of going up to your room, stay down here."

Rebecca wanted the company of her daughters after everything she had been through.

Katie ran upstairs for the book and then the two girls settled in the rockers in the sitting room. Rebecca went into the kitchen to put on some water for tea as she listened to Katie read to her little sister. Her heart was full.

A moment later, Jake slipped into the kitchen. "The news crew is packing up. I called the sheriff. He promised them a statement if they came down to the station. He also promised them a photo op with Tommy if they hurried."

"A photo op?" Rebecca repeated, confused.

"Bottom line, they're gone. I also told the sheriff about Tommy's statement that Samuel was innocent. They'll work on Tommy. See if they can get an official statement."

Rebecca closed her eyes and felt the weight lifting from her chest. "Thank you again."

In the privacy of the kitchen, Jake took her two hands in his. "I'm glad I was there for you. We are both truly blessed."

Rebecca felt her cheeks heat and she turned her face away. She could still hear Katie's soft voice reading to her sister. "After everything that happened with Willard, and then Samuel, I had often felt uncomfortable in my own home. But tonight, when I realized I might never get to return, I realized that a house doesn't make a home. It's the people." She lifted her eyes to meet his. "Oh, listen to me ramble on." She shook her head and smiled up at him. "I'm happy to be home with my daughters."

She met his gaze and with a burst of courage she didn't know she had, she said, "I'm glad you're here, too."

He pressed a kiss to her forehead and her heart expanded.

Then with even more courage she said, "I'm never leaving the Amish. If you want to become Amish, you need to do it because it's best for you. I don't want you to resent the decision."

Jake dragged the tie of her bonnet through his fingers. "You talked about home. I've never felt more at home than when I'm with you."

Her pulse beat steadily in her ears. The voice of her daughter faded off into the distance.

"My parents left the Amish in search of something else," Jake said. "I've been searching all my life for someplace to belong. The army. College. Through my research. But I always felt at a distance." He pointed to his chest. "I know my place is with you." He grazed her cheek with the back of his hand. "I need to be baptized to court you."

All the world disappeared and the only thing she could see was his handsome face. She wanted to tell him once again that if he joined the Amish it had to be for his own reasons. Not for her. But she couldn't get the words out.

Knowing this warm, compassionate man had tender feelings toward her made her heart soar. He brushed a soft kiss across her lips and whispered, "Wait for me."

Epilogue

Sixteen months later...

"Why didn't *Mem* go ice-skating with us?" Katie asked as she held out her arms and did a shaky twirl.

Jake skated over to her, ready to catch her if she hit a rough patch on the frozen pond. "I suppose she had other things to do."

Grace skated toward them with short choppy steps. Jake had been working with the girls for an hour each day, ever since the pond had safely frozen over two weeks ago.

"Maybe *Mem*'ll have hot chocolate waiting for us," Grace said, her words came out on an icy puff of air. She clapped her blue mittens and said, "I'm cold."

"How about you, Katie? Ready to go in?" Jake squinted against the flurries. The sun low in the sky reflected off an ominous, gunmetal cloud in the distance. "Looks like more snow is on the way."

"No school!" Katie said as she glided to the edge of the pond.

Jake smiled. Some things were universal.

It took a few minutes for the three of them to change from their skates into their boots. Jake had set up a little wooden bench by the edge of the water for just this purpose. He had grown to love the simplicity of life since quitting his job at the university and becoming Amish. He worked the land and built things, and he finally had time to work on a book about the Amish he had long been planning. He wasn't sure how the church elders would feel about that, but he figured he'd present it to them before he published it.

He vowed to show the Amish in the best possible light while also sharing some of their struggles. Struggles that were real. The Yoder brothers were currently both in prison for their involvement in aiding Tommy in his drug venture. Tommy was in prison, too, but his sentence was much longer. Maybe there would be a role for someone like Jake to work with young Amish men who wrestled with the decisions facing them as they moved into adulthood, bridging the gap between the Amish world and the one outside.

"Last one to the house is a rotten egg," Grace hollered as soon as she had slipped on her second boot. She was off like a shot over the fields to the tiny dot that was his home now.

Katie rolled her eyes as she tied the laces of her skates together and hiked them up on her shoulder. "Let her run ahead. I don't really care if I'm a rotten egg." She smiled, and it reminded him of his Rebecca.

The two walked across the field, their boots crunching the snow underneath. "We might have to put snowshoes on next time we come out here. It's really starting to snow."

When they reached the steps, Katie slowed down and looked up at him. She had yet to hit her teenage years, but every so often, in her mannerisms, he detected a hint of the woman she was becoming.

"*Denki* for being nice to me and my little sister."

Jake's chest tightened. "Of course." How could he be anything but to these two precious girls?

"My *dat* was very strict and made my sister and me afraid. It's just…" She seemed to be struggling with the words. "It's nice to have peace in the home."

"Yes, it is." He held out his hand, encouraging her to go ahead of him, but she paused.

"Is it okay if Grace and I call you *Dat*?" Katie glanced down and drew circles in the freshly fallen snow with her boot. "Grace and I have talked about it, but we wanted to ask first. You and *Mem are* married and everything."

A knot formed in Jake's throat. "Of course, I'd like that."

"Okay, then." Katie slipped the ties of her skates off her shoulder and hustled inside.

Jake turned and canvased the land. God's land. He was truly home.

The door swung open and Grace ran in, leaving a trail of wet puddles from the snow in her wake.

"Slow down there," Rebecca admonished.

Grace stopped and smiled, panting. "Katie's a rotten egg."

"Oh, stop that. No one's a rotten egg." Rebecca couldn't help but smile. This past year had brought much happiness to her little family. Jake had followed through and had been baptized this past summer. They were married in October, as soon as the harvest season was over. Now a few months later they had settled into a nice routine.

The only time Rebecca went to the diner now was to meet her friend Hannah for lunch. It was also nice to catch up with Flo. Jake had saved up some money, allowing Rebecca to stay home with the girls on the farm, and allowing them to plan for the future. Meanwhile, Jake had thrown himself into working the farm the summer before their marriage and truly seemed satisfied with it. Now in the dead of winter, he spent his time with the family and his writing.

Rebecca had feared he'd regret becoming Amish, but he truly seemed at peace.

The door opened again and Katie stepped in, followed by Jake. He smiled at her and her heart fluttered, a reaction only his smile inspired. They all took off their winter gear and settled around the heating stove.

"*Mem*, you should come skating with us tomorrow. I want to show you how I can skate," Grace said, rubbing her hands together near the stove. "Can you come with us?"

Rebecca looked up, meeting Jake's eyes. "I don't know if that's such a good idea." She placed her hand on her belly. She had felt sick this past week, but after a quick visit to the doctor today, she knew for certain.

Over the heads of their two daughters, Jake raised his eyebrows. *Really?* he mouthed.

Love expanding in her chest, Rebecca nodded. Jake

closed the distance between them and pulled her into a tight embrace.

She closed her eyes and breathed in his scent, the fresh smell of soap mixed with the great outdoors. When she opened her eyes, Katie and Grace were staring up at them with curiosity.

With his arm still wrapped around his wife, Jake placed his other hand on her belly, an intimate gesture reserved for husband and wife. He met her gaze, getting her unspoken approval.

"Katie, Grace," he said, "how would you like to have a baby brother or sister?"

They both scrambled to their feet and came to their mother's side. "Is it true?" Katie asked, always the more conservative of the two.

Rebecca reached out and cupped her eldest daughter's cheek. "Yes, honey. Are you happy?"

Katie nodded, but her lower lip quivered.

"What's wrong?" Rebecca whispered.

Jake put a hand on Katie's shoulder.

"I'm happy."

"Then why are you crying?" Grace asked in the way only little sisters can.

Rebecca brushed away the tears with her thumb. "Those are happy tears."

Katie nodded. "I can't wait to tell Samuel. When will we see him? He gets to be a big brother again."

"He and Marian are coming for a visit next week if the weather's good."

After all the drug charges had been dropped, Samuel had remained near Rochester in an Amish district in communion with Apple Creek. He'd been baptized around the same time as Jake and had married a pleasant Amish girl from a big family there.

"I hope the weather's good," Grace said.

Rebecca gently tapped her daughters' bonnets. "You girls warm up and I'll make you hot chocolate."

Katie and Grace held up their palms to the heating stove.

Jake wrapped his arms around Rebecca and whispered into her neck. "You make me the happiest man alive." A warm tingle ran down her spine.

Her face flushed. She'd never get used to Jake's warm affection. Some of his outsider ways were welcomed. She held her hand to his chest. "I need to make hot chocolate."

Slowly he shook his head. "*Neh*, sit." His hand brushed her stomach. "I'll make some for everyone."

Reluctantly, Rebecca relaxed and picked up her knitting. She watched as Jake walked into the kitchen. He glanced over his shoulder and smiled at her.

A warm feeling swirled around her heart. Love. Happiness. Contentment.

And peace.

Most definitely peace.

* * * * *

WE HOPE YOU ENJOYED THESE **LOVE INSPIRED** AND **LOVE INSPIRED SUSPENSE** BOOKS.

Whether you prefer heartwarming contemporary romance or heart-pounding suspense, Love Inspired® books has it all!

Look for 6 new titles available every month from both Love Inspired® and Love Inspired® Suspense.